CONFESSIONS of a CURIOUS BOOKSELLER

Center Point
Large Print

This Large Print Book carries the
Seal of Approval of N.A.V.H.

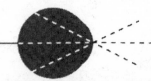

CONFESSIONS
of a
CURIOUS BOOKSELLER

ELIZABETH GREEN

CENTER POINT LARGE PRINT
THORNDIKE, MAINE

This Center Point Large Print edition
is published in the year 2021 by arrangement with
Amazon Publishing, www.apub.com.

Originally published in the United States
by Amazon Publishing, 2021.

The text of this Large Print edition is unabridged.
In other aspects, this book may vary
from the original edition.
Printed in the United States of America
on permanent paper.
Set in 16-point Times New Roman type.

ISBN: 978-1-64358-875-9

The Library of Congress has cataloged this record
under Library of Congress Control Number: 2020952795

For Matt, because of everything.
And for the boys.

Advertisement

WE'RE HIRING!

In West Philadelphia, steps from Clark Park and the Green Line, sits the most renowned and beloved bookstore in the city: the Curious Cat Book Emporium. And as luck would have it, we're hiring!

Full-time assistance needed for the upcoming holidays (and beyond). Duties: Stocking shelves, counting inventory, greeting customers, answering phones, tidying up, running the register, smiling, and being a rock star! Must not be allergic to cats. Must like cats. (I will know if you are pretending!) Pay is fair. Sorry, no benefits. EOE.

From: Fawn Birchill
Sent: Sat, Nov 3, 2018 at 10:20 PM
To: Kyle Krazinsky
Subject: Application for employment

Dear Kyle,

Congratulations! You have been selected for the new role of cashier/tech support at the

Curious Cat Book Emporium! Please arrive Monday, November 5 at 8 a.m. to begin your shift. Along with a smile and a willingness to make a difference, please wear jeans and a nice shirt or sweater (it can be drafty in here) and shoes with strong toe protection. As I stated in the interview, you will be lifting!

Before I forget, the store opens at 9:30 a.m. I ask my employees to arrive thirty minutes early, but I would like you to arrive at 8 a.m. to assist with the register's computer as it has been freezing up lately. Also, my phone doesn't ring anymore when people call me. It's fine if it's my mother, but if it's something important, I'd like to know!

Congratulations!
Fawn, Owner

●●

phillysmallbiz.com
Mon, Nov 5, 2018

Top Review—The Curious Cat Book Emporium
I thought there would be a poetry section? I came in looking for some Charles Bukowski. If you have a poetry section, it's not well marked. I couldn't find it last time I was in.

—Jiancheng P.

phillysmallbiz.com
Mon, Nov 5, 2018

Dear Jiancheng P.,

We in fact do have a poetry section! It is on the second floor by the historical fiction. Unfortunately I have only four full shelves of it, but I always found that the quality of poetry should overshadow the quantity. Don't you agree? We have Emily Dickinson, Wallace Stevens, Pablo Neruda, and Alfred, Lord Tennyson to name a few. I apologize, for we do not carry Charles Bukowski, as you requested in your PSB review. Do you know how PSB works? I only ask because you shouldn't give us one heart simply because we aren't carrying the book you were looking for. Do return and I will personally show you the poetry section, though most likely Charles will not be there. He is far too edgy to be tucked between William Blake and Emily Dickinson. Imagine the conversation! Oddly, I do have Allen Ginsberg—a fact I had forgotten because I borrowed the book to read one day and never returned it. "A Supermarket in California" is probably my favorite poem. Have you read it?

Fawn, Owner, The Curious Cat Book Emporium

From: Sam Asimov
Sent: Tue, Nov 6, 2018 at 5:08 PM
To: Fawn Birchill, Staff
Subject: New Bookstore Opening

Hi Fawn,

It looks like a new bookstore is moving in down the street. Do you know anything about this?

Sam

From: Fawn Birchill
Sent: Tue, Nov 6, 2018 at 6:17 PM
To: Sam Asimov, Staff
Re: New Bookstore Opening

Dear Staff,

Yes, I am aware of this and have been for many months. By no means will this change anything. I cannot press this enough—we will see no changes, and there is no reason to panic. In fact, this may be an excellent boon for us, as it will help to heighten people's awareness of the importance of books and perhaps spark interest in people who have never before been readers, ultimately bringing them to us. I assure you this is not a negative development. Furthermore, I plan on going over and introducing myself to the staff as soon as they are up and running. Here, I must make my supposed enemy my friend and see if we can even work together somehow.

Stiff upper lip,
Fawn, Owner

●●

phillysmallbiz.com
Tue, Nov 6, 2018

Top Review—The Curious Cat Book Emporium
It took me twenty minutes to find the book I was looking for and when I found it, it was in the travel section. I must ask: Why was Upton Sinclair's *The Jungle* in the travel section?? They know that it's a novel, right?

—Alex S.

phillysmallbiz.com
Tue, Nov 6, 2018

Dear Alex S.,

I am so glad you were able to find the book you needed; however, I am sorry that it took you so long to find it. I am perplexed as to why you did not reach out to me or to one of my many employees for assistance. I purposefully hire people who are not intimidating creatures, so you should have no trouble approaching them for help. The fact that you found *The Jungle* in the travel section is a fault of one of my employees, and I do thank you for bringing it to my attention. I always strive to hire people who are well read, but we can't have perfection all the time. A person who hasn't read *The Jungle* might look at it and think it is perhaps a study on the flora and fauna of, say, Borneo, and not, as we know, a horribly depressing novel about poor Lithuanian immigrants coming to Chicago and butchering animals all day. I will have to tell my employees that Upton Sinclair was not, in fact, another Bill Bryson but a novelist and does not belong tucked beside *The Adventures of Lewis and Clark*. How fortuitous then that you thought to look in the travel section at all. You are either a detective or a skilled peruser, or you are spinning me quite a yarn. I give you the benefit of the doubt and think that you love perusing and so came upon it by happy accident. Sometimes that is how the greatest books are found.

Best wishes,
Fawn, Owner, The Curious Cat Book Emporium

From: Kyle Krazinsky
Sent: Tue, Nov 6, 2018 at 7:11 PM
To: Fawn Birchill
Subject: Cat food

Hey Fawn,

Just wanted to let you know that I went out tonight and picked up some food for the alley cats behind the store because I noticed your bag was running low. I'll bring it in tomorrow, so don't feel like you have to go out and buy more tonight.

Kyle

From: Fawn Birchill
Sent: Wed, Nov 7, 2018 at 8:02 PM
To: Florence Eakins
Subject: Richard

Dear Florence,

I fear that I have little patience left for Richard. Hopefully you have told Mother nothing of him, and as far as she knows I am not dating or seeing anyone at the moment. I do hope, Florence, that you have managed to keep this secret for me. Please also remember that the only reason I've told you anything is because I do not have many female friends that I can trust and confide in, and so I hold you to this promise that you made to me in the beginning to *not tell Mother about Richard*. If he were any other kind of man, I would brag about him. I would be bringing him around all the time. But Richard? I often wonder late at night as I lie alone in the bed how it ever got to this point with him. How did I complacently allow this dating to go on as long as it has? Can you believe it's been three months? Just last week, he took me out to dinner and paid for it himself! If this doesn't smell like commitment, then I don't know what does! He tried to kiss me that night after dinner as he was dropping me off (I tell him to stop four blocks away from my actual house because I don't want him to know where I live). After watching him eat that soup all night, he really expects me to kiss him? The dribbling, Florence! The front of his shirt was sodden in vegetable broth before the main course had even arrived.

Once, while walking down the street, sweating in the October heat, he told me all about how he had a deep and affectionate love for freight trains and begged me, like a little boy, to go down to the Schuylkill with him where the freight train runs to see it go by. I was only tempted to say yes insofar as I might have gotten the chance to push him in front of it.

Florence, how do I do it? How do I rid myself of this man (besides the unthinkable freight train idea)?

How do I break it off gently?

Many thanks,
Fawn

••

November 8, 2018
Sometimes asking for help only presents a hindrance. Yesterday, for example, it rained so much that water began pouring into the store through the closed windows! And as I was running around directing my team of three to close the shutters, water was dripping all over my bed upstairs! And so instead of catching it with buckets like I should have been, I had to micromanage their efforts. One would think that putting three heads together is an advantage, but in their case the outcome is more akin to a head injury.

But they mean well, and I can't fault them for trying. They are good workers and, like me, have a soft spot for feeding the alley cats behind the store. Even though my employees can be forgetful at times, I never have to remind them to keep the bowls filled. The other day my newest employee noticed that my cat food was getting low and went out and bought another bag. He didn't even ask for money! This gives me hope for the future.

When I was their age—no, much younger, in fact—I was running my father's general store with my sister with perfect competence. While our father was out on deliveries and Florence handled the books, I was front and center, selling cigarettes and milk while sweeping up spills and telling the town drunk to take a hike. The responsibility I had! I have to admit it, and it pains me to say it, but without this experience I might not be so brazen and successful. Sadly, I can't say the same for my sister, Florence, who has Falstaff's work ethic, but to each her own. I am not sure how the two of us, who had the same upbringing, could turn out so differently, but alas, life is funny. All I can do is seek to better myself.

The holidays are approaching. I am nervous as usual that I won't hit my numbers, especially now with the advent of this new little bookstore just down the street. All these negative business reviews aren't helping, but they are par for the course ever since I added my business to the platform. The truth of it is that most people who come in are quite satisfied, but generally speaking, happy people don't leave reviews. So we hear the negativity far more frequently. Over the years I've learned not to take any of this personally, but I do hope it doesn't sadden my employees too much. No one is born with thick skin; instead it is battle-tested on the rough seas of the business world. I hope they can survive.

●●

phillysmallbiz.com
Thu, Nov 8, 2018

Top Review—The Curious Cat Book Emporium
Before I went all the way to their store, I called to make sure they had *Great Expectations*. I need it for school, like yesterday. Anyway, I got all the way there only to hear from one of the employees that it wasn't there, and when I told him I had even called to make sure it was there, he said that it must have been purchased. I live five minutes away. Am I supposed to believe that in the time it took me to hang up and go outside, someone else came in and bought their only copy of *Great Expectations*? I guess I should have lowered my own before entering their store.

—Beth G.

phillysmallbiz.com
Thu, Nov 8, 2018

Dear Beth G.,

As a Luddite, I find it unpalatable to even

log on to the internet, let alone find my way to phillysmallbiz.com and my listing therein. However, I want my customers to know that I go to great lengths to make them satisfied with their experience. The fact that you couldn't find your book is a testament to how many customers we get in a given day. Yes, I agree that one of my employees made a mistake by not putting it aside, but I think that if you needed it badly enough for school and were a responsible young woman, you wouldn't have waited until the last minute to read such a thick novel. If you're interested, however, I do have *A Tale of Two Cities*, which is also by Dickens and has quite a bit of murder in it, unlike *Great Expectations*, wherein the only interesting thing that happens is that some old hag catches on fire and dies.

Sincerely,
Fawn, Owner, The Curious Cat Book Emporium

From: Florence Eakins
Sent: Thu, Nov 8, 2018 at 7:43 PM
To: Fawn Birchill
Re: Richard

Fawn,

To be honest, this sounds like you're leading the poor man on. Good thing is you haven't gotten that far with him yet, so you can always break it off. I mean, of course you can break it off at any time, but the earlier the better. I'm curious why you're bothering with this guy in the first place if you don't really like him?

Flo

P.S. Saw Dad yesterday. He seems okay.

From: Fawn Birchill
Sent: Thu, Nov 8, 2018 at 8:24 PM
To: Florence Eakins
Re: Richard

Dear Florence,

Thank you for your prompt reply regarding my dilemma.

You asked me quite frankly why I would bother with such a creature in the first place. Well, if you must know, my reasons are twofold: Richard isn't a bad-looking man. In fact, part of his initial appeal were his looks and his occupation. A handsome librarian who was interested in me sounded too good to be true, and sadly, it turns out that it was. Unfortunately, it is his behavior that I find insufferable. I do not have to tell you how long it's been since I've been out in the dating scene. Running a successful bookstore is extremely tiring and saps all my energy. It also makes it quite difficult to have a social life, and so it was flattering and welcome when this stranger at the library asked me out for coffee. How, as one who spends her time among shelves of books all day, could I say no to such a proposal? Please do not blame me and instead help me out of this mess.

Sincerely,
Fawn

From: Florence Eakins
Sent: Thu, Nov 8, 2018 at 9:02 PM
To: Fawn Birchill
Re: Richard

Fawn,

Sometimes the hardest thing is the right thing. Remember when Dad used to say that to us whenever we had a dilemma? He wasn't much for giving advice, of course. It pretty much began and ended with that statement, but at least he tried. I take that advice with work a lot and most of the time it turns out paying off. I'm up for a promotion soon, so I'm doing the hard thing and taking on more work than ever. Can you believe I've been a marketing coordinator for going on five years now? I'm so ready to move on. A director role has opened up, and I've got my sights on it. So of course lately I'm staying a bit later at work, which Joseph isn't thrilled about since he's the one having to take care of the kids after a long day at Macy's, but this is what I want and in the end it will be best for all of us. Maybe he could even one day quit his job and do something that he really wants to do—whatever that is.

I guess all I'm saying is that it's going to be hard to break it off with this Richard guy, but if that is what you want to do, then you must. Honestly, he doesn't sound so terrible if you take away the soup slurping. Everyone has their quirks. The question is, Is it the price you're willing to pay to be with him? If not, bite the bullet, Fawn. But do it kindly.

Also, Dad asks about you every time I visit him. I'm getting tired of feeding him the same line about you being busy. Why don't you stop by sometime?

Flo

From: Fawn Birchill
Sent: Thu, Nov 8, 2018 at 10:00 PM
To: Richard Saunders
Subject: You and I

Dear Richard,

As much as I have enjoyed our time together, I must regretfully bring it to a close. Please know that this had nothing at all to do with you and everything to do with my invalid father who needs someone to care for him in his last dying days. I will be splitting my time between Philadelphia and Norristown and will therefore be far too busy to date. Perhaps when my father finally passes, I will have time. However, for now, I must close the book on this. You are probably wondering why I would be so kind to my father after I have told you so many terrible things about him. Well, when parents age, as I'm sure you already know, the children come to a realization that they must be there for them whether they harbor ill will or not. Please do not blame yourself for this—you are merely a bystander caught up in the whirlwind that is my life. You are charming and generous and no doubt will find someone else to slurp soup with. By the way, were you able to get that vegetable broth out of your shirt? I do hope it didn't stain. Dry cleaning bills on top of a restaurant tab would be enough to make my stomach turn.

Sincerely,
Fawn

●●

November 8, 2018 (continued)

I just ended it with Richard. I hit "Send" five minutes ago and I'm still pacing, not because I think I have made a mistake but because as annoying as he was, I really don't enjoy the idea of hurting his feelings. Especially this late at night. Perhaps I should have waited until the morning, but I couldn't put this off any longer.

I am simply tired of going at this alone, otherwise I wouldn't have led him on this long. It's quite nice to have my own business and good employees and a geographically close family, but in these later years I'm beginning to long for more. Richard was merely the man who seemed interesting at the moment. And now because of my flighty interest and fickle tastes, his feelings have been hurt. There is nothing really wrong with Richard; he's just not the man for me. Just as a shoe that is two sizes too large is not for me. It's no fault of the shoe's, nor is it any fault of my foot's. Oh, here I am trying to make myself feel better. I hope I still have some wine left in the fridge! Most of the time that works better than any reasoning and logic.

●●

From: Fawn Birchill
Sent: Fri, Nov 9, 2018 at 9:30 AM
To: Staff
Subject: Richard

Dear Staff,

If a man named Richard comes into the store looking for me, tell him I am out and let me know immediately so that I can disappear until he decides to leave. He is handsome, about 6’3” with thinning brown hair and large green eyes. I told him my father is dying and even though he isn’t, please play along if Richard mentions it.

Thanks!
Fawn, Owner

●●

phillysmallbiz.com
Fri, Nov 9, 2018

Top Review—The Curious Cat Book Emporium
I stopped in here today to just peruse. After leaving I realized another bookstore is moving in just down the street and looks kind of amazing. I’m really glad a new place is coming

in because the Curious Cat Book Emporium is an unorganized dump, and its time has come!

—David P.

phillysmallbiz.com
Fri, Nov 9, 2018

David P.,

Your comment was both hurtful and inaccurate. Please do not use phillysmallbiz .com to tout your slanderous remarks, but keep them to yourself. No doubt this new store will be wildly different from ours, and there will be no competition between us whatsoever. Most likely they will specialize in certain books or (god forbid) have a poor selection but a great atmosphere—the death sentence for a new bookstore.

Thanks for stopping in to the store (even though you gave it two hearts). I do hope you found the book you wanted!

Best wishes,
Fawn, Owner, The Curious Cat Book Emporium

●●

From: Richard Saunders
Sent: Fri, Nov 9, 2018 at 11:04 AM
To: Fawn Birchill
Re: You and I

Hi Fawn,

I understand the pressing need to care for family, and I appreciate your honesty. You seemed distracted the last few times we were out, so this explains it. I was a little concerned it had something to do with me.

And just to set the record straight, I was mildly embarrassed that I managed to splash soup all over the front of my shirt. I actually hadn't realized it happened until I was home and looked in the mirror. It would have been nice had you told me the moment you noticed it so I could have done something about it before it got out of hand. Maybe this is all for the best.

I wish you well.

—Rich

From: Fawn Birchill
Sent: Fri, Nov 9, 2018 at 11:26 AM
To: Richard Saunders
Re: You and I

Richard,

If you must know, yes, the soup incident was a bit difficult to stomach. I can't help but advise you that if you know from the start that you are an avid slurper and dribbler, then do not order soup on a date. And you are correct: this has nothing to do with you personally. I simply cannot take care of two men at once, and it is only because of blood connection that I choose my father.

Additionally, a new bookstore is moving in literally a block from mine. Thus far they haven't contacted me or acknowledged my store, so I fear I am stuck with neighbors who lack decorum and manners. I stood outside to watch them unload trendy couches and large boxes of who knows what while my eye twitched ever so slightly. In the twenty years I've owned this business, something like this has never happened. As you can see, there is much cause for stress in my life.

Sincerely,
Fawn

From: Richard Saunders
Sent: Fri, Nov 9, 2018 at 12:16 PM
To: Fawn Birchill
Re: You and I

Hi Fawn,

Actually, I didn't need to know that the soup bothered you so much, as it wasn't my fault. And since we're going there, it's probably a good idea for me to remind you that I live on a librarian's salary, so insisting we eat at swanky steak houses every time we go to a restaurant is a bit gauche.

This has been very illuminating.

—Rich

P.S. I hope your store isn't too affected by the new neighbor and that your father feels better soon.

From: Fawn Birchill
Sent: Fri, Nov 9, 2018 at 1:45 PM
To: Richard Saunders
Re: You and I

Richard,

I fail to believe that one doesn't feel hot soup cascading down one's shirt. Maybe all that time in the library has made you quite the great storyteller. Ever consider writing fiction?

Thank you for your concern regarding my store and my father.

Fawn

From: Richard Saunders
Sent: Fri, Nov 9, 2018 at 1:56 PM
To: Fawn Birchill
Re: You and I

Fawn,

That was unnecessary and over the line, but I will assume it's because you are stressed, so I won't fault you for it.

Regarding your store, I have an acquaintance through my work at the library who has an impressive inventory of books that he is looking to off-load for the right price. His grandfather just died—he was a bit of a mad collector—so he's holding an estate sale. His info is attached.

I wish you well.

—Rich

From: Fawn Birchill
Sent: Fri, Nov 9, 2018 at 2:02 PM
To: Richard Saunders
Re: You and I

Richard,

You’re right: I apologize. That was over the line. I get very sensitive when people are petty. You are a kind man with many excellent qualities that I know someone else will appreciate. I am just too busy right now. And yes, if you must know, the soup really pushed me over the edge. But this is about my father, let me remind you, and not the soup or your childish love of freight trains.

To leave this on a positive note, thank you very much for the estate sale contact. Did you say he would reach out to me? If so, I will wait to hear from him. I am excited to see the kind of volume he has. You are a true friend to think of me. Keep in touch.

Best,
Fawn

From: Jacob Whitney
Sent: Mon, Nov 12, 2018 at 7:55 PM
To: Fawn Birchill
Subject: Books for sale

Greetings!

Our mutual friend, Richard, mentioned you might be interested in some of my late grandfather's books. He was quite the collector, as you will find. For example, I have some first-edition Faulkners and a second edition of *The Waste Land* by T. S. Eliot. Also, I have a lot of Mark Twain. I would be happy to work something out with you and support your store in this way.

Regards,
Jacob

From: Fawn Birchill
Sent: Mon, Nov 12, 2018 at 8:12 PM
To: Jacob Whitney
Re: Books for sale

Dear Mr. Whitney,

Thank you for your interest in my bookstore and for reaching out to me. My store has two floors of used books (some rather rare) and a basement full of inventory waiting to go up on the shelves. That said, I would be happy to take whatever you have. May I ask: What exactly do you mean by, "I have a lot of Mark Twain"? I'll take it all regardless, but I'm already running out of room in the basement, so I have to be somewhat cautious. What is your price, and can you send me a manifest?

This is quite fortuitous timing, as a new bookstore (literally a block away) is opening its doors later this month, and I am strategizing ways to stand apart. There was an article in the paper about how it will have cats and a coffee shop / bar inside, which worries me—but only slightly, as the article left out nearly any mention of the types of books they will be selling. Either it's bad journalism or someone at that store is covering up the fact that its inventory is shamefully scarce!

Additionally, thank you for your kind words. They say times are changing, and I see it myself: everyone in Philadelphia has an electronic reading device like a Kindle or an iPad, it seems. But I think there are still people out there who want to hold on to the printed page like a newborn baby or a small animal—gently, lovingly, and viscerally. And even though I see a resurgence in people's interest in books and the independent bookstore (thank god!), my store, it seems, is left behind. It is a truth I regularly keep from my staff, for if while on the raging seas a captain points out a leak in the hull, she might find her weaker crew members abandoning ship, which is not the result I seek. I suppose a captain would tell her crew the ship was sinking only if it were absolutely necessary to do so. No need to stir up panic just because of a little deficit in the finances. It's not as if I am looking to file for bankruptcy! Anyway, let us keep that between us businesspeople, shall we? I will catch this wave and ride it yet, and I believe your books may be just the ticket. For that, I thank you.

Will it be possible to deliver the books prior to Black Friday?

Sincerely,
Fawn Birchill, Owner, The Curious Cat Book Emporium

From: Fawn Birchill
Sent: Tue, Nov 13, 2018 at 10:45 AM
To: Staff
Subject: Store Cleaning

Dear Staff,

I will be staying late on Thursday to do a quick cleaning of the store. It should take only a few hours. I need some willing volunteers because I can't do it on my own or I'll be cleaning until 3 a.m. again.

A general note: do not leave the toilet seat up. That goes for the ladies too. PLEASE, SHUT THE LID. Butterscotch likes to play in the water, and last time somebody not only left the lid up, but they also didn't bother to flush.

Many thanks,
Fawn, Owner

November 14, 2018
My only tenant, an elderly woman named Jane, is so quiet that I sometimes worry she's dead. There are spans of time in which I don't hear a thing from her—not even running water or a flushing toilet. Last night was such a circumstance, where it dawned on me that it had been three days since I'd heard anything. I had leftover chicken parmesan, so I crept downstairs with it. The last time I'd spoken with her was when I had to go in to collect a couple of dead mice in their traps; the woman hates rodents. So I pushed open the door and said hello. She was very surprised to see me and grateful for the chicken. However, she spoke to me while holding a tissue to her nose, claiming to be ill. She directed me to put her dinner in the refrigerator and to stay away from her, as she was contagious. I wanted to clean up all the tissues scattered on the floor, but she wouldn't let me, so I didn't push the subject. She is a very nice woman, and I think she might appreciate a home-cooked meal from time to time.

I received an email from my pen pal, Gregory,

tonight! It was just what I needed to brighten my evening. Now to my tradition of pouring a large glass of wine, turning on Chopin, and replying.

••

From: Gregory Harris
Sent: Wed, Nov 14, 2018 at 8:31 PM
To: Fawn Windsor
Subject: Yoo-hoo!

Dear Fawn,

I had some time between meetings, so I'm taking the opportunity to say a quick hello. Right now, I'm at a café on the Liffey drinking a cappuccino and watching passersby, and I can't help but think of you and how much you'd enjoy this. At this very moment, in fact, I'm witnessing a young man propose to his girlfriend. She seems completely flabbergasted. Oh, this is good.

Anyway, I'm very busy. Just flipped a multi-unit residential building not far from where I'm sitting. Hoping the capital gains are worth it. This one came in over budget.

Oh dear. I think she said no. This is quite uncomfortable. Dublin is a hell of a town.

Tell me how your life is going lately. Talk soon.

Gregory

From: Fawn Windsor
Sent: Wed, Nov 14, 2018 at 10:00 PM
To: Gregory Harris
Re: Yoo-hoo!

Dearest Gregory,

I had a whisper of a notion that you might be emailing me, and I was right! I'm so glad you did, as I have much to recount from my recent trip to Croatia. Have you been? No doubt in your line of work, travel is forced upon you. I was able to leave my father's estate for an entire month (imagine the freedom!) and entrust the horses to Pierre. I put my finger on a globe in the study and spun it, only to land on Croatia!

I got my affairs in order and left, worried the place may burn to the ground under the watch of my house staff, but I couldn't deny myself a little freedom. I won't be young forever—I'm already going rather grey, even though I dye. And sometimes when I see myself in the mirror, I realize with horror that my feet have a natural splay to them, almost like that of Daffy Duck. I can only imagine how ridiculous I appear when I walk. I am always trying to correct this, but my efforts are like swimming upstream—I am getting nowhere. Do you know, despite all that, a stranger came up to me the other day and told me that I look like an older Keira Knightley? Needless to say, I was flattered. Had he seen me walking or standing he might have rescinded, but luckily I was sitting at the time and no one was the wiser. Do you know who Keira Knightley is? I recommend looking her up and imagining her a little older, with splayed feet, and it may be as good as any photograph that I could send you.

Croatia, contrary to popular belief, is no longer going through any major conflict and is therefore a best-kept secret for discerning travelers like myself. While most are traversing the beaches of Monte Carlo and skiing the Alps, those in the know are drinking fabulous Croatian wine and walking through its amazing parks. The waterfalls, Gregory! I've never been able to drink an entire bottle of wine and then wake up the next day for a hike around waterfalls. One simply doesn't get hungover on Croatian wine! Incidentally, the same gentleman who commented that I looked like Ms. Knightley ended up being a love interest while I was on my travels. However, it did not work out. He is a charming, handsome man from the South of France and owns acres of seaside real estate; however, he cannot properly eat soup to save his life. By the time we were finished with our meal, his white Versace shirt was covered in tomato bisque. And how childish he was! He had the strangest obsession with trains. Anyway, I ditched him in Split (no pun intended!). I think I broke his tomato-covered heart, but alas, it was for the best.

Here I am rambling on. I just wanted to say hello and let you know how things are going on my end. A failed proposal! How terribly awkward! I am so happy to hear your real estate business is getting on well. Dublin must be lovely this time of year. It's been so long since I've traversed those city streets or drunk a pint of real Guinness!

Incidentally, one of my cousins (a duke in southern England) has passed away and left me with a mountain of Mark Twain books. An odd gift but I believe a lucrative one if I play my cards right. I would very much like to sell them and see what I can get. Some are very old indeed. Funny for a Brit to love Mark Twain so much, but my cousin was eccentric. I hear he paid for everything in rolls of shillings, despite his millions.

Much love,
Fawn Windsor

November 14

Dear Fawn,

Enclosed please find your birthday gift. Sorry there isn't much this year. How are the store and Philly in general these days? I haven't been to Philly since last year when I went for the Macy's Christmas light show with Florence and the kids.

I wanted to let you know that your father was moved into hospice care two days ago. Most of the time these days he doesn't even know who I am. I do wish you would visit when you can find the time. It would mean so much to him, even though he might not recognize you. He often calls Florence by your name, and lately we've decided to stop correcting him.

Sorry to include this morose news with your birthday card, but such is life. Personally, I'd rather know what's going on than have people sugarcoat everything for me, only to find out how terrible things really are when it's far too late.

Anyway, happy birthday, my firstborn child. Yours was an extraordinarily difficult birth, but you were absolutely worth it. I hope you have fun birthday plans.

Much love,
Mother

November 15, 2018

I didn't sleep well last night. The pressure to see my father is overwhelming. It would be one thing if the guilt was only coming from my mother and sister, but there is some self-generated guilt as well that's making this particularly challenging. Not that I owe him anything. I sacrificed my childhood and teenage years for his pitiful store. And for what? So people would have somewhere to buy cigarettes and Pepsi? So that they wouldn't have to drive or walk another five blocks to the Wawa? And he wants to see me. Does he want to see me? Or is this something Mother is doing—a last-ditch attempt to get the scattered family back together again one last time? Not so that Florence and I can see our father but so that we can see our jailer. So that he can feel less guilty because our presence alone indicates forgiveness or at the very least an attempt at it. And my mother can sit back and see us all together and feel absolved of her complacency in our lost childhood.

And yet, shouldn't I see him? This man who never said a tender word to me in my whole life? Should I rise above by picking up the phone or jumping on the train? Frankly, at the moment, all I can think about is going back to sleep. I must stop drinking in bed.

Dear Fawn,

I found chicken parmesan in my refrigerator. Did you or my daughter leave it? I heated it in the microwave, and it was good.

—Jane, your tenant

From: Mark Nilsen
Sent: Thu, Nov 15, 2018 at 8:02 AM
To: Fawn Birchill
Subject: Introduction

Good morning, Fawn,

My name is Mark, and I'm the owner of the new bookstore down the street. I'm so sorry I haven't stopped by in person yet, but things have been nonstop here since we moved in. I would love to sit down with you sometime for coffee and a talk. Do you have a free half hour in the coming weeks? Maybe we can discuss ways in which we can work together. At the very least, it would be great to sit down with a fellow bibliophile. ☺

Sincerely,
Mark

From: Fawn Birchill
Sent: Thu, Nov 15, 2018 at 8:17 AM
To: Mark Nilsen
Re: Introduction

Dear Mark,

How nice of you to reach out to me! Though it would be lovely to meet, I am so very busy with Black Friday approaching. Surely you understand (or maybe not?) that it is a very busy time for successful businesses like mine and so next to impossible to meet each and every local store owner that reaches out to me. As you may know, I have been in business for a very long time and have established quite a loyal following, so it is paramount that I meet the needs of my customers first and meet fellow business owners second.

I couldn't help but notice that you are closed on Sundays. Is this for religious reasons, or do you close because you'd like to have a day off? It might be wiser to be closed on Mondays and Tuesdays, as most people are working weekdays and shopping on the weekends. Food for thought!

Perhaps another time we can make introductions, and I can give you some advice on your new business. At the start, I would suggest doing a better job landscaping your small front lawn, as it is the outside of your store as much as the inside that will draw people in. I'm sure you're simply hoping it will snow soon and cover the dead leaves, grass, and ever-present candy wrappers and soda cups; however, I hear this winter is supposed to have minimal snow, so I certainly wouldn't rely on nature in this case!

Best of luck!
Fawn Birchill, Owner, The Curious Cat Book Emporium (a Mark Twain specialist store)

From: Jacob Whitney
Sent: Thu, Nov 15, 2018 at 9:52 AM
To: Fawn Birchill
Subject: Manifest

Greetings!

Attached please find the manifest. I'll see what I can do about getting the books out to you before Black Friday. Since there are so many, this will be costly both in time and money. No promises, but I'll do my best.

Regards,
Jacob

From: Fawn Birchill
Sent: Thu, Nov 15, 2018 at 12:20 PM
To: Jacob Whitney
Re: Manifest

Dear Mr. Whitney,

Though it was somewhat helpful for volume's sake, the manifest you sent me certainly wasn't what I was hoping for, which was to receive the titles of these many books and not simply the number of books you will sell to me. Nevertheless, I will take them off your hands. I cannot spend my time arguing about the manifest since Black Friday is approaching. I have mailed you the check as requested, so you should see it in your mailbox soon. Perhaps this will drive the idea home that I am very serious about having these books *before* the most important selling day of the year. I will pay the extra delivery costs to ensure they arrive sooner than early December. Though I understand that life moves a bit slower out in Paoli, please remember that I am the owner of a retail store and as such it would be detrimental not to have this exciting inventory to incentivize customers to walk through my door. Please reconsider.

Many thanks,
Fawn Birchill, Owner, The Curious Cat Book Emporium (a Mark Twain specialist store)

●●

From: Fawn Birchill
Sent: Thu, Nov 15, 2018 at 11:30 PM
To: Tabitha Birchill
Subject: Thank you

Mother,

Thank you for the birthday card and the Starbucks gift card! I had never been in a Starbucks before to order a drink—I usually go just to buy their coffee beans—but the card inspired me to give it a try. I have never been so overwhelmed in all my life. There are code names for sizes and variants on how much flavor one pumps into the cup to determine the strength of the drink. The young woman in front of me ordered a two-pump nonfat no-whip venti white mocha (I wrote it down). Instead of decoding the menu and holding up the lengthening line, I just asked the cashier to duplicate her order. It was actually quite good. I don't know how the young men and women keep it all together behind the counter. I have never done anything like it before, aside from that horrible job busing tables when I was sixteen. I kept confusing the regular with the decaf coffee. I hope those baristas are paid a hefty salary for their wizardry. I am fortunate to have such a slow-paced occupation.

I wish you would come visit the store. Your dust allergies can be regulated with medicine, and Butterscotch is declawed and therefore completely harmless. He's a very interesting cat in that he is so uncatlike and reminds me more of a rabbit or a lamb. My staff consists of three young people, all in their twenties. Sometimes I think they are some of my closest friends. As you know, I never had many growing up (Father kept us too busy with his store), so it's important to me that I have found camaraderie in them. Our tight-knit friendship would be apparent if you could see it yourself. I feel truly rich. Do visit soon; I am getting an embarrassment of Mark Twain books shortly, and I'd love for you to see it all shelved and alphabetized in its glory.

Thank you for the update on Father. I would see him, but I am so busy with these books that things are extremely difficult—no doubt being a former proprietor himself, he would understand. The impending winter is pushing me unwillingly toward the holidays and my busiest time, and therefore I can't leave for

Thanksgiving or otherwise. I know Father would understand, even if you may not. The holiday season is the determining time of year in which businesses know whether they will sink or swim. Need I mention Black Friday? That is the single most important day, and I cannot be traipsing around Pennsylvania on visits like some carefree prima donna. Surely you must understand on some level that this is all that I have and all that I am. I cannot risk ruin. Father knows only too well the sacrifices one must make for one's livelihood. Or have you forgotten those mornings when he would drag Florence and me out of bed at 4 a.m. to help him open his shop before we had to go to school? To comfort us, he would quote Winston Churchill: "If you are going through hell, keep going."

Perhaps I can visit when things slow down in the spring if he is still in hospice. What a horrible place, by the way. Last time I was there, I noticed that their sitting-room library (if you want to call it that) consisted of nothing but Jesus books, cookbooks (how are they going to cook?), and travel books. How very depressing—though the book on Croatia was fascinating. Did you know that they have a city called Split and also a Dalmatian Coast? I imagine countless dalmatians running in packs along the cliffs, as common as white-tailed deer.

Fawn

From: Fawn Birchill
Sent: Fri, Nov 16, 2018 at 1:30 AM
To: Staff
Re: Store Cleaning

Dear Staff,

Thank you for your effort in helping me clean tonight. Although only Kyle bothered to show up, it was still a great help, and he was able to leave around midnight. We ordered pizza, had some wine, and listened to his music. It was a nice time despite the duties, and you all missed out.

DO NOT SMOKE with the back door open. Not only does it let the cold air in, but also Butterscotch could wander out and get in a scuffle with the alley cats. Additionally, the smoke's cancerous tendrils have a way of reaching my old used books and permeating the very fibers of the fragile pages, burrowing in and sticking there for eternity. If I wanted my business to smell like cigarettes, I would have opened a bowling alley.

Best,
Fawn, Owner

P.S. Does anyone know how to fix a leaky toilet? Every time the toilet flushes, water seeps from the pipe that connects the floor with the tank. Help!

●●

November 16

Dear Fawn,
I found this article in the paper about how ship captains would keep cats on board to mitigate the mouse and rat population. I thought you would enjoy it because of your alley-cat-feeding hobby, so I cut it out for you. It seems that you are doing the neighborhood a favor! Also, I've included a few CVS coupons for toothpaste and aspirin.

Much love,
Mother

●●

From: Fawn Birchill
Sent: Sat, Nov 17, 2018 at 8:07 AM
To: Philly Small Biz Journal
Subject: My Annual Ad

Dear Sir or Madam,

For nearly twenty years, I have been putting my ad in your journal, so understand my shock when I opened the front page and saw not my Black Friday sale advertisement but the Grumpy Mug's. I turned each page with haste, trying to find mine, only to see that you had put it toward the very back by the hardware store ad.

I know I didn't submit it as early as I normally do, but as a longtime patron and advertiser of your journal, I thought we had a gentleman's agreement that the front page is where it would surely go? Did Mark offer to pay you more money than I normally do? I'm just trying to get to the bottom of his scheme, for not only does it devastate me, but also the public expects to see it there each year. I know it is too late to change it now that you've distributed all the journals, but is there any way that we can ensure this will not recur next year? Name your price, and I will pay it.

Many thanks,
Fawn Birchill, Owner, The Curious Cat Book Emporium (a Mark Twain specialist store)

From: Fawn Birchill
Sent: Sun, Nov 18, 2018 at 11:23 AM
To: Mark Nilsen
Subject: Black Friday Advertisement

Dear Mark,

I would like to know how much you paid the *Journal* to replace my long-standing Black Friday ad (which is always found on the inner front page of the paper) with yours? Surely you do not live under a rock and saw the ad there these many years. What inspired you to do such a nefarious thing to me? Are you really that threatened? Do you have friends over at the *Journal*?

Curiously yours,
Fawn Birchill, Owner, The Curious Cat Book Emporium (a Mark Twain specialist store)

From: Mark Nilsen
Sent: Sun, Nov 18, 2018 at 2:51 PM
To: Fawn Birchill
Re: Black Friday Advertisement

Hi Fawn,

Nice to hear from you again. I paid the *Journal* the standard amount for a full-page spread and absolutely did not dictate to them where my ad should go. I believe that is 100 percent their decision, so it must have been an honest mistake on their part. I am sorry for any stress this might have caused you.

Take care,
Mark

From: Fawn Birchill
Sent: Sun, Nov 18, 2018 at 2:56 PM
To: Mark Nilsen
Re: Black Friday Advertisement

Dear Mark,

I'm sorry, but I can't believe that for a minute. I have an excellent sense for sniffing out deception. I thought we might be able to have a functioning, amicable relationship, but sadly that will not be.

I would love to give you the benefit of the doubt. Perhaps you can try to earn back my trust this year and we can, in fact, someday be friends.

Best wishes,
Fawn Birchill, Owner, The Curious Cat Book Emporium (a Mark Twain specialist store)

From: Florence Eakins
Sent: Sun, Nov 18, 2018 at 5:16 PM
To: Fawn Birchill
Subject: Pics

Fawn,

Sharing these cute pics we took when visiting Dad the other day. I think number two is particularly funny because Charles is crying in it. He was getting tired, as kids do. Dad looks good in it, doesn't he? It was a good day for him cognitively. He remembered their names and asked me where Joseph was, which he never does. Most of the time he ignores him when he's there, so Mom and I were a bit shocked.

Little Joe sang for him. He seemed to like it. Wish you were there to be in the pictures!

Flo

●●

From: Fawn Birchill
Sent: Mon, Nov 19, 2018 at 8:12 AM
To: Jacob Whitney
Subject: Black Friday?

Mr. Whitney,

I have been patient and have given you four days to reply to my email regarding the delivery of the books. Black Friday is November 23, if you aren't aware, and therefore I have very little time to spare if we are to have a decent inventory of this exciting new stock for our Black Friday customers. This is not a joke, nor a hobby, nor do I ask for these things to happen on a whim. This is strategy. Let us set up a time. Please email me ASAP or give me your phone number, and I will call you.

Many thanks,
Fawn Birchill, Owner, The Curious Cat Book Emporium (a Mark Twain specialist store)

●●

November 19, 2018
I must defend myself here. I've run this store for twenty years, and I've dealt with my share of questionable characters in my time. Therefore, I know better than to just send a check to someone I've never met who claims to have a thousand books for me. You might ask, What exactly were you thinking? Honestly, I shouldn't have been so trigger-happy. I was so wrapped up in the fantasy of actually having something unique to offer that it clouded all judgment. Perhaps he is just disorganized and busy? I will have to believe this, because to think otherwise would inflict me with insomnia for the next few months.

I should call Florence and see what she thinks. Or perhaps I should call her husband, who is in retail. But I can't! I can't possibly ask them. If this turns out disastrously, understand that I didn't have a good feeling about this, but my desperation got the better of me. Like that time I got asked to a sleepover by the popular girls only to discover that I had been invited so they could make fun of me and send me on errands the entire night. I should know better than this. I should know better.

The toilet continues to leak, so I've closed off the bathroom to customers and employees. I let Sam, Kyle, and Angela use my personal bathroom, which works for now. Kyle tried to fix the bookstore bathroom, but the leak only became worse. I drained the tank, and when trying to unhook the connection I managed to break one of the pieces. After the store closed, I spent a good hour on the floor, despite my bad back, and taped the broken connection with so much duct tape that I was sure it would work. Well, I turned the water back on, flushed the toilet, and discovered firsthand just how much water is used to flush. Now soaked, I grabbed what towels I could find and laid them out on the floor. I don't know what to do. I can't afford a plumber right now.

From: Fawn Birchill
Sent: Mon, Nov 19, 2018 at 3:09 PM
To: Staff
Subject: Thanksgiving, Black Friday

Dear Staff,

I'm sure it is rather unnecessary to announce this, but the store will be closed on Thanksgiving Day, Thursday, November 22. Equally obvious, the store will be open on Friday, November 23. Unlike last year when I spent exorbitant amounts of money on advertisements for doorbuster sales that amounted to a piddling show of about ten people at 7 a.m.—most of whom bought nothing but drank all my free coffee (Kyle and Sam, this was before your time)—this year we shall do something a little differently. We shall be open during our usual Black Friday hours of 7 a.m. to 8 p.m., and since it is a fairly popular day without the need for advertisement, we will simply let people know when they come in that the entire store is 40 percent off. Meanwhile, I am trying very hard to get Mr. Whitney to deliver the books prior to Black Friday, but he is being extremely unresponsive and irresponsible. If we end up getting this inventory early (fingers crossed), I will require all of you to help shelve the books.

Black Friday is a mandatory, all-hands-on-deck day. Come to me if you have an issue with this, but unless you are bleeding from your neck or any necessary appendage, you are REQUIRED to show.

Many thanks and enjoy your Thanksgivings!!

Fawn, Owner

From: Sam Asimov
Sent: Mon, Nov 19, 2018 at 8:07 PM
To: Fawn Birchill
Re: Thanksgiving, Black Friday

Hi Fawn,

Would it be all right with you if I took off Black Friday? My grandpa is very old, and it might be his last Thanksgiving. He lives in Pittsburgh, so it's a haul to get there and would be impossible to get back in time for Black Friday. My grandpa and I are pretty close, so it would mean a lot if I could do this.

Thank you,
Sam

From: Fawn Birchill
Sent: Mon, Nov 19, 2018 at 9:18 PM
To: Sam Asimov
Re: Thanksgiving, Black Friday

Sam,

I understand that your grandfather is old (my father is old as well), but please be reminded that I am not taking away your Thanksgiving. You will, no doubt, still have plenty of time to eat with him and drive back from Pittsburgh as long as you don't leave too late. Need I remind you, as I needed to remind both Angela and Kyle, who had the courage to approach me directly, that you are in retail, and you must understand that this commitment comes with the territory. I will not be visiting my family on Thanksgiving as I will be here preparing for Friday. You should count yourself lucky that I am not asking you to come in the evening before Thanksgiving—or worse, the evening of—and help me. I make sacrifices so that the three of you can have a semblance (in fact, more than a semblance) of a family life while still working in retail. My brother-in-law has been in retail for fifteen years and has never had a long Thanksgiving weekend or a decent Christmas break, and he is still a functioning family member. This should give you some comfort.

See you Friday,
Fawn, Owner

From: Fawn Birchill
Sent: Wed, Nov 21, 2018 at 7:00 PM
To: Jacob Whitney
Subject: HIGH IMPORTANCE: Please Advise

Dear Mr. Whitney,

I can only assume that you are either injured or with family in a location that does not have the internet. I have been informed that my nemesis, the bookstore down the street, will be opening its nefarious doors for the first time on Black Friday! Though this is a potentially cataclysmic event, what would greatly allow us to stand a chance against this monster is if we simply had the Mark Twain books. I have paid you the money and saw that you cashed the check. PLEASE deliver the books before Friday, and I will be eternally grateful.

Stressed but hopeful,
Fawn Birchill, Owner, The Curious Cat Book Emporium (a Mark Twain specialist store)

P.S. When I close my eyes and go to sleep at night, three words float around in my head like lava in a lamp: chapter 7 bankruptcy. Don't be the leak in my ship, Mr. Whitney.

November 21

Dear Fawn,
I cut out some CVS coupons and have enclosed them here. I thought they might be of use to you. I am also enclosing a funny *Cathy* comic that made me LOL. I hope you like it.

Hope to see you at Thanksgiving!
Mother

From: Fawn Birchill
Sent: Wed, Nov 21, 2018 at 8:14 PM
To: Staff
Subject: Please Advise

Dear Staff,

As you may be aware, the new bookstore's official opening will be on Black Friday. Before we all panic, I have a strategy! I went to CVS and bought some poster supplies so we can announce our 40 percent off sale. We will put posters in the windows and adhere them to the telephone pole outside the store. I have taken photos of the posters with the digital camera and am having trouble uploading them to show you, but if you have free time tonight to stop by the store and give me your opinion, I would be very grateful.

If anyone can offer me some tech support through email regarding uploading the photos from this hellish device, I would be equally grateful. When I connect the wire from the camera to the computer, it doesn't prompt me to do anything but assumes I know exactly what to hit or what program to open, as if I am some kind of technical savant. The thing about computers is that they are presumptuous machines and show neither patience nor adaptability based on the user's level of comprehension. Although I understand they are insentient machines, this still infuriates me, as I am forced to write to my dear employees for help the night before Thanksgiving when most of you are no doubt hitting the booze. I, too, am minutes away from that myself—not because of relaxation, but because I can't handle this project sober for another minute.

Any assistance is greatly appreciated!

Best wishes,
Fawn, Owner

From: Jacob Whitney
Sent: Wed, Nov 21, 2018 at 9:03 PM
To: Fawn Birchill
Re: HIGH IMPORTANCE: Please Advise

Greetings!

Terribly sorry for the delay on my part. As Black Friday is right around the corner, this would be a very costly, last-minute request. I'll see what I can do.

Regards,
Jacob

From: Fawn Birchill
Sent: Wed, Nov 21, 2018 at 9:09 PM
To: Jacob Whitney
Re: HIGH IMPORTANCE: Please Advise

Dear Mr. Whitney,

Thank you for your reply!! If you had been paying attention to my emails from the beginning, you would have had plenty of time to arrange a delivery of these books *before* Black Friday. As it stands, we are too late for traditional shipping, but please understand that I am willing to rent a truck, drive to Paoli, and pick them up myself right now. Though I haven't driven in many years and am terrified of highways, I am willing to do this because it is that important to me. Or, you could simply hire a delivery service to bring them here tonight. I will pay for it.

Sincerely,
Fawn Birchill, Owner, The Curious Cat Book Emporium (a Mark Twain specialist store)

From: Fawn Birchill
Sent: Wed, Nov 21, 2018 at 9:18 PM
To: Staff
Subject: Please Advise

Hello again!

Can someone please assist me through email or phone on how to send the photographs of the posters over to you all for final approval? I'm not sure if they look right and I could use your opinions. I took the pictures with my camera, but I can't figure out how to get them onto the computer.

Many thanks!
Fawn, Owner

From: Angela Washington
Sent: Wed, Nov 21, 2018 at 9:31 PM
To: Fawn Birchill
Re: Please Advise

What are you seeing when you plug the camera in? There's a drive that recognizes devices when you plug them in.

—A

From: Fawn Birchill
Sent: Wed, Nov 21, 2018 at 9:50 PM
To: Angela Washington
Re: Please Advise

Angela, you are so kind to write back! I have the wire connected, but when I click "Start" and then "Drives," there is nothing there but the C drive, something else I don't recognize, and the D drive with a little boxy-looking picture. Could that be it?

Many thanks,
Fawn, Owner

P.S. I know, I know. I realize I'm the last person in the universe to give in and buy a smartphone. :(

From: Angela Washington
Sent: Wed, Nov 21, 2018 at 10:05 PM
To: Fawn Birchill
Re: Please Advise

Can you take a pic on your phone and send me what you're seeing? I think you want the D drive.

—A

From: Fawn Birchill
Sent: Wed, Nov 21, 2018 at 10:16 PM
To: Angela Washington

Re: Please Advise

Well, I would take a picture of it and show you if I could. I guess the boxy-looking thing could be a camera. Is the camera usually on the D drive? Why don't they just call it a camera drive?

I just clicked on it, but then nothing happens. I give up. The posters will have to do as they are. If they are ugly and not to anyone's liking, feel free to blame the D drive.

Fawn, Owner

From: Fawn Birchill
Sent: Fri, Nov 23, 2018 at 7:15 AM
To: Staff
Subject: Black Friday Doughnuts!!!

Dear Staff,

There are doughnuts and bagels in the kitchen. Please help yourselves! It's important to stay energized on this very important day! (Please do not eat in front of the customers.)

Fawn, Owner

P.S. Has anyone heard from Angela? She won't pick up her phone.

●●

From: Fawn Birchill
Sent: Fri, Nov 23, 2018 at 12:30 PM
To: Angela Washington
Subject: Edible Arrangements

Angela,

Simply sending an Edible Arrangements basket in lieu of your presence on Black Friday (the most important retail day of the year) is ludicrous and inadequate. How dare you assume that this is a suitable apology for a no-show? I understand family is important, but family is constant, unlike a paycheck.

Still, we are enjoying the fruit. When you return, we will discuss a proper punishment.

Fawn, Owner

●●

From: Fawn Birchill
Sent: Fri, Nov 23, 2018 at 8:59 PM
To: Staff
Subject: A Success!

Dear Staff,

Thank you so much for your efforts today! Although customers only started to trickle in around 9 a.m., I still think we had a very successful day, even without Angela's presence. And even though we did not have the Mark Twain inventory delivered in time as I had hoped, I don't think I've heard the cash register pop open that much since last year at this time! Truly, you should all be commended. You stayed positive during the slow morning hours, kept your energy up as we cleaned up from the madness of the day, and ignored the long and pretentious line of people down the street for the grand opening of a store they had no idea about. They must have paid those people to stand in line.

I am truly blessed to have you all helping out today, and I appreciate your stiff upper lips in the face of the adversity of new store openings and absent employees. Also, thank you, Sam, for jumping on the register so that I could lie down. My back is really getting worse, and the eye twitching seems to be somehow connected.

Fawn, Owner

P.S. Who names a bookstore the Grumpy Mug Bookstop? I can't tell if it's a photo booth for criminals or a store that sells heavy tomes as doorstops. Confusing? Misleading? I think so!

●●

Dear Fawn,

Somebody left a ziplock bag of pizza in my refrigerator. Did you leave it? It was good.

—Jane, your tenant

●●

From: Fawn Birchill
Sent: Sat, Nov 24, 2018 at 1:03 PM
To: Jacob Whitney
Subject: Black Friday Hell

Dear Mr. Whitney,

Although I stayed positive throughout the day and afterward commended my employees for their excellent job in the face of adversity, I am sickened by how poorly our Black Friday actually went. I looked at the numbers, and it was surely the most abysmal Black Friday I have on record. I am able to tell you, with utmost surety, that Black Friday's sales were akin to a typical rainy day in February. Do you understand what this means? I will help you if you do not. What this means is that we did not get the proper inventory in for the busiest day of the year, customers were disappointed to find NOTHING new to buy, and I lost hundreds of dollars while my nemesis gained not only happy customers but all the money that was rightfully mine for the taking. I am almost too upset to go on, and so I will instead plan my next move. Wallowing does a person not a shred of good.

And so, when will you be able to have the books delivered? Let's please aim for before Christmas and spare me from another cruel circumstance.

Fawn Birchill, Owner, The Curious Cat Book Emporium (a Mark Twain specialist store)

From: Jacob Whitney
Sent: Sat, Nov 24, 2018 at 3:56 PM
To: Fawn Birchill
Re: Black Friday Hell

Fawn,

Please expect the books to arrive within the next couple of weeks.

Best wishes,
Jacob

••

From: Fawn Birchill
Sent: Sat, Nov 24, 2018 at 4:09 PM
To: Angela Washington
Subject: Punishment

Angela,

I have thought about it long and hard, and I believe the proper step to take is suspension without pay for one week. I will see you back here on Monday, December 3.

I looked up the price of the arrangement you sent us, and it almost knocked me to the floor. Though it was an expensive apology, it doesn't take away the sting of abandonment. Enjoy your week off.

Fawn, Owner

••

Advertisement

ANNOUNCING THE NEW MARK TWAIN ROOM!

In West Philadelphia, steps from Clark Park and the Green Line, sits one of the most renowned and beloved bookstores in the city: the Curious Cat Book Emporium.

This neighborhood staple has recently gained a niche in the bookselling world by being the ONLY MARK TWAIN SPECIALIST in Pennsylvania. Doors will open Friday, December 14, to reveal the new Mark Twain Room, where over a thousand old tomes of various Mark Twain titles will be on sale. Prices will vary depending on the rarity and edition of the books, but Ms. Birchill will ensure that the books are professionally appraised.

A selection of this magnitude has never before been available to the Philadelphia public. Stop by December 14 and get your copy. One day, perhaps you will tell your grandchildren with pride that you were there when the Mark Twain Room was opened for the first time, and it forever changed your perspective on life. This is the past coming to the present; this is happening now, so take advantage and don't miss out!

*Free coffee will be available along with home-baked cookies. (One cup of coffee and one cookie per customer, and you must show receipt of sale to receive the coffee and cookie.)

December 1

Dear Florence,
Enclosed please find three CDs I found at a thrift store that I thought Little Joe might like to have as he practices his singing skills. I realize Sarah Brightman and Charlotte Church might be out of his vocal range, but they are lovely to listen to all the same. The Josh Groban CD skips a little, and Sarah Brightman's "Moon River" is a disaster, as it skips throughout the entirety of the song, so he might want to forego that one altogether. Otherwise the CDs are in good shape. I hope he enjoys!

Fawn

December 4

Fawn,
Thank you so much for the CDs! When Little Joe opened them, he screamed loud enough to scare the parakeet. She made a beeline toward the cage bars and landed on the ground in her own seeds and poo. It was funny (only after we realized she was okay). So, yeah, the scream proves that Little Joe can definitely reach the range of Charlotte Church and Sarah Brightman! It was very nice of you to think of us while you were out shopping. He is currently listening to Sarah Brightman in his room. I had to pull out my old boom box from the basement because we don't have a CD player in the house anymore. Guess what was inside the CD player: the Chopin CD you let me borrow a million years ago. Do you want it back? I had completely forgotten you let me listen to it.

Thanks again, Fawn.
Flo

P.S. You were missed at Thanksgiving this year.

From: Fawn Birchill
Sent: Thu, Dec 6, 2018 at 8:13 PM
To: Staff
Subject: Customer Bathroom

Dear Staff,

This evening I discovered that despite the out-of-order sign and the water on the floor, someone is still using the customer bathroom. I do not know if it is our illiterate customers or employees who can't seem to hold it long enough to climb the stairs to my abode, but *please* do your best to not let this continue! It is unsanitary and an eyesore. I am in the process of trying to fix it myself—I promise—but until then we must endure this setback.

Thank you for your patience!
Fawn, Owner

P.S. Speaking of eyesores, I have left a live trap outside the alley for one of the cats that has a perpetually watery eye. If you see it in there, let me know. I plan to take it to the vet.

phillysmallbiz.com
Sun, Dec 9, 2018

Top Review—The Curious Cat Book Emporium
Ah, every time I walk through these doors it makes my day! I came in looking for *Les Misérables*, and one of their fine employees (the handsome one with the beard) was able to help me very quickly. In all my travels around the globe, this is by far the finest bookstore I have ever been in. And that Butterscotch! Ah, what a darling! Clearly, he is well cared for and deeply loved. And this cannot be just me who thinks this, but I have to ask: Doesn't the owner bear an uncanny resemblance to an older Keira Knightley?

And let me also say that I have been to the new store down the street, and it doesn't hold a candle to the emporium. Its dullness is palpable. I can feel it emanating off the street like a rank odor from the moors in which I grew up. I feel sorry for whoever must work in that drab establishment all day.

Can't wait to return to the emporium! Keep up the great work!

—Sybil C.

phillysmallbiz.com
Sun, Dec 9, 2018

Dear Sybil C.,

Thank you for your five-heart review of my bookstore. It means so much when I know my hard work has paid off. I'm also glad we were able to locate *Les Misérables* for you. It is on my reading list, so please let me know what you think of it. I have a feeling that we have similar tastes. When it comes to literature, I find that it's less about the books themselves and more the moments we take in the day to read the books. I often look back and remember the rain on the window or the tea in the cup. I remember the angle of a splash of sunlight, or the purring of my cat on my lap. The book is only a companion to these moments, but without the book, these moments may not have happened. Therefore, it is all the better, I think, to have as excellent a book as possible. Don't you agree? I think you would.

You flatter me, and saying that my store is the best you've run into in all your world travels speaks volumes to me. And yes, Butterscotch really adds a flare of life and homeyness to the store. I haven't been in the new store down the street, but I will take your word that mine is superior, although I do not wish to engage in competitive behavior, as we are both clearly after the same thing: providing excellent literature to the West Philadelphia area.

Personally, I do not believe I resemble Keira Knightley, but if you say so then I must accept. Ha ha! Do keep in touch.

Sincerely,
Fawn, Owner, The Curious Cat Book Emporium (a Mark Twain specialist store)

••

From: Fawn Birchill
Sent: Mon, Dec 10, 2018 at 8:09 AM
To: Florence Eakins
Subject: Father

Dear Florence,

I received a voice mail from Mother begging me to see our father. Sometimes I think I can't live far enough away or be busy enough to make her understand that I can't handle being in hospice centers. All that I think of is death and my own future. Luckily for you, your children will take you on as their burden in forty years, but I have no one. A facility will be my doom. They might as well keep the bed warm for me after Father goes. Doesn't she understand that? It's like staring down the barrel of a loaded gun. Does that sound selfish? By the way, this is not to say that I wish I had children; it is merely to say that I wish I had loads and loads of money to pay nurses to take care of me in my home, so I can be comfortable there and not among cold hallways with thin blankets and the constant smell of death.

In other news, my life is about to turn a very important corner! In a little less than a week, I am to receive nearly a thousand Mark Twain books. They are not all worth much, but by sheer volume alone I will be the only Mark Twain specialist in all Pennsylvania. I've done some Google searches, and no one has the kind of volume that I will have. It is extremely exciting and surely puts me up to a new criterion of bookseller. Perhaps I will start being recognized at conventions. Won't that be something!

If Father were still lucid, I'd like to think he would be proud of me for my success. No doubt he would claim responsibility for anything good that happens in my store—he always had a way of letting me know that everything I ever learned was gleaned through him. I might have received much of my business acumen from Father, but let's not forget that he ended up in financial ruin, so I learned as much from his mistakes as I did from his infrequent successes.

How is your husband? Is he still selling perfumes at Macy's? Shoplifting must be terrible there this time of year. How are the kids? Has Charles got his braces off yet? Remember, don't stop moving during the holidays. This is that time in which even skinny people like us gain a few pounds if we're not careful!

Fawn

From: Florence Eakins
Sent: Mon, Dec 10, 2018 at 10:13 AM
To: Fawn Birchill
Re: Father

Hi Fawn,

I'm not sure what to address here first. I guess I'll start with Joseph, who doesn't work in the perfumes section anymore but has been moved to the home section. He seems happier there—"seems" being the operative word since he doesn't like talking about his job very much because it depresses him.

I hope you know that I don't intend for Little Joe or Charles to take care of me when I'm unable to care for myself. It would be nice, but it's certainly not something I'm expecting, nor did I have kids for this purpose. God, I hope you don't think that. Also, the hospice center isn't that bad, Fawn. The medical staff there have an incredibly difficult job, and they do their very best to make it as nice as possible for their patients. It's not like Mom and I are asking you to crawl into a grave with us. I think your perspective is in dire need of a shift. Actually, going to the hospice center once in a while might help with that.

In other news, I'm happy to hear about the Mark Twain books. I know running a business is tough, and it's important these days to find ways to stand out from the crowd, for sure. I'm glad you've found something after all these years.

Flo

●●

December 10, 2018

I managed to trap the cat with the runny eye. According to the vet, I am supposed to put drops in his eye, but I can't bring him inside, as Butterscotch's safety is my priority. And it's not as if I can chase him around the neighborhood with an eyedropper! Anyway, I told them I couldn't possibly, and they seemed to understand. They gave him a shot of something and said the eye trouble will likely clear up on its own. I let him go tonight. The vet bill was atrocious, but it was worth it. I hope he gets better, the poor thing.

If I could slip away from my family without them worrying, I would. I would go somewhere exotic maybe, and let thousands of miles be my excuse. I suppose I could, money or no money. People have picked up and left before and somehow made it.

I do the best I can, but I can't shake the feeling that my family's eyes are on me all the time. I can't shake the feeling that they are, for some reason, worried about me. I don't know why they would be. And using Father as an excuse to check on me, which is what I think is happening, angers me to the point where I simply want to dig my heels in. I wish Philadelphia were hours from Norristown. I wish I didn't love this city, this store, or this building as much as I do. If I could pick this city up and move it to Borneo just to be away from my family, I would.

When I'm here, I'm not the awkward girl who swept up cigarette butts and candy wrappers, who fell asleep at the cash register and hit her face on it so hard one day that she chipped her front tooth. I am not the older sister who was constantly abandoned at the register so Florence could balance the books. I am not the daughter of a mother who constantly mixed up our too-similar names. I am not the daughter of a father who saw his children more as workhorses than young girls. Who showed his love in paltry allowances and swift knocks upside the head. I am Fawn, simply Fawn, who is an adult now but is still waiting for that to sink in. I thought that maybe when I developed lines and gray hair, I would finally molt my arduous past, but sadly I am still waiting. I am a snake carrying around old skin. What a disgusting analogy. This is what happens when I run out of wine: my thoughts turn strange. To the liquor store!

••

From: Fawn Birchill
Sent: Mon, Dec 10, 2018 at 6:08 PM
To: Staff
Subject: Closing Tills

Dear Staff,

I was taking a look at the closing tills this evening and found to my horror that they were dreadfully low for mid-December. I want to make sure that no one is giving away any books without my permission. If so, please let me know. No one will be in trouble but merely educated. Now that we have a direct competitor a block away, we must be as stringent as ever with our numbers and less generous than we used to be. This saddens me, but it's the way life goes.

I am considering that we run the batch twice at the end of the night to ensure the numbers are correct. It's an old machine, so I wonder if maybe it is inaccurate.

Also, one of the windows toward the back is open. I do not know how long it has been like that, but it may explain the draft and the high energy bills. I tried shutting it, but it wouldn't budge. I even stood up on a chair and hit the top of it with a hammer to try and knock it down, but it did nothing. Kyle, when you get in tomorrow morning, I will need your help.

Many thanks!
Fawn, Owner

••

From: Fawn Birchill
Sent: Mon, Dec 10, 2018 at 6:34 PM
To: Fortieth Street Catering
Subject: Delightful Mouthfuls

Dear Fortieth Street Catering,

Ah, the cookies! The sandwiches! The salads! Your food is beyond delightful. I was lucky enough to have some at a function at the Cira Centre that, I daresay, I may not have been invited to, but because I was wearing a fur coat on my way to the Amtrak station, they let me beyond the velvet ropes and into the soiree without question! I missed my train, but it was okay; I was only going to see my mother. Long story short, the party was for the unveiling of a memorial for a local artist whose name escapes me, but no doubt her sculpture is still there. As I milled about amid the upper strata of Philadelphia society, I mostly stayed glued to the catering table. Luckily it was an open bar, and most everyone was too drunk to notice me sneaking the mini sandwiches into my overnight bag. The olive array was, by far, my favorite—though they are rather difficult to sneak into anything but one's mouth! I made off with about eight sandwiches, five cookies, and a mouthful of olives. The sandwiches, to my pleasant surprise, were just as good the following day! (A testament to your culinary genius.) Before I ramble on any further, I will get to the purpose of my correspondence. I am hoping to hold a holiday party for my staff. As you may know, I own the Curious Cat Book Emporium, and I'm sure I don't need to tell you what we do, as most Philadelphians in even a tenuous state of awareness know of us. We are a small company (there are only four of us including myself), but I want to pull out all the stops, as they say, as it's been a wonderfully successful year. I am most interested in the pepperoni platter, the prosciutto wraps, the veggie tray for our vegetarian employee, and the cookie tray. For a main course I'd like the same sandwiches that you had at the Cira Centre. I'm sure if you look through your records, you will find the right ones. Since I am a local business owner and right around the corner from you, I was hoping you could offer us some kind of discount. Somewhere in the 40 percent off category? Please write back soon and let me know what you think. Or stop by the store!

Yours in business,
Fawn, Owner, The Curious Cat Book
Emporium (a Mark Twain specialist store)

From: Fortieth Street Catering
Sent: Mon, Dec 10, 2018 at 7:18 PM
To: Fawn Birchill
Re: Delightful Mouthfuls

Hi Fawn,

Thank you for reaching out to us regarding your holiday party. The price breakdown is attached for our standard corporate party trays, but feel free to mix and match items as you see fit. For example, you can swap out the vegetarian sandwiches for roast beef if everyone is a meat eater.

And unfortunately, we do not offer a discount for fellow business owners. By the nature of our business, most of our customers are business owners, so it wouldn't make much sense for us to offer a reduced rate for nearly 90 percent of our clientele. Sorry!

Please let us know if you have any questions at all and thanks again!

Have a good night,
Carl Suzuki

From: Fawn Birchill
Sent: Mon, Dec 10, 2018 at 10:03 PM
To: Fortieth Street Catering
Re: Delightful Mouthfuls

Dear Carl,

Thank you for getting back to me so quickly regarding the holiday party, though I must admit the price you threw at me almost gave me a heart attack. Luckily, I was seated at the time! For a sandwich platter, prosciutto wraps, pepperoni tray, veggies, and a cookie platter, you'd think I was asking Gordon Ramsay to cater the queen of England's jubilee. I worry that I may have given you the wrong impression of my financial status when I told you that I was wearing a fur coat. The coat was a hand-me-down from my great aunt Mabel who ran with the mob in New York during the Prohibition era. It's falling apart in many places, but you can't tell unless you look closely. My aunt Mabel was the only person in our entire family who had money, and that's only because she was pretty and sometimes poisoned people for money.

And may I remind you that, though quite successful, I am not ready to spend $300 for four people. I really don't want to resort to a pizza delivery for our holiday party, but it's looking closer to reality. What if we left out the pepperoni and the prosciutto? That would leave it at $200, and then with the discount of 40 percent it would only come to $120—quite affordable! And since nothing should be done for free, I will offer you a lifetime discount of 20 percent on all my books. How does that strike you? Do let me know.

Yours in business,
Fawn, Owner, The Curious Cat Book Emporium (a Mark Twain specialist store)

P.S. What does a catering company do for a holiday party? Do you eat your own food, or do you hire another catering company? I've always wondered.

From: Fawn Birchill
Sent: Tue, Dec 11, 2018 at 8:45 AM
To: Staff
Subject: Alphabetization

Dear Staff,

A comes before *b*, and *b* comes before *c*. If you cannot learn to properly alphabetize, then I will hold an after-hours seminar on the fundamentals. I wonder how many people walked out of my store and went to the Grumpy Mug when they couldn't locate Dickens because he was tucked between Tolkien and Tolstoy.

Joyce comes *after* Ben Jonson, not before.

Fawn, Owner

●●

From: Gregory Harris
Sent: Tue, Dec 11, 2018 at 9:12 AM
To: Fawn Windsor
Subject: Christmas in the tropics

Fawn!

Writing to you from a beach in Turks and Caicos. Just went for a morning run, and now I'm bumming around. I wish I could take off my real estate hat and just enjoy myself, but like a lion amid a herd of gazelle, I look around and all I see is fresh meat.

I'll be here until mid-January. My family is joining me in a couple of days. We rented a beach house together that overlooks a cove. It's very desolate out here, which I prefer. In order to get anything in town, I have to hop on a quad and drive it down the beach! How are your holidays so far?

Gregory

From: Fawn Windsor
Sent: Tue, Dec 11, 2018 at 9:34 AM
To: Gregory Harris
Re: Christmas in the tropics

Dear Gregory,

A Christmas gathering in Turks and Caicos sounds lovely. I think your family has the right idea. I for one will be shackled to the family estate assisting with a large event where we will attempt to be merry and bright but will instead probably end up trying to push each other into the fireplace. It doesn't matter how much tinsel I place around or how big and decorated the tree is. It never seems to push the holiday spirit beyond our hard, stubborn exteriors. Christmas is a strange holiday for families that don't get along. We dislike each other for 364 days out of the year and then childishly expect a single day of gift giving to wash all the bad blood away. Being around my family during the holidays is like watching a bad play. Phrases like "thank you," "so delighted to see you," and "Happy Christmas" are jumbled in their mouths and caught between their teeth, struggling to make their way out and to sound halfway truthful. We playact liking anything that is given to us. Instead of being grateful as I turn the horrible knitted hat in my hands, I instead think of how I can sneak it into the bin when no one's looking . . .

One of these years, Gregory, I am going to adopt your idea and flee to somewhere tropical, leaving the tepid festivities to my miserable sister who cracks her signature pained smile when she gets something she doesn't like. Pretending to like something you hate is so important on Christmas, for it keeps the peace. If we end up fighting on what should be the happiest day of the year, then we are all doomed. In a funny way, though, I love the comfort of being surrounded by people on Christmas, even if I can barely stand them. As of late, the numbers of family and friends stopping by during Christmas have decreased, and I find myself less surrounded by those that were once so loyal to me during the holiday season; however, I cannot take it too personally. I understand that things change, and people can be as transitory as the tides. That said, it is a comfort to have loyal people by my side because their presence teaches me that I am not all that horrid to be around after all.

Have a wonderful time down there, and wear lots of sunscreen!

Much love,
Fawn Windsor

From: Fawn Birchill
Sent: Tue, Dec 11, 2018 at 8:07 PM
To: Staff
Subject: Tills

Dear Staff,

For those of you who left early today and didn't settle the tills with Angela, I want to inform you that the machine is accurate and that sales are indeed abysmal. I know during our meeting we all denied giving away books to people who come into the store, but I cannot stress how important it is to no longer do that. I see bodies in the store, but no one is buying. Can you please watch where they go after they leave? I fear it is to the Grumpy Mug. If that is the case, we need to pull out all the stops this Christmas. We shall not be donning our gay apparel this Christmas, shipmates, but instead donning full battle gear. Report back to me as to how many customers go to the Grumpy Mug, and if the numbers are what I think they are, we have to change tack.

Fawn, Owner

●●

December 11, 2018

We will get through this. I will get through this.

I don't visit my bank account landing page anymore because the numbers are enough to invoke the eye twitch, so lately I just wait for the email alert telling me that I have less than fifty dollars in my account. That's when I throw another fifty in from my paltry savings and have a glass of wine.

Even though I've drained the toilet in the customer bathroom, there is still water leaking from somewhere. The floor is growing soft, and I don't know what to do. On top of that, Kyle, Sam, Angela, and I all tried shutting the jammed window together but nothing happened. And then a customer suggested I use WD-40. So I sprayed some in the sides and voilà! The window shut. This was after I cracked the glass from trying to hammer it shut. Now there is another air leak, albeit comparatively modest.

It's always a good day when I receive Jane's rent. Her daughter, who happens to live in Hawaii, always sends it on time, thankfully. Last night I went down to check on her again. I stood outside the door and pressed my ear to it. The television volume was so loud that it sounded more like an air-raid announcement. There was another noise that I recognized but couldn't place.

I was back in my apartment when I realized that it was the sound of Jane's recliner. My father had the same one; I know because of the mechanical sound it makes when the lever is pulled and the whump of the upholstered footrest knocks against the chair's frame. It made me shudder. It immediately brought me right back to my childhood. In instances like this, I doubt the linearity of time. If it were linear, how is it possible that a single sound can transport me to another place?

Because of my inexhaustible love of culture and all things ethnic, I once went to a Serbian food festival in North Philly—maybe about three years ago at this point—and wandered the small church grounds while a handsome man with an accordion deftly played Serbian songs. I ate delicious food that I've since forgotten the names of, but I do remember there were a lot of meats and vegetables. In any case, they were offering a tour of the church, so of course I signed up, as I knew nothing about Eastern Orthodoxy. And because no one else signed up, I was given the private tour! The priest, a bearded, middle-aged man, led me up the creaky, cloistered stairs. He apologized for walking so slowly due to his knee problems. (This was before my bad back.)

Upon entering I was struck by the iconography, the beautiful paintings on the walls depicting the saints, and the cozy warmth of the quiet, dark place. It smelled of incense, polished wood, and summer. I took a seat in one of the pews and immediately felt transported to medieval Europe. He told me many things that I've since forgotten about Eastern Orthodoxy, but a few facts linger like an old song that you can never quite shake. He said that traditionally the congregation doesn't sit, and the only reason this church had seating was because they bought a Roman Catholic church and didn't feel like ripping out all the nice old pews. He said people traditionally stand because the service is interactive. You are not checking out, sitting back, and relaxing while the priest goes on, but you are an active participant in the word of God. Along those lines, he also explained that it is their belief that time isn't linear. They are not only reading about the

Last Supper, telling a story set thousands of miles away and thousands of years in the past, but they are actually there, watching it take place. They are transported. They fully live the Bible through the course of the year. And when he said this to me, it made perfect sense. I often feel as if my past is my present—that it follows me around, and all I need to do is take a moment to step into it and all the feelings, fears, and desires come screaming back at me. I can see my sister in the back room, working on her homework while organizing invoices. I can see myself changing a light bulb on a ladder so worn with age that every time I climbed it, I crossed myself. I can see my father standing in the doorway of his store and hear the rubbery squeak of his old boots on the dusty floor as he shifted his weight and talked to a customer about a boxing match the night before. How can time be linear if it only takes a single sound, a whump of upholstery, to send me back?

If I happened to believe in God anymore or saw any personal benefit to religion, I'd like to think I'd convert to Eastern Orthodoxy. There is something so perfectly honest about it that appeals to my sensibilities.

Tomorrow we will begin brainstorming about holiday decorations. I've never bothered to decorate in the past, but this year we truly need all the help we can get. Perhaps this will distract me from my worries and get me into the holiday spirit!

From: Fawn Birchill
Sent: Wed, Dec 12, 2018 at 5:10 PM
To: Staff
Subject: Decorations?

Dear Staff,

Normally we don't decorate for the holidays, but due to the fact that there has been no snowfall whatsoever, I am concerned that none of my customers are in the holiday spirit. Therefore, let me know what you think about decorating the store this year to evoke some holiday cheer and hopefully make wallets more slippery than usual.

I was thinking garlands on the staircases and a Christmas tree in the front foyer by the discount books. We can add a menorah in one of the smaller rooms to be inclusive. Thoughts?

Fawn, Owner

From: Angela Washington
Sent: Wed, Dec 12, 2018 at 7:27 PM
To: Fawn Birchill, Staff
Re: Decorations?

What about a snow machine like they have at ski resorts? We can spray snow on the roof and in front of the store.

—A

From: Fawn Birchill
Sent: Wed, Dec 12, 2018 at 7:30 PM
To: Staff
Re: Decorations?

Angela,

I like your suggestion, but how would we get it over the roof?

Fawn, Owner

From: Kyle Krazinsky
Sent: Wed, Dec 12, 2018 at 7:32 PM
To: Fawn Birchill, Staff
Re: Decorations?

Hey Fawn,

For inclusivity, I can try to pick up a Kwanzaa kinara.

Kyle

From: Fawn Birchill
Sent: Wed, Dec 12, 2018 at 7:45 PM
To: Staff
Re: Decorations?

Kyle,

All right, if you can find one. Should we put it in the same room as the menorah or another room? The only other room that is big enough to hold a table with candles is the romance and erotica section, and I don't think it would be an appropriate location.

Fawn, Owner

From: Sam Asimov
Sent: Wed, Dec 12, 2018 at 8:03 PM
To: Fawn Birchill, Staff
Re: Decorations?

Fawn,

Speaking of inclusivity, what if we did something a little different and put the menorah in the front and the Xmas tree elsewhere in the store? That way you don't have to spend as much money on a giant tree.

Sam

From: Fawn Birchill
Sent: Wed, Dec 12, 2018 at 8:12 PM
To: Staff
Re: Decorations?

Sam,

We have to put the Christmas tree in the front because it's the biggest holiday fixture. Blame the pagans, not me.

And a small tree wouldn't work. I think it should be as big as possible because, quite honestly, a big Christmas tree will make people shop more than a giant menorah would.

Fawn, Owner

From: Angela Washington
Sent: Wed, Dec 12, 2018 at 8:20 PM
To: Fawn Birchill, Staff
Re: Decorations?

My dad is in construction and might be able to get us a crane that would lift the snow machine over the roof. Also, we have a small machine in our basement that spits fake snow for front window displays. My mom bought it from the Philly Lord + Taylor when they were going out of business.

—A

From: Fawn Birchill
Sent: Wed, Dec 12, 2018 at 8:34 PM
To: Staff
Re: Decorations?

Angela,

Even if you have access to a snow machine, renting a crane would be extremely costly unless you think you can get a good deal on a crane as well.

This all seems very dangerous.

Fawn, Owner

From: Kyle Krazinsky
Sent: Wed, Dec 12, 2018 at 9:13 PM
To: Fawn Birchill, Staff
Re: Decorations?

Hey Fawn,

We should not leave out the Muslim people.

I looked up what they are celebrating at this time, and I found this thing called Ashura. Can we include it somehow?

Kyle

From: Fawn Birchill
Sent: Wed, Dec 12, 2018 at 9:35 PM
To: Staff
Re: Decorations?

Kyle,

I know very little about Ashura, and I understand that it's important to be inclusive of Muslims, but as far as I could tell they do not have candles or a tree of any kind to showcase it. From what I could find on it, it is a time of mourning and I don't believe that's what we are looking to evoke here. Additionally, I think it already took place in September.

Fawn, Owner

From: Sam Asimov
Sent: Wed, Dec 12, 2018 at 9:43 PM
To: Fawn Birchill, Staff
Re: Decorations?

Fawn,

I think all this inclusivity is overly complicating things. What if we get rid of all the religious stuff and just make it secular? So, Frosty the Snowman, wreaths, garlands, etc. All this religious stuff might turn people off anyway.

Sam

From: Fawn Birchill
Sent: Wed, Dec 12, 2018 at 9:50 PM
To: Staff
Re: Decorations?

Sam,

I don't think it will bother anyone as long as we are inclusive and go about this in the right way. Simply omitting a tree, a menorah, and a Kwanzaa display is not what I had in mind. Garland and wreaths alone would be nice but would come across as entirely Christian by default. Frosty the Snowman is a Christian-inspired fabrication, as is any intimation involving candy canes and trumpets, so window stickers of that sort would be exclusive to Christians.

Fawn, Owner

From: Kyle Krazinsky
Sent: Wed, Dec 12, 2018 at 9:55 PM
To: Fawn Birchill, Staff
Re: Decorations?

Hey Fawn,

What about something for the atheists?

Kyle

From: Fawn Birchill
Sent: Wed, Dec 12, 2018 at 10:05 PM
To: Staff
Re: Decorations?

Kyle,

The atheists that I know (that do celebrate the idea of Christmas) have a tree in their homes and only celebrate the gift-giving aspect of it, cutting out the idea of Christ altogether. Sounds like a cop-out to me. So I don't believe they have any kind of candle fixture to celebrate their disbelief structure. I think simply by having a tree in the front, they will see it as a present-giving mechanism and will feel included.

Fawn, Owner

From: Sam Asimov
Sent: Wed, Dec 12, 2018 at 10:36 PM
To: Fawn Birchill, Staff
Re: Decorations?

Fawn,

So then, I have to to ask. Where do your beliefs lie? I'm Jewish, so it's nice to have a menorah, but I really don't care ether way. That said, we should definitely probably make sure to include the owners sensibilities in all this after all . . .

Sam

From: Fawn Birchill
Sent: Wed, Dec 12, 2018 at 10:55 PM
To: Staff
Re: Decorations?

Sam,

What I believe is not important. The idea of inclusion of all people is all that I care about.

Fawn, Owner

From: Angela Washington
Sent: Wed, Dec 12, 2018 at 11:01 PM
To: Fawn Birchill, Staff
Re: Decorations?

Oh, come on!!!!11 Sam's Jewish, and I'm a Baptist. Kyle???

—A

From: Kyle Krazinsky
Sent: Wed, Dec 12, 2018 at 11:02 PM
To: Fawn Birchill, Staff
Re: Decorations?

Kyle is trying to sleep. Phone is going off.

Kyle

From: Fawn Birchill
Sent: Wed, Dec 12, 2018 at 11:05 PM
To: Staff
Re: Decorations?

Kyle, Angela, Sam,

Fine. I dabbled in paganism in college and studied witchcraft shortly thereafter. If I were to say what I am now, I am an agnostic who believes that if there is a God, he is definitely a man because of how badly women are put together.

Fawn, Owner

From: Angela Washington
Sent: Wed, Dec 12, 2018 at 11:13 PM
To: Fawn Birchill, Staff
Re: Decorations?

Fawn,

I still think the snow machine idea is the best idea. Also, I just did a double take on that last email about women being put together badly. WTF? LOL. But seriously . . . ?

—A

From: Fawn Birchill
Sent: Wed, Dec 12, 2018 at 11:30 PM
To: Staff
Re: Decorations?

Angela,

That might work. How much is it to rent per day from your father? I doubt the Grumpy Mug will have this in their arsenal!

Fawn, Owner

P.S. I'm sorry. I meant nothing by it. I was mostly referring to the ridiculousness of monthly bleeding. I'm not sure how well that worked out for us in our caveman days as we traipsed across the African savanna smelling like blood to any lions or leopards nearby.

We must have been as enticing as a street-taco truck to a college kid. On the other hand, perhaps the fact that women survived that is indeed a testament to how strong we are!

From: Sam Asimov
Sent: Wed, Dec 12, 2018 at 11:39 PM
To: Fawn Birchill, Staff
Re: Decorations?

Hi Fawn,

Okay, I think I got this figured out. Let's just put everything together to to make this super PC. No single religion is thrown into some back room. Also, let's include your Wiccan background! Why not?/ I'm sure there are cool things to display in that regard.

Also holiday music! – Hanukkah and Christma for sure. We need that.

Sam

From: Fawn Birchill
Sent: Wed, Dec 12, 2018 at 11:45 PM
To: Staff
Re: Decorations?

Sam,

I think putting the Kwanzaa candles and

menorah next to the tree is a fire hazard. There is a safety issue here that goes beyond the idea of being fair to all belief structures. Therefore, I will stick with the idea of putting them all in separate rooms.

I also think that including any Wiccan paraphernalia in the scene might confuse and anger people, so I will opt to leave that out. Also, are you drinking while writing to your boss?

Fawn, Owner

From: Angela Washington
Sent: Wed, Dec 12, 2018 at 11:54 PM
To: Fawn Birchill, Staff
Re: Decorations?

No one would know any different. You said yourself that Christmas comes from the pagans or whatever.

—A

From: Fawn Birchill
Sent: Thu, Dec 13, 2018 at 12:10 AM
To: Staff
Re: Decorations?

Kyle, Sam, Angela,

A final decision has been made. Thank you all for your after-hours assistance with this! We will have a tree in the front foyer, a menorah in the romance section, and a Kwanzaa display in the future Mark Twain Room. We will hang a cinnamon besom near the door and put pine-scented rings in the lighting fixtures. We will wrap garland around the staircase banisters, and Angela's father will stop by and blow some snow onto the front walkway. Kyle, I will need you to shovel because of my back.

Sam suggested a mixture of Hanukkah and Christmas music, so he will put together a playlist. Please, no Adam Sandler.

Additionally, I have purchased some mini reindeer antlers for Butterscotch. If you see him trying to remove them, let me know. He always has such an incomprehensible problem with them.

Fawn, Owner

●●

From: Fawn Birchill
Sent: Thu, Dec 13, 2018 at 12:30 AM
To: Florence Eakins
Subject: Christmas!

Dear Florence,

It was so nice to hear back from you, and sorry it's taken me this long to reply. I'm glad to hear that Joseph is doing well. Forgive me; I thought he was still in the perfume section. I see his move as a definitive step up for his masculinity, and I'm sure he agrees. Spraying eau de toilette on old ladies' baggy necks can't be very rewarding or confidence boosting.

This is by far the busiest holiday season we've had. I should have asked to have the Mark Twain collection shipped after Christmas, but something told me they would go faster if they were put into inventory before the holidays. Call it retail common sense. So I've worked myself into a pretty corner where not only are we receiving the shipment tomorrow morning, but we have to have the entire store fully decorated Saturday night. I can't believe there is only a week left before Christmas!

Speaking of, what would you like? Anything from the bookstore (except for the rare books) can be yours—just name a title! For me, I don't want much. As an aside, do you think Joseph can get good deals on microwaves? The "2" and the "Minute Plus" button are defunct on my current microwave, so instead of putting the timer on for 12:00 minutes, I have to put it on for 11:59. I also use "Defrost" quite a bit, and lately that button has been finicky.

I must be getting old because I have started to freeze my baked goods and leftover dinners just like Mother does. Call me crazy, but it sounds like something that only a Depression-era survivor would do. Or perhaps it is lengthening her life span and her memory—preserving her baked goods, thereby preserving her life and her imprint on the world. If this is true, she probably can't bear to see her own food go moldy. It must feel like someone walking over her grave.

Wish me luck tomorrow. I will be very busy in the next two months, so don't get your hopes up for me visiting you or the parents. I will stay young by staying busy—even if it kills me!

Fawn

From: Florence Eakins
Sent: Thu, Dec 13, 2018 at 10:23 AM
To: Fawn Birchill
Re: Christmas!

Hi Fawn,

Please don't do too much for us this year for Christmas. To be honest, I'd do away with our gift exchange altogether, but I know how much it means to you to have something to open. If that hasn't changed, let's keep things modest? I'll see what we can do about a microwave, but no promises. Joseph's employee discount isn't as great as you'd think, and of course the boys want literally everything they lay their eyes on, haha, so Christmas is always an expensive endeavor.

Is Mom sending you coupons in the mail? She keeps bringing paper-clipped stacks over to us every time she visits, along with cutout comic strips, and I almost went berserk on her yesterday. We literally don't have the time to sift through those coupons or read the comics that she insists we adhere to the fridge. I can't sometimes with her. I'm this close to telling her to stop.

Flo

● ●

From: Fawn Birchill
Sent: Thu, Dec 13, 2018 at 11:39 AM
To: Jacob Whitney
Subject: Important Issue, Pick Up Phone

Dear Mr. Whitney,

Thank you for delivering the books this morning as promised; however, there is one thing blatantly wrong that I fear you were, might I say, keeping from me throughout our correspondence.

I'll put it rather bluntly, Mr. Whitney. I believe I have been fooled, and I believe you think me a total idiot to accept these books. If I had been there receiving the shipment myself, I would have noticed the issue immediately and refused them. Unfortunately, my slow-witted employee accepted the books and not only that but has loaded the shelves of the Mark Twain Room with 850 copies of *The Adventures of Tom Sawyer*.

What, Mr. Whitney, am I to do with 850 copies of the same book? Do you honestly believe that 850 people will walk into my store *all* wanting *Tom Sawyer*? Additionally, they all seem to be from the 1960s at the earliest, and many bear childish renderings of male genitalia in the margins.

You may have seen the advert I recently published in the *Philly Weekly* announcing that I will have close to a thousand *various* Mark Twain books. I have already received emails from people all over Pennsylvania regarding this, excited to see the diversity of the rare and varying books I will have for sale. So not only have I been cheated, I have subsequently cheated my customer base, and that I cannot abide. What am I to tell them?

I demand that you refund me the money and come by to take back the books, for I do not have any use for them in my store. This has been an enormous disappointment, and I am just sick to my stomach over it. My eye alone has broken its twitch record. I can barely see out of it! And this all culminating with the advent of the Grumpy Mug down the street and their delightful CONSTANT Christmas music pumping from their store eight hours a day, welcoming in passersby with promises of hot chocolate and a bright, warm, comfy place to sit while they read whatever books they sell (probably a measly variety, I'm sure). I thought for certain my business would be turning a new corner this year, but clearly I was wrong. How on earth am I to offer anything different now? Without a specialization, how am I to compete?

You may collect the books Monday through Thursday anytime before noon. Just let me know ahead of time so that Kyle has time to pack the books back up. I would deliver them myself, but the only address I have for you is a post office box, and I doubt the post office will let me leave 850 books on the floor by your box.

I appreciate your prompt response.

Best,
Fawn Birchill, Owner, The Curious Cat Book Emporium (a Mark Twain specialist store)

••

Dear Fawn,

I know this couldn't have been my daughter's meat loaf because hers isn't as good. Did you leave this or did someone else? Thank you if it was you. It makes me think of my daughter.

—Jane, your tenant

••

From: Fawn Birchill
Sent: Thu, Dec 13, 2018 at 8:32 PM
To: Staff
Subject: Strategy

Dear Staff,

Due to the plethora of *Tom Sawyer* books, I have had to think long and hard about a solution. I've decided against putting out another advert stating that the books have sold out before I said they were to go on sale. I feel that is also going to be cheating my customers. I have not yet heard back from Mr. Whitney regarding when he will be coming by to pick up the books and refund me the money, so it might be best to just keep going with the sale as planned and see what, if anything, we can sell. I believe we should be up-front about it to our customers, but spin it in a rather positive way by telling them that *Tom Sawyer* is by far Twain's best book and everyone should own a copy. And with every *Tom Sawyer* sold, we will throw in a free candy cane. I am hopeful. This snafu couldn't have come at a better time of year, where almost anyone will buy anything as long as it is pushed enough and something free is thrown in.

Good luck!

Fawn, Owner

P.S. Kyle, after lunch tomorrow I will give you ten dollars. Please go out and buy as many candy canes as you can with it (and get a receipt). Buy Bob's brand—everything else tastes like peppermint-flavored glue.

From: Florence Eakins
Sent: Thu, Dec 13, 2018 at 9:45 PM
To: Fawn Birchill
Subject: Video

Hi Fawn,

Wanted to share this video I made of Little Joe singing for Dad. He is doing his best Josh Groban impression, clearly. He just loves that singer so much. It's so cute. ☺ Also, this isn't in the video, but right after, Dad started talking to me like I was you. I should have caught it on tape. He said you didn't sweep the front steps this morning like he asked and now his customers are going to drag in the dirt. Remember when he used to rail about that all the time? "You're gonna drag in the dirt!" Hahaha, as if the store wasn't filthy already. So glad those days are over. (I guess for him they're not.)

Hope you enjoy this. I love the smile on Dad's face.

Flo

••

From: Fawn Birchill
Sent: Fri, Dec 14, 2018 at 4:30 PM
To: Fortieth Street Catering
Re: Delightful Mouthfuls

Dear Carl,

I am following up on my email about reconsidering the pricing for our humble company party. Please reply because if you cannot make this work, I will need to start seeking alternatives soon.

Thank you ever so much,
Fawn Birchill, Owner, The Curious Cat Book Emporium (a Mark Twain specialist store)

From: Fawn Birchill
Sent: Fri, Dec 14, 2018 at 6:00 PM
To: Staff
Subject: Closing Tills

Dear Staff,

Thank you for informing me that many of our usual customers have wandered over to the Grumpy Mug after visiting our store without buying anything. The fact is, we have books and so do they (though I imagine their inventory is less impressive), and so I must assume that they are merely dropping in for some coffee before heading home. This could explain our horrible closing till reports. People have grown to connect drinking hot liquids with reading—a century-long tradition that smart bookstores have taken advantage of. Therefore, let us do the same. This might turn things around!

Do not despair, dear staff!

With high hopes,
Fawn, Owner

●●

From: Fawn Birchill
Sent: Fri, Dec 14, 2018 at 6:32 PM
To: Missy's Co-op
Subject: We could make quite a pear!

Dear Missy's Co-op,

As you may very well know, my name is Fawn and I frequent your co-op every Saturday for various goods such as fruit, vegetables, teas, rice, barley, oats, nuts, etc. I just love your little shop. It reminds me of my father's small general store in Norristown—though he didn't have the kind of selection or homey feel. Instead of wood floors, he had broken and chipped linoleum; instead of wainscoting, he had cheap faux-wood paneling out of the seventies. I toiled many hours weighing out the rice and the oats until I thought I could eyeball a bag and know the volume without needing to weigh it. Anyway, since I feel such a strong connection to your store both nostalgically and on a community level, I would love it if we could pair up. Perhaps you could sell some of your coffee at my store? We can split it 80/20 since I am offering the venue and you are receiving the free advertisement. I believe that as fellow small business owners, we must reach out to each other and see what needs doing. Since I am a frequent customer and so well connected in the community, and since I don't believe you've ever stopped by for a visit, the time to officially acknowledge each other's professional presence is long overdue! Think on it? See you Saturday!

Fawn Birchill, Owner, The Curious Cat Book Emporium (a Mark Twain specialist store)

From: Missy's Co-op
Sent: Fri, Dec 14, 2018 at 7:07 PM
To: Fawn Birchill
Re: We could make quite a pear!

Dear Fern,

Thank you for your interest in partnering with our co-op! We are already in a partnership (as of two weeks ago) with the Grumpy Mug Bookstop, and their demand has been so high that we have been struggling to keep up our inventory! At this time we are not able to partner, but as an aside, an 80/20 split in your favor would also not be tenable for us. We would, however, be happy to offer you a 10 percent discount off any of our whole bean bags for the purpose of selling coffee in your store.

Thank you again for your interest!
Missy's Co-op

From: Fawn Birchill
Sent: Sat, Dec 15, 2018 at 8:16 AM
To: Missy's Co-op
Re: We could make quite a pear!

Dear Missy's Co-op,

I am sorry that you will not be taking me up on this mutually beneficial offer. I think the fact that you partnered with the Grumpy Mug should in no way stop you from also partnering with me. Regarding your offer, the coffee is quite expensive, so I'm sorry but a 10 percent discount just isn't sufficient. A partnership with a more favorable split would be better.

Like the Grumpy Mug, we also get many customers, and I think we can agree that the only reason the Grumpy Mug is getting such excellent business is because they are new. Eventually when the thrill wears off, my customers will return like the prodigal son to my charming, literature-loving store. We are not *très chic* like the Grumpy Mug, and because of that we often get your most common clientele: vagabonds. I know because I can smell them minutes after they've left. They leave in their wake a sad afterglow of an unaccomplished life that smells of unwashed skin and patchouli. I'd much rather be smelling your coffee. Wouldn't you agree?

Yours in business,
Fawn Birchill, Owner, The Curious Cat Book Emporium (a Mark Twain specialist store)

P.S. My name is *Fawn*, not *Fern*. I understand how you can confuse the two, but one is a low-lying leafy plant and the other is an elegant, forest-dwelling deer. Surely I remind you of the latter? Just think of me thusly and it will be easier for your memory.

Dear Fawn,

My daughter stopped leaving the bags of food in my refrigerator. She is hard to reach at times, so can you please ask her to leave the bags again?

—Jane, your tenant

From: Fawn Birchill
Sent: Sat, Dec 15, 2018 at 10:17 PM
To: O'Hare Repair
Subject: Business Arrangement

Dear O'Hare Repair,

Greetings! I am writing to inquire about your prices. You may have heard of my bookstore, the Curious Cat Book Emporium, located in West Philadelphia steps from the Green Line. I mainly focus on old, used books; some are rare and extremely valuable, which is partly the reason that I am writing.

I live just above the store in a spacious Victorian apartment (I believe it was the maid's quarters for the family that was downstairs over a hundred years ago). It is dusty, and it tends to be cold in the winter but rather cool in the summer. I get a lot of light, and the hardwood floors are stunning and in great shape for their age. The bathroom is decorated with white porcelain tiles, and the bath is an old marble claw-foot. Before you start thinking I'm only writing to brag about the romantic quarters in which I live, I must say that the toilet in the customer bathroom has been leaking for quite some time, and what has now developed could arguably be described as damage to the floor's integrity. In addition, my claw-foot has been leaking black water onto my fiction section for some time. I realized this when I went down to get Jane Austen's *Emma* and found that she was covered in black mold. She, Louisa May Alcott, and Hans Christian Andersen were just wet with sludgy decay. How long they have been enduring these harsh conditions I'll never know.

Perhaps this week you can stop by and let me know how quickly this can be remedied? Our Christmas season has begun, and any mishap may cost me an important sale. Additionally, I saw my cat, Butterscotch, catching the black liquid with his tongue. There is simply nothing this cat won't eat! Do you think this will harm him?

Thank you very much for your time.

Sincerely,
Fawn, Owner, The Curious Cat Book Emporium (a Mark Twain specialist store)

From: Fawn Birchill
Sent: Sat, Dec 15, 2018 at 11:54 PM
To: Jacob Whitney
Subject: Mark Twain is overstaying his welcome

Dear Mr. Whitney,

I am starting to wonder if you have changed your email address, as I still haven't heard from you. Yesterday, two of your Mark Twain books sold. If you take the inventory back at this point, I will call that much a profit so you would not have to pay me back for the two books. I had hoped to sell many more than that, but given the weak selection, I am not surprised.

Please respond and let me know when you can collect your books. I check the mailbox each day with the hope that I will find my money returned. Incidentally I've developed a leak in my ceiling (the Twain books are fine), and I fear it will cost me money I don't have to repair.

Sincerely,
Fawn Birchill, Owner, The Curious Cat Book Emporium (a Mark Twain specialist store)

● ●

Dear Fawn,

Thank you for asking my daughter to make the food again. The spaghetti heated up well. She dislikes spaghetti, so it was a wonder she made it. I really do like it very much.

—Jane, your tenant

From: Fawn Birchill
Sent: Sun, Dec 16, 2018 at 7:15 PM
To: O'Hare Repair
Re: Business Arrangement

Dear Mr. O'Hare,

Thank you for stopping by and taking a look at the leak. After much consideration, I've decided that I can afford your services if we can make some kind of arrangement. As $500 is a lot of money for anyone to spend on a leak around the holidays, would you be interested in knocking the price down by one hundred if I were to throw in a third edition *The Adventures of Tom Sawyer*? It is a most excellent book that adults and children alike can enjoy. I know you mentioned you are not the bookish type, but perhaps your young sons would like it for Christmas? If you think about it, it would be at absolutely no cost to you, and you'd be helping out a local business owner around the holidays who is already quite strapped.

Also, thank you for your help and concern with Butterscotch. I believe you are correct when you say he ingests much worse on a daily basis just by being a cat.

I look forward to hearing from you. By the way, Cahill is a lovely name. Is it Irish? I love the Irish. I grew up down the street from a large Irish Catholic family who said they were originally from Cork. They had dark hair and blue eyes like you, so perhaps you are related? Food for thought!

Sincerely,
Fawn

●●

December 16

Dear Fawn,
Enclosed please find a coupon for cat food. I know you feed the alley cats the premium stuff, but they are just strays, and the fact that you are feeding them at all should be enough. Food is food, right? Especially when you are a street cat. Also, I thought this *Far Side* comic was cute.

Mother

phillysmallbiz.com
Sun, Dec 16, 2018

Top Review—The Curious Cat Book Emporium
So, maybe it's my fault for not calling ahead, but I drove all the way from Connecticut thinking I'd find a nice selection of books by Mark Twain. Instead I found mostly *The Adventures of Tom Sawyer*, which I've read before and actually own.

I'm disappointed to say the least. That said, I've never been to Philly. Might as well enjoy it while I'm here.

—George N.

phillysmallbiz.com
Sun, Dec 16, 2018

Dear George N.,

You are not alone in that the selection turned out to be not what was expected. However, had I sent out a notice, I don't think anyone would have stopped by, which would have made sales unspeakably dismal. Hearing that you drove in all the way from Connecticut saddens me. It must have been somewhat of a disappointment to get here and see nothing but the same book. Trust me when I say that this is not how I had hoped it would turn out and that this is the end of my transaction with a certain seller who shall remain nameless.

I am glad you are looking at it the way Mark Twain may have: as an adventure. Philadelphia is a lovely city with much to see and explore, so while you are here you might as well go on some sightseeing tours and make the most of it. Don't let something like this bring you down. I'm sure that if Mark Twain had spent a significant amount of time in Philadelphia, he may have written books on it.

Were you not offered a candy cane for the inconvenience?

Sincerely,
Fawn, Owner, The Curious Cat Book Emporium (a Mark Twain specialist store)

••

From: Fawn Birchill
Sent: Mon, Dec 17, 2018 at 8:05 AM
To: Staff
Subject: Candy Canes

Dear Staff,

Please make sure you are handing out candy canes to our customers who are disappointed in the Mark Twain selection. It may not seem like it, but it makes a difference!

Fawn, Owner

From: Fortieth Street Catering
Sent: Mon, Dec 17, 2018 at 9:10 AM
To: Fawn Birchill
Re: Delightful Mouthfuls

Hi Fawn,

With regrets, we cannot offer any discounts. Sorry about that.

Best,
Carl Suzuki

From: Fawn Birchill
Sent: Mon, Dec 17, 2018 at 11:14 AM
To: Fortieth Street Catering
Re: Delightful Mouthfuls

Dear Carl,

Thank you for your reply, but because you cannot provide me with the discounts that I requested, I will have to look for other means by which to feed my staff for our humble holiday party.

I miss the days when local businesses helped each other out, acted like neighbors, and got to know each other. Now everyone operates like they've been outsourced to China. There is no sense of community, and it saddens me. For most of my childhood and young adulthood, my father owned a general store and, though this was another time, he would pay for his milk deliveries in cigarettes. He would also give away free items to his loyal customers, rewarding them for their patronage. I knew his cognitive decline had begun, however, when I caught him giving away our cash register to the paperboy. Luckily, he couldn't fit it on his bike, and I was there just in time to stop him. That said, my father had the right idea. Anyhow, this is just to say that the world is changing, I suppose. Sad and lonely times we live in.

Your neighbor in business,
Fawn, Owner, The Curious Cat Book
Emporium (a Mark Twain specialist store)

●●

phillysmallbiz.com
Mon, Dec 17, 2018

Top Review—Fortieth Street Catering
I can't give more than one heart when it comes to poor service involving food. I hired them for a company function and not only were they forty minutes late, but the delivery boy smelled of marijuana. The food was thrown on the table like hunks of meat in a butcher shop; the receipt was oily with some strange substance stuck to

it, and the food itself tasted like Ritz crackers without the salt. Even the baklava tasted like it had been in the refrigerator with an open can of old olives for a year before being served. The prices are extraordinarily high for what you get.

—Butterscotch

From: O'Hare Repair
Sent: Mon, Dec 17, 2018 at 1:02 PM
To: Fawn Birchill
Re: Business Arrangement

Fawn,

Sorry but price is fixed, and I only take hard American currency. I raise my two boys on my own so I gotta make a living. My families from Kerry, I think. Least that's what my Dad said.

Cahill

From: Fawn Birchill
Sent: Mon, Dec 17, 2018 at 2:19 PM
To: O'Hare Repair
Re: Business Arrangement

Dear Cahill,

I find it absolutely fascinating that you know

the exact county your ancestors came from (though you say you are first-generation, so that shouldn't make it a challenge)! I hear Kerry is lovely. Have you ever visited the homeland? I have always wanted to be Irish myself. There is something appealing about it that I can't put my finger on. A romanticism perhaps? An exoticism? A harkening back to an old world from long ago colored with songs of rebellion, gorgeous literature, attractive people, and heavy drinking? This is why, I believe, on Saint Patrick's Day everyone claims to be a little Irish. It is similar to how white people claim to have Native American heritage—except, in the case of the Irish, it is for only one day a year and not all year round.

My background, on the other hand, is strictly English, but my father always pressed the idea that we were nothing more than American, which I always found dreadfully dull. It must be nice to have a sense of belonging and heritage elsewhere as well as here.

On to other matters at hand! I understand your hesitation to take a book as payment, but if you returned to look at it, you would see it is in excellent condition and quite old. I have contacted other repairmen regarding this, and they all charge a little less than you do.

I believe that is due to the fact that you are probably the best in Philadelphia. Otherwise why would you charge so much? Incidentally I would rather go with your services as you have been the nicest to deal with, and I would love to support you as a single father of two.

Please reconsider?

Sincerely,
Fawn

From: Fawn Birchill
Sent: Mon, Dec 17, 2018 at 3:09 PM
To: Staff
Subject: Theft

Dear Staff,

I believe someone has stolen the Kwanzaa display from the Mark Twain Room. Can you please look around the store for it? This is why we give out the candy canes: so people don't feel cheated and steal from us. Also, feel free to check the Grumpy Mug. I wouldn't be surprised if they stooped this low. I walked by their store yesterday and glanced in, and I think I saw one candy cane window sticker. How sad.

Fawn, Owner

From: Angela Washington
Sent: Mon, Dec 17, 2018 at 3:20 PM
To: Fawn Birchill, Staff
Re: Theft

No one stole it! I was cleaning the table it was on and forgot to put it back. It was on the floor behind a stack of books. Sorry about that.

—A

••

December 17, 2018

I think I understand what it's like to be a diplomat or the secretary of state during wartime. Getting fellow business owners to work with me has been a herculean effort. Who thought this would be so difficult? Is it that I run a used bookstore that's not hip enough for them to be associated with? I wish I knew what the magic answer was for this because I would pay a hefty price to learn. I have reached out to numerous businesses in these twenty years and have either had no one offer to give me cheaper rates or I've been completely ignored. It's been twenty years, and it still hurts as much as if it just happened for the first time.

Tonight I had managed to fall asleep right away, a rare event indeed, until I was awakened by what sounded, in my foggy waking state, like plates crashing to the floor. With a little more clarity and time, I realized that what I was listening to was applause. I got out of bed, went to the window to peek through the curtains, and found that the Grumpy Mug was still open and holding some kind of event! At 10:30 at night! Instead of going back to bed, I listened for a little longer. I couldn't help myself. I barely felt the cold seep up from the floorboards to my bare feet as I listened to the muffled but amplified voice of a single person in front of a microphone, then a pause followed by another uproarious bout of applause and whooping. Trembling, I drew back from the window, skin now hot with a sensation that I knew too well but had not known as rawly and intimately as I did in that moment. I couldn't sleep after that, even though I tried. Eventually the crowd dispersed, and the store officially closed. I could hear his customers walking by my own store, laughing. I pulled the blankets over my head and waited for that hot sensation to fade.

In better news, the cat with the runny eye is looking better! What a relief and joy to see. I'm not sure what it was that finally cured him. Maybe he just needed to be shown a little love. Sometimes that's the best tonic.

●●

From: Fawn Birchill
Sent: Tue, Dec 18, 2018 at 7:05 AM
To: Jacob Whitney
Subject: Smooth Criminal?

Dear Mr. Whitney,

I am beginning to think that you are a common criminal and are currently sunning yourself in Belize, using the money I've paid you to buy yourself rum and Caribbean cruises.

I have considered taking legal action but have run into some financial straits. I may take action in due time, so don't go too far because the Philadelphia justice system may be calling you back home.

Fawn Birchill, Owner, The Curious Cat Book Emporium (a Mark Twain specialist store)

From: Fawn Birchill
Sent: Tue, Dec 18, 2018 at 11:17 AM
To: O'Hare Repair
Re: Business Arrangement

Dear Cahill,

Thank you so much for stopping by and reconsidering. I believe the number we arrived at suits us both very well. The job you did on the leak is wonderful. Aside from a little staining on the ceiling, one would never know that there was ever any black mold dripping onto my inventory. One of my staff members, Angela (the tall girl with the slumped stature), has taken on the task of wiping the mold from the books. So far we have rescued one and thrown out three—not terrible for such a disaster.

Would you like to have coffee with me? Please do not think of me as forward. If you decline, be simply flattered and nothing more, for I respect you very much and would never want to put you in an uncomfortable position. There is a La Colombe on Rittenhouse Square that I think would be a nice middle ground since you live so far south. We could get our coffees and sit inside (it is so romantically Italian in there!) or perhaps walk around the park and see the holiday lights. You must get these inquiries all the time, so please forgive me. I have been struggling with what to say and how to say it, and I think through email is best. That way you can think on it, too, and not have to answer right away. Oh, here I am rambling on like a teenager! I rarely do this, which explains why I am so terrible at it.

Sincerely,
Fawn

From: Tabitha Birchill
Sent: Tue, Dec 18, 2018 at 12:40 PM
To: Fawn Birchill
Subject: How are things?

My dear Fawn,

How are things faring this holiday season? Florence tells me you are holding a special sale. I have been very busy with your father. Over the last two days he has shown some improvement, but I fear that it is only because he loves Christmas and is expecting to be taken home. It's heartbreaking.

Nothing is new here. The neighbors bought a new mailbox, and Harriett Winfield finally quit at the grocery store to take care of her mother full time. Do you remember her? I always pictured bigger things for her. Florence is taking Little Joe to a vocal intensive in the Poconos in the next few days. He is really improving, and I am so proud of him.

Hope you are well. Are you getting my coupons?

Mother

From: Fawn Birchill
Sent: Tue, Dec 18, 2018 at 2:00 PM
To: Tabitha Birchill
Re: How are things?

Mother,

The sale is going really well, thank you! This is probably the busiest Christmas yet on record, and I think it is compounded by the plethora of Mark Twain books I have acquired. I know *Tom Sawyer* is your favorite novel of his, and I may have one or two left if you would like me to put one aside for you. (Just let me know soon!)

I am glad Father is improving slightly. The cold can be rough on the elderly. How are you faring? How is Beaker? Is he still ripping his feathers out? I can't imagine what makes him so neurotic. It's just about the easiest life to be a bird and have to do nothing but sit in a cage and eat seeds. He's practically the queen of England.

Speaking of, do you know where in England our family originated? I am going on a date with an Irishman, and I want to sound somewhat in touch with my background for he is very in touch with his. He is tall with dark hair and bright blue eyes. He has very strong cheekbones, and when he talks he likes to scratch the back of his neck. I think he is a tad younger than me, but I think once you get into your midfifties, ten years or so has less of an impact.

Florence may have mentioned to you that there is a new bookstore down the street, but business has been so good that it's as if it isn't even there. It might as well be selling anchovies with the impact it has had on my store. I was a little worried at first, but time revealed that there was simply nothing to worry about. Things are looking up!

Also, yes, I am getting the coupons and I truly appreciate them—especially the funny comics you send. It is nice to get things like that in the mail. Thank you.

Much love,
Fawn

From: Fawn Birchill
Sent: Tue, Dec 18, 2018 at 7:09 PM
To: Staff
Subject: Holiday Party

Dear Staff,

We will close at three o'clock on the twenty-fourth and reopen on the twenty-sixth. We will also close at three o'clock on the thirty-first and reopen on the second (though I will be here working all those days, so if anyone would like to join me, they are most welcome).

Also, I will be hosting a company holiday party January 2. Yes, it will be after the holidays, because I believe we must first focus on those big sales before we can sit back and relax over some mulled wine. Location details to follow, but please RSVP!

Fawn, Owner

phillysmallbiz.com
Tue, Dec 18, 2018

Top Review—The Curious Cat Book Emporium
When I go into stores to buy stuff, it never occurs to me that I might witness a murder, but I did today. It was between a cat and a mouse, and it was horrifying. Basically, I walk into this store, and on my way to the history section is this big yellowish cat batting around this squeaking, defenseless little mouse. I like, tell the cat to stop, but it won't listen. Instead it sits on the mouse and stares at me! And then when the cat is like, sure I won't intervene, it starts beating the mouse again. I even got pics

of it because I couldn't believe how long it was going on for. Seriously, it took like ten minutes for the thing to die. Maybe not something to have on display for your customers to see? Traumatized.

—Juanita A.

phillysmallbiz.com
Tue, Dec 18, 2018

Dear Juanita A.,

Given that this is an old building and mice are extremely common in places such as this, it is an inevitable fact of life. Butterscotch, having been declawed, is relatively harmless unless you are a tiny mouse. And that, Juanita, is simply the way the world works.

The fact that Butterscotch did not kill the mouse right away but tortured it with his useless mitten-paws, bludgeoning it and sitting upon it until it expired, is simply his killing technique. His previous owners cruelly declawed him, so he must resort to these tactics. True, he could simply take the mouse's neck in his teeth and kill it quickly, but Butterscotch enjoys the sport of it. Aside from ripping the already brain-dead mouse from Butterscotch's grasp, there is nothing we can do but watch or simply walk away, which is exactly what you probably should have done instead of taking photos of the murder on your iPhone and posting them on PSB.

By the way, did you happen to find the book you were looking for?

Best,
Fawn, Owner, The Curious Cat Book Emporium (a Mark Twain specialist store)

● ●

From: Tabitha Birchill
Sent: Tue, Dec 18, 2018 at 9:12 PM
To: Fawn Birchill
Re: How are things?

Dear Fawn,

I'm so glad you're enjoying the coupons and comics! I'll keep them coming. ☺

Regarding our family background, I don't know much about my mother's since, as you know, she was adopted, but my father's side is supposed to have been from England, I believe. Your father's side hails from Southampton, England, and he's always said there was a nobility connection somewhere in the past—not the Birchill name but another name that escapes me. Phipps maybe? In any case, I hope that answers your questions. Take the nobility rumor with a grain of salt.

I fear it is something that many people like to claim about themselves to be true.

Much love,
Mother

●●

Dear Fawn,

Please tell my daughter that the beef thing that was left in my refrigerator last night was good but that I don't like peanuts. I think peanuts were in there. In any case, it was still good once I picked them out. Please tell her thank you.

—Jane, your tenant

●●

From: O'Hare Repair
Sent: Wed, Dec 19, 2018 at 8:45 PM
To: Fawn Birchill
Re: Business Arrangement

Hi Fawn,

I'm flattered and I appreciate it but I got to decline the offer. Its my policy not to date my customers.

Thank you,
Cahill

From: Fawn Birchill
Sent: Wed, Dec 19, 2018 at 8:56 PM
To: O'Hare Repair
Re: Business Arrangement

Dear Cahill,

I appreciate your honesty and your gentlemanly rule to never fraternize with customers. I can see how that would be a potential lawsuit waiting to happen. If we had perhaps gone on a date and happened to have feelings for each other, and somewhere down the line I were to leave you, I could perhaps use our history to get free work out of you. Or perhaps I could say that you were inappropriate not as a boyfriend but in a business setting. This I understand.

However, rarely do I experience such chemistry with a person, and though I'm not sure if it was requited, I would like to think that it could be. Hypothetically speaking, let's say we met in Paris on a moonlit path by the Seine. If I were not your customer, would you consider me fair game? Rereading that, I realize it sounds as if I'm proposing that you might force yourself on me, which is not at all the intention. I suppose what I meant was that if there were no strings attached in our already stringy relationship, would you ever consider me to be more than a friend?

According to my mother, my family is originally from Southampton, and we have ties to British nobility, which may explain some of my eccentricities and rather expensive taste for things. Wouldn't it be a match if we were to get together after knowing this! Wasn't it the crown that committed all those atrocities to your people? To think that you would be consorting with the enemy! We would have a regular *Romeo and Juliet* story on our hands.

Please reconsider?

Sincerely,
Fawn

phillysmallbiz.com
Thu, Dec 20, 2018

Top Review—The Curious Cat Book Emporium
I was so happy to go in and find *The Adventures of Tom Sawyer*. It is such a wonderful story and highly underrated. All right, now on to the true matter of this message! I am curious to find out if the owner is married. Does anyone know? I have a lovely, handsome, wealthy cousin who was recently made a widower due to an

equestrian accident. I just know he and the lovely owner—who looks so much like Keira Knightley—would get along splendidly.

Also, I must divulge and confess! I was at the Grumpy Mug earlier this week, and their bathrooms are atrocious! They smell like a filthy porta potty, and the coffee they sell tastes like it was made with dirty dishwater and filtered with an old cheesecloth. Their cats look like inbred barn dwellers, and the owner is a total snob that probably doesn't even read what he sells. There! I feel relieved of my burden. Let the people hear the truth and make of it what they wish.

—Sybil C.

phillysmallbiz.com
Thu, Dec 20, 2018

Dear Sybil C.,

Once again, you flatter me!

In answer to your question: I am not married and therefore am open to finding the right person. I obviously don't know your cousin and have no idea what he looks like, but if he is half of what you have described, he sounds like a wonderful man; please do bring him by. I am sorry to hear about his wife. I imagine that horse-riding accidents are among the greatest causes of nobility deaths in England.

Once again, I do not believe that I look a thing like Keira Knightley. She is much younger and more demure than I could ever hope to be, but if you must use her to describe me to your cousin, then I will not object to it. Incidentally, I have recently discovered that my family is British nobility (now far removed in these modern times), so perhaps we would have more in common than previously thought?

Regarding the store down the street, I understand that it is not to your taste, but please do not say such things about it, as they are unable to defend themselves. I understand you are championing my bookstore and that you are its greatest fan, but please, my dear Sybil, let's try to stay positive for them, as no doubt they are struggling to lure customers in these questionable economic times.

Sincerely,
Fawn, Owner, The Curious Cat Book
Emporium (a Mark Twain specialist store)

December 20

Hi Fawn,
I wanted to send the Chopin CD back to you since it was just collecting dust, and now that Little Joe is obsessed with playing the Josh Groban CD 24-7, it's only getting in the way. I think I have the entire CD memorized. Yesterday he came down the stairs and insisted we all call him Josh. Ugh. In any case, I hope this CD is still in good shape.

Mom has decided that she's worried about how much money you spend on taking care of the alley cats, as if it's her business. And the coupons! OMG, she won't stop with the coupons. If you haven't heard from me in a few months, send a search party. The coupons have likely crushed me to death.

Flo

● ●

From: Angela Washington
Sent: Thu, Dec 20, 2018 at 7:18 PM
To: Fawn Birchill, Staff
Subject: Mark Twain books

I was thinking about the books, and I got this idea. What if we put out an ad to schools and youth organizations and stuff like that? They tend to buy in bulk, right?

—A

From: Fawn Birchill
Sent: Thu, Dec 20, 2018 at 8:01 PM
To: Staff
Re: Mark Twain books

Angela,

What a fine idea! Surely that will be an easy way to rid us of these albatrosses. It is a comfort to know my employees care enough to strategize on off-hours.

I'll send out an advertisement at once!

Many thanks,
Fawn, Owner

●●

From: Fawn Birchill
Sent: Thu, Dec 20, 2018 at 9:30 PM
To: Jacob Whitney
Subject: You Win

Dear Mr. Whitney,

I am writing to concede my position on this book dilemma. I hereby relieve you of all ownership or responsibility of these books.

I have devised a strategy, and I may be able to spin this manure-covered straw into gold. Simply put, our correspondence here is over. Enjoy your rum, and don't stand directly under the coconut trees—the fruit tends to fall.

Sincerely,
Fawn Birchill, Owner, The Curious Cat Book Emporium (a Mark Twain specialist store)

Advertisement

HUGE SALE!

In West Philadelphia, steps from Clark Park and the Green Line, sits one of the most renowned and beloved bookstores in the city: the Curious Cat Book Emporium.

Calling all teachers, homeschool parents, and youth leaders—if you are to give your class one book to read this year, make it *The Adventures of Tom Sawyer*. And what adventures he has! From getting into fights to witnessing murder, going on treasure hunts, and testifying in court, this novel is rife with life lessons and peppered with fun.

Running this weekend only, buy twenty books published after 1965 and get 10% off your purchase! Nowhere else will you find such a volume of *The Adventures of Tom Sawyer*. Hurry while supplies last!

••

From: Mark Nilsen
Sent: Fri, Dec 21, 2018 at 4:09 PM
To: Fawn Birchill
Subject: Gossip about my store

Hi Fawn,

So, I saw that review where "Sybil C." complained about my store, and I'm a little shocked. We keep our bathrooms exceptionally clean. Also, to attack my five cats is a pretty low blow. I'm not sure why you're doing this. Can we talk?

And also, I know it's you. Sybil C. is supposed to stand for Sybil Crawley from *Downton Abbey*, right?
Mark

From: Fawn Birchill
Sent: Fri, Dec 21, 2018 at 5:01 PM
To: Mark Nilsen
Re: Gossip about my store

Dear Mark,

Though I haven't been inside your store, many of my customers have. Unfortunately, I cannot control their opinions regarding your establishment. If some find the bathroom to resemble a filthy porta potty, then there is nothing I can do. Or if they feel as if your (is it really five?) cats all act as if they fell into a can of paint and had to drink their way out, there is also absolutely nothing I can do. Surely you saw that I attempted to defend your store, and what I was writing was not slanderous, as Sybil wrote it first. Your claim that I am Sybil is both insulting and sickening. You may not know me very well yet, Mark, but understand that as you get to know me, you'll find that I am nothing but honest, upstanding, and fair. Regarding what else I've been writing on phillysmallbiz.com, it is not slanderous in any way. Perhaps if anything I am being too kind, as I have never set foot in your store and have nothing on which to base my kindness.

This effort to explain myself has gone on far too long. I am too busy to put out petty fires and must go back to my helm and run my ship like the admiral that I am. I do hope that we can put this misunderstanding behind us and become friends. Stop by the store sometime!

Sincerely,
Fawn Birchill, Owner, The Curious Cat Book Emporium (a *The Adventures of Tom Sawyer* specialist store)

P.S. I hear that you sell alcohol after five and your store becomes a sort of book bar. It is an interesting combination, mixing alcohol and reading. Whenever I try this at home, I end up falling asleep and waking in the middle of the night confused and dehydrated. Do you often have to scrape dozing people off couches and chairs? Sounds like more trouble than it's worth!

From: Fawn Birchill
Sent: Fri, Dec 21, 2018 at 6:34 PM
To: Staff
Subject: Staff Cuts

Dear Staff,

I am going to cut one of you the week of Christmas (twenty-sixth to the twenty-eighth). It isn't worth me paying all three of you to sit around sucking on candy canes and dusting the banisters. You can draw straws and let me know who wins!

Also, the holiday party will be held January 2 from 5 p.m. to 9 p.m. at the store. There will be Domino's pizza, mulled wine, and soda. Feel free to bring something like beer or a tray of sandwiches or cookies. I will try to make some cookies if I find the time. Please RSVP, and feel free to bring any significant others!

Best,
Fawn, Owner

From: Angela Washington
Sent: Fri, Dec 21, 2018 at 6:38 PM
To: Fawn Birchill, Staff
Re: Staff Cuts

Wait, so is somebody being fired?

—A

From: Fawn Birchill
Sent: Fri, Dec 21, 2018 at 6:56 PM
To: Staff
Re: Staff Cuts

Dear Staff,

No, I am not firing anyone! This is temporary—only for the twenty-sixth through the twenty-eighth. I assure you, no one is being let go! Apologies for the vagueness.

Besides, why would I announce that I am firing someone and then immediately invite them to the holiday party? They would definitely not be invited!

Best,
Fawn, Owner

••

phillysmallbiz.com
Fri, Dec 21, 2018

Top Review—The Grumpy Mug Bookstop
Where do I begin? I must confess that the owner of the Curious Cat Book Emporium contacted me and informed me that she received a scathing, threatening letter from Mark, the owner of the Grumpy Mug Bookstop, about my review of his store on phillysmallbiz .com. Have we honestly all lost our collective minds? Has the time come when a customer can no longer write an honest review about a store without starting a war? Or throwing the threatened owner (Mark) into a fit of such jealousy that instead of focusing on his store, he must write a letter to a competitor because he was unhappy with how I felt? Why do you feel the need to blame Fawn for this, Mark? It is a true indication of your character that you find it so difficult to take criticism—truer still when

you accuse Fawn of this. The woman does not have the resources you have and therefore doesn't have time to field your insecure little emails.

Get a life, Mark Nilsen! And focus on your store, please. It could use the attention.

—Sybil C.

From: Fawn Birchill
Sent: Fri, Dec 21, 2018 at 10:23 PM
To: Staff
Subject: Please help

Sam and Kyle,

I have fashioned a lovely green poster from CVS with cutout bold neon-pink lettering that says **GREAT DEALS THIS WAY**! First thing tomorrow, I need you to come in and trade off sign duty every hour. I thought things would pick up as we approached Christmas, but I seem to be dreadfully wrong. If a neon sign doesn't do it, then our customers are either blind or completely lost to us. I am holding out hope that they are merely awestruck by the opening of Mark's cheap store and will come to their senses. Perhaps this sign will help sway them and let them know that we are not fooling around.

Many thanks!
Fawn, Owner

From: Fawn Birchill
Sent: Sat, Dec 22, 2018 at 5:19 PM
To: Florence Eakins
Subject: Thank you!

Dear Florence,

I received the Christmas package! Thank you in advance—I will not open it until Christmas!! I, too, have sent you a box, so please let me know when you get it. Don't have the kids lift it—it is very heavy.

Sales are really out of control this season. My extensive Mark Twain collection is to thank for that!

Has Mother told you about the man I'm seeing? He is Irish American and quite beautiful, though I'm not sure how long the relationship will last. I tend to favor men with a little more sophistication and worldly wisdom. He is not much of a reader, but his South Philadelphia accent is dreamy. Also, he turns heads on a dime. We shall see!

Has Joseph been able to find a deal on a new microwave? My "Start" button has become questionable, so I must walk over to my tenant's across the hall and use hers. It is helpful, however, that she is ninety-six and thinks that I'm her daughter visiting from Hawaii. It's a win-win for all! Funny she doesn't question why her daughter from Hawaii only stops in for two minutes, heats up wet cat food, and then disappears.

Aloha!

Best,
Fawn

From: O'Hare Repair
Sent: Sat, Dec 22, 2018 at 6:07 PM
To: Fawn Birchill
Re: Business Arrangement

Hi Fawn,

I'm sorry, but I can't reconsider going on a date. If you ever need plumbing, though, please keep me in mind.

Cahill

From: Fawn Birchill
Sent: Sat, Dec 22, 2018 at 7:08 PM
To: O'Hare Repair
Re: Business Arrangement

Dear Mr. O'Hare,

I understand. Thank you for your professionalism. I enjoyed our short-lived chats very much. If you happen to change your mind, you know where to find me: wrapped up in a blanket with tea, a book, and Butterscotch (the cat, not the food).

Happy holidays!

Fawn

●●

From: Fawn Windsor
Sent: Sat, Dec 22, 2018 at 10:09 PM
To: Gregory Harris
Subject: Happy Christmas!

Dear Gregory,

The Christmas season is fast approaching, so I wanted to send you a brief hullo for the holidays before I go on radio silence until January. Funny that I will be wishing you happy Christmas for the thirty-ninth time since your message attached to that balloon landed on my uncle's farm in Pennsylvania and we became pen pals. So advantageous that I happened to be visiting from the UK and equally so that I was able to pry the balloon strand quickly from that goat's mouth before it choked and perished! I still have the little note to this day, though I've memorized it:

Dear Whoever:

Will you be my pen pal? I have no siblings—just a dog—and I'm homeschooled.

Write back if you want a friend.

—Greg

You may be my oldest consistent friend! I may have thought it strange at first that a sixteen-year-old boy was looking for a pen pal, but after spending some years in the Pennsylvania countryside, I was able to understand how deeply lonely it can be out there. However odd it may have been at first, I am so glad that we maintained this relationship through the years. At first we corresponded through my uncle's post because—let's just be honest—I did not trust the Royal Mail to safely fly my letters to your house in Pennsylvania. It just made more sense to write back when I had the chance to visit my uncle. And then, ah! The glorious advent of the email! I daresay our correspondence picked up a bit after that. I detest technology but am thankful for it in this case.

As you know, at our estate it has been a tradition to have the family visit during the holidays (some travel here from as far away as northern Scotland). We ride horses in the snow and try to catch a few pheasants. I'm not sure if I told you this, but there is a rather large marble fireplace in the main sitting room that the maid takes excellent care of. (We usually have about ten maids, but we have significantly cut down for the holidays so that they can go home to their families. We manage, albeit barely!) The fireplace is the cornerstone of our Christmas celebration. There is nothing like sitting by the fire with hot cocoa on Christmas Eve. As you know, we don't all get along perfectly well, but for Christmas Eve we manage to rein in the ill will—that is, until presents are exchanged and we find out how much we really don't know about each other. One year my sister, who lives in London with two boys and a rather awkward husband, gave me some awful fuzzy socks that looked like fungus. I have about five pairs accumulated from previous Christmases, and each year a new one gets shoved to the back of my sock drawer. I am thinking of regifting them to the maids. It turns out this year that nearly the entire family "had other things to do," and they didn't let me know until the very last minute. After I had arranged a banquet of food and had the maids clean the house top to bottom, my family have the nerve to skip out on my Christmas. I was livid, though also a bit relieved not to have a great showing. Sometimes the feeling of abandonment is rather a relief, as you have no one's expectations to live up to but your own.

How are your holidays treating you? Have you purchased any new buildings lately? I imagine it slows down a bit in the winter months. Do you only purchase and restore old buildings and homes, or do you work with modern ones as well? I ask because there are many modern but deteriorating buildings in London and in the States that could use a face-lift.

All for now. Do take care. Happy Christmas and New Year!

Much love,
Fawn Windsor

P.S. Do you think a Mercedes-Benz for my little brother is too generous a gift? My sister is appalled!

December 23

Fawn,
I can't believe it, but I found a coupon for premium cat food! Enjoy. Not you personally, of course.

Mother

●●

From: Fawn Birchill
Sent: Mon, Dec 24, 2018 at 8:09 AM
To: Angela Washington
Subject: More Snow TODAY?

Angela,

Does your father have any more snow he can spare? It seems to draw people into the store; however, it has blown away and so have our sales figures.

Thank you,
Fawn, Owner

From: Angela Washington
Sent: Mon, Dec 24, 2018 at 8:17 AM
To: Fawn Birchill
Re: More Snow TODAY?

I'm glad this snow directly correlates with your sales figures. I think it's time we talk compensation. Let's say every time we blow that snow for you, I get 10 percent of daily sales?

—A

From: Fawn Birchill
Sent: Mon, Dec 24, 2018 at 8:23 AM
To: Angela Washington
Re: More Snow TODAY?

Angela,

I am not implying the snow is the only reason sales were good that day, nor am I offering you a commission on sales for the snow machine. When I was young, I lived in a world where employees helped out without expecting that they would be rewarded for every little thing that they did.

Never mind about my request. I am no longer interested in your blood snow.

Fawn, Owner

From: Angela Washington
Sent: Mon, Dec 24, 2018 at 8:28 AM
To: Fawn Birchill
Re: More Snow TODAY?

Holy hell on earth, I was only kidding.

—A

From: Fawn Birchill
Sent: Mon, Dec 24, 2018 at 8:34 AM
To: Angela Washington
Re: More Snow TODAY?

Angela,

I apologize profusely. I never meant to send that email to you. I was just getting my anger out and must have gotten carried away enough to hit "Send." Forgive me.

The holidays tend to make me a little edgy.

That said, my word still stands: you cannot get a commission on books sold due to your father's snow machine. I will still utilize the snow machine if you are offering, however.

Fawn, Owner

From: Fawn Birchill
Sent: Mon, Dec 24, 2018 at 3:45 PM
To: Staff
Subject: Thank you!

Dear Staff,

Truly, I am moved. The fuzzy socks will be so warm in my cold Victorian apartment! And the Starbucks gift card—how thoughtful.

Butterscotch says meow and thank you for the treats.

I am so lucky to have such a caring group of people working for me. Every time I put on these socks, I will think of you.

Happy holidays,
Fawn, Owner

From: Fawn Birchill
Sent: Mon, Dec 24, 2018 at 4:34 PM
To: Staff
Subject: Inventory

Dear Staff,

I am going to start counting our inventory each month to try to determine if our inventory tracker numbers are correct. I have looked for *Finnegans Wake*, for example, knowing our inventory tracker says that we have four copies, only to find just one copy on the shelf. Kyle, since you are the head of inventory, I will need you to focus on this task each month. You do not have to count the entire store each month; instead tackle each section, rotating until you get through the whole store, and then start over again. If you have any questions, please come find me. If you require assistance, please recruit Sam or Angela.

Thank you for your understanding in this important matter.

Fawn, Owner

From: Sam Asimov
Sent: Mon, Dec 24, 2018 at 5:13 PM
To: Fawn Birchill, Staff
Re: Inventory

Hi Fawn,

Just being honest here, and I mean this respectfully, but we've all witnessed you give books away to customers, friends, and family regularly. Could that possibly be the issue?

Sam

From: Fawn Birchill
Sent: Mon, Dec 24, 2018 at 5:23 PM
To: Staff
Re: Inventory

Sam,

I appreciate your input, but though in the past I have given books away to foster loyalty and build relationships with my customers, I have always made it my top priority to correctly check the book out of the inventory log. The numbers have been off for years, so either we have little gnomes running around stealing books and using them as kindling, or someone here or possibly our customers are little thieves.

Fawn, Owner

From: Sam Asimov
Sent: Mon, Dec 24, 2018 at 5:50 PM
To: Fawn Birchill, Staff
Re: Inventory

Hi Fawn,

I think if you caught us doing what you do, you'd call it stealing and fire us immediately.

Respectfully,
Sam

From: Fawn Birchill
Sent: Mon, Dec 24, 2018 at 6:07 PM
To: Staff
Re: Inventory

Sam,

I do not believe that my actions constitute stealing since it is my own store, and therefore it is acceptable for me to give away a book now and then.

Fawn, Owner

••

From: Fawn Birchill
Sent: Tue, Dec 25, 2018 at 9:05 AM
To: Tabitha Birchill
Subject: Christmas

Dear Mother,

As I sit here in my drafty apartment on Christmas Day, I wish I had instead taken the train out to see you. You must be so lonely without Father, though I think Florence is going to visit with her brood?

Thank you so much for the ribbon candy, the nonpareils, the fuzzy socks, and the Shakespeare mug. You have been so generous this year, as always.

There is something romantic and whimsical about being alone on Christmas. At the moment I am listening to Chopin, drinking peppermint tea, and sitting on the floor near my small tree watching Butterscotch bat the wrapping paper around. I am reminded of one childhood Christmas when Father bought me a children's easel and drew Santa on the first page. He was always such a great artist. I believed with all my heart that it was Santa who drew himself and wished me a merry Christmas. Or there was the time Father collected deer droppings from the woods, sprinkled them on the kitchen floor, and told us that Rudolph had been inside (though the evidence was swiftly eaten by the dog). And while, if you can remember, Florence began to cry at Rudolph's blatant disregard for decency, I was instead blown away by the idea and managed to believe in Santa for at least another three years. These things you did for us as parents make me want to keep the Christmas spirit alive, even to this day. On days such as Christmas I wish I had children of my own, though it is a passing fancy. I have neither the patience nor the necessary hip width to bear motherhood.

Speaking of, the young Irishman did not work out. I had to break up with him, though we parted on amicable terms. I won't divulge the reasons, as they are strictly personal. I will simply ask: Why are all the crazy ones so beautiful? That said, he has whetted my desire to find a male companion. Next time, however, I will be far more careful!

Merry Christmas,
Fawn

●●

From: Angela Washington
Sent: Tue, Dec 25, 2018 at 11:09 AM
To: Fawn Birchill
Subject: Thank you!

Hi Fawn,

Thanks for the nice Christmas card and the fifty bucks! Whoa! Definitely wasn't expecting this—not because it was from you. I mean it was just really special to get.

Thanks!!

—A

From: Sam Asimov
Sent: Tue, Dec 25, 2018 at 5:04 PM
To: Fawn Birchill
Subject: Thanks for the card and the money

Fawn,

Thank you very much for the card and the money. I hope you had a memorable Christmas.

Sam

From: Kyle Krazinsky
Sent: Tue, Dec 25, 2018 at 11:23 PM
To: Fawn Birchill
Subject: [No Subject]

Hey Fawn,

You're the best. You did not have to do this, but know it was appreciated. I went out for Chinese with the money today and have some left over for booze.

Merry Christmas,
Kyle

P.S. I'll be at the holiday thing, and I'll be bringing Aiden.

From: Florence Eakins
Sent: Wed, Dec 26, 2018 at 3:30 PM
To: Fawn Birchill
Subject: Merry Christmas!

Hi Fawn,

I tried calling, but of course you didn't pick up. Just wanted to say thank you so much for the Christmas gifts. They must have been expensive to ship.

I hope you had a nice Christmas! Ours was very relaxing, with minimal tears and fighting over toys this year. And the kids behaved pretty well too. ☺

Flo

●●

From: Fawn Birchill
Sent: Wed, Dec 26, 2018 at 8:17 PM
To: Staff
Subject: Holiday Party

Dear Staff,

Do not forget to RSVP. So far I have only heard from Kyle, who will be bringing his boyfriend.

Also, who tacked up the Season's Greetings card from the Grumpy Mug? Did he hand deliver it, or was it mailed? If he thinks a card is going to put out the fire he started, he is truly delusional. Please do not display anything in our store that comes from him.

Fawn, Owner

From: Fawn Birchill
Sent: Thu, Dec 27, 2018 at 9:18 PM
To: Angela Washington
Subject: Posting

Dear Angela,

Thank you for your help with the Philly Love Finder posting. Please do not tell Sam or Kyle about this. It will be our secret!! Hope you are enjoying your week off!!

Many thanks,
Fawn, Owner

PHILLY LOVE FINDER

MY SUMMARY

I am a fiftysomething woman who enjoys traipsing the aisles of bookstores and tickling the spines of old, dusty books. I love being among that which is old and antique, for it holds a mystery that, as much as I study and learn about and dive into history, I will never fully comprehend. I love cats and have only one after his brothers, Juniper and Mistletoe, died of old age. For his own privacy I won't reveal his name, but he is a sweet little lamb of a cat and has never lashed out at a single human being in his long life.

I am at once both afraid and in wonder of the city I live in. Being underground and riding public transportation makes me feel like a rat, while being up in high-rises makes me feel like a bird. I feel like an ant among ants on the sidewalk. In the city, we are forced to feel like animals, and so animals we become. In the country, where animals live among humans, we are made self-aware of our place in the world and do not need the reminder that we are human beings, and so we behave accordingly. I am not good at cities, as you may have gathered, and so I mostly stick to my five-block radius, where I can walk to the grocery store and the pharmacy. I would move, but I love the building in which I live and the safe life I have carved out for myself.

People generally find me to look much like a slightly older Keira Knightley. You may notice my unique feet and the way that they splay out when I walk. It is something you sometimes see in ballet dancers; however, I have no such excuse, as I have never taken formal dance lessons outside of one interpretive dance class in college. Most of all, I believe I have an illuminating intelligence and warmth that I bring to all conversations. It is overwhelmingly the most noticeable thing about me.

I love adventure but have never left the East Coast. One day, I would like to do that very much. I like Chopin, F. Scott Fitzgerald, honey in my tea, and back rubs. I used to be a Wiccan and a pagan, but now I am an agnostic.

OCCUPATION

I own a successful used bookstore in Philadelphia. It is the heart and soul of the neighborhood, a cornerstone of culture, a place for families to spend quality time, and a melting pot for diversity.

TALENTS

I am quite skilled at taking care of myself in all aspects of life. That is to say, I would never be a burden on a man should he choose to be with me. I am very good at riding bicycles and can pick up M&M's with chopsticks (a talent I discovered when I was quite young at a carnival where I won a Chinese coin).

A FEW FAVORITE THINGS . . .

I just LOVE *The Great Gatsby* and *Madame Bovary*. Those two books say the most about my personality. As I read them, I am also aiming a mirror deep down into my very soul. If you were to read these books before meeting me, you would have a head start on getting to know me. I have extremely varied tastes in food, but my favorites include rice, Wheat Thins, and crème brûlée. My favorite music leans toward classical, with a few modern choices sprinkled in: Chopin, Ella Fitzgerald, and Édith Piaf. I love *Titanic*, *Gone with the Wind*, and *A Streetcar Named Desire*. Ah, that Blanche. And for shows, I absolutely ADORE *Downton Abbey*. If you dislike *Downton Abbey*, it's very possible I will dislike you.

AGE RANGE OF MEN

I do not discriminate based on age. I believe I could learn as much and have as equally fine a time with a twenty-year-old as with a fifty-year-old. If you are young at heart, I will consider you even if you are in your seventies. I hope that answers the question.

ASTROLOGICAL SIGN

I no longer buy into this.

MY IDEA OF A GREAT EVENING

Writing letters and emails to all my friends with a bottle of wine at my side.

SECRET TIME! DISH WHAT YOU CAN . . .

Sometimes while writing letters, I fall asleep at my desk and wake up the next morning with the letter stuck to my face. This is not the secret. The secret is that each morning I wish there had been someone to lift me up and tuck me into bed.

PHAVORITE PHILLY LOCATION

I'm not sure if I'm supposed to pick a bar or a historic landmark or what, so I suppose I'll wing it. I love walking from Washington Square park and across the other parks (it might all be one park for all I know, but to me they are different) until I get to Penn's Landing, where I can walk along the river. Old City has such a romantic layout, with cobblestones, horse-drawn carriages (make sure to look where you are stepping!), and people dressed in colonial garb. I have always wanted to walk through there arm in arm with a nice man. Perhaps someday I will. The cemetery on Pine Street is also quite lovely and relaxing. Sometimes there is a man who sits among the graves wearing a Viking helmet (horns and all) and just stares out at nothing. One can never know what one might stumble on in Philly, which is why it is such a glorious city.

THE BRASS TACKS

A man. (I am not a lesbian, though I did kiss a girl on the playground when I was five. I don't remember much except for the cat poop we discovered shortly thereafter in the sandbox.)

Preferably of Irish descent, though I am open to all cultures and backgrounds.

You must like cats.

You must like reading books.

You must be okay with me drinking a little.

I am not a social butterfly, so maybe a more socially adept man would be good for me?

Muscular.

Hygienic.

Handy.

I respect your religious beliefs, but I am not interested in going to church/temple/mosque with you or hearing about your superstitions.

CONCLUSION

If you are tired of casual, meaningless couplings, are looking for a long-term relationship, and are okay with gray-haired women (I will not dye it for you), then we might have a shot. Additionally, you MUST be okay with being third in importance after my cat and my bookstore.

● ●

From: Fawn Birchill
Sent: Fri, Dec 28, 2018 at 9:04 AM
To: Staff
Subject: Excrement

Dear Sam or Kyle,

Can one of you please own the task of donning some rubber gloves and taking care of the biohazard outside the front door this morning? I would appreciate it if we handled it before opening the store.

At the moment I am indisposed in my upstairs apartment dealing with a sudden refrigerator leak, so thank you in advance for your swift attention to this matter.

Thank you,
Fawn, Owner

From: Sam Asimov
Sent: Fri, Dec 28, 2018 at 9:08 AM
To: Fawn Birchill, Staff
Re: Excrement

Gross! Is it human?? Why would someone do this?

Sam

From: Fawn Birchill
Sent: Fri, Dec 28, 2018 at 9:13 AM
To: Staff
Re: Excrement

Sam, Kyle,

I do believe it is human. I think I saw a Corn Pop in there. Also, I don't know why someone would choose to make a bowel movement on the front steps of our store. In times like this,

I ask not why but how we can solve the issue and move on.

Fawn, Owner

From: Sam Asimov
Sent: Fri, Dec 28, 2018 at 9:15 AM
To: Fawn Birchill, Staff
Re: Excrement

Hi Fawn,

Respectfully, this is a biohazard, so maybe we should get the city involved.

Sam

From: Fawn Birchill
Sent: Fri, Dec 28, 2018 at 9:19 AM
To: Staff
Re: Excrement

Respectfully, Sam, I don't believe you will become sick if you put on gloves, throw it in a plastic bag, and dispose of it in the trash can outside at the corner.

Fawn, Owner

From: Kyle Krazinsky
Sent: Fri, Dec 28, 2018 at 9:23 AM
To: Fawn Birchill, Staff
Re: Excrement

Hey Fawn,

How about we just wait for it to freeze over and pick it up then? And while we wait, just throw a blanket over it?

Best,
Kyle

From: Fawn Birchill
Sent: Fri, Dec 28, 2018 at 9:30 AM
To: Staff
Re: Excrement

Staff,

I'll clean it up.

Fawn, Owner

From: Fawn Birchill
Sent: Fri, Dec 28, 2018 at 7:18 PM
To: Staff
Subject: The Grumpy Mug Calling

Dear Staff,

After we closed, I received a call from Mark at the Grumpy Mug accusing one of us of placing the excrement in front of his store. If he calls accusing us of such things again, please inform me immediately. I am sickened that he would think I was capable of such a heinous act.

Along those same lines, we cannot keep going as we are and hope to stay successful. We all need to put our heads together and think up what we can do to help turn things around. I believe a good start would be adding a coffee stand to our arsenal. It will be at no extra cost to us, as I have a large jug of Folgers that has been sitting on my refrigerator for god knows how long and plenty of plastic cups from a picnic a couple of years ago. Please let me know what you can contribute from your own homes, and that way it won't end up costing us anything extra!

Also, many thanks to whoever filled up the bowls of food for the alley cats. If you do so and notice the bag is getting low, please let me know and I'll run out and buy more.

Fawn, Owner

From: Fawn Birchill
Sent: Sat, Dec 29, 2018 at 8:18 AM
To: Mark Nilsen
Subject: Garbage

Dear Mark,

Today I walked outside to discover a trash bag in front of our building with old food and other questionable and rancid substances within. I went through it (with rubber gloves) and found, much to my surprise, that it was from your store due to the many receipts inside. Congratulations, by the way—it looks like your hippie customers are big spenders indeed. Either they have excellent jobs or (more likely) they are running up their credit cards—an unsustainable act to be certain, so it would be unwise to rely on their business for much longer if that's the case.

Is this because of the feces incident? I want to let you know that I did not place the feces in front of your store. I wouldn't put the act past one of my dangerously loyal employees, however, and if that was the case then I apologize. Please note that I can be fined for having trash (a health hazard) in front of my place of business.

Yours in business,
Fawn Birchill, The Curious Cat Book

Emporium (a *The Adventures of Tom Sawyer* specialist store)

P.S. I can't help but notice that the events you are holding in your store, quite late at night, seem to be rather boisterous for a weeknight. Often the events wake me on the rare occasions that I am actually able to go to sleep. Might it be possible for you to ask them to not be so loud, as it is a predominantly residential block?

From: Mark Nilsen
Sent: Sat, Dec 29, 2018 at 4:23 PM
To: Fawn Birchill
Re: Garbage

Hi Fawn,

The sanitation workers must have failed to pick that one up. It was also a windy day, so it's possible it just blew out of the truck while it was going down the street. I'm sorry it landed on your property. I can't believe I have to say this, but in the future please don't go through our garbage.

Thanks,
Mark

From: Fawn Birchill
Sent: Thu, Jan 3, 2019 at 8:14 AM
To: Staff
Subject: Holiday Party

Dear Staff,

For those of you who showed up to the party, thank you. Thank you to Kyle and Aiden, who both stayed for most of the party, and to Angela, who showed up for an hour, drank most of the wine, and left. I purchased a lot of pizza and a fair number of libations for this party, so I would appreciate it if you could take some of it home after work tomorrow. Sam, I don't know where you were (you told me that you would be there), but you truly missed out on a lovely wintry evening full of mirth and merriment. We even played a few quick rounds of charades where I impersonated a snake by dancing like one of those belly dancers. No one got it! What fun!

Happy holidays!

Fawn, Owner

••

January 3, 2019
My store is falling apart, and I don't know what to do. Last night I came downstairs to the heater making loud banging noises. I turned it off and

tried to turn it back on, but now it won't turn on.

I dragged my two space heaters up from the basement. One I gave to Jane, asking that she does not so much as walk by it, as it is such a fire hazard. No doubt she's already forgotten what it is. I am imagining her pushing it out of her way and innocently turning it toward the wall or her curtains. Needless to say, I don't plan on sleeping tonight. For now the other space heater is keeping me warm, but I do not know what I'll do when the store opens. Space heaters and books do not mix.

To make matters worse, Mark is having one of his events again. He clearly did not tell his customers to keep it down, as they are loud as ever.

Luckily for me, I found a bottle of wine in my cabinet that I didn't know I had. I am drinking it now. I hope it will calm me.

It isn't always this way, but there are days, and they are becoming more frequent, when I ask myself why I'm still doing this. I don't know sometimes. I don't know.

From: Fawn Birchill
Sent: Fri, Jan 4, 2019 at 6:05 AM
To: Angela Washington
Subject: Posting

Angela,

It has been over a week since my posting, and I haven't heard anything from a single person. Perhaps we did it wrong? And I know things take time, but this is ridiculous. Do you think it is my picture? It is the only one I have of myself that is decent, but now that I think about it, that hat with the bird on it makes me look like a kook. Would you help me tweak a few things? I'll pay you extra.

Fawn, Owner

P.S. Please do not tell the boys.

From: Fawn Birchill
Sent: Fri, Jan 4, 2019 at 7:45 AM
To: Staff
Subject: Space Heaters

Dear Staff,

Please do not move the space heaters. I have positioned them specifically so they will not burn the building down. This morning I came downstairs to find one of them turned off (thankfully!) but facing the *Tom Sawyer* books. Need I point out that is not a viable way of getting rid of them?

Thank you for your cooperation,
Fawn, Owner

From: Kyle Krazinsky
Sent: Fri, Jan 4, 2019 at 8:02 AM
To: Fawn Birchill, Staff
Re: Space Heaters

Hey Fawn,

Maybe you're sleepwalking? We definitely didn't touch it.

Kyle

From: Fawn Birchill
Sent: Fri, Jan 4, 2019 at 8:15 AM
To: Staff
Re: Space Heaters

Dear Staff,

I have never sleepwalked before. Although, I suppose since I've lived alone these many years, I would not know.

Is everyone certain that they have no knowledge of how to fix a heater? Or do you know someone who could cut me a deal?

Fawn, Owner

January 6, 2019

As strange as it is to admit, I hope Mark is the saboteur. He is an enemy I understand and can go toe-to-toe with. By the very nature of what he does, I inherently understand him more than he could ever know, and perhaps because of that he understands me. Truly, I hope he isn't the culprit of this latest rash of tomfoolery, because I don't want us to be enemies. I never did.

But if it has to be someone, let it be him. Better him than Missy from Missy's Co-op or those losers at Fortieth Street Catering. Or Richard—though I doubt he has the energy to do much of anything against me when he's busy drooling over the freight trains at the Schuylkill like some simpleton.

Yesterday I walked down to the Schuylkill, and in the woodpile beside the tracks was a mother cat and a large litter of kittens. Two of them were playing just outside the woodpile while another little gray one was drinking from a puddle of questionable origin. The mother seemed to be stalking something. When the train came barreling through, I watched as they all ran with practiced dexterity and timing into the safety of their improvised house. I wanted to bring them all home with me, but it was clear that they were perfectly fine without my interference. Their mother was providing them with everything they needed. For a long time, I stood there and imagined what it would be like to grow up in an environment of play, warmth, and love. I let myself wonder how things would be different, if they would be different, and most importantly, if they should be different. Maybe it isn't for me to decide what should have been. The world simply is, and we must do our best to make the most out of it. Some are born into a household that shows love through spankings and assignments; others are born on sprawling estates with royal blood in their veins and no cares in the world, while others still are born by the train tracks under a woodpile. And there is no deep meaning to any of it.

It is useless to lament what could have been. I didn't see the kitten complaining as she drank from the oily puddle by the tracks. Why should I lament? And yet . . . and yet I do. Because if my life were different growing up, would I be here putting myself through this? Would I have been happier? Would I have known what happiness was if I encountered it? And am I able to discern it now? The other day I went to heat up cat food in Jane's apartment, and she took one look at me and said, "Oh, you poor thing." I couldn't believe it, and I didn't have the gumption to ask her what exactly made her say that. Instead I just smiled and left as quickly as I could. But what did she see there as the seconds wound down, as I watched the wet food rotate on the little plate? What did she see?

From: Fawn Birchill
Sent: Mon, Jan 7, 2019 at 8:15 AM
To: Mark Nilsen
Subject: The trash police

Dear Mark,

I have been putting my trash out at six thirty every Friday night for the past couple of decades, and I have never had anyone call and complain. I know it was you because the ornery woman who handed me the fifty-dollar fine had no qualms revealing the identity of the man who called the sanitation department on me. After five we get very little foot traffic, so the likelihood of someone walking down this well-lit street and stumbling over my trash is about as high as winning the Powerball.

How easily threatened you are by my business. I would be flattered if I wasn't so angry.

Fawn Birchill, Owner, The Curious Cat Book Emporium (a *The Adventures of Tom Sawyer* specialist store)

From: Fawn Birchill
Sent: Mon, Jan 7, 2019 at 9:56 AM
To: Staff
Subject: Sales Numbers

Dear Staff,

I have never seen sales numbers this dismal around Christmas (attached). Since I have heard absolutely nothing from anyone as far as ideas go, I feel I must introduce an incentive. I believe our top priority right now is that we have to move these Mark Twain books to make room for some variety. With that goal in mind, please bring me your suggestions by the end of the week. The winning suggestion will receive a fifty-dollar gift card to the Fresh Grocer. And no, you cannot suggest nuking the Grumpy Mug, even though it would be an easy fix—ha ha!

Thank you,
Fawn, Owner

From: Sam Asimov
Sent: Mon, Jan 7, 2019 at 10:08 AM
To: Fawn Birchill, Staff
Re: Sales Numbers

Hi Fawn,

What about selling your books online? I'll gladly help in any way I can.

Sam

From: Fawn Birchill
Sent: Mon, Jan 7, 2019 at 12:13 PM
To: Staff
Re: Sales Numbers

Dear Sam,

If I do that, we might lose our physical customer base and become nothing better than a warehouse. I don't like using the internet to sell—it feels like an easy-way-out solution, and I want to be a bit more creative. Plus, I don't like computers, so though you have kindly offered to spearhead the operation, I will politely decline.

Fawn, Owner

From: Kyle Krazinsky
Sent: Mon, Jan 7, 2019 at 1:32 PM
To: Fawn Birchill, Staff
Re: Sales Numbers

Hey Fawn,

What about just having more of an internet presence? I've attached a list of websites that might be good to start with. I know the Grumpy Mug uses the Parrot, and they have a lot of followers. (It's like Twitter.)

If you build a presence, they will come.

Kyle

From: Fawn Birchill
Sent: Mon, Jan 7, 2019 at 3:00 PM
To: Staff
Re: Sales Numbers

All,

I don't know anything about Twitter, but if the Parrot works for the Grumpy Mug then we should give it a try!

Sam, I would like you to spearhead the operation, posting as much as you think is realistic. Angela and Kyle should certainly help you. Please keep it relevant to the goings-on in the store, and keep it positive. This is an excellent and necessary idea now that we have competition, so we must take such measures as these and leave our comfort zones.

Many thanks,
Fawn, Owner

phillysmallbiz.com
Mon, Jan 7, 2019

Top Review—The Curious Cat Book Emporium
I was so disappointed by the customer service in their store. None of the books I wanted were in stock, and no one seemed interested in doing anything about it. I went to the Grumpy Mug after, and they were super nice and helpful. I honestly don't know how the emporium is going to make it now that this new place has moved in. It's going to need a lot of luck, and I think they should be very worried.

—Kenji O.

phillysmallbiz.com
Mon, Jan 7, 2019

Dear Kenji O.,

To be quite frank, if a book is not in the inventory, then we cannot retrieve it for you. We are not magicians. However, our employees should have certainly offered to order you a copy of this book, and for that oversight I apologize. And yes, even though we are a used bookstore, we certainly can order books. Not only do I have an amazing array of books in the basement not yet shelved, but I also have internet access and can order anything you need. If you return, we will remedy this.

No, I am not worried about the Grumpy Mug Bookstop down the street. The owner knows very little about running a business. If he thinks that having coffee, craft beer, and cats hides the fact that he knows nothing about literature and the business of bookselling, then he has another thing coming. I, in contrast, went to business school. I didn't fall off the trust-fund hippie wagon and whimsically decide to open a small business for the heck of it. I know exactly what I'm doing, and I've been doing it for years, so please rest assured, Kenji: the Curious Cat Book Emporium isn't going anywhere.

Best,
Fawn, Owner, The Curious Cat Book Emporium (a *The Adventures of Tom Sawyer* specialist store)

From: Mark Nilsen
Sent: Mon, Jan 7, 2019 at 6:04 PM
To: Fawn Birchill
Subject: Hippie Wagon?

Hi Fawn,

I don't understand this animosity, and frankly, don't bother explaining it to me, though I'm sure you will try. Can you please just agree to stop libeling my store on phillysmallbiz .com? I do not want to report you and get you kicked off, as I know it has been a useful platform for you. Also, understand that I am always willing to put this behind us and start fresh. You are always welcome to stop by the store and meet everyone.

Regards,
Mark

From: Fawn Birchill
Sent: Mon, Jan 7, 2019 at 8:45 PM
To: Mark Nilsen
Re: Hippie Wagon?

Mark,

After you stole all my customers on Black Friday, the most important sales day of the year, I can no longer be friendly with you. My store was doing quite well before you came along with your bright track lighting, new books, craft beer, and feel-good coffee. You might be a bit shinier, but we are no different, Mark, so I will ask you straight: Why this block? Why my neighborhood?

And no, I have no interest in meeting your staff or seeing your store. So far you have been nothing but a scheming, two-faced marauder, and I will not support such behavior by paying a visit.

As much as I stand by what I say on phillysmallbiz.com, I do not wish to lose my listing over this silly feud, so I will refrain from all further mention of you or your store. I hope you are satisfied and no longer feel the need to report me.

Speaking of, your little reading events, or whatever they are, are still keeping me up at night. Please tell your guests to keep quiet. I would hate to get the authorities involved.

Best wishes,
Fawn Birchill, Owner, The Curious Cat Book Emporium (a *The Adventures of Tom Sawyer* specialist store)

From: Mark Nilsen
Sent: Mon, Jan 7, 2019 at 9:20 PM
To: Fawn Birchill
Re: Hippie Wagon?

Hi Fawn,

Thank you. Also, to set the record straight, I sell

as many used books as I sell new ones. If you bothered to stop by, you'd know that already.

We'll try to keep it down. Remember that when I first came here, I offered that we work together. I'm sorry this has been so difficult.

Mark

● ●

From: Fawn Birchill
Sent: Mon, Jan 7, 2019 at 10:34 PM
To: Florence Eakins
Subject: Just what I wanted

Dear Florence,

I'm so glad you liked the Christmas presents. *Ulysses* is a bear of a book, but I know it is not above your capabilities. If Joseph doesn't like *Madame Bovary* then I recommend you give it a chance. I gave each of the kids their own *Tom Sawyer* so they would not fight over it!

Thank you for the jellies and for the truffles. Butterscotch loves his catnip. You are too generous with your gifts. I imagine a microwave was too heavy to ship—gas prices are astronomical—so I understand your choice to instead give me jelly and truffle, though the obvious greater need is for a microwave. In this dubious economy, expensive but necessary gifts are difficult to come by (though Mother told me you bought her a sound system). Next year perhaps instead of getting me physical things, you can save the money you would have spent and just send me a Macy's gift card?

Many thanks again, and merry Christmas! (Sorry it has taken me this long to write a thank-you! I have been so very busy!!!)

Fawn

From: Tabitha Birchill
Sent: Tue, Jan 8, 2019 at 7:45 AM
To: Fawn Birchill
Subject: Microwave

Dear Fawn,

I feel the need to mediate. Florence spoke with me about the rather rude email you sent her regarding the fact that you did not receive a microwave for Christmas. I am sorry you did not receive something that you needed, but please understand that Florence is not made of money and gives what she can. There is love behind it. You should see that, appreciate the gesture, and not obsess over the perceived inadequacy of the gift. I thought I raised you better.

I understand that your store is going through a rough patch, but it is not appropriate to take it out on your sister. I hate to say it, but this sounds like the behavior of one who is generally unhappy and a little, dare I say it, envious. It is not a way to behave at any time but especially not around the holidays. It would mean a lot to her if you apologize. And before you assume that I am blowing it out of proportion, Florence is capable of reading between the lines and sees right through what you are doing.

I hope you are okay. I am worried about you.

Love,
Mother

From: Fawn Birchill
Sent: Tue, Jan 8, 2019 at 8:19 AM
To: Tabitha Birchill
Re: Microwave

Dear Mother,

I would like to say first that what I wrote to Florence was not rude but honest. Only in America do people confuse honesty with rudeness. If we were French or German, she would have thanked me for the refreshing insight on how I really feel about things.

Florence has always been a bit spoiled, and the spoiled tend to be awful at giving presents. For you to accuse me of being envious of her life and unhappy—I have no words to describe my disappointment in your horribly confused misconception of the way things truly are. I will have you know that I am very happy indeed. Because I have an inquisitive mind, because I read, and because I am a business owner on her own, you think that I am lacking something? As if the presence of a husband or a couple of kids would complete me? I have all that I need, thank you.

Contrary to family rumor, the store is doing exceedingly well. The fact that I do not have a new microwave is not because I cannot afford one but because I am too busy to go out and get one myself. The Grumpy Mug has merely made things more interesting, and there is nothing to worry about. The owner is a bit of a kook. I haven't had a good look at him, but he is young, bearded, and tattooed—the new physical criteria that seem to promise successful entrepreneurship in Philadelphia. They did an article on him last week with a full-color spread. He had a cat on his shoulders, his favorite books lined up in front of him, and a steaming mug of coffee in his hand. There is nothing special about him except for the fact that he is from South Philly and just lost his mother to emphysema. Maybe I'll ask the paper to do an article on me, and I can tell them all about my father in hospice and all the cats I've watched grow old and die in my lifetime. Maybe then I'll get some pity customers! What a desperate cry for attention.

Fawn

From: Mark Nilsen
Sent: Tue, Jan 8, 2019 at 11:04 AM
To: Fawn Birchill
Subject: Feb 8 Gala to Benefit Inner City Youth Centers

Hello Fawn,

I would like to officially invite you to our gala on February 8. It will be held at the Grumpy Mug, starting at 7 p.m. and concluding whenever. ☺ Proceeds (books and greenbacks) will benefit the Youth Centers of West Philadelphia. I will send you an official invite in the mail, but I thought I'd reach out electronically to make sure you knew about it.

Hope to see you there,
Mark

From: Fawn Birchill
Sent: Tue, Jan 8, 2019 at 1:12 PM
To: Mark Nilsen
Re: Feb 8 Gala to Benefit Inner City Youth Centers

Dear Mark,

Though I am flattered, I am regretfully declining the offer, as I have already made plans to attend the ballet with a date. He got us special box seats by the stage. Apparently he is a subscriber! That said, I believe the cause is very just, and I wish you all the best donating books to inner city youth centers. Perhaps you were inspired by my similar idea when I sent out an advertisement welcoming teachers and schools to purchase *The Adventures of Tom Sawyer*. Even if it was subconscious mimicry, I find it flattering and adorable.

Good luck with your gala, and I do hope it concludes at a reasonable hour!

Sincerely,
Fawn Birchill, Owner, The Curious Cat Book Emporium (a *The Adventures of Tom Sawyer* specialist store)

From: Fawn Birchill
Sent: Tue, Jan 8, 2019 at 3:46 PM
To: Angela Washington
Subject: Revised Posting—Please Approve

Angela,

Per your suggestions, the revisions to my profile are attached here in red. I have taken out all mention of my cat but for one instance. I have taken out the comment on my feet being noticeable. For books, I have added Chuck Palahniuk (though I have only seen half of *Fight Club* due to the violent and sexual nature of it). I have added that I enjoy rock music of all kinds, and for shows I have added *Breaking Bad*, though I've never seen it. For my idea of a great evening, I added drinking socially and spending time with friends (a slight stretch from the truth). I have removed my preference for the Irish as well as my religious intolerance at the end.

Hope that helps!!
Fawn, Owner

From: Angela Washington
Sent: Tue, Jan 8, 2019 at 4:30 PM
To: Fawn Birchill, Staff
Subject: Sales Numbers

Okay, what about this? Crazy thought, but have you ever considered reaching out to, like, Mark Twain's estate to see if they'd be willing to sign some of these books? I found this contact info online. I don't know if it's totally right, but it's worth a try???

—A

From: Fawn Birchill
Sent: Tue, Jan 8, 2019 at 4:55 PM
To: Staff
Re: Sales Numbers

Dear Angela,

That's the best idea I've heard all day. Thank you for providing the address—I would have had no idea how to begin to get in touch with them otherwise, as everything is on the internet these days and navigating that feels to me like rounding the Cape of Good Hope without a paddle.

I will get in touch with his estate immediately!

Many thanks,
Fawn, Owner

From: Fawn Birchill
Sent: Tue, Jan 8, 2019 at 8:17 PM
To: Twain Estates
Subject: Business Opportunity

To the estate of Mark Twain:

I do not doubt that you have heard of my store and me in the Mark Twain circuit recently. If your head has been in the literary sand for the past two months, then I have included the news article regarding my bookstore and its specialty in Mark Twain literature. Without getting too deep into the bookstore (it is all included in the article), I will cut to the chase, as I imagine you are extremely busy and have very little time to read letters from strangers.

I have a proposition for you. Though I have sold many of my books, I still have an enormous number of *Tom Sawyer* books that have not yet been purchased. This is no reflection of the unpopularity of my store, but perhaps these incredible pieces of history could be even more valuable with the stroke of your pen.

Would you help me in this endeavor by putting your pen to them, increasing their value and making them pieces of history and collector's items? My idea is this: If you were to come down to Philadelphia, I would put you up in the Best Western (a fine hotel near the art museum), or alternatively you may stay with me in my apartment. I will create a workstation in the back office of the bookstore where you may sign your name and stamp "Official Mark Twain Collector's Item, Authenticated by the Estate of Mark Twain." I will purchase the stamp.

Thoughts? If you agree to this, you will collect 10 percent of the profits sold on each book. Regardless of copyright date, I will value each book at no less than one hundred dollars, which means that for each book sold you will walk away with at least ten dollars. We have about eight hundred of these books, so you could stand to make, at the worst, $8,000!

Please consider this and respond as soon as possible.

Thank you for your time, and happy New Year!

Best,
Fawn Birchill, Owner, The Curious Cat Book Emporium (a *The Adventures of Tom Sawyer* specialist store)

Advertisement

BOOK SIGNING!

Starting in February, the Curious Cat Book Emporium, located in beautiful West Philadelphia, will give the Philadelphia community a once-in-a-lifetime opportunity to meet the estate of Mark Twain. Books signed by the estate will be sold through February, but the time in which you can meet the estate member(s) is limited; therefore, you may purchase tickets in advance by calling the number below. Tickets will be going fast, so ACT NOW!!

Ticket Price: $15 for a five-minute Meet the Author's Estate on **February 8 and 9**. (Tickets are nonrefundable under any circumstance.)

Book Price Range: $100 and up

Store Hours (Extended through February): 8 a.m.–8 p.m.

Event Hours: 6 p.m.–9 p.m.

Coffee/snacks provided for purchase

From: Sam Asimov
Sent: Wed, Jan 9, 2019 at 8:17 AM
To: Fawn Birchill, Staff
Re: Sales Numbers

Hi Fawn,

What about starting a blog about your store? It will drive interest, and it might give people a chance to see another side of you, the store, and Butterscotch that they don't normally see. Thoughts?

Sam

From: Fawn Birchill
Sent: Wed, Jan 9, 2019 at 9:58 AM
To: Staff
Re: Sales Numbers

Dear Sam,

Though Angela has already won the gift certificate, I do like this idea as well. Can you please help me set that up? I know very little about blogging, but it might be a good way in which to drive interest, like you said. How is the Parrot going? Have you started?

Thank you for your suggestions,
Fawn, Owner

From: Fawn Birchill
Sent: Wed, Jan 9, 2019 at 9:59 PM
To: Staff
Subject: Gala Event

Dear Staff,

Upon closing the store tonight, I discovered that someone had put a poster on our door advertising Mark's gala event. Surely I know it wasn't one of you, but please let me know which one of our turncoat customers did this so that I can reprimand them. Or perhaps maybe Mark snuck over when we weren't looking and put it up? On second thought, I believe that to be more likely.

And let me just ask: How did he get sponsorship from phillysmallbiz.com and every nonprofit in the city? This nobody, who appeared out of the woodwork, seems to have connections like the mob. Watch your backs, everyone.

Sincerely,
Fawn, Owner

PHILLY LOVE FINDER

Butterscotch,

Would you be interested in a date?

Mr-Pants

PHILLY LOVE FINDER

Mr-Pants,

What would a date consist of in your book? I will admit that it's been a long time since I've been on what anyone would define as a date.

Also, is that scrap metal in the back of that pickup truck in your photo?

What does your alias mean? Does the hyphen suggest that you are without pants, or is that just because Philly Love Finder does not allow one to use periods in one's username? I haven't tried myself.

Butterscotch

PHILLY LOVE FINDER

Butterscotch,

How about Afghan? It's very savory. Lots of spinach, rice, and tender meat. It's some of my favorite food in the entire world. What do you think? Feeling adventurous?

And yeah—that's my art project in the making. I use scrap metal and whatever various crap I can get my hands on.

Mr-Pants

PHILLY LOVE FINDER

Mr-Pants,

I have never had Afghan food before, but the

way you describe it, it sounds lovely. When and where?

You make art out of scrap metal!!?? I would just LOVE to see that!

You did not answer my question about the pants.

Butterscotch

• •

Jan 11, 2019

If anything happens to me and anyone (particularly family) comes across my journal and decides to violate my privacy, I encourage and urge you to stop reading at this moment. Do not continue. Shut the book. Perhaps burn it? I would be eternally grateful. It's not that I have many great secrets or that you will come across a horrible truth that you hadn't known about me. In fact, my life is both dull and full: two qualities that ensure an incredibly boring journal.

I am extremely disappointed in my Christmas gifts, but that is par for the course once you hit your fifties and stop consorting with family on a regular basis. Having a life tends to lead one to this fate.

I think my Christmases may have been better had I been given a brother and not a sister. Men tend to give money as gifts, are far less apologetic, and waste very little time in stores hunting for the right thing only to settle on the dreadful 50 percent off bin with the fluffy hats and the self-help books.

It would have also been nice to have a brother because ever since I was a little girl, I have wanted to be a Caddy to someone. I have always loved the character from The Sound and the Fury, though I don't believe it was Faulkner's aim to create a female character that young girls could look up to. It was less what Caddy did and more her absence that interested me, as well as her brothers' fascination with her and her untouchable beauty—untouchable mostly because it was so hard to see. She is in the book so little, although the entire story revolves around her. Her brothers are absolute worshippers of her whether they like it or not, and worship they do, mostly because she is absent! And here I am: the absent daughter whom nobody knows is gone. I have always been the capable older sister, while Florence floundered through life like a rag doll, yelping and crying at the first sign of trouble. Once, my family accidentally left me behind on a camping trip. I wandered through the woods and pretended I was a beaver before they found me a few hours later, chewing on a stump. That was me: self-sufficient Fawn. You see, it didn't take long for me to adapt to my new environment, not unlike the character Buck in The Call of the Wild. Truth be told, I was rather disappointed when they found me.

After the holidays, life is as dull as ever. The world turns gray, and people stop being nice to each other because there are no more gifts to open. No more surprises. Some people need the promise of a reward.

The issue with Mark and the Grumpy Mug is escalating. The other day he invited me to his gala, as if he really wants me there! And that holiday card that he had all his employees sign. He must be doing rather poorly to kiss butt as much as he does. I have no intention of ever setting foot in that awful place, but I will say that when I walk by and glance in from across the street, there are many people there. However, I know it is only because they sell coffee and beer—a clever trick all the same, and so I say touché. I know my Folgers probably won't stand a chance against his organic, fair trade, arabica hippie sludge, but I suppose it's better than nothing. If I charge a dollar a cup, I'll be bringing in more money, and it won't cost me nearly a thing since it will be stuff from my kitchen that I already own. I'll just have to buy some sugar and powdered creamer. Everyone knows it's the smarter choice since it lasts longer.

The Mark Twain event is the thing—the way I vanquish him, once and for all. I can sell as much coffee as I would like or make a multitude of posters, but what will really wreck him is if my event is a success. I will advertise, and I will garner such interest that by the night of my event, he will be shaking in his Converse shoes and I will finally have the money I need to fix or replace my heating system. (Due to the space heaters, my electric bill has risen significantly.)

In other news, Butterscotch has been ripping out his fur. I have been finding little tufts of hair throughout the store. Sometimes I wish cats were taken seriously enough that we could hire licensed therapists for them.

It snowed today! A little late since now no one is in the mood to shop—only to return unwanted gifts. By the way, I plan to try and exchange the awful socks at Target. As much as I hate the socks, every time I return a gift from my family I feel as if I'm giving up a piece of them, and it makes me sad. As I stand in line, I have to keep telling myself that it's really nothing personal and that they are just bad at picking out gifts. They can't help it. And to be honest, I'm always so busy with my business that I make it impossible for them to know what to get me. So there, that makes me feel better. Off to Target!

PHILLY LOVE FINDER

Dear Mr-Pants,

I am so looking forward to dinner! So that you will recognize me, I will be wearing a purple dress and a blue silk scarf with small golden chariots on it. Though . . . I may wear a black skirt and a green silk blouse with the blue scarf. Either way I will have the silk scarf. It was a gift from Paris, so I think it makes me appear quite worldly. You be the judge!

See you then.

Sincerely,

Butterscotch

PHILLY LOVE FINDER

Dear Mr-Pants,

Did you fall ill? We were supposed to meet at the restaurant at six, but you were nowhere to be found! I figured you were running a little late, so I went inside out of the cold and waited on that velvet bench by the door for twenty minutes, but you still never showed up. Meanwhile the door kept opening as more people arrived, and each time I suffered a horrible blast of air with which my silk scarf could not contend. There was one instance when I thought it was you, for a tall man in a black coat hurried in as if he was late (and he resembled you, strongly). He stopped, looked down at me where I was sitting, and let out a horrid chuckle before turning red in the face, pulling out his cell phone, and walking out the door. Surely that couldn't have been you because you would have said something upon recognizing the silk scarf. Perhaps an apology for being so late? I believe this man had the wrong restaurant, for there are two side by side on this street—a worry I had until I verified the name of it (I had it written on a piece of paper).

At seven, just as I was about to leave, a handsome man came in and, looking quite sad, sat down on the bench beside me. I asked him what was the trouble, and he said he had recently broken up with his girlfriend and needed to go out on the town. I offered to be his informal date for the night—an offer he accepted—so we spent the evening laughing, talking, and having a wonderful time. He looks a bit like Hugh Jackman but more toned down in looks and so comes across as a bit ragged at first, though his obvious aristocratic persona came out the moment he smiled. Needless to say, I was quite happy with last night and don't mind at all that you didn't show, for I had a wonderful time. Hope you are all right and not in a ditch somewhere.

Butterscotch

From: Mark Nilsen
Sent: Sat, Jan 12, 2019 at 7:56 AM
To: Fawn Birchill
Subject: 50 Percent Sale Sign

Hi Fawn,

One of my employees walked by this morning on their way in and saw that you or someone who works for you pulled one of our 50 percent off sale signs from the trash and repurposed it. Can you please take it down?

Best,
Mark

From: Fawn Birchill
Sent: Sat, Jan 12, 2019 at 8:08 AM
To: Mark Nilsen
Re: 50 Percent Sale Sign

Dear Mark,

Well, the sign was in the dumpster, undestroyed, available for anyone to use. I'll have you know that to appease to your sensibilities, I had my employee cross out where it says **GRUMPY MUG BOOKSTOP**.

Hope that satisfies you.

Best,
Fawn

From: Mark Nilsen
Sent: Sat, Jan 12, 2019 at 8:18 AM
To: Fawn Birchill
Re: 50 Percent Sale Sign

Hi Fawn,

No, sorry, but that doesn't satisfy me. It's still my property, and I would like you not to use it and to also no longer pick through our trash. I don't want to have to call the police.

Best,
Mark

From: Fawn Birchill
Sent: Sat, Jan 12, 2019 at 8:20 AM
To: Mark Nilsen
Re: 50 Percent Sale Sign

Mark,

It doesn't say your store name anymore, so I don't see the issue or the need to call the cops. I don't believe going through the garbage is a crime, but I'd be happy to challenge that with you in person.

Fawn

From: Mark Nilsen
Sent: Sat, Jan 12, 2019 at 8:34 AM
To: Fawn Birchill
Re: 50 Percent Sale Sign

Hi Fawn,

In order to have accessed my garbage bin, you would have had to trespass onto my property, which is a crime and something I could call the cops over.

Best,
Mark

From: Fawn Birchill
Sent: Sat, Jan 12, 2019 at 8:50 AM
To: Mark Nilsen
Re: 50 Percent Sale Sign

Dear Mark,

You win. The sign has come down, so you can call off the dogs. Perhaps next time you should shred your old signage if you are so afraid of people reusing it.

Fawn

From: Mark Nilsen
Sent: Sat, Jan 12, 2019 at 10:45 PM
To: Fawn Birchill
Subject: Cops

Hi Fawn,

Someone called the cops on our store this evening due to a noise complaint. Do you know anything about this?

Best,
Mark

From: Fawn Birchill
Sent: Sat, Jan 12, 2019 at 11:09 PM
To: Mark Nilsen
Re: Cops

Dear Mark,

I believe it was my downstairs tenant, who is very old and needs sleep. I hope you know that I would at least walk over and ask in person before doing such a thing. I believe the only reason she called the cops on your admittedly boisterous event was because she has a very difficult time getting around, and calling is more convenient.

Best wishes,
Fawn

From: Fawn Windsor
Sent: Sun, Jan 13, 2019 at 8:17 AM
To: Gregory Harris
Subject: Winter romance

Dear Gregory,

I don't want to pry into your love life, but I feel as if I must divulge mine to you. I went on a blind date last night to find, much to my surprise, that it was a celebrity! Now, I won't reveal to you who he is because it might very well end, but he took me to the finest restaurant in London and then afterward we walked along the Thames together, not quite hand in hand but close! And when we parted, I gave him a kiss!

It's quite possible nothing will happen with this, and I know if not for my illustrious status we probably would have never met, but it is something I will look back on fondly. Are you still single? Do you go on many dates? The dating world can be very difficult—especially when one is busy. You might not think someone like me can be very busy, but lately I have willingly taken on more work around the estate (mostly due to extreme boredom), and I find there is so little time for myself these days! Work is truly the thing that keeps my mind from running out of control, because otherwise I find myself sitting around this grand estate wondering what exactly I'm even doing here anymore. Think about it, Gregory! I am only here because I was born into it, because I was told that this was the life I was supposed to lead. No one ever took Fawn Windsor aside and asked her what she wanted. Of course, what child wouldn't want sprawling acres, teams of horses, and being waited on hand and foot? So of course, I understand why they never bothered to ask.

Once, to quell my boredom, I tried my hand at writing romance novels, but it was a miserable failure. I lack the imagination to conjure up romance out of thin air, and I refuse to use my own whirlwind romances, as they are ever so personal. And so, I feed the horses and help Pierre outfit them with new shoes. I brush them and exercise them. Last fall I even painted one of the barns! I just love getting dirty once in a while with the peasants—it makes me feel so alive!

Here I am going on. I just wanted to say hullo and keep you updated on the romantic whirlwind that is my life!

How did you like Turks and Caicos? What I wouldn't give to lie on a sandy beach right now, but alas, I promised Pierre I would help him with the horses this week. Perhaps the week after . . .

Much love,
Fawn Windsor

From: Gregory Harris
Sent: Mon, Jan 14, 2019 at 1:12 AM
To: Fawn Windsor
Re: Winter romance

Hello there, my dear,

What a romantic tumult you've found yourself in! I have to say I'm a bit envious—most of my blind dates don't end up so exciting. I think my nearest brush with a celebrity was briefly dating some baseball player's personal assistant. I have no idea who the baseball player was because sports are terribly boring to me. But to each his own, I suppose. My date went on incessantly about the baseball player, and it was clear by my second martini that they would have rather been dating their boss than sitting there with me. Oh well.

Where was I? It's late, and I'm exhausted from a hard day of real estate work, so I thought I'd send off a quick reply before crashing.

Fawn, my dear, Turks and Caicos was DIVINE. It's too much to write about. Perhaps more later.

Gregory

●●

From: Fawn Birchill
Sent: Mon, Jan 14, 2019 at 10:16 AM
To: Staff
Subject: Mark Twain Estate Guests

Dear Staff,

We have received some phone calls inquiring about the event this February and have sold a few tickets, but numbers are still not as impressive as I had hoped. Please mention the event to customers as they come in. They may buy tickets in-store. Feel free to give them a complimentary cup of coffee when they buy a ticket.

Fawn, Owner

●●

From: Mark Nilsen
Sent: Mon, Jan 14, 2019 at 11:09 AM
To: Fawn Birchill
Subject: Gala Event Invitation

Hi Fawn,

I hope you received the official gala invitation. If your plans fall through, you are always welcome to stop in.

I couldn't help but notice that the sign in your window has been taken down. Your employee Kyle said it would be fine to put it up, especially since it is to benefit youth centers and not the Grumpy Mug whatsoever. Since it has been taken down, could I get it back?

Thank you,
Mark

P.S. We managed to get the mayor to come to our event! Might be cool to meet him. :)

From: Fawn Birchill
Sent: Mon, Jan 14, 2019 at 11:45 AM
To: Mark Nilsen
Re: Gala Event Invitation

Dear Mark,

I appreciate the invite; however, as I stated before, I simply cannot make it. Because you have literally no history in the Philadelphia business scene, I am surprised that you managed to get the mayor to attend your gala. I am not sure if you are trying to impress me or intimidate me, but please know that I am not easily intimidated nor am I impressed.

Fawn, Owner, The Curious Cat Book Emporium (a *The Adventures of Tom Sawyer* specialist store)

P.S. I appreciate you coming forward and admitting that you put your gala poster up in my doorway, and that you got permission from Kyle to do so. I have spoken to Kyle and told him that we unfortunately cannot support our immediate competition, and so the poster was taken down. I'm sorry, but I recycled it (I hope posters are recyclable!) and cannot return it to you.

From: Fawn Birchill
Sent: Tue, Jan 15, 2019 at 6:09 PM
To: Angela Washington
Subject: Philly Love Finder (CONFIDENTIAL)

Dear Angela,

Is there somewhere on this service where I can write a bad review of an individual so as to warn the other potential dates? I am beginning to remember why I swore off the dating scene in the eighties. The world hasn't improved much in that regard.

Fawn, Owner

THE CURIOUS CAT BOOK EMPORIUM

Blog Post #1

An Interview with the Proprietor

June Marchland is a journalist who has worked with the* New York Times *covering the Syrian conflict as well as the war in Afghanistan. June began her journalistic work at Harvard, where she founded their quarterly women's newsletter. She currently holds a PhD in philosophy and journalism studies and is extremely exclusive about whom she chooses to interview. The Curious Cat Book Emporium is honored and humbled to have her here with us today.

JM: What was your inspiration for such a store?

FB: When I was a child, my father owned a general store in our hometown of Norristown. He worked tirelessly day and night, with my sister and me assisting him. My sister often remained in the back working on the books while I was in charge of all up-front matters, no doubt due to my positive and customer-oriented personality. Often businessmen would come in on their way into the city and flirt with me, but never with my poor sister, who was stuck in the back room and I believe grew to resent me for it. My inspiration came as I watched all the mistakes Father made.

He would not treat us well and paid us only enough to get a school lunch that day. My grades slipped because I was always so tired from getting up early, and I would often fall asleep in class. This spawned my dream of opening my own store and doing it right. Treating people right, rewarding customers (but not too much)—not to the detriment of my business—and always being deeply rooted in the community.

JM: Do you feel rooted in your community?

FB: I do. I am always looking for ways to get the local businesses to work with me on what would be mutually beneficial opportunities. Not all have taken to it. I believe the times we live in have forced people—even hippies that run co-ops—to be rather paranoid, but some have proven me wrong. The owner of O'Hare Repair is an example of an excellent businessman, rooted in his community. I daresay I have also inspired local fellow bookstore owners to become more involved in grassroots community efforts. If you watch closely, you may see a pattern where I come up with a great idea, and shortly thereafter they duplicate it but vary it enough to make it their own. An insecure person would take this as an affront and perhaps even accuse them of being completely unimaginative and desperate, whereas I see it as a healthy and welcome exchange of ideas.

JM: That leads perfectly into my next question. Some have said that you are a pioneer in the field of used bookstores. Why do you think that is, if you agree?

FB: I humbly agree, June. And that is because not only are our sales numbers steadily increasing each year, but I have also managed to diversify and become the only bookseller in Philadelphia, or perhaps Pennsylvania, with such an inventory of Mark Twain books as to set me far above the others. I am aware that certain sellers down the street may be jealous of my situation, but they needn't be. They should do as I do, learn from my successes, and emulate when possible—as long as it's not selling Mark Twain books!

(Laughter)

JM: They didn't tell me you were so funny.

FB: I like to surprise people with that.

JM: Would you say you are popular among your employees?

FB: My employees are like family to me. They are my closest friends. We share my great Victorian space for eight hours a day, so we have no choice but to become close and reliant on each other. I liken it to how sailors must feel on ships, stuck on the ocean for months at a time, building friendships, alliances, and lifelong memories.

Recently we had a wonderfully fun holiday party at the store. Everyone came and brought their friends, and we talked and laughed into the night just as I, as a little girl, had dreamed my family would always do.

JM: Are you close with your family?

FB: I have always felt like a stranger in my family, and as much as I would like to be closer to them, I have to choose my work. It is the one thing that has brought me more happiness and satisfaction than anything in my life before. And if anything were to happen to this place . . . well, failure is simply not an option. I watched my father fail, and it's an ugly, terrible thing. My father and I were never close, but ever since I opened my store twenty years ago, I believe that I have been in a silent competition with him—even though he has been practically bedridden these last twenty years. I often think on the Ginsberg poem "A Supermarket in California" when I think of my father. I believe Ginsberg was speaking of Whitman when he referred to "father, graybeard, lonely old courage-teacher," though I have never seen this poem as referring to anyone but my father, and my questions to him, which I believe are similar to Ginsberg's: What kind of America did you get to see? And more personally for me, what did you leave me to deal with? Why haven't we spoken? Why can't we speak? Why must you,

Father, be on a ferry to death while I'm left to pick up the various pieces of confusion in my life that you left littered around me like broken glass?

JM: You are quite a poet yourself, yes?

FB: When it comes to my father, I think I can throw out a lot of feelings at the drop of a hat. That is what happens with neglect. The child is left with so many unsaid words, so they become poets, artists, or bookstore proprietors. But getting back to your question, the quiet competition between my father and me has forced me to become close to him in a strange, ethereal way that's rather hard to explain. I suppose I am showing him, with my success, that I am doing it right. I am showing my entire family this truth, and I think it's hard for them to watch me rise and be happy. Some families just like being miserable together.

JM: Before you owned the bookstore, what was your occupation? Did you own another business, or did you work for someone else?

FB: I went through a time in my life when I wasn't completely sure of what I wanted to do, even though I knew I wanted to own my own business. It's very frightening to be in your thirties and decide to start a business completely on your own, knowing that you will be putting your personal life on hold until things even out. While

I was in that state of flux, right after graduating from college with a business degree, my father tried to sell me his business, presumptuously assuming that I would want it. But that store was a giant sinkhole, and neither my sister nor I wanted anything to do with it. It was in terrible physical condition and he owed a lot of money, which he eventually handled with bankruptcy. While that was happening, I took a few years to live at home and reevaluate things before taking the plunge into opening my own business.

JM: Why books?

FB: What a great question! Without books, I may have never had a way to disappear from the reality I faced every day under my father's rule. Without books, I wouldn't have been able to flex my imagination and pretend to be, for example, such vivid characters as Caddy Compson or Madame Bovary. Books allowed me to see that there was more to this world than the town I grew up in or the nearby cities we sometimes visited so my father could exercise his gambling habit. I suppose I could have opened up any store at all, but I chose books because, quite frankly, they might be solely responsible for having kept me fighting all my life for what I wanted. Because of this, it seemed only right to be able to share such a gift with others—and at discounted rates!

JM: What was it like twenty years ago, starting a business from the ground up the way that you did?

FB: It was challenging in that West Philadelphia was a very different place twenty years ago. My greatest challenges were vandalism and robbery, but I will have you know that even though it was considered a rough area, I was unafraid. I saw this as an opportunity to bring books to the community. Also, the building, despite needing a lot of repair work, was incredibly affordable; however, that was not my main motivation for the purchase. I knew this neighborhood would turn around, and sometimes, I daresay, I credit my store for the start of its gentrification.

JM: If you had one piece of advice for a new business owner, what would that be?

FB: Pay your bills without taking out too many loans and pay them on time. Be creative, and you cannot fail. I suppose that's three.

(Laughter)

JM: We'll let that one go.

(More laughter)

JM: It has been so wonderful to sit in your shop and get to know you. I have interviewed many people—from world leaders to intellectuals—and this has been a true highlight.

FB: I am humbled. Thank you, June. It's my pleasure.

JM: The pleasure is mine.

An audio clip of this transcript is unavailable due to technical difficulties. Fawn Birchill apologizes for the inconvenience.

●●

From: Tabitha Birchill
Sent: Tue, Jan 15, 2019 at 8:18 PM
To: Fawn Birchill
Subject: Building Collapse

Dear Fawn,

I heard on the news of a building collapse in the city. Did you know about it? Was it near you? I tried calling, but you didn't pick up.

Love you,
Mother

From: Fawn Birchill
Sent: Tue, Jan 15, 2019 at 10:05 PM
To: Tabitha Birchill
Re: Building Collapse

Dear Mother,

Please do not worry. It happened down in

South Philly, not West Philly where I live. Apparently no one was injured or hurt. I hear it was being torn down, and it happened to come down faster than they planned. Even though I am far from the epicenter, I appreciate your concern. I happen to live in a very sturdy building, however imperfect it may appear on the outside.

Have you been reading my new blog? I have cut and pasted the link below!

Fawn

●●

January 15, 2019

I wish I knew how to recall emails. Immediately upon sending my mother the link to the blog, I read over the interview again and regretted ever telling her about it. It isn't the nicest portrayal of her and our family. Thank god that a few moments later, she wrote back saying that the link didn't work and to resend. I think I will simply tell her that the page is under construction and forever leave it at that. In the future, I should be more careful.

Jane, the old woman who thinks I am her daughter from Hawaii, is getting worse cognitively, so I have made my trips to her apartment much more frequently to see if there's anything she needs. Butterscotch loves following me in and playing jungle cat in the aloe plants, and I think Jane likes petting him when he sometimes walks by her recliner. Sometimes she calls me by my name, and other times she calls me by her daughter's name. When she thinks I am her daughter, before I leave I say that I had a wonderful weekend with her and that I will send the kids her love (though if her daughter has kids I wouldn't know, and I doubt she would know, either, at this point). She sits alone in a recliner by the drafty window and watches reruns of Touched by an Angel *and* Murder, She Wrote. *There is always an unopened box of chocolates on her lap that I believe was a gift from the last Valentine's Day. Sometimes I wonder what horrible things she did to end up so alone. What scares me most is that she probably did nothing horrible—that this is simply what being unlucky looks like. She has a terrible family, and I, too, have a terrible family. Sometimes I hurry through her apartment because I fear that if I were to stick around too long, I may become her—that I may forget how to open the door, how to extricate myself, and instead sit on her floor staring at the cabinets, only to become a human vegetable. Perhaps that is how her family feels? I opened the cabinets once to see what kind of food she had, and there was nothing but a half-eaten box of Triscuits. Her freezer is filled with those little instant microwave meals, which I think she lives off when she isn't eating the dinners I leave for her. She also keeps numerous open boxes of rat poison all over her apartment. It is thick with dust in there and bears the odor of medication and quilts—a combination of smells that reminds me of visits to my father and also reminds me of why I no longer do it. I hope that I am never this alone one day, or if I am, that I do not care or realize it—that I am too far mentally gone.*

When I went to the store, I couldn't help myself and bought her some herbal tea, bananas, and saltine crackers. She seemed to appreciate it.

●●

Sam Asimov/*CuriousCatBooks*/1d

So psyched to read To Keep the Sun Alive by Rabeah Ghaffari! #newrelease #fiction #novel

Sam Asimov/*CuriousCatBooks*/5h

Can't believe I'm just finding out about Ohio by Stephen Markley. What an amazing book! #novel #fiction #betterlatethannever

●●

From: Fawn Birchill
Sent: Wed, Jan 16, 2019 at 9:00 AM
To: Staff
Subject: The Parrot

Sam,

I have seen some of the things that you are posting, and I must say that nearly none involve my bookstore. Talking about new books coming out would be fine except for the fact that the store in which you are employed does not carry them. I thought the point of this was to boost *our* business? Please stick to what we have in inventory.

Many thanks,
Fawn, Owner

●●

Angela Washington/*CuriousCatBooks*/10m
Good day at CCBE! Butterscotch the cat smells less like mildew this a.m. #miraclesdohappen #smellycat

●●

From: Fawn Birchill
Sent: Wed, Jan 16, 2019 at 10:13 AM
To: Staff
Subject: Butterscotch

Angela,

Please explain to me how your post about Butterscotch is supposed to bolster sales. Do you honestly think people will flock from far and wide? Now is not the time to be bringing into question the cleanliness of Butterscotch since we have five supposedly "adorable" feline competitors down the block. We have to be nothing but positive when we speak of him. And please, post about books that are in the inventory, for the one hundredth time!

Fawn, Owner

P.S. Sometimes Butterscotch likes to sleep in the basement and drink from the pipes. I believe he is playing survivor cat and merely imagining that he is living off the land that is the unfurnished basement. If this bothers you, then perhaps you should merely stay away from him?

From: Fawn Birchill
Sent: Wed, Jan 16, 2019 at 1:13 PM
To: Twain Estates
Subject: Business Opportunity?

To the estate of Mark Twain:

It has been over a week, and I have not heard back from you regarding my proposition. I understand how busy you must be as the estate of Mark Twain. I do not know how many of you there are, but I only need one individual to assist. If you do not reply, you are actually throwing money away. You might as well put eight grand in an envelope and burn it. I hear burning money is illegal, however, so I do not encourage it but only use it as an example of the madness of your decisions. If someone were to make me an equivalent offer, I would buy a first-class ticket and be there in a flash—though I assume a first-class airline ticket can be about eight grand, so I would probably ride coach with the bourgeoisie and live off the complimentary airline food to make it as profitable a journey as possible. If you go this route, I recommend putting any handouts in your pockets and saving them for later, because that way if you are hungry around dinnertime you need only to pull them out and save yourself the price of a meal at a restaurant. That is, if you must fly to get here. I personally love the train myself. Anything invented after 1900 reeks of mass industry and sameness. After the Victorian era, the world unquestionably began to fall apart; don't you agree?

Awaiting your reply!

Best,
Fawn

Kyle Krazinsky/*CuriousCatBooks*/5m
Just finished Anna Karenina. Good except for Levin getting all weirdly religious at the end. #letdown #wtf

From: Fawn Birchill
Sent: Wed, Jan 16, 2019 at 2:40 PM
To: Staff
Subject: Books

Kyle,

Writing Parrot posts about books in-store that you dislike is also not a good idea. I don't understand how this is such a difficult concept for all of you! Are you intentionally trying to undermine this project? I would honestly wonder this if I didn't know that you all truly care so much and are really trying to help. For that I thank you, but I think I'll need to take over. Some of us need to go to business school to have good sense, some of us are born with it, and some will simply never grasp the concept.

Fawn, Owner

From: Fawn Birchill
Sent: Thu, Jan 17, 2019 at 8:17 AM
To: Staff
Subject: ATTENTION REQUIRED

Dear Staff,

Will somebody please explain why I walked downstairs this morning to find the *Philly Small Biz Journal* open to a glowing article about the Grumpy Mug Bookstop on the counter for all customers to see? And then, to make matters even worse, on top of it a steaming to-go mug of coffee with a Grumpy Mug insulator jacket advertising our competitor!? When we have coffee here? Folgers, no less? There are two mugs I desperately never want to see first thing in the morning: their coffee mug and his bearded hippie face.

And to think I was considering giving you all raises. One of you better fess up to this, or you will all be equally to blame for this transgression. We are supposed to be like a supportive family, not a bunch of Judases!

This article is full of falsehoods anyway. This writer states that "the Grumpy Mug Bookstop has revitalized a neighborhood where before there was no reason to set foot on the street except to get a check cashed or to cross over to Clark Park." If they are trying to insult me, they are doing a fine job. Crediting HIM for gentrifying the neighborhood? Mark, who looks more like a criminal himself with his tattoos and creepy affection for his cats?

Please come to me by noon today, and I will forgive the guilty party. If no one comes to me, then you can forget your raises.

Fawn, Owner

From: Fawn Birchill
Sent: Thu, Jan 17, 2019 at 1:32 PM
To: Mark Nilsen
Subject: Bold Tactics

Dear Mark,

It's interesting to me the level to which you choose to stoop just because you happen to be a little threatened by my store, which unlike yours is a neighborhood staple and has as much of a foothold in Philadelphia as the Liberty Bell. I understand the stressful feeling you must have, being in competition with me day to day, but that is no excuse for your behavior. My employees came to me and unanimously said that you showed up this morning, placed your article open on our checkout counter along with a steaming mug of your coffee, and left without a word.

I feel the need to explain to you that, though the article paints you in a Jesus-like light, you and your business do not threaten me. So, please refrain from using guerilla tactics to undermine my store and steal my customers. If you are really as successful as the papers claim you to be, don't you have better things to do?

Sincerely,
Fawn Birchill, Owner, The Curious Cat Book Emporium (a *The Adventures of Tom Sawyer* specialist store)

From: Mark Nilsen
Sent: Thu, Jan 17, 2019 at 2:45 PM
To: Fawn Birchill
Re: Bold Tactics

Hi Fawn,

I walked in to say hello and to see if you were there, but they said you were out. Then I got a call from my little brother about something important, so I took the call outside. It was an emergency, so I went back to the store, completely forgetting my stuff. And for the record, I certainly didn't leave it open to that page. One of your employees must have been leafing through it and never closed it back up.

Sorry for any distress this might have caused.

Mark

From: Fawn Birchill
Sent: Thu, Jan 17, 2019 at 3:03 PM
To: Mark Nilsen
Re: Bold Tactics

Mark,

I'm sorry, but I just can't buy that line. My employees said you came in without a word and dropped this stuff off, so are you asking me to believe you over my own employees? After you've already done so many obnoxious and childish things? It's simply impossible for me to see it any other way. Since there is no empirical evidence aside from your word against theirs, I'm going to have to leave it at that, but please spare us this battle in the future and do not come in here again with your marketing materials.

Fawn Birchill, Owner, The Curious Cat Book Emporium (a *The Adventures of Tom Sawyer* specialist store)

Fawn Birchill/*CuriousCatBooks*/5m
Butterscotch is sleeping on top of the travel section this morning! Come and see him dreaming of exploring the West with Lewis and Clark!

Fawn Birchill/*CuriousCatBooks*/4m
Mention the above post and get a 10% discount!

From: Fawn Birchill
Sent: Sun, Jan 20, 2019 at 10:04 AM
To: Sam Asimov
Subject: The Parrot

Sam,

The Parrot is infuriating! I cannot send a message unless it's incredibly short and therefore practically useless! How is this supposed to be at all helpful!? For someone as verbose as me, it makes me feel as if I am in a cage with my feet and hands tied together. I want to run through my apartment screaming! You must admit that it is absolutely draconian.

Nevertheless, I already have ten followers, so it must be doing some good.

Many thanks,
Fawn, Owner

Fawn Birchill/*CuriousCatBooks*/2m

Joy of #reading #sale today at the #Curious #Cat #Book #Emporium! Discounts for mentioning author #Chekhov! (Discounts apply to any #books.)

From: Gregory Harris
Sent: Mon, Jan 21, 2019 at 4:08 PM
To: Fawn Windsor
Subject: A London Get-Together?

Hello, my dear,

I will be in London January 31 to February 3 on business. We are converting a late 1800s millinery into a swanky bar. First time doing something like this and I'm a little nervous, but it should be fun!

I'm rarely over there, so if you'd like to get together at any point, please let me know. It would be fun to finally meet you.

Tell me what is new with you.

Sincerely,
Gregory

From: Fawn Windsor
Sent: Mon, Jan 21, 2019 at 9:30 PM
To: Gregory Harris
Re: A London Get-Together?

Dearest Gregory,

The horses are all wrapped up in their stables for the night, braying and kicking their shoes against the hay-covered floor. I sit by the window at the fire, taking in the crackling of wood and the smell of musky smoke, and bask in the silence of the house—minus the servants' constant shuffling and murmuring of course. Sometimes they sound like mice in the walls. The servants will be taking down the tree tomorrow and restoring the estate to its usual utilitarian body without the mirth and mistletoe.

Incidentally an American has moved into the estate three miles down the road and is bringing in horse after horse. Apparently he is going to start a polo club at his home. He came over to introduce himself to me the other day, riding up on what I believe was an Arabian horse. He told me, without dismounting, that he would be moving in indefinitely and not to mind the shouting crowds but that I was more than invited to attend his ridiculous events (my emphasis).

He wears a mustache and goatee combination like Tolstoy, and his eyes are so dark that they bear an air of mischief despite his kind words. I don't trust him, Gregory. It seems he aims to make my haven into a hell of ceaseless noise.

Ah, I almost forgot! Thank you for your interest in wanting to meet me in London in late January. Though it would only be a skip over there by train, I plan to visit the Canary Islands at that time, taking care of some boring paperwork regarding another estate we own there. But even if I weren't leaving on family business, I would be hesitant to meet you, as the mystique and intrigue of our relationship has always been fueled by the fact that neither of us have met nor do we know what the other looks like. There is a reason I correspond through email instead of the post, which is my usual preferred way. One day, I know I would accidentally put my return address on the envelope, and you would show up with flowers in your arms at my door (platonically, of course)! Though you would need to be buzzed in through the gate and then walk the mile down the road (presumably you would drive), to get to the front entrance. My butler is a bit serious about his job (think Mr. Carson from *Downton Abbey*) and usually won't let a stranger within feet of the steps! He is very protective of me as I am more like his Mary Crawley figure and therefore his favorite of the household.

I do hope you understand and have a nice time in London! Do you have to do much restoration on the building or is it in decent shape? I imagine a Victorian-era millinery would be in questionable condition. I greatly share your interest in Victorians, though I do hope you maintain their charm and don't modernize them too greatly.

I hear the Tower of London is very interesting and historical, and I do encourage you to go. My family suffered in those cold cavernous cells when they fell out of the king's favor during the Protestant Reformation. Thankfully only a handful met the chopping block, and quickly thereafter the family was restored to title and property. Phew! There's my family saga in twenty seconds flat! Personally I have never been to the tower because it's a typical tourist trap, though we would never look down on Americans for finding it incredible—for no doubt it is an amazing piece of history.

Much love,
Fawn Windsor

●●

Fawn Birchill/*CuriousCatBooks*/5m
Mention #Downton Abbey and receive 25% discount on #Victorian Era #novels! (We do not have #Downton Abbey DVDs.)

From: Mark Nilsen
Sent: Thu, Jan 24, 2019 at 11:45 PM
To: Fawn Birchill
Subject: Police

Hi Fawn,

Our decibel levels are not violating any ordinances. I don't understand why you feel the need to keep calling the police.

I will try to stop by tomorrow, though I'm sure your employees will feed me the usual line that you are out.

Mark

From: Fawn Birchill
Sent: Fri, Jan 25, 2019 at 10:09 AM
To: Mark Nilsen
Re: Police

Dear Mark,

The police are simply doing their job. If your events are so loud that they are called, it is not my problem nor am I the one to blame. Perhaps, as I said before, you can ask your guests to reel in the enthusiasm. I do not know who called the police on your extremely loud event, but I assure you on my mother's life it was not me. (And I'll have you know that my mother and I are very close, and so I don't throw that around lightly!)

Fawn Birchill, Owner, The Curious Cat Book Emporium (a *The Adventures of Tom Sawyer* specialist store)

From: Fawn Birchill
Sent: Fri, Jan 25, 2019 at 8:56 PM
To: Staff
Subject: Raises

Dear Staff,

Thank you for following up in person regarding the status of your pay increases. Yes, you are all excellent employees. You are loyal and take the success of this business very seriously. Sadly, I am unable to give you raises this year. Yes, I said I was considering it, and especially given the fact that you came forward about Mark's unwanted visit the other day, you certainly deserve it. But thanks to Mark's business, money is tight. You can blame him for your lack of a raise if you'd like to blame anyone. I'm sure you've seen the change in customer volume since he's moved in. And yes, of course it's a painful pill to swallow, but I believe that things will turn around when they realize his store is no different than mine and quite frankly, not as good. Simply having more cats does not a successful store make.

I am sorry I am unable to give you raises this year, but I believe if we stick with it, we will see a greater possibility of a raise in 2020.

Sincerely,
Fawn, Owner

●●

Fawn Birchill/*CuriousCatBooks*/3m
Fawn here! Who loves #learning? Stop by today ONLY for a 50% discount on #Encyclopedias published before 1975!

●●

January 25, 2019
Januarys are hard. The only thing worse than January is February, and the only thing worse than either is attempting to get through them sober. That is not to say I'm a lush. I would be mortified if someone found these ramblings and assumed such a thing. Truly, I say this in jest,

but as with all humorous musings, therein lies truth. Now that the holidays—which bring their own cavalcade of issues—are over, most nights I am opening and polishing off a bottle of red by the defunct fireplace. There are always years in which I'm tempted to try to get through these two months without fumbling through the cabinets for my liquid crutch, but I am either too weak or too stuck in my ways. I suppose there are worse ways to spend evenings alone. And when the wind whistles through the cracks in the panes and the building groans and pops from the pipes, I sit in my chair with my blanket, Butterscotch, a book, and my booze and I do not feel alone at all. Not at all.

Lately my mind wanders to Jane. I find myself going into her apartment to see how she is faring in these dark, drawn-out months. The woman is a real trouper—she seems as content in January as she does in May. I would stay longer and have considered bringing her some wine or at least a deck of cards, but I hold back. I am not so good with face-to-face interaction. Perhaps this is all thanks to the many years I spent ringing up local regulars and passing-through strangers alike, when I had to engage in small talk and occasionally bear the brunt of their bad day. Once my father told me, after watching me engage for a longer time than usual with a young man, that no one really wanted to speak to me and that it's best to let them get on with their day. The way he put it, I was holding the man hostage, even though—at least as best as I can remember—he was the one asking me the questions. I never saw him again. It doesn't matter. It doesn't matter that I never saw him again, I mean. I do remain rather baffled, though, that the first truly kind person who ever seemed interested in what I had to say was shooed off like a dog picking up scraps around tables at a restaurant. He was right, after all. When engaging in transactions, be they business or personal, people don't really want to lollygag. Especially with someone like me who is "better off keeping her nose to the grindstone," as my father put it.

The more I drink on these cold nights, the louder his voice becomes. But at the same time, the more ridiculous it sounds.

I have half a bottle remaining and then another in the pantry. It should last me the rest of the week until I can get back to the liquor store. I would like to say they know me by name there, but the cashier thinks my name is Fran no matter how many times I've shown him my ID. I don't have the heart to correct him since I have to see him every Sunday.

From: Kyle Krazinsky
Sent: Mon, Jan 28, 2019 at 8:36 AM
To: Fawn Birchill, Staff
Re: Inventory Update

Hey Fawn,

I just finished up physical inventory this morning, and it appears as if we are missing about $2,800 worth of books. Could some of these be the ones you give away on occasion?

Kyle

From: Fawn Birchill
Sent: Mon, Jan 28, 2019 at 8:45 AM
To: Staff
Re: Inventory Update

Dear Kyle,

Sometimes I give away a book here and there but I have not, in the twenty years that I have owned this business, given away nearly $3,000 worth of books. Either your numbers are off or we have a thief among us.

Fawn, Owner

From: Angela Washington
Sent: Mon, Jan 28, 2019 at 9:08 AM
To: Fawn Birchill, Staff
Re: Inventory Update

Sometimes vagrants wander in and sleep on the couch upstairs. Could that be it maybe? What if we like, put a fence around our store and screen people who enter? Like maybe ask for their home address to make sure they're not hobos or whatever?

—A

From: Fawn Birchill
Sent: Mon, Jan 28, 2019 at 9:18 AM
To: Staff
Re: Inventory Update

Dear Angela,

Vagabonds do wander in, but we can hardly do anything reasonable to stop it. I think your idea of asking people for their home address is smart but unrealistic since they could easily lie. Besides, people who live in houses are capable of theft. Though I lived in a dormitory in college, I stole frequently and with abandon from the local grocery stores—it was the only way I kept myself fed and healthy those four arduous years.

We will simply continue to keep an eye out. As Dogberry says in *Much Ado About Nothing*, "Adieu, be vigitant, I beseech you."

Fawn, Owner

●●

January 28, 2019

I am trying so hard to be positive, but it is a struggle. Today we had a cold snap, and I noticed customers walking out sooner than usual due to our frigid temperatures. It is challenging to heat a large Victorian store with only three space heaters.

So after the store closed, I went downstairs with a flashlight and tried to fix it myself. I believe the monstrous mechanism is about thirty-five years old and so well past its expiration. I took the panel off and, despite the many warnings of electric shock and explosion, unhooked some wires. And then, not knowing what to do once they were unhooked, reattached them. From the basement, even underground, I could hear the applause from Mark's store. The laughter. The whooping. I rested my head against the unit and breathed, but the anger grew. I don't know how it started. The desire to kick it bubbled up from a place deep inside of me. And I listened to that desire as it lashed its way out. I kicked the unit until there were dents all over the sides. I kicked it until it rattled and snapped from within. I kicked it until my back started to protest, and still I didn't stop. I screamed at it. Something inside the unit popped, and I heard what sounded like a screw fall. Out of curiosity more than anything, I flipped the switch to see if by some miracle all it needed was some tough love, but sadly, the banging noise persisted. I could have been imagining it, but I thought I smelled gas. Of course, I turned it right off and went upstairs, defeated.

I stood at the window for a long time after that. I could see the warm lights from Mark's store spill out onto the street. I don't know how long I cried.

I believe that I need a distraction to get me through these winter months.

From: Fawn Birchill
Sent: Tue, Jan 29, 2019 at 3:30 PM
To: Schuylkill Photo
Subject: Glamour Photos?

Dear Schuylkill Photo,

Do you do glamour? I think your prices are quite reasonable, and I am willing to give you a try. On your website I saw mostly black-and-white photos of babies and sepia-toned wedding photography. Are you capable of incorporating color? If so, I would like a quote for a glamour/modeling portfolio with some props that I will provide (boas, books, and parasols to name a few). I will do my own makeup and have four wardrobe changes. I would like to use music if possible, and if you do not have speakers, I can bring a small boom box. I tried to do the photos on my own, but I can't figure out how to use my computer's built-in camera, so I am resorting to this.

Thank you,
Fawn

From: Schuylkill Photo
Sent: Wed, Jan 30, 2019 at 7:24 AM
To: Fawn Birchill
Re: Glamour Photos?

Good morning,

We certainly offer modeling packages (please see attached breakdown). I would be happy to jump on the phone with you in the next few days to set something up. It is okay to bring props/makeup and have costume changes. I believe you will find the quality of these photos will far exceed anything your computer's camera could do.

Best wishes,
Sarah

January 30

Fawn,
Enclosed please find numerous CVS and Giant coupons. There are some for litter and cat food as well as bacon, which is astronomically expensive these days. You'd think pigs were going extinct!

Please reach out to your sister. She is still angry and probably won't do it even though I've begged her.

Mother

From: Fawn Birchill
Sent: Wed, Jan 30, 2019 at 8:09 AM
To: Staff
Subject: Customer Bathroom

Dear Staff,

Please do not go into the bathroom to wash your hands anymore. We have a kitchen sink in the back for that purpose. Yesterday, upon checking the bathroom, I noticed that the floorboards have the consistency of wet newspaper. If something were to happen, I do not have the money to pay for your medical bills.

Fawn, Owner

●●

From: Fawn Birchill
Sent: Wed, Jan 30, 2019 at 9:24 AM
To: Twain Estates
Subject: Counteroffer?

To the estate of Mark Twain:

Regarding my proposition, as I have not heard from you, I will take it as a sign that 10 percent is not enough. I will raise it to an even 15 percent but can go no higher, as I am the one with the product and wish to see some profit from this.

Please reply shortly as my patience is wearing thin.

Best wishes,
Fawn Birchill, Owner, The Curious Cat Book Emporium (a *The Adventures of Tom Sawyer* specialist store)

●●

From: Fawn Birchill
Sent: Wed, Jan 30, 2019 at 10:43 AM
To: Mark Nilsen
Subject: Grumpy Mug Sign

I was walking by today on my way from Missy's Co-op and saw to my dismay that the sign for your business is dangerously close to the fire escape that hangs suspended just above your first floor. In the event of a fire, whoever was on the second floor would find themselves in dire circumstances indeed, since your sign seems to impede the extension of the fire escape stairway. I highly recommend that you deal with this situation posthaste before I am forced to inform the police of this safety violation. Please know that I am thinking of your customers and you, not trying to undermine your business by encouraging you to take down your lovely store sign.

Have a beautiful day,
Fawn Birchill, Owner, The Curious Cat Book Emporium (a *The Adventures of Tom Sawyer* specialist store)

From: Mark Nilsen
Sent: Wed, Jan 30, 2019 at 11:02 AM
To: Fawn Birchill
Re: Grumpy Mug Sign

Hi Fawn,

Wow, thank you so much for letting me know about that. I never even noticed it. I think it would only be fair if I let you know that there seem to be no exit signs in your store. That could be an issue if a similar emergency occurs.

Thanks again!
Mark

From: Fawn Birchill
Sent: Wed, Jan 30, 2019 at 11:12 AM
To: Mark Nilsen
Re: Grumpy Mug Sign

Dear Mark,

You are most welcome! And let me thank you for bringing the exit sign issue to my attention. I am surprised that you have been in my store long enough to notice this and find it worrisome. I have been operating for twenty years and not a single person has pointed out the lack of a back door exit sign, nor have I been fined. That happens when you are a neighborhood staple—people tend to overlook things because they are so focused on the contents of the store and not the safety.

Thanking you ever so much for the input,
Fawn Birchill, Owner, The Curious Cat Book Emporium (a *The Adventures of Tom Sawyer* specialist store)

phillysmallbiz.com
Wed, Jan 30, 2019

Top Review—The Curious Cat Book Emporium
Okay, so I went into this store to look for a book for my niece's birthday (I am a regular customer) and this time I noticed that the store has taken on a weird dank smell, particularly toward the back. Also, why is there cat hair all over the books all of a sudden? It never used to be this bad. I don't want to go to the Grumpy Mug, but I might have to start.

Please get the cat and filth situation figured out STAT.

—Tamara J.

phillysmallbiz.com
Wed, Jan 30, 2019

Dear Tamara J.,

Since you say you are one of my most loyal customers (though I've never met you, I'll take your word for it), I will accept your criticism of the layout with the utmost sensitivity. I apologize if you find the cleanliness questionable. The smell in the back is from a leaky pipe where black mold has been collecting for years, and seeing how I have been here for twenty years and have not yet dropped dead from it, I doubt you will do the same. In regard to the animal fur on the books, I also apologize. Butterscotch likes to tuck himself between the books and sleep on the shelves. I always found it a rather charming hobby of his. Nevertheless, I will have you know that my customers' comfort (especially regular ones, as you claim to be), are paramount. That is why I have stopped allowing Butterscotch his usual happiness and no longer allow him to sit on the shelves with the books. Even though you are in here for only ten minutes and he is in here all day, every day, it is much more important that you are more comfortable because you are a human being—an accepted double standard that we, as business owners and pet parents, adhere to.

Today, for example, he was tucked away in

the self-help section, so I took it upon myself to pull a chair up to the shelf, stand on top and, balancing carefully on uneven flooring, reach my arms out to extract him. He would not be moved. He has been declawed so he cannot scratch, but he has spent so many years bludgeoning animals that his little fists are like boxing gloves. He hissed at me and turned around in place, knocking down about five books. I tried again, this time successfully grabbing him. With cat in arms, I turned to step off the chair, but the leg slipped along the uneven flooring and the chair went completely upright. I flew, Butterscotch howling and twisting in the air above me, and I landed hard on my back. I will have you know that I have previous back problems. Butterscotch landed on his feet and took off while I remained on the floor with the wind knocked out of me, waiting for one of my employees to find me, though no one seemed to hear the crash or the cat's howling. A book landed open, covering my face like a paper tent. The book was aptly titled *Finding Happiness*. Well, I must say that a nosebleed, and not happiness, is what I found in that moment. I remained on the floor for thirty minutes, regaining my breath and slowly moving each limb to check for paralysis or a broken back. I was happy to find out that nothing too serious befell me. On the floor, surrounded by my self-help books, listening to my employees move around on the first floor below me, I thought for some time about all the sacrifices I've made for this store. I have cut family from my life and only see them once a year for funerals. Friends are rare, as I do not have time for them. This place is my life; this is who I am. As I lay on the floor like a soldier wounded on the battlefield, fighting for his country, I realized that I had just done the same for you, Tamara. The difference is, I do not get a medal for my hard work. I do not get recognition of any kind for running a small used bookstore. I am the ultimate sacrificial lamb, and I will fight for my cause, my store, my life. So please, return and take back what you said about never coming back again until we "get the cat and filth situation figured out." As you can see, I do my very best every time—more, I'm sure, than my competitor down the block.

By the way, the store is no dirtier than when you first started coming here. Nothing has changed in the way we clean, so I wonder why you've donned white gloves and decided to criticize me now?

All the best,
Fawn, Owner, The Curious Cat Book Emporium (a *The Adventures of Tom Sawyer* specialist store)

From: Fawn Birchill
Sent: Wed, Jan 30, 2019 at 2:12 PM
To: Staff
Subject: January Numbers

Dear Staff,

I have never seen sales this low in all the years I have been running this store. I am adamant that we keep morale high during these dark times, but things are not as good as they used to be, and I may have to let one of you go permanently if things do not turn around—a horrible act that I always feared I may have to do.

Still, let us keep positive. Stiff upper lip and all that! I'm not saying this is a sure thing but if it comes to this, I do not want anyone to be blindsided.

Fawn, Owner

From: Fawn Birchill
Sent: Wed, Jan 30, 2019 at 3:40 PM
To: Twain Estates
Subject: Please respond

To the estate of Mark Twain:

If you are not interested in this amazing opportunity, at least do me the decency of writing back. Incidentally, I have already advertised in all the Philadelphia papers as well as in the Wilmington, Princeton, and Trenton papers that we will be graced with your presence. It would be most embarrassing for your good name if you were to simply not show up to your own event.

Additionally, there will be coffee, fresh baked goods, and a lovely declawed cat for the children to play with and pet—so feel free to bring any little ones. To assuage your concerns, this cat has been given its rabies shots, wears a flea collar, and has been free of tapeworms for nearly four months.

Best wishes,
Fawn, Owner, The Curious Cat Book Emporium (a *The Adventures of Tom Sawyer* specialist store)

●●

From: Tabitha Birchill
Sent: Wed, Jan 30, 2019 at 6:53 PM
To: Fawn Birchill
Subject: Check-in

My dear Fawn,

How are you? Forgive me; I need to brag. I won a bowling tournament last night! First time ever winning.

How is the store?

I should also let you know that your father has decided to give most of his savings to the church upon his death. I was helping him write up his will a couple of nights ago during a rare, lucid evening. I am not a fan of this, but it is his money and his decision.

Please, for all that is good, reach out to Florence. You are the older sister.

Love you,
Mother

From: Fawn Birchill
Sent: Wed, Jan 30, 2019 at 9:45 PM
To: Tabitha Birchill
Re: Check-in

Dear Mother,

Thanks for the email, and congratulations on the win the other night. I'm sure if Father were lucid, he would be very proud.

Things at the store are interesting. Life is interesting. I went twenty years in this neighborhood without dealing with a single copycat. I truly believe I was the first store those twenty years ago to make cats an intregral part of a bookstore. And a draw to customers. And I mean all over America not just my block of Philadelphia. I think I was a pioneer! And here I am facing a copycat that the papers are calling a pioneer??? That was me! Just because he's young nad has a beard like a pritae? Does he really think he is special? Jjjjjjjjjjjjjhisuye89sf//o

Svd\]'

B'

That was Butterscotch saying hello!! He almost tipped over my wine glass too—he does that sometimes. I think he must miss you, ha ha!

Father isn't really giving all his money to the church, is he? They are doing so well. They have a pool for Christ's sake. Why is it that teh rich get all the money all the time? Why is that? How can a man that was so money-oriented and aware of his own lack of funds give money to an organization that doesn't really need it?? When there are bookstore owners that might need to sell their own furniture to pay their employees? When bankruptcy looms only to be scared away by the rare good day?

I am having an event in Febuayray that will turn everything around! I am getting rather sleepy. So I better get to bed before I fall asleep here at the computer again!

Fawn

From: Fawn Birchill
Sent: Thu, Jan 31, 2019 at 8:13 AM
To: Tabitha Birchill
Re: Check-in

Dear Mother,

I apologize not only for my horrendous spelling, but also for writing to you intoxicated last night. I really shouldn't have done that. Things are much better than Drunk Fawn likes to claim they are. The man down the block is harmless and won't last. I have a feeling about it. Being in the business for so long, you get a sense of who will last and who is just a passing fad.

I will tell you more about the event in February when I get a chance, but for now just know that it will be very exciting.

Talk to you soon!

Fawn

P.S. I will reach out to Florence.

••

From: Fawn Birchill
Sent: Thu, Jan 31, 2019 at 11:21 AM
To: Florence Eakins
Subject: Sorry

Hi Florence,

I am sorry about Christmas and my complaints about the microwave. I was stressed and took it out on you.

Best,
Fawn

••

Fawn Birchill/*CuriousCatBooks*/5m
Fawn here! Dress as Your Favorite #Book #Character Day at #CCBE Feb 1! Fawn (owner) will be #Caddy Compson!

Fawn Birchill/*CuriousCatBooks*/2m
(Continued from post above) Guess the #book and get a 10% discount on #book!

••

From: Fawn Birchill
Sent: Thu, Jan 31, 2019 at 9:18 PM
To: Staff
Subject: Favorite Book Character Day!

Sam, Angela, Kyle,

I am sorry to write to you after hours when you are home, but I came up with the most splendid idea! If you look at the Parrot feed, you will see what I mean. Tomorrow, your wardrobe will be quite important, as it will be the first annual Dress as Your Favorite Book Character Day! (I know, the title is rather verbose, and I am trying to amend that.)

To help with ideas, I shall be Caddy Compson from William Faulkner's *The Sound and the Fury*. Butterscotch will dress as Miss Havisham from *Great Expectations*. If you catch him biting, fighting, or otherwise getting caught up in his little dress, please let me know. I shall be using old lace curtains that are of no value; however, I'd rather he didn't make a giant spectacle, so please alert me if he starts trying to undress himself.

Do let me know if you need assistance with ideas! This will be SUCH fun!

Fawn, Owner

From: Angela Washington
Sent: Thu, Jan 31, 2019 at 9:24 PM
To: Fawn Birchill, Staff
Re: Favorite Book Character Day!

Bella from the Twilight books.

—A

From: Sam Asimov
Sent: Thu, Jan 31, 2019 at 9:30 PM
To: Fawn Birchill, Staff
Re: Favorite Book Character Day!

Great idea. I'll be Kostya from *The Seagull*, my favorite play.

Sam

From: Fawn Birchill
Sent: Thu, Jan 31, 2019 at 9:48 PM
To: Staff
Re: Favorite Book Character Day!

Sam, Angela,

Angela, I believe Bella would be a bit of a cheat. Sorry to be harsh, but I looked this person up and not only do we not sell the Twilight series, but Bella dresses as you already dress: flannel shirts and jeans. What, may I ask, would be the difference?

Sam, I like your idea to dress as Kostya, especially since we do carry that play; however, you already dress like Kostya every day. Often you wear a ridiculous train conductor's cap, no doubt an attempt to give the impression of worldliness and antiquity. Often you wear vests over your button-down shirts and faded jeans (something Kostya definitely didn't wear), so I fail to see a great difference. Sorry to be so detailed, but I fear that Kyle and I will be the only ones actually looking any different tomorrow.

Fawn, Owner

From: Kyle Krazinsky
Sent: Thu, Jan 31, 2019 at 10:03 PM
To: Fawn Birchill, Staff
Re: Favorite Book Character Day!

Hey Fawn,

I pick Pip from *Great Expectations*. Aiden says I kind of look like Ethan Hawke anyway.

Kyle

From: Fawn Birchill
Sent: Thu, Jan 31, 2019 at 10:30 PM
To: Staff
Re: Favorite Book Character Day!

Sam, Kyle, Angela,

Kyle, Pip is fine but you must be Pip from the book, not from the movie that came out in the nineties. Do you understand that there is a difference? *Great Expectations* is supposed to have occurred in the nineteenth century.

Fawn, Owner

From: Sam Asimov
Sent: Thu, Jan 31, 2019 at 11:03 PM
To: Fawn Birchill, Staff
Re: Favorite Book Character Day!

Hey,

I think any iteration of a book you like is fair game. It's unfair to dictate strict rules this late at night.

Sam

From: Fawn Birchill
Sent: Thu, Jan 31, 2019 at 11:36 PM
To: Staff
Re: Favorite Book Character Day!

Sam, Kyle, Angela,

I fear you are all having a hard time understanding exactly what I am looking for. I would be tempted to pull the plug based on everyone's apparent confusion; however, I have already Parroted this, and therefore we must stick to our guns.

Sam, you will come in tomorrow as Huck Finn.

Kyle, you will come in tomorrow as Shane from the book *Shane*. Look it up if you don't know it.

Angela, you will come in tomorrow as young Lolita from *Lolita*. If you don't know this book, I am appalled.

Again, you will not be alone in this as not only are Butterscotch and I dressing up for this, our customers most likely will as well.

Failure to follow this dress code tomorrow may result in immediate suspension without pay. Please know that I do not mean to be harsh, and I am merely trying to drum up business and put this Parrot account to good use. If anything, blame Sam for the idea of us utilizing the Parrot in the first place. It has resulted in many beneficial ideas that some of you may find hard to stomach, but I believe in the long run it is good for the sake of the business.

Looking forward to tomorrow! ☺
Fawn, Owner

Fawn Birchill/*CuriousCatBooks*/2m
Fawn here! Today only! Dress as Your Favorite #Book Character! Come see #Huck Finn, #Shane and #Lolita! What will you be???

From: Fawn Birchill
Sent: Fri, Feb 1, 2019 at 8:08 PM
To: Staff
Subject: Thank you for dressing up

Dear Sam, Kyle, and Angela,

I know it wasn't your favorite thing to do, so I appreciate wholeheartedly that you stepped it up and dressed up today. I like to believe that without my threats of suspension, you still would have pulled together and done it; however, I shall never know for sure.

I find it charming but also slightly intrusive that Mark showed up dressed as Long John Silver and brought his cat dressed as Captain Flint, donning a parrot beak with two wings strapped to his back, the poor thing. It's not even a clever costume because apparently that's already the cat's name. Yes, it was annoying that he was the only "customer" to appear wearing a costume, but we all did a very fine job not showcasing our obvious distaste. You all did a fine job keeping a stiff upper lip as he went around talking to customers about his own store, luring them in his creepy hippie way, parading his confused and bedraggled feline as if it were nothing more than a sideshow spectacle. At least I let Butterscotch wander freely (or as freely as he can while dressed as Miss Havisham). Unfortunately Mark's pitching to my customers got so frequent that I had to ask him to kindly cease and desist. You won't believe it, but he actually told me that they were asking him about his store and that he hadn't been the one to bring it up in the first place. With all things that come out of his mouth, I have learned to take it all with a large grain of salt.

I will say that I appreciated him purchasing *The Adventures of Tom Sawyer* but couldn't help but see this as an attempt to case the place for more ideas he could steal from us. Though he is welcome, please watch him carefully. I don't trust him and find it rather suiting that he came in dressed as a pirate.

Thank you all,
Fawn, Owner

P.S. Who left the giant bag of cat food by the front counter?

From: Angela Washington
Sent: Fri, Feb 1, 2019 at 9:12 PM
To: Fawn Birchill, Staff
Re: Thank you for dressing up

He stole more than ideas. I saw like five people go over to his store after the event.

—A

From: Fawn Birchill
Sent: Fri, Feb 1, 2019 at 10:09 PM
To: Staff
Re: Thank you for dressing up

Angela,

Basically what you are saying is that this entire day was nothing but a clever way for the Grumpy Mug to gain more customers. Fantastic. Thank you for letting me know.

Fawn, Owner

From: Sam Asimov
Sent: Fri, Feb 1, 2019 at 10:15 PM
To: Fawn Birchill, Staff
Re: Thank you for dressing up

Hi Fawn,

Mark left that bag. I think Kyle told him we feed the alley cats, and he was pretty moved by that so he brought some stuff over. I don't think he wanted to make a big thing out of it, so he just left it by the front and asked that we use it.

Sam

● ●

From: Fawn Birchill
Sent: Fri, Feb 1, 2019 at 11:13 PM
To: Mark Nilsen
Subject: Cat food

Mark,

I didn't realize or notice that you had left the giant bag of cat food by the front register. What a thoughtful thing to think of all the cats we feed. It kind of makes up for all the customers you stole from me today.

I've been feeding the alley cats for about twenty years, and the price of cat food has only skyrocketed. Every little bit helps, so the kitties and I thank you much.

Best,
Fawn

From: Florence Eakins
Sent: Sat, Feb 2, 2019 at 9:18 AM
To: Fawn Birchill
Re: Sorry

Hi Fawn,

Thanks for the email. Sorry it took me a while to reply. Life has been hectic here. I really do wish we could have gotten you that microwave. Maybe next Christmas and all Christmases following, we adults should just skip gifts?

Flo

February 2, 2019

I fear that I will need to let one of my staff go.

I fear that I have made a terrible mistake with the advertisements for the Mark Twain event. I am beginning to sell tickets, but I am unable to deposit the money in my account for fear that the estate won't accept my offer. I did say the tickets were nonrefundable, but I am suffering from some unexpected bouts of guilt and regret. I need the money desperately, and what is fifteen dollars to one person? Surely with this influx of money, I may not have to fire one of my employees . . .

Jane just called me and asked that I come over

to pick something up that she dropped. When I came in, I found her struggling and reaching for it with a cane. It was that box of Valentine's chocolates, still unopened. So not only did I pick it up, but I opened it for her and she was very pleased. The chocolates looked fine even though it's hard to tell how old they are. Those drugstore chocolates are incredibly resilient—ironically, perhaps more so than most relationships.

Anyway, I helped her back into her chair and as I started to move away, she gripped me by the arm and looked deep into my eyes. She said, "You poor, poor thing."

"I'm not poor," I said. "I'm fine. I'm wonderful." I hoped she didn't detect the catch in my voice. Her eyes were so kind, but I don't appreciate being pitied, even if the person means well. Then she said the most extraordinary thing.

She looked around her small apartment and said, "I have so much. So many things I don't use anymore. If certain things were to go missing from here, I probably wouldn't even notice." She put a chocolate in her mouth and continued to gaze around the room. "It's so nice," she said, "when you have reached the point where you can let things go."

"Thank you, Jane," I said. I think I knew what she meant.

"For what?" she said, her mouth packed with chocolate.

I have decided that I will do everything I can not to let any of my staff go. It frightens me to think that I could be alone in this drafty place with no one to speak to, for if one goes, the two remaining may band together and quit. And as much as I complain about them, I must admit that I not only enjoy their company but I need it. In all my years running this store, I've never had a staff of less than four, including myself, but none of them have stayed long. And each time they leave, it hurts because I get so attached and I can't help but take it personally even though I know I shouldn't. What am I doing wrong? I honestly want to know what I'm doing wrong.

● ●

From: Fawn Birchill
Sent: Sun, Feb 3, 2019 at 10:20 PM
To: Schuylkill Photo
Subject: Thank you!

Dear Schuylkill Photo,

Thank you for the enjoyable time at your photo studio and for the warm hospitality I received therein. The photos themselves were quite acceptable for what I needed; however, I was hoping that you could have done something about hiding my double chin. I know you will say, "What double chin?" And though it may be quite hard for others to notice, it stands out to me. Perhaps you can fix it with your computer program?

I also wanted to apologize for the boa. It was not my intention to "egg on" your dog, as you said that I might have done. I hear Labs eat a lot of garbage and household objects and will not hesitate to eat an entire pink boa if given the opportunity. I imagine it will pass through his system naturally in the next two days or so. When the feathers stop appearing in the feces, you can rest assured it has passed. My cat ate a Christmas ribbon once, and it passed completely through his system as one whole strand over the course of a couple of days. Imagine what *that* looked like!

Additionally, I thank you for being such a friendly, affordable company. Money is tight these days, so I give myself few allowances to splurge. I find that it is not only healthy but necessary to treat oneself sometimes. You have allowed me, for at least an hour, to forget the things that are going on right now in my life, and for that I thank you.

I await your response regarding the double chin.

Best wishes,
Fawn

From: Schuylkill Photo
Sent: Mon, Feb 4, 2019 at 8:00 AM
To: Fawn Birchill
Re: Thank you!

Hi Fawn,

It was great having you here, and we are thankful for your patronage. Regarding the double chin, it is not something that we are able to erase; however, it is minimal and very hard to notice, so I wouldn't worry.

Also, the boa has already passed through Buster without any complications, so all is well. In fact, when the last of it came through, he appeared completely thrilled, like a jackpot winner at a slot machine, and started going for it again, but this time we were quick enough to grab the remains from his exuberant jaws.

We are glad to be of service. This is why we went into this business in the first place—to brighten days and capture moments with grace, sometimes humor, and skill. So happy that you were satisfied.

Take care,
Sarah

From: Fawn Birchill
Sent: Mon, Feb 4, 2019 at 10:11 AM
To: Angela Washington
Subject: Blog Entry

Angela,

I just came up with the most fabulous idea! Will you please write a blog entry for the store? Theme will be a day in the life of an employee (or something like that). I think it would be fantastic for the public to hear from someone other than me. Please have it to me within the next few days. Only a page will do.

Thank you,
Fawn, Owner

From: Fawn Birchill
Sent: Mon, Feb 4, 2019 at 11:00 AM
To: Staff
Subject: PIZZA LUNCH!

Dear Staff,

Due to low morale, I have ordered Domino's! It will be delivered at noon, so you don't need to leave for lunch today. I ordered a large half-plain/half-pepperoni and a large Philly cheese steak pizza. Hope that's enough food for the four of us!

This is not necessary, but if you wouldn't mind throwing me five dollars toward the pizza, it would be much appreciated.

Fawn, Owner

●●

From: Fawn Birchill
Sent: Mon, Feb 4, 2019 at 1:13 PM
To: Mark Nilsen
Re: Grumpy Mug Sign

Dear Mark,

I am surprised at how fast you remedied the issue. I believe your sign was only down for about twenty minutes, which thankfully wasn't enough time to impede any possible sales. It would have been terrible if a fire broke out or any other disaster came to pass and whoever was on the second floor was stuck, forced to crash onto the sidewalk below.

Happy to help!
Fawn, Owner, The Curious Cat Book Emporium (a *The Adventures of Tom Sawyer* specialist store)

P.S. Thank you for checking in regarding my exit sign. I am taking care of it in my own time. ☺ Many thanks again!

PSB Classifieds

Rectangular End Table ($50)

Romantic, solid, and young—what more could one want in a man? Can't find a man with these qualities? Why not settle for an end table!?

Parquet design

Strong

No dimensions (sorry, do not have tape measure)

In good shape. Used gently by an elderly woman to hold pills and Kleenex—needs a new good home!

Please see "pic"

<LOCATED IN WEST PHILADELPHIA>

From: Fawn Birchill
Sent: Tue, Feb 5, 2019 at 9:44 AM
To: Twain Estates
Subject: Last Chance

To the estate of Mark Twain:

This is your last chance to accept my offer. Had I known you would all be so uncommunicative, I would have never made the effort. Surely you are not too busy or important to do some marketing for your own books. I am disappointed and shocked at your silence.

Please reach out to me in no more than twenty-four hours upon receiving this letter. I have sold over a hundred tickets, and most guests are traveling from Wilmington and Princeton, so it would be exceptionally cruel to continue in this way.

In case you have a change of heart, I have reserved three rooms at the Best Western, so please let me know by Friday if you can't make it so I can cancel on time without penalty. I've also cleaned my apartment militaristically and rid it of all if not most of the cat hair. For a shorthair, Butterscotch loses fur like a golden retriever.

Best wishes,
Fawn, Owner, The Curious Cat Book Emporium (a *The Adventures of Tom Sawyer* specialist store)

PSB Classifieds

Seeking Actor/Actress for Lucrative Job

I am currently seeking an actor or actress with an open mind and a sense of confidentiality to participate in an improvisational, unscripted acting role. Details to follow if interested. Pay is good and negotiable. Must be or look over 25 years of age. Please email if interested.

<LOCATED IN WEST PHILADELPHIA>

PHILLY LOVE FINDER

Butterscotch,

These photographs are the most vivacious and unique I've seen on here by far. I'm intrigued! My eye is drawn, admittedly, because I'm a bit of a photographer. I mostly dabble in modeling photos, but I do some weddings on the side for money.

What are the things on the parasol? Some of them look a little phallic, so I have to ask where the heck you got something like that.

Would you like to have a drink sometime?

Capitan_Murphy

Dear Capitan_Murphy,

Thank you for your interest in my profile. I appreciate your feedback on the photography work. What kind of camera do you use? I run into so many photographers that say they would like to take more modeling photos, but I imagine it is difficult to find attractive people who are also good in front of the lens. As you can tell, I was a little shy in these, and the camera never lies! I was also distressed, as I had hoped to use my pink boa for most of them, but the dog in the studio ate it when we were all taking a break.

The parasol was a gift from my mother when I was a little girl. The figures thereon are of sea life such as seals, whales, and squid. I understand that the squid may look like something lewd, but that is not the intention of the parasol manufacturers nor my own. I do not want to give anyone the wrong impression, so I will take the parasol photos down. Thank you for your concern with this.

Incidentally, it has been some years (count ten) since I have been intimate with a man, which is fine with me. No doubt my married sister may be able to claim the same thing. Ha! However, due to this my mind rarely goes to these sensitive places where I would be so astute and perhaps lewd enough to see what a squid looks like at a certain angle.

I enjoy going to bars, though I haven't been to one in over a year. I would be interested in going to one with you, I believe. When and where?

Are you really a captain?

Fondly,
Butterscotch

••

From: Scott Farmer
Sent: Wed, Feb 6, 2019 at 9:32 AM
To: Fawn Birchill
Subject: Job Posting

Hi Fawn,

I hope this finds you well. As you will see on my résumé, I have been in the Philadelphia theater scene for many years after moving here from Toronto. I have experience in television (soap opera), Shakespearean theater, and my passion, improv, with which I have been involved these past ten years.

What is the nature of the work?

Many thanks,
Scott

From: Fawn Birchill
Sent: Wed, Feb 6, 2019 at 11:35 AM
To: Scott Farmer
Re: Job Posting

Dear Scott,

Thank you for your interest. This is an unconventional request, and so your work in Shakespeare and soap opera is rather unnecessary, however impressive. I am most interested in your work with the local improv companies, with which you have been working for ten years.

Long story short, if you were to take this job, it would be a monthlong gig wherein you would be acting as a member of the estate of Mark Twain inside a bookshop. You will simply sit behind a desk and sign copies of old Mark Twain books for twelve-hour shifts wherein you will be given two half-hour breaks. Housing is available if needed. Pay is negotiable, but for each book signed you will get a 5 percent profit. And these books are not cheap. Additionally, you will receive a flat $200 stipend for the month.

Hope this lights your fire. Please let me know if interested ASAP.

Thank you,
Fawn

P.S. Are you recognizable in the community? It would be better if you were an unknown so as not to accidentally get recognized by someone, thereby ruining the illusion.

●●

From: Fawn Birchill
Sent: Thu, Feb 7, 2019 at 7:05 AM
To: Angela Washington
Subject: Please Help

Dear Angela,

I have been reported in the PSB classifieds as a scam and have been taken down. How do I fix this?

Thank you,
Fawn, Owner

●●

From: Fawn Birchill
Sent: Thu, Feb 7, 2019 at 7:11 AM
To: Scott Farmer
Re: Job Posting

Dear Scott,

Did you report me to PSB classifieds as a scam? If so, I believe you are mistaken, as

I am not. Furthermore, I will no longer need your services, as I was able to hire an excellent New York City actor who doesn't demonize unorthodox artistic projects.

Best wishes,
Fawn

From: Keith Vandetty
Sent: Thu, Feb 7, 2019 at 9:07 AM
To: Fawn Birchill
Subject: Job Posting

Fawn,

My buddy Scott told me about this ad. I'd be interested in this, but I need to know more about it. Sounds a bit ethically and morally questionable.

Keith

From: Fawn Birchill
Sent: Thu, Feb 7, 2019 at 9:50 AM
To: Keith Vandetty
Re: Job Posting

Dear Keith,

Thank you for your interest; however, I must assure you that there is nothing questionable going on here. You may even feign ignorance and say very little as you sit at the desk, as far as I'm concerned. You need only to stamp some books, sign a false name (last name should be Clemens), and when people ask if you really are from the estate, you need only to nod politely in their direction. If it helps, think of it as simply helping out a local bookstore owner whose profits have sunk to an all-time low (at no fault of her own).

Best,
Fawn

From: Keith Vandetty
Sent: Thu, Feb 7, 2019 at 12:01 PM
To: Fawn Birchill
Re: Job Posting

Hi Fawn,

Yeah, that all sounds good to me. I got no problem doing unethical things for profit, especially since I've been out of work for a year. Think you could up the rate a little? Like, how about a 10 percent cut instead of 5 percent?

Keith

From: Fawn Birchill
Sent: Thu, Feb 7, 2019 at 1:34 PM
To: Keith Vandetty
Re: Job Posting

Dear Keith,

I assure you that this is not a scheme or a plot that would land either of us in trouble if caught. Look at it instead as a social experiment or a charitable opportunity for which you get paid.

Speaking of, I'm sorry but I cannot raise my pay. I am already taking a substantial blow just by hiring someone to deal with this. I won't tell you the exact number of people who have already bought tickets, but let's just say it's well over a hundred. I'm sure that a clever and charitable man such as yourself can make this work.

Please consider,

Fawn

●●

From: Fawn Birchill
Sent: Thu, Feb 7, 2019 at 3:13 PM
To: Angela Washington
Re: Blog Post

Angela,

As you have not taken the initiative to write the blog entry as asked, I will write it for you. I apologize in advance if you do not like it, but take it as a lesson in business. It is always better to do your own work instead of lazily passing it off to others.

Best,
Fawn, Owner

From: Fawn Birchill
Sent: Thu, Feb 7, 2019 at 3:20 PM
To: Staff
Subject: Sagging stair

Dear Staff,

The top stair is beginning to sag dangerously from its usual 90-degree angle. I fear the nails are losing their hold on the wood. Can someone please take care of this issue before a customer slips and goes barreling down the staircase?

Many thanks!

Fawn, Owner

P.S. Sam, please go out and buy more cat food for the strays at some point today. Please take it out of petty cash.

From: Tabitha Birchill
Sent: Thu, Feb 7, 2019 at 4:25 PM
To: Fawn Birchill
Subject: Tried calling. Visit soon?

Dear Fawn,

When is your event? I would very much like to come and support! And how are you doing otherwise? I have been thinking of paying a visit lately if you have a little time to spare. It would be so nice to catch up.

There is not much new around here. The neighbor's new mailbox has been stolen, and we got a new mailman. Or should I say mailperson? Also, I don't know if you remember Mr. Federman, your fifth-grade math teacher, but he passed away yesterday.

Talk soon!

Love you,
Mother

From: Fawn Birchill
Sent: Thu, Feb 7, 2019 at 5:05 PM
To: Tabitha Birchill
Re: Tried calling. Visit soon?

Dear Mother,

This is not the best of times to visit. I must admit I was a bit shocked by your offer, seeing how you are always "too busy," but the timing is just awful. Thank you for asking about my event! I believe I *finally* have a few minutes to brief you on it! There will be celebrities gracing the many rooms of my shop, along with wall-to-wall customers and high-society socializing. I think if anything you would be bored and intimidated by the intellectual crowd. This will take place tomorrow evening and will close on Feb 9. You may ask how I plan to keep up my energy? Well, of course good sleep goes without saying! But I have the help of a very handsome new boyfriend whom I met at an Afghan restaurant. He is tall and wealthy, and after this we plan to take a trip to Italy, for I've never been. Then perhaps in April we can get together? I can take the train out, and we can go to that diner you like. Or if you'd like to come here, you can stay on the pullout futon in the living room (this time I promise to remember to vacuum up the cracker crumbs). Please feel free to inform Florence of the good news both business-wise and romantically, though if you choose to leave it out, I understand, as I know she usually takes other people's good news rather poorly.

Much love,

Fawn

P.S. I rarely keep my phone on me, as you know. My new smartphone is only so that I can conveniently shoot emails off to my employees when necessary. You know as well as I how much I hate talking on the phone.

From: Fawn Birchill
Sent: Thu, Feb 7, 2019 at 6:05 PM
To: Mark Nilsen
Subject: Invitation to Mark Twain Estate Event

Dear Mark,

I would like to cordially invite you to attend our two-day Mark Twain estate event that will be taking place on February 8 and 9. I have placed an official invite in your mailbox; however, I wanted to send you this email to ensure that you were aware of it.

Best wishes,
Fawn

From: Mark Nilsen
Sent: Thu, Feb 7, 2019 at 8:14 PM
To: Fawn Birchill
Re: Invitation to Mark Twain Estate Event

Hi Fawn,

I appreciate the invite! It sounds like a lot of fun. Sadly our gala event happens to fall on February 8, and then on the ninth I made plans with my dad, so I won't be able to make it.

I thought you were seeing the ballet on the eighth?

Thank you again!

Mark

From: Fawn Birchill
Sent: Thu, Feb 7, 2019 at 10:20 PM
To: Mark Nilsen
Re: Invitation to Mark Twain Estate Event

Dear Mark,

Yes, I understand, but I thought I would extend an invitation to you since you so kindly did the same for me! How funny that they have landed on the same evening! And yes, I absolutely planned on going to the ballet that night, but my date insisted we choose Feb 8 and 9 and go to the ballet the following week, since his favorite ballerina won't be performing that night anyway. Ah, c'est la vie.

So, if your event isn't as successful or populated as you hoped, feel free to stop by for some excellent food and schmoozing with the Philadelphia elite. I'm sure you can get that *Tom Sawyer* book signed if you'd like, but just to warn you, there will naturally be a fee.

Wishing you all the best with your event,
Fawn, Owner, The Curious Cat Book Emporium (a *The Adventures of Tom Sawyer* specialist store)

February 7

Dear Fawn,
More coupons! Sometimes I swear Florence just throws them out, but the other day she told me she bought two bikes for the boys with one of the Walmart coupons I gave her. They have been wanting to learn to ride. She is such a good mother. I'm glad you two have patched things up, even if it's tenuous.

Mother

Blog Post #2
The Outlook of an Employee

My staff member Angela has volunteered to write a brief blog post on what it is like to be an employee at the Curious Cat Book Emporium. The below entry is unedited and, I'm sure much to the surprise of some of our readers, completely truthful on all accounts.

As an employee of the Curious Cat Book Emporium, I am never more satisfied than when ringing up customers and seeing the smiles on their faces as they walk out of the store with a surefire, good purchase. Even if one does not like a book, reading it was still an experience. Take, for example, a person you run into on the street. You may not like them, but they have taught you something about yourself—perhaps that you find smoking in public to be unspeakably rude and disgusting.

I feel a sense of ownership in this store. A sense of belonging. I do not feel as if I am going to work when I leave my tiny, dismal apartment in Center City but rather that I am going home. This is how every single person should feel about work, but so few do. For this I am fortunate. I thank Fawn for the continued opportunity to work in her store. Without her, I might be getting into trouble with men or smoking too much marijuana, waking one day to find myself on my way to cleaning up highways in an orange vest. This is not to say that I am prone to criminal behavior, but purpose gives me a sense of responsibility, as does ownership.

Eventually when I marry, have children, and leave this wonderful job for another, I will look back and think fondly on my experiences, on my family among the books, and of course, on Butterscotch.

●●

February 7, 2019

Tomorrow it begins. The money from the ticket sales is in my bank account, and I am currently set to be able to pay my employees for another three months without letting them go. It is a real miracle.

Keith has been calling me all day to get the right wardrobe picked out. It's all coming together quite well!

However, I am having trouble sleeping. Sometimes when I look in the mirror, I don't know who is looking back at me. I often find myself caught in the doorways of my apartment just staring at my feet, terrified to move into the next room. I am so frightened that something terrible will happen, so continuing on in my day is doing nothing but hastening it. I want to curl up into a ball and force time to stop. And though all these dark thoughts have been running through my head, things are going so well! Is this what happiness feels like? Perhaps it is, since I only feel truly alive when the bookstore is packed with people. It's as if my purpose in life has been fulfilled, and I am frightened to see it all end. I am frightened of March, frightened that after the event people will move on and forget about my store, frightened that the turnout won't be all that I had hoped. Unlike for my sister, mediocrity was never an option in my life. I always aspired to be something so much greater than the circumstances into which I was born, so it never occurred to me that I could ever be anything less. Achieving this, surpassing this, and waking up with the knowledge that I could turn a great corner in my business this month makes the hairs on the back of my neck tingle with life. Because of my ingenuity and my unorthodox business skills, it has come to this. Everything feels different: Butterscotch is softer! The sun is brighter! The colors are more vivid! This must also be what success feels like.

Sometimes I think that if my father were aware of all that I do for my business, he would turn green with envy but never admit how impressed he is. He never allowed Florence and me to make suggestions about his store or decide what to sell, although without us it would have gone under years before it did. He preferred the company of mindless servants and would rather that we simply work, keeping our heads down and our mouths closed, than be a true part of his business. We were nothing more than cogs. So to see me now, strategizing and working around challenges like I do, might just shock him right into a coma.

And then there is Florence, the prize of the family, who is praised for everything she does, right down to buying bikes for her sons. Buying things is easy. Putting in time is the difficult part—something that I know so well and for which I have not been praised. If one doesn't see the outward, constant fruits of one's labors, then it is hard to understand or believe how hard one is trying. It's funny: no matter how accomplished I may become with my bookstore, they will never be capable of caring as much as I expect them to. This is no fault of Florence's but merely the environment in which she was raised. I wish I could go on with my life without holding resentment like this, but I'm not sure how to begin. It is much harder, I suppose, to let things go. One is then forced to deal with oneself. But then again, I deal with myself every day. And once in a while it feels good to hold on to resentment. Sometimes, it's all that I have to hold on to.

Fawn Birchill/*CuriousCatBooks*/3m

Fawn here! How excited are we for the #Mark Twain #Event tomorrow!? Post your adjectives!

Fawn Birchill/*CuriousCatBooks*/2m

Fawn here! #Fabulously, #voraciously, #rapaciously, #loquaciously, #exuberantly, #buoyantly, #over-the-top, #heart-poundingly . . .

Fawn Birchill/*CuriousCatBooks*/1m

(continued) #shout-it-from-the-rooftops, #head-over-heels #excited for the #Mark Twain #Event!

From: Fawn Birchill
Sent: Fri, Feb 8, 2019 at 5:09 PM
To: Staff
Subject: Gum

Dear Staff,

Will someone please own the problem of scraping the gum off the sidewalk out front? If you squirt Goo Gone over it and then apply a paint scraper, it should come right up.

Many thanks,
Fawn, Owner

From: Kyle Krazinsky
Sent: Fri, Feb 8, 2019 at 5:16 PM
To: Fawn Birchill, Staff
Re: Gum

Hey Fawn,

Um, do you know how much old gum is out there?

Kyle

From: Fawn Birchill
Sent: Fri, Feb 8, 2019 at 5:24 PM
To: Staff
Re: Gum

Dear Kyle,

I do not want our refined guests walking over forty-year-old gum to get into my store. Additionally, Angela, can you please dust? And all of you: please ensure NO ONE uses the customer bathroom, as the floor's integrity is still questionable. For relief they may use my personal bathroom. Please direct them there if they must go. As there were no volunteers, thank you in advance, Kyle, for taking care of the gum problem.

Fawn, Owner

From: Fawn Birchill
Sent: Fri, Feb 8, 2019 at 5:30 PM
To: Keith Vandetty
Subject: URGENT: Missing your cue

Dear Keith,

I am emailing you because you are not picking up your phone. You were supposed to be here twenty minutes ago, and I already have people lined up outside begging to be let in. Are you okay? Please get here.

Fawn

From: Fawn Birchill
Sent: Fri, Feb 8, 2019 at 5:45 PM
To: Keith Vandetty
Subject: URGENT: The show must go on

Keith,

I've opened the doors and told people that you would be a little late because your limo got into a minor accident on the way over—who knew I was so good at improvisation? Many have purchased the books and are now standing about eating my pepperoni and cheese and talking about West Philadelphia as if they've been here before and are not frightened of it. Some have come from as far as Princeton. There are BMWs parked outside! Please, please for all that is good, get your tush over here! I don't know how long I can keep them here and keep them happy!

Fawn

●●

From: Fawn Birchill
Sent: Fri, Feb 8, 2019 at 6:00 PM
To: Staff
Subject: Two things <URGENT>

Dear Staff,

1. Have you seen Butterscotch?

2. Help me think of an excuse for Keith's absence that won't make these people feel cheated! I doubt he is going to show himself at this point. I see them eyeing the windows. I don't think they like being out here after dark.

Fawn, Owner

From: Angela Washington
Sent: Fri, Feb 8, 2019 at 6:08 PM
To: Fawn Birchill, Staff
Re: Two things <URGENT>

Haven't seen Butterscotch.

What if we say this guy just died on the way here in a terrible car accident?

—A

From: Fawn Birchill
Sent: Fri, Feb 8, 2019 at 6:14 PM
To: Staff
Re: Two things <URGENT>

Dear Angela,

Perhaps a heart attack would be better?

Fawn, Owner

From: Sam Asimov
Sent: Fri, Feb 8, 2019 at 6:20 PM
To: Fawn Birchill, Staff
Re: Two things <URGENT>

Hi Fawn,

A heart attack isn't tragic enough. You want people to buy stuff, right? Also, maybe the car accident wasn't so bad and he can come in tomorrow? A heart attack would lay him out for days.

Also, can we please group text instead?

Sam

From: Fawn Birchill
Sent: Fri, Feb 8, 2019 at 6:23 PM
To: Staff
Re: Two things <URGENT>

Dear Sam,

Good point. I don't know how to group text, and since you're responding so quickly to my emails, I see no reason to fix what isn't broken.

Thank you,
Fawn, Owner

P.S. No one has seen Butterscotch?

February 8, 2019
Disaster doesn't quite sum it up enough. After telling everyone that their guest couldn't make it due to minor injuries from an accident on the way over, I was forced, after much protesting by my customers, to refund the tickets. I felt like Marie Antoinette kneeling at the chopping block! I sat gallantly behind my counter with Kyle at my side and issued refunds until I thought my fingers were going to fall off. I also gave them all discounts on their already-purchased books.

To make matters even worse, instead of going home, more than half my guests went down the block to the Grumpy Mug. All that advertising and hard work was not all for naught—it was all for Mark! So in the end, I lost a great amount of money and at the same time provided him with an influx of wealthy customers—all primed to spend good money at a bookstore.

After they had left and the sound of the last BMW engine dissipated into the night, I wearily asked that my staff take five minutes and look for Butterscotch—but the search was in vain.

All I can think about is having to do this all over again tomorrow: another crowd of disappointed rich people, another multitude of discounted books and refunds. I can't help but hear my father's nefarious laughter in the distance. I know I made a mess of things, but it is too late now. It's too late. Maybe I should have asked for help, but that would have been harder than any of this. There isn't a greater sense of loneliness than when you know you're making a mistake and you still don't ask for help. And then when it's been made and everything falls apart, and you're standing there in the ruins of your decisions, you either give up or you keep going. I have learned that I am the kind of leader that keeps going. In some instances, that must be an admirable quality, right?

I am very frightened that one of my guests made off with Butterscotch out of spite. Or perhaps they let him run out the front door? He has disappeared in the past, and I have found him tucked into the bookshelves or sleeping under the bed—but I have never held an event like this. He is not used to this kind of crowd. I will have to take some pills because I just cannot sleep tonight. This Tuesday I am supposed to go on a date with one of my contacts on Philly Love Finder, but I don't know if I can with Butterscotch missing.

Money is once again a problem, but I think that goes without saying. Angela suggested getting a credit card, but after watching my father max out his credit cards, I fear that I may do the same. I have one credit card that I use to buy cat food and kitty litter, and I pay it off promptly every month. It has helped my credit, which is a positive thing, but never will I use it for anything so great as an event, the mortgage, or payroll. When I was very young, I witnessed my father dragging out my mother's hutch, which was an heirloom from her family going back a few generations. He set it on the lawn, and it was gone in about ten minutes. I believe he got $500 for it, enough to put a small dent in his credit card debt. He then broke the lock on our front door and called the police. When Mother came home, he told her burglars came in and took the hutch and some of the cash he had out on the table. Little did he know, I was watching the entire thing from upstairs. When the cops asked me where I was, I told them I was upstairs sleeping and didn't hear *anything. Father said he was outside mowing. The story didn't exactly add up, and the cops had a hard time buying that burglars would walk in on a sunny Saturday and steal an old hutch while the man of the house was home working in the backyard. However, my father has a flare for the theatrical, and he expertly turned red and embarrassed by the emasculation of having been robbed in broad daylight. If I had been more clever, I may have been able to use my knowledge as blackmail against him. I suppose I still could; however, he is harmless these days, like a crocodile that's lost its teeth, and I am not such a terrible person as to do that to my father, as awful as he is and was.*

From: Mark Nilsen
Sent: Sat, Feb 9, 2019 at 4:09 PM
To: Fawn Birchill
Subject: Thank you for the business!

Hi Fawn,

Just want to say thanks for all the customers you sent over to my store after your event. It was moving to see such an influx of people still willing to buy and donate after they had probably spent a lot at your place.

I am overwhelmed by the amount of money we made and by the number of books donated. What a great neighborhood we share.

I hope your event was as successful as mine.

Best wishes,
Mark

From: Fawn Birchill
Sent: Sat, Feb 9, 2019 at 7:54 PM
To: Mark Nilsen
Re: Thank you for the business!

Dear Mark,

Oh, the pleasure was all mine! Great events all around, for sure! I, too, am overwhelmed by the success we had over here. And now, I'm just super exhausted, ha ha!

And to think we have to do it all over again tonight! Must find coffee!!

Best wishes,
Fawn, Owner, The Curious Cat Book Emporium (a *The Adventures of Tom Sawyer* specialist store)

PSB Classifieds

Antique Wingback Chair in Good Shape ($400)

Bold, barely used, with a story to tell—take this chair home and live like royalty.

Original upholstery

Some wear on the feet

Orange with a green flower design

<LOCATED IN WEST PHILADELPHIA>

PSB Classifieds

Coffee Table for Sale! ($40)

Hey, Don Draper called. He wants his coffee table back!

From the 1950s. Only two coffee-stain rings! Classy yet modern. Live in style.

<LOCATED IN WEST PHILADELPHIA>

PSB Classifieds

VHS Tapes!! ($5 Each)

These rare tapes are going fast! All work just fine (I played all of them through to the end to make sure). Tapes include but are not limited to:

Storyteller Café—the complete set

The 700 Club (good quality!)

Rigoletto

Sister Act

Milton Berle, the Second Time Around

Fight Club

Touched by an Angel reruns (good quality!)

Richard Simmons's *Stretchin' to the Classics*, *Tonin' to the Oldies*, *Sit Tight*, and more!

. . . and much, much, MUCH more!!!

<LOCATED IN WEST PHILADELPHIA>

Advertisement

MISSING MY BELOVED CAT

Nine-year-old tan cat that sometimes answers to "Butterscotch" went missing

February 8. He is sweet, kind, and usually bears the expression of a lost little lamb (even when not lost). He is declawed, so he will not scratch you if you pick him up. He wears a white flea collar. He really likes raw tuna, so if everyone who reads this puts a plate out tonight, one of you may draw him in. Call me if so.

Thank you.

●●

Fawn Birchill/*CuriousCatBooks*/5m

Fawn here. Missing #Butterscotch, my cat. Ran off after #Mark Twain #Event. If seen please post or email me. Tan cat, declawed, friendly. Please help.

●●

THE CURIOUS CAT BOOK EMPORIUM

Blog Post #3

Butterscotch Is Missing!

Fawn was planning to write a fun and lighthearted entry for Valentine's Day but will have to postpone due to unforeseen circumstances. Instead, she will write a profile of her beloved cat, Butterscotch, to heighten the community's awareness of his recent disappearance.

Name: Butterscotch

Color: A milky blondish-orange with faint cream-colored stripes

Appearance: He has the face of a little lamb and big brown eyes. He is quite small in size. He is declawed by a previous owner and so, if wandering the streets, has NO WAY OF DEFENDING HIMSELF. No fleas or worms!

Personality: The sweetest cat to ever walk the earth—wouldn't hurt another being in a million years (except the occasional mouse)

Favorite Toy: A raggedy squirrel with catnip housed inside its belly

Favorite Show: *Downton Abbey* (He likes the dog in the opening credits, and each time it appears in a scene he stares fixedly as if reconnecting with a long-lost friend.)

Favorite Foods: Hot dogs, tuna, and candle wax

Went missing on February 8 in the Clark Park area of West Philadelphia. Please, if you are reading this, keep an eye out for him. He is no doubt malnourished, cold, and frightened.

From: Fawn Birchill
Sent: Mon, Feb 11, 2019 at 5:00 PM
To: Staff
Subject: Today

Dear Staff,

For those advance ticket holders that didn't show up at the event on the ninth but are requesting a refund, please grant them this. We are ceasing discounts on the Mark Twain books.

If anyone sees Butterscotch, tell me immediately.

Fawn, Owner

PHILLY LOVE FINDER

Dear Capitan_Murphy,

I am going to have to postpone our date tonight due to unforeseen events in my family. My dearest younger brother has gone missing, and the family is banding together with authorities to search for him. I am sorry, but my life has become wrapped up in this quest, and so I must decline until he is found. He is very adventurous and often hitchhikes and climbs bridges without any rope, so any number of things could have happened to him.

I wouldn't say he willfully ran off, as he and I are about the closest two siblings the world has seen. Needless to say, I am up night and day and in no shape to participate in small talk and niceties. Thank you for your interest and patience in this matter.

Best,
Butterscotch

••

February 16, 2019

I have lost the will to date. My Philly Love Finder profile is down until Butterscotch is found.

Phillysmallbiz.com did an article on my Mark Twain book sale. They were there incognito the very first night of the mayhem, and they have recently published a terrible review and a false representation of my store. I've picked out some choice quotes: "The shop smells like a stable, and one can hear mice in the walls, even over the owner's incessant chatter." "Most of the books are marked up, moth-eaten, and stained with god-knows-what on the pages." "The books are well organized, but the selection is limited, as one will find five copies of The Sound and the Fury *and no copies of* As I Lay Dying*." "The Mark Twain Room looks as if a tornado blew through. All of this, on top of the fact that the guest of the night failed to show, is a testament to Ms. Birchill's disorganization and overall lack of planning.*

Thankfully, the Grumpy Mug Bookstop was holding its event next door, offering an unwitting haven for the disappointed customers. . . ."

Need I go on? If this reviewer bothered to run a store of her own for five minutes, she'd see it's no walk in the park and would think twice about publishing this tactless slop. Needless to say, since then customer numbers have further decreased.

I must engage in some damage control. I did not want to go to war with the Grumpy Mug, but I fear that I have been given no choice in the matter. For the past day and a half I haven't left my bed, but I can certainly strategize from here. I am distracted, however, by the many negative reviews on PSB, and I can't keep up in replying to them. I have a collection of saltine cracker remnants in the folds of the sheets, and last night I kept rolling on their sharp little edges. I keep finding bits of cracker in my hair and in the wrinkles of my nightclothes. Sometimes I smell my breath in disbelief of how bad it's gotten in a little over twenty-four hours. It's nice to still be able to surprise myself these days. Besides saltines, I have been living off sliced American cheese and dry Frosted Flakes. I don't want to drink very much because that means going to the bathroom and looking in the mirror. Butterscotch going missing only exacerbates the situation. I haven't cried. I think the state I am in is beyond tears. What I feel is a deep hurt that goes down into the bones. It is despair and ennui. It is as if a great hot wave has come down over me, dragging me out to sea. But I will not be dragged into obscurity, marooned, or otherwise vanquished by that bearded nobody. If he wants to steal my customers, he won't get them without some serious repercussions. Clearly, it is a war that he is asking for, and I am more than willing to give it to him.

●●

From: Mark Nilsen
Sent: Mon, Feb 18, 2019 at 3:04 PM
To: Fawn Birchill
Subject: Poster outside my store

Hi Fawn,

Can you please remove the poster you have stapled to the telephone pole on my property? It's very distracting and a bit of an eyesore.

Thank you,
Mark

From: Fawn Birchill
Sent: Mon, Feb 18, 2019 at 3:30 PM
To: Mark Nilsen
Re: Poster outside my store

Dear Mark,

I wasn't aware that the telephone pole directly in front of your store is your property and not the property of the city of Philadelphia. Therefore, I apologize for putting my poster there. Since that pole is surely the property of the Grimy Mug, then can you please climb up there and take care of the poor connection that has always afflicted my landline? I'm so glad to have come in contact with a real person that can take ownership of this issue so that I no longer have to wrestle with the soulless telephone company to get things done.

Please provide proof that the pole is in fact your property, and I will swiftly take the poster down. Otherwise, it shall remain.

Best wishes,
Fawn, Owner, The Curious Cat Book Emporium

From: Mark Nilsen
Sent: Mon, Feb 18, 2019 at 4:03 PM
To: Fawn Birchill
Re: Poster outside my store

Hi Fawn,

Not only is it dangerous to staple anything

to utility poles, but it is illegal. Please take down the ad.

Best,
Mark

From: Fawn Birchill
Sent: Mon, Feb 18, 2019 at 4:50 PM
To: Mark Nilsen
Re: Poster outside my store

Dear Mark,

I fail to see how it is illegal to post anything on telephone poles. And your warning that it is dangerous is preposterous. I am nowhere near the wire itself. I will look this up online, as I think you are starting to make things up out of fear that I may entice people to come to my store over yours. How sad.

Best,
Fawn, Owner, The Curious Cat Book Emporium

P.S. Sorry I mistyped your store as the Grimy Mug. It's an easy mistake to make, as the two words are so similar.

From: Fawn Birchill
Sent: Mon, Feb 18, 2019, 5:03 PM
To: Staff
Subject: Poster

Dear Sam,

Please walk over and remove the poster from the telephone pole. No need to try to save it; just rip it off and come back. Apparently I can get a citation from the city for posting an advertisement on a telephone pole. Who knew?

Many thanks,
Fawn, Owner

••

PSB Classifieds

Aloe Plants for Sale ($10–$40)

Various plants, mostly aloe, for sale. Make your home a jungle paradise! Suffering from a cut or burn? Just break off a hunk of the aloe plant and slather it on the wound! Over fifty to choose from!!

Call if interested.

<LOCATED IN WEST PHILADELPHIA>

PSB Classifieds

Oriental Runner for Sale ($95)

Introduce some class to your apartment with this oriental runner. Possibly antique. Small stain of what appears to be chocolate on the edge, but no doubt easily cleanable.

Serious inquiries only.

<LOCATED IN WEST PHILADELPHIA>

February 22, 2019

For the first time in my career, I have had to dip into my savings account to pay my employees. For some time now, I have been using it to pay the bills, but paying employees with a credit card is like paying in pounds of flesh—there is only so much one can give. I don't know how I will keep it up. I don't want to fire any of them. Angela is kind, Kyle is indispensable because he'll do almost anything, and Sam is . . . well, Sam has some positive qualities, I suppose. At least he's not terrible to look at.

The stairs to the second floor are in worsening shape. Securing that sagging step on the way up to the romance and children's sections seemed to do nothing. Perhaps it was due to the many guests from the Mark Twain event. In any case,

I decided to try and fix it myself last night with a sledgehammer and crowbar and some nails. It took some time getting the old step to come up but eventually and with enough pounding and wrenching it released—and so quickly that I nearly tumbled down the stairs! I replaced it with a new plank of wood; however, the wood I had bought was too short so I did my best to center it. As long as people don't walk up the sides of the step, no one should fall into the little well underneath. It was a real workout when it was all said and done—three hours later! The wine helped.

I'm beginning to wonder more and more if one of those rich snobs from Princeton stole Butterscotch. I can almost picture him batting the windows of their BMW SUV with his impotent little paws, begging to be back with his mother. I can see them driving with that self-righteous smug look on their face—so sure they are getting justice. The thought breaks my heart, but it's much better than the thought of him being out in the street fighting off cats and dogs with no claws—with only his wits and will to survive. In this way, he and I must be in very similar situations. I hope we both come out of it together intact.

● ●

From: Fawn Birchill
Sent: Mon, Feb 25, 2019 at 9:02 AM
To: Staff
Subject: Reconnoitering

Kyle,

Please do me a favor and go to the Grumpy Mug and look for Butterscotch. I had an epiphany in the middle of the night that he might have been stolen by Mark or one of his minions and is currently being held in captivity. Please try to be very inconspicuous. Buy some coffee, peruse the shelves, ask questions about what books they have, and keep an eye out for Butterscotch. Keep an ear open too! I would go, but I have sworn to never set foot in that awful place.

Fawn, Owner

From: Fawn Windsor
Sent: Fri, Mar 15, 2019 at 7:18 PM
To: Gregory Harris
Subject: Springtime Greetings!

Dear Gregory,

Ah, the beginnings of spring! The snow has melted, and the horses are shaking off their wintry dispositions. The birds in the barns are cooing, coaxing the burgeoning sun to its grandeur.

The weather is fine, but the situation at the estate has become rather questionable. My younger brother, Gordon, has been missing for over a month! Do not take the exclamation point the wrong way—it is not my intention to cheapen the news with hyperbole. I am merely trying to translate my shock. Gordon was never much of an adventurer. He spent most of his time in one place: Russia. He studied Turgenev with a Fulbright scholarship and when that ended, he went back each year, having fallen in love with the drinking of vodka and with the various Russian men and women (but mostly women, if you know what I mean). Am I surprised he is missing? Yes, I am—but I would not be surprised if he showed up at my door saying that he squandered all the money our father had given him to pursue his studies in Moscow. I hope he is all right.

Truth be told, the countryside of England in the springtime can be a bit lonely. I wonder if it is all the melting that gives me this strange sinking feeling that my life is slipping away from me. I am getting older—it is just the reality of it, as I'm sure you understand. But being surrounded by servants and stable workers gives me a strange sense that I am useless—merely a figurehead of sorts with nothing worthwhile to do. I'm considering letting some of my servants go permanently. It isn't money so much as it's that I feel like I have grown completely out of touch with my own surroundings. Perhaps fluffing some pillows and dusting the chandeliers would help get me back on track, but I'm not sure.

For the first time in my life, I look around this grand place and wonder if this is the very best thing for me.

Much love,
Fawn Windsor

From: Gregory Harris
Sent: Sat, Mar 16, 2019 at 8:13 AM
To: Fawn Windsor
Re: Springtime Greetings!

Hi there, my dear,

I'm so sorry to hear about your brother. I hope they find him soon. I'll keep my fingers crossed that he's simply at the bottom of a bottle somewhere in a swanky out-of-the-way Russian hotel, cozying up with lovely women, good books, and cigarettes.

I know what you mean, as I am also throwing into question everything I've built these many years. This happens to me, though, around this time of year. I get itchy for change. I begin to ask myself if flipping buildings is really the right path to have taken in life. But is there a right path? Because if so, such a notion assumes that there is something predestined about life, that there is something pulling the strings for us, and despite the desperate pulling and corralling, we dumb humans go the other way. It could be true, since my whole life I've felt as if I always zigged when I should have zagged. Not that I'm unhappy. But I think it's healthy to question, as much as possible, whether or not you are content.

I believe, wholly, that we are allowed to change our paths if we want to, and we do not have to feel guilty about it. But putting that into practice is hard. All I'm saying, my dear, is that if you are tired of running your father's estate and the status quo no longer makes you happy, you have every right to walk down a different path. I certainly wouldn't blame you. So many people don't have that ability because of money, family obligations, or illness. Some people are entirely trapped where they are in life, but inversely you seem to be free. Unmoor yourself, my dear, if you wish. Do it for those who can't, and ask yourself: What *does* make you happy?

Nothing new for me. Spring tends to make me a bit sad until I start to see the first daffodils pushing up in the park.

Much love,
Gregory

●●

From: Fawn Birchill
Sent: Sat, Mar 16, 2019 at 9:30 PM
To: Kyle Krazinsky
Subject: Job Performance Meeting

Kyle,

Please come in a bit earlier tomorrow (say 7:30?) so that we can sit down together and discuss your future with the company.

Many thanks,
Fawn, Owner

●●

From: Fawn Birchill
Sent: Sat, Mar 16, 2019 at 9:33 PM
To: Sam Asimov
Subject: Job Performance Meeting

Sam,

Please come in a bit earlier tomorrow (say 7:45?) so that we can sit down together and discuss your future with the company.

Many thanks,
Fawn, Owner

●●

From: Fawn Birchill
Sent: Mon, Mar 18, 2019 at 8:19 AM
To: Angela Washington
Subject: Coffee

Dear Angela,

Just because they have coffee, that doesn't justify your patronage. This is what I'm talking about. You do understand that we have coffee here? And I would even let you drink it for free if it meant you wouldn't go support the enemy. And the only reason Kyle was there was because I asked him to go search for Butterscotch. Stealing cats is a pastime I wouldn't put past Mark and his band of hooligans.

By supporting them, Angela, you are stealing from your own paycheck. The stronger they get, the weaker we become. Don't you see that? I would hate to see it get worse around here and be forced to let you go just as I did the others.

Best,
Fawn, Owner

••

Fawn Birchill/*CuriousCatBooks*/8h
Fawn here! What is your favorite #book!? #Post it to us to win a #discount! Just come in and let us know you participated!

••

From: Florence Eakins
Sent: Mon, Mar 18, 2019 at 3:23 PM
To: Fawn Birchill
Subject: The Pirates of Penzanse

Hi Fawn,

I hope you are well! I just wanted to fill you in on what's happening in our neck of the woods. Little Joe got the main part in *The Pirates of Penzanse*. He is absolutely thrilled about it, and I'm so proud of him. It would be great to see you there for a performance if you have the time. I know you're very busy.

In other news, I got that promotion at work—finally! It will mean more hours, and I'll be managing a small group of people, but honestly I've wanted more responsibility for years so this has been way overdue. It's crazy to think that I am now director of marketing. Doesn't it sound so authoritative??

How is your store doing? I hope that other store down the street isn't giving you too much trouble. Let's stay in touch more!

Talk to you soon,
Flo

From: Fawn Birchill
Sent: Mon, Mar 18, 2019 at 10:20 PM
To: Florence Eakins
Re: The Pirates of Penzanse

Florence,

I am glad to hear that Little Joe got the part, though I am not at all surprised. He has always had a flare for the theatrical, just like his father—but also just like me! It runs on both sides of the family, I believe! Let me know the dates, and I will see if I can make it. I am also happy to hear about your promotion. That repetitive office work can't be easy or at all stimulating, so I have great respect for it. I imagine that day after day it really starts to wear you down, and you begin to see the world as a very repetitive and gray place indeed. But you somehow rise above with your vivacious personality! Sometimes I think about what we wanted to do as children and how our lives are now, and I imagine what I would pay the devil to take me back to my childhood so that I don't make the same mistakes.

I am so happy to hear of the good family news. In my news, Butterscotch has been missing for well over a month. I have posters everywhere but haven't heard a peep from anyone. I do not sleep anymore and when I do, I need to take Ambien. Don't be alarmed; it's not something I've gone to the doctor over. My neighbor has a plethora of pills that she lets me take for emergencies, so it's nothing serious. I just have to make sure I am in bed before taking the Ambien—a fact I learned the hard way when I woke up one afternoon facedown on the kitchen floor. I am missing a part of myself with Butterscotch gone. I feel like half a person all the time, and this despair makes it impossible to sleep. I don't mean to burden you with this. Lately circumstances have been challenging and I've found that sometimes, indeed most of the time, it's best not to shut down, to turn away, to hide. So I'm compelled to tell you the truth. I'm sorry if it's uncomfortable.

The store is doing well. I let two of my staff members go because it is a slow time of the year, but no doubt they will return when things pick up. The new bookstore (thank you for asking) has made very little impact on the business (which I'm not surprised to find). I am not threatened by them and even encourage my staff to browse the new store's aisles on their lunch break.

Miss you much!

Fawn

P.S. *Penzance* is spelled as such. ☺

From: Florence Eakins
Sent: Mon, Mar 18, 2019 at 11:40 PM
To: Fawn Birchill
Re: The Pirates of Penzanse

Hi Fawn,

Actually, my job is extremely stimulating. Otherwise I wouldn't be doing it. Not all of us want to be business owners. I could really use your support right now without the snide, thinly veiled blows to my "office worker" status. Joseph is not as thrilled about my promotion as I hoped he would be, and it's weighing on me. I kind of expected him to at least say that he was proud of me, but I came home from a very happy day at the office only to be greeted by him complaining about every little thing. So, I'm a bit sensitive tonight. I could use a kind word, thank you very much.

Flo

P.S. I'm so sorry about Butterscotch. He is a lovely kitty, and I hope you find him soon.

From: Fawn Birchill
Sent: Tue, Mar 19, 2019 at 1:12 AM
To: Florence Eakins
Re: The Pirates of Penzanse

Dear Florence,

I am so very sorry for my transgression. Plase forgive me. I am trly excited to for you and your win at the office. I know you are a hard worker and Joseph should see that and appreciate it about you.

Have a good night,
Fawn

March 19, 2019

I think it's important to mark the date on which I shared an honest exchange with my sister (even if I was a little tipsy for it). I can truly say, now in the sober light of morning, that it was freeing. It doesn't make any logical sense as to why it would be, but I suppose life isn't always logical. In fact it's quite messy, and sometimes things don't fit the way one would assume they should.

My sister, though somewhat intolerable in the way she raises her boys and the way she interacts with the world around her, is not a bad person. She doesn't deserve to be alienated by anyone but especially not by me. We have been through the war together, and I am finding it hard to suss out why I have pushed her away all these years. I suppose it could be because she reminds me of my past. Sometimes when I look at myself in the mirror, I see traces of my father—in the shape of my eyes and the curve of my chin. I hate mirrors because of this. Perhaps these two things are related.

••

From: Fawn Birchill
Sent: Tue, Mar 19, 2019 at 8:17 AM
To: Angela Washington
Subject: Windowpane

Angela,

When you get here, please find some cardboard in the back, cut it to size, and duct tape it to the broken window. Some smart aleck decided to throw a softball at our store.

Fawn, Owner

From: Gregory Harris
Sent: Wed, Mar 20, 2019 at 4:32 PM
To: Fawn Windsor
Subject: Hello

Dear Fawn,

I hope I didn't overstep the other day. Since you haven't written back, I'm worried I may have upset you. I didn't mean to push my opinion on what you should do in such a forthright manner. To be honest, I am going through a bit of an identity crisis these days, so I was taking a lot of my angst out on my unsuspecting friend across the pond. Forgive me.

Regards,
Gregory

From: Fawn Windsor
Sent: Wed, Mar 20, 2019 at 4:59 PM
To: Gregory Harris
Re: Hello

Dear Gregory,

Please don't think my lack of response was due to anger! I wouldn't be able to live with myself if I thought we weren't friends. Life got a little hectic (Gordon is still missing), so I've been scattered. Your words and opinions are always welcome. Don't feel as if you ever have to censor yourself or your advice toward me.

I hope you are doing well. You may always, always share your angst with me.

Much love,
Fawn

● ●

March 23, 2019

It has been three days since I found Butterscotch, and it's still difficult for me to remain calm enough to sit down and write. I have spent the last two days feverishly cleaning and doing calisthenics, only to be interrupted briefly by intermittent sobbing episodes. I should have known not to allow Jane to keep open boxes of rat poison all over her apartment. I should have seen it as a hazard and discarded them.

It unfolded like this: I went in the other day to see if Jane needed help with anything or if anything needed to be tidied up. She asked for a book in her hallway on the shelf, White Fang. *Why this sweet old woman wants to read a book about animals tearing into each other all day is beyond me, but I suppose it shows what I know. So I went to the bookshelf and immediately smelled something strange. I don't know how I didn't notice it earlier. Perhaps I was always in and out so fast that I couldn't register the odor. I stood before the bookshelf for some time without looking at it, working up the courage to crouch and take a closer look—my thoughts already turning to the worst of possibilities. The smell was nearly unbearable by the time I knelt down to the rows of books to find Butterscotch huddled atop them, six weeks dead.*

Spring is one of my favorite times of the year. I don't know if I have it in me to walk to the art museum, which is what I usually do in the spring, but I think I will open the windows today. It's becoming a bit stale in my apartment, and since I haven't showered, it's hard to tell if it is me who needs airing out or if it is my apartment.

I do not wish to write about the emptiness at the loss of a loved one. I do not think that whoever is still reading this wants to be told about feelings and pain when they very well may understand them well enough. But if you can imagine the worst moment of your life thus far and how it cripples your knees and turns your stomach inside out—it would be close enough to the truth. We all mourn in our own way. Ever since I was a little girl, my mourning rituals have been energetically cathartic. I would clean my bedroom, run laps around the house, and punch the trees until I wore myself out and fell into a stupor of emotional denouement, unable to leave my bed for days. I have memories of my father literally pulling me out of bed by the ankles, shoving shoes on my feet and carrying me to his shop while my sister looked on smugly, my knuckles still covered in dried blood from the birch bark. I used to be quite combative, but that all changed with puberty when I became quite the demure Scarlett O'Hara. I'm not sure exactly when this change took place, but instead of punching things when someone or something died, I simply cleaned and then, my head swimming in chemicals, fell onto my bed and sobbed into my pillow. Even at sixteen, however, my father was pulling me by the ankles. That did not ever change.

Every day I appear to be aging—I can actually see the changes in the reflections in the windows at night (I will not look in the mirror). Last night I went up to the dark window and pulled the skin of my face back and up until I thought I resembled Keira Knightley—especially from the side. Then I noticed someone looking at me across the way, and I pulled down the blinds. There is not a shred of privacy in this city anymore.

I plan to adopt a rescue cat in the coming days, and it has to be very clean in here. It has to be right, and there must not be any hazards. I have a lot of work to do.

From: Fawn Birchill
Sent: Sun, Mar 24, 2019 at 9:50 PM
To: Angela Washington
Subject: New lodger

Dear Angela,

You may notice a new presence wandering the store with regularity. Please do not be alarmed, as she is meant to be here. I met her outside Missy's Co-op yesterday when purchasing sundries. You may be wondering why in the world I would still patronize such a cold place that turned its back on me with impunity; however, I am doing my best these days to forgive when forgiveness is due. Also, they have the best steel cut oats this side of the Schuylkill River and quite frankly, I will not deny myself such pleasures.

I digress. This new lodger, who says her name is Rainbow, was seated outside performing card tricks. With a lovely little rabbit at her side that goes by the name of Jellybean, she was able to divine my card eight out of ten times—an impressive percentage! She also pulled dollar bills from behind my ear! As I am gregarious to a fault, we got to talking, and I soon learned that she had been kicked out by her landlord for not paying the rent on time and had nowhere to stay. I then asked her, "Well, if you can pull dollar bills from my ear, why can't you materialize rent?" But I think the joke was lost on her. Anyway, perhaps the recent tragedy of Butterscotch got the better of me, but I offered that she could stay in my spare room with her sweet little rabbit for the very reasonable price of fifty dollars a month—until she can get back on her feet. She tells me she is saving up to go to Vegas where she will "shock and inspire millions with her illusions." I would not classify what I've seen so far as shocking or inspiring; however, this is perhaps simply an example of my ignorance when it comes to magic.

She will stay with me in my apartment and will keep her things in the kitchen/break room area downstairs, as I simply don't have room to store her groceries in my small but romantic Victorian kitchen. I gave her permission to do her card tricks outside the store, so if you see her performing please don't ask her to leave as we've done a few times before with others. Also, because she is an artist, she asks that when she is doing her card tricks or otherwise practicing around the store, please let her concentrate and give her the space she needs to perfect her skills for

Vegas. Also, you must call her Rainbow and not shorten it to Rain, which she hates.

I am terribly excited to be living in such proximity to a true artist! I know you will give her a warm Curious Cat welcome!

See you tomorrow!

Many thanks,
Fawn, Owner

From: Angela Washington
Sent: Sun, March 24, 2019 at 10:45 PM
To: Fawn Birchill
Re: New Lodger

Wow, okay. Cool.

—A

●●

March 25, 2019

My new lodger is a true gem! Angela, of course, is baffled by her presence, and I often catch her staring at Rainbow in disbelief as she practices her magic on the staircase or by the front door, but I think she'll come around in time.

I believe it was in the fifteenth century when aristocrats and various wealthy patrons of the arts would take artists under their wing and support them financially so that they would be able to pursue their dreams and hone their craft. I daresay that today, as I watched Rainbow light a cigar and stick it up her nose, I found that our arrangement is not so dissimilar. She is the Botticelli to my Medici, but instead of painting the Madonna, my artist is attempting a straitjacket escape. If both bring joy, I fail to see a great difference.

●●

From: Fawn Birchill
Sent: Tue, Mar 26, 2019 at 9:18 AM
To: Hank Turo
Subject: Cats for sale

Dear Hank,

I came across your ad in the classifieds regarding the six cats, and since your price is very reasonable, I would like to ask you a few questions:

- Are they declawed?
- How are they with rabbits?
- Are they aloof or friendly?
- Are they litter-box trained?
- Are they wormed, spayed/neutered, tick-free, flea-free, up to date with shots?
- Have they scratched, hissed, bitten?

It is a hobby of mine to feed the strays outside my building, and though I would love to take one of them in, it is far too costly for me to pay for what will certainly be a hefty vet bill getting one neutered/spayed and up to date with shots. Money is tight these days, so please understand that I am only asking for a cat that has already been made suitable for domestic life.

I eagerly await your response.

Many thanks,
Fawn, Owner, The Curious Cat Book Emporium

●●

From: Angela Washington
Sent: Wed, Mar 27, 2019 at 11:01 AM
To: Fawn Birchill
Subject: Rainbow

Rainbow is hanging upside down on the second-floor banister. I don't know what to do.

—A

From: Fawn Birchill
Sent: Wed, Mar 27, 2019 at 11:13 AM
To: Angela Washington
Re: Rainbow

Dear Angela,

Please allow Rainbow to express herself however she pleases. She is a professional and no doubt knows exactly what she is doing. We do not ask electricians to cease operations just because they are removing outlets. We do not interrogate plumbers when they cut through pipes. If Rainbow doesn't feel safe to stretch her limitations in her own (temporary) home, she will never achieve her goal of shocking and inspiring.

Therefore, my advice would be to simply sit back and enjoy the show!

Many thanks,
Fawn, Owner

March 30, 2019

Rainbow and I visited Jane last night with a bottle of red wine. I feel that these days, after the loss of Butterscotch, this is the best way for me to cope: with good company and decent wine. Rainbow performed magic tricks for Jane, which positively thrilled her to the point of nearly spilling her drink all over herself. More than that, Jane loved Jellybean, who cuddled up on her lap as we all turned our attention to Star Trek *reruns, per Rainbow's request. Jane did not seem to mind the show, which is good because it is my default to allow the artist whatever she needs, as every little thing could lead to a great artistic breakthrough or further inspiration for a new act. Often when I am around Rainbow, I feel as if I am watching history in the making.*

All that said, it would be nice to hear something from my family. They don't know about Butterscotch because I haven't told them, which I can't fault them for. Still, it would be appreciated if someone reached out to check on things. Just because they are not hearing from me does not mean I am okay.

●●

From: Angela Washington
Sent: Sat, Apr 6, 2019 at 9:34 AM
To: Fawn Birchill
Subject: Jellybean

So Rainbow bounced to go do some tricks in Center City and left me with Jellybean. It is now pooping on the floor and chewing on cables. Not sure what to do here.

—A

From: Fawn Birchill
Sent: Sat, Apr 6, 2019 at 10:24 AM
To: Angela Washington
Re: Jellybean

Angela,

I'm sorry that I only just saw this. I hope Jellybean is okay. Also, Jellybean is a *she,* a pronoun that Rainbow insists upon, as she says, "Animals have souls and are not 'its.' "

I am currently dealing with a refrigerator leak but I will be down shortly to retrieve her and put her in the cage. I am not sure why Rainbow didn't do that initially.

Many thanks,
Fawn, Owner

From: Angela Washington
Sent: Sat, Apr 6, 2019 at 10:29 AM
To: Fawn Birchill
Re: Jellybean

I don't know why she didn't think of it either. It could have had something to do with Rainbow being "struck by sudden inspiration" to run off to Center City and do some magic. She actually used the words, "The muse is attacking me." She barely had time to put her shoes on before running out the door, so I guess Jellybean was far from her mind.

Thanks.

—A

From: Fawn Birchill
Sent: Mon, Apr 8, 2019 at 12:13 PM
To: Angela Washington
Subject: Internet games

Dear Angela,

I don't mind that you check email or the news once in a while, but please don't sit at the front register and play on the internet all day. From the middle of the stairs, I can see your screen. It wasn't my intention to come down and spy on you; I merely wanted to see the kind of customer volume we have today, and my eyes were drawn to the glowing screen. A good way to spend your time might be to clean up the Mark Twain Room, as according to a local "journalist," it looks like a tornado blew through.

Many thanks,
Fawn, Owner

From: Hank Turo
Sent: Mon, Apr 8, 2019 at 2:42 PM
To: Fawn Birchill
Re: Cats for sale

Answers below.

- Are they declawed? *No*
- How are they with rabbits? *No clue*
- Are they aloof or friendly? *All are friendly*
- Are they litter-box trained? *Yes*
- Are they wormed, spayed/neutered, tick-free, flea-free? *Yes*
- Have they scratched, hissed, bitten? *Yes, they are cats*

Hank

From: Fawn Birchill
Sent: Mon, Apr 8, 2019 at 3:30 PM
To: Hank Turo
Re: Cats for sale

Hank,

Thank you for answering all my questions. I would only be interested in one cat. How did you come about acquiring six adult cats? Did a grandmother recently die, or are you a Good Samaritan who collects strays off the street? You could easily put them in shelters but instead you sell them, so I want to be sure that this is an admirable, philanthropic venture and that you are not, for example, breaking into people's homes and robbing them of their cats to turn a profit. I wouldn't want to support such a scheme.

Where are you located so that I can perhaps visit them? That is, after you answer me on how you acquired these animals.

Best wishes,
Fawn, Owner, The Curious Cat Book Emporium

From: Hank Turo
Sent: Tue, Apr 9, 2019 at 9:33 AM
To: Fawn Birchill
Re: Cats for sale

I did not steal these cats. Three are from my sister who recently divorced her husband and had to move to a smaller place. Two have been taken in from the street and cared for and the last one I've had for years, but he won't stop humping the other cats. Mainly, I'm just looking to get rid of the five so the humper doesn't have anyone to violate, but you can take him if you want.

I don't like being accused of crimes I didn't commit.

I live in South Philly.

Let me know if you're still interested.

Hank

From: Fawn Birchill
Sent: Tue, Apr 9, 2019 at 12:26 PM
To: Hank Turo
Re: Cats for sale

Hank,

In no way was it my goal to offend. I am a sensitive person when it comes to animals and the cruelty and moneygrubbing that often befalls them. As they cannot speak for themselves, it is so much more important that we stand up for them. Hence my accusation was well intentioned.

Now, on to the matter of the cats. I am looking for a cat that can help me run my popular bookstore. Since you are down in South Philadelphia, I am unsure if you have ventured across the river for reading material, as there are some good bookstores down there, unfriendly though they may be. But perhaps only to me? A year ago I contacted a store in your area to team up, but they outright refused to have any business with me, stating that they have heard of my store and think that I "make other used bookstores look bad." Ridiculous! Aside from the rather shocking words (I realize now they were only jealous), I am often mystified by this standoffish behavior.

But I digress, and for that I apologize. I have been rather glum lately, so I tend to do the lonely thing and go on and on about anything my heart desires. It is even more convenient for me while writing an email, as you cannot walk away. Ha ha! I suppose you could stop reading, and for that reason I will get back on track!

Case in point, I nearly spilled my wine glass all over my keyboard! Time to focus!

Since you came about these cats by virtuous means, I would love to stop by—perhaps tomorrow—and meet them. I only need a cat who is friendly enough, as I plan not to get too attached. I will not go into the sadness of the passing of my last cat, but I will tell you that when I love something, I love it with all my being. So much harder is it then when it's taken from me.

Well, that is all for now. Let us set up a kitty date?

Many thanks,
Fawn, Owner, The Curious Cat Book Emporium

From: Florence Eakins
Sent: Tue, Apr 9, 2019 at 3:33 PM
To: Fawn Birchill
Subject: Pirates

Okay! So *Pirates* tickets are ten bucks each. There is only one comp ticket, and we've decided to give it to Mom.

Hope to see you there!

Flo

From: Fawn Birchill
Sent: Tue, Apr 9, 2019 at 7:18 PM
To: Florence Eakins
Re: Pirates

Dear Florence,

That's what they want to charge people for a middle school show? Who's in the play with them, Pavarotti? If Mother is taking the comp ticket, that's fine. I know she is on a very fixed income.

I am very much looking forward to seeing it!

Regards,
Fawn

From: Hank Turo
Sent: Tue, Apr 9, 2019 at 8:42 PM
To: Fawn Birchill
Re: Cats for sale

Sure, let's meet tomorrow at noon in Palumbo Park instead. My wife and I will bring them all in crates, and you can check them out. I don't like to let strangers into my house.

Hank

From: Fawn Birchill
Sent: Tue, Apr 9, 2019 at 9:18 PM
To: Hank Turo
Re: Cats for sale

Hank,

I understand. Since my home is attached to my business, I have no choice but to let Philadelphians stomp around underneath my sacred apartment. It is often an odd feeling and spurs many strange dreams. Often I wake in the middle of the night to find that I am sitting up in bed, handing imaginary people their change and bidding them good day. My hands do this dance around my imaginary cash register for hours before I realize, through a sleepy fog, that I have been up all night conducting business in bed with no one there at all!

I digress again! I apologize. Since my cat died, I have been in quite a state; however, I have recently taken in a new lodger who has been a much-needed ray of sunshine. Appropriately, her name is Rainbow. Go figure!

Tomorrow at Palumbo Park sounds splendid! I will be wearing a sun hat with a red ribbon. How many cats will you be bringing?

Many thanks,
Fawn

From: Angela Washington
Sent: Wed, Apr 10, 2019 at 1:23 PM
To: Fawn Birchill
Subject: Rainbow

Rainbow is on the roof doing headstands because she told me it was "headstand Wednesday." I thought you should know because people walking by are concerned. Also, I don't know how much this has to do with magic tricks, so I think asking her to stop would be okay and not get in the way of her "artistry."

—A

From: Fawn Birchill
Sent: Wed, Apr 10, 2019 at 1:45 PM
To: Angela Washington
Re: Rainbow

Angela,

Thank you for letting me know. I will ask her to come down unless she can justify what this has to do with magic. Thank you for being concerned for her safety.

Fawn, Owner

From: Angela Washington
Sent: Wed, Apr 10, 2019 at 2:02 PM
To: Fawn Birchill
Re: Rainbow

More than anything, I'm concerned that her falling would be a huge liability. Not sure that's something you want to risk.

—A

●●

From: Fawn Birchill
Sent: Sat, Apr 13, 2019 at 1:09 AM
To: Hank Turo
Re: Cats for sale

Hank!

I have decided! After MUCH internal debating, I choose the overweight gray one. He is sluggish and dull but has lovely, kind eyes. Would you be able to deliver him?

Fawn

From: Fawn Birchill
Sent: Sat, Apr 13, 2019 at 2:20 AM
To: Hank Turo
Re: Cats for sale

Hank,

It was so lovey meeting you and your wife the other day. No doubt she has won the the jackpot as not only are you a young self-reliant urban farmer, but an attractive one at that! Also I get the impression that you are a democrat and an athest by the Darwin t-shirt you were wearing when we met. You are a gem and I cannot help but think how lucky your wife is . . . not that she is not beautiful! She is quite somewhat pretty indeed, but I got the feeling that she was a little protective of you and I dare admit say, I would behave the same if you were my husband, as you are a real steal. She did come across as mildly hyperaware of me, aloof and slightly threatend. I do hope I didn't frighten her, as I pose no threat whatsoever! Sometimes my cherry nature is mistaken for flirtation, and so I do hope hope that impression was not given.

Did I say I waned the gray cat? If I didn't and sipped all that accidentally then please yes, I will take the gray cat.

Many thanks,
Fawn

From: Fawn Birchill
Sent: Sat, Apr 13, 2019 at 10:30 AM
To: Hank Turo
Subject: Apologies

Hank,

I couldn't remember if I wrote to tell you that I had decided on the cat, so I checked to see if I sent any emails last night to find, to my horror, that I in fact did tell you and rather drunkenly to boot. I apologize profusely for making you a victim of my tipsy emails. Of course, it could be worse. Luckily I don't get into cars and hit people, but I do believe drunk emailing is one of those unspoken awful truths that we tend to forget happens until we find ourselves the victim or the instigator. I hope this doesn't make you change your mind about adopting out one of your cats. I am so embarrassed and beg for your understanding and forgiveness.

Many thanks,
Fawn

From: Fawn Birchill
Sent: Sat, Apr 13, 2019 at 1:12 PM
To: Mark Nilsen
Subject: Author reading

Dear Mark,

I was surprised to be walking by your store today to see a poster in the window advertising an author reading. Upon closer inspection, I discovered that it was none other than Ian McEwan. I am impressed that you were able to snag someone as enormously famous and successful as he, so my question to you is: Being as small-time and new as you are, how much did you offer him? I can only assume that two scenarios exist here: either you are fabulously wealthy and no one is the wiser or you have astounding connections. I believe the former to be truer, for if you did have excellent connections you wouldn't have purchased a store on a street that constantly floods, is laden with potholes, and has a severe mildew problem (it's in every building, trust me on that). I realize money could have bought you a nice high-rent spot on Rittenhouse, but let's be honest with ourselves and admit that it is not wealth that helps us make intelligent decisions but the know-how and ingenuity that good connections can bring.

So surely, unlike me, you cannot lure him on merit alone, having only been open a few months. I imagine someone like you must utilize other tactics—financial tactics, perhaps? Don't worry about divulging such things to me, as you know I am only asking out of curiosity from one business owner to another. I've oft thought of dragging authors in from their busy and reclusive lives to do a reading but it seems, in a strange way, to be such a selfish move on my part. Shouldn't they be churning out new material and not languishing in the past, wallowing in what they've already accomplished? Why not have someone else read their material so they can get back to work!? It's all the same on paper! Anyway, I am not saying this to convince you to halt this lofty idea, but think on what it might mean to Mr. McEwan, who no doubt has to give up precious writing time to read from a book.

Best wishes,
Fawn Birchill, Owner, The Curious Cat Book Emporium

From: Mark Nilsen
Sent: Sat, Apr 13, 2019 at 2:41 PM
To: Fawn Birchill
Re: Author reading

Hi Fawn,

Sorry, I can't share what I'm paying Ian to come and read. That said, it would be great to have you here. Perhaps you can meet him and do some networking of your own—that wouldn't bother me in the slightest. And then next time around he might be interested in coming to your store instead?

Best,
Mark

P.S. Lately I've noticed a woman hanging around performing magic tricks outside your store. Is she one of your employees? If not, and if you do not wish her to be there, you have every right to ask her to move on.

From: Fawn Birchill
Sent: Sat, Apr 13, 2019 at 3:00 PM
To: Mark Nilsen
Re: Author reading

Dear Mark,

Thank you for inviting me to the reading, even though it is a public event and if I wanted to go I would simply show up. However, I believe you know me by now to be a staunch businesswoman who never goes halfway. Since you appear to be adamant in continuing your course with Mr. McEwan, I intend, as selfish as it sounds, to request that he visit my store as well (this time around, not some nebulous next time). I was simply asking the price so that I can offer him a competitive rate. And because you will not divulge this, I see that we cannot be colleagues with like-minded interests but that we must be alienated from each other—foes that, if seen within cannon range in the dead of night, may fire shots. This saddens me. Please know I will always be open to being friends and that it is your stubborn attitude that halts the progress of mutual amicability.

Yours in business,
Fawn Birchill, Owner, The Curious Cat Book Emporium

P.S. The magician you speak of is named Rainbow, and she is one of my tenants. Even though things are rocky between you and me, you should feel free to say hello, as she is a lovely person of many talents! Oh, and she has corrected me many times, so I feel the need to pay in kind. She calls them *illusions,* not tricks. ☺

From: Fawn Birchill
Sent: Sat, Apr 13, 2019 at 6:40 PM
To: Ian McEwan
Subject: A visit to my humble store?

Dear Mr. McEwan,

First let me start out by stating that you are an incredible author and no doubt extremely busy with all the obligations that come with constant success, that is, book tours, interviews, seminars—oh, and *writing!* But please take a moment and consider this thought. I own one of the most unquestionably successful used bookstores in Philadelphia. People come from everywhere to peruse my tomes, so it is with great humbleness that I implore you to deviate only slightly from your book tour route and pay a visit (and perhaps sign a few books) at my shop. I learned about your trip as I was passing by the Grumpy Mug Bookstop down the block from my shop, and was thrilled—and I daresay a little hopeful—that you would be gracing our sidewalks.

May I ask: Are you being paid for the tour? I imagine so. And if you are used to expecting a stipend for your time, I only find it suitable to treat you as the Grumpy Mug would, if not a little better, as we are a small and personable store and not a business that is all about the bottom line. Would one hundred dollars be fair? You may scoff at first, but please remember that the pleasure may very well be all yours. You will be treated like a king and will have very little to do except to run your pen over a few of my used books (I of course cannot promise that these books will be yours). Think on it, and let me know before your tour!

It must be so perpetually romantic to be from England. I believe it is the same for those from the Mediterranean or Switzerland—such beautiful landscapes! I have never been to England, but just like you, my family's heritage is British. It is my goal to one day see London. Did you know I have never been out of the country? My parents never took us on trips besides horrible camping excursions in Pennsylvania where at least one of us would end up getting bit by something or burning ourselves in the campfire. We have never been a graceful family. I always thought the nicest part about the camping trips was packing up and leaving. I found great joy in pulling the tent from its place, seeing the squashed leaves and writhing worms underneath. It was the one shred of proof of what I had endured over a weekend, besides the smoke inhalation and spider bites. However, I had always wanted to do more to leave my mark on that most terrible place. It didn't seem enough to merely leave a burned circle of char and a few squashed worms. When I was thirteen, I actually considered trying to light that camping spot on fire, but I came to my senses when I realized that my father would just have us camp somewhere else. There are a lot of woods in Pennsylvania. In fact, the name of our state literally means "Penn's woods." Did you know that?? Here I am, going on. Long story short, despite my lack of worldly experience, I believe you will find me to be quite worldly and intelligent, and I think we will get on very well.

Do consider, and let me know as soon as possible!

Many thanks,
Fawn, Owner, The Curious Cat Book Emporium

April 13, 2019

In an interesting turn of events, my mother showed up out of the blue. Apparently she is "worried" about me. Unfortunately I answered the door in my bathrobe at about 3 p.m. with my hair in a horrible state, empty wine bottles everywhere, and my breath smelling as stale as old fish left out in the sun. My immediate reaction—a terrible one in hindsight—was shutting the door in her face. I shouted my apologies, threw on some clothing, pulled back my hair in its usual noble bun, and hastily chewed on some Tic Tacs (I must have looked like a rabid squirrel to the nosy neighbor across the way). I may not have been a new woman, but it was close enough. (Thankfully Rainbow was out performing in Clark Park and missed this display.)

As usual, my mother didn't say much, and also as usual, I caught myself taking on bits of Florence's flighty and bright personality just to survive the two hours she occupied my home. She sat at my kitchen table while I heated up some old V8 soup and asked me if I had been keeping a journal—and of course I said I wasn't. She told me about Florence and Joseph and how they are going through marriage counseling—something that I wasn't made aware of in her emails but wasn't surprised to hear in the least.

I told her about Butterscotch. As usual she sat on the subject for literally two seconds, offering her tepid condolences, and moved swiftly on to Father. Apparently for Christmas one of the nurses gave him a Pendleton blanket, and it's all he talks about. Mother says he will call her and tell her every time, as if it's the first time, that he's been given a Pendleton blanket. "Guess what I got this morning!" he'll say. And then he goes on to tell her the different colors, often repeating them as such: "Blue, red, orange, brown, brown, red, green, blue . . ." and so on. And apparently—an unthinkable thought to Mother—he takes it to the bathroom with him (on good days when he can get to the bathroom). All this was supposed to lure me to him. Sometimes I do envy him. It must be exciting to wake up each morning to see, as if for the first time, the gift of a new blanket draped across one's body, and be as excited as if it were a stack of money. How nice would it have been if, in his youth, Father were even a little like the way he seems to be these days. I always find it rather interesting how people generally grow nicer as they age, as if they've wised-up to the idea that if they are not nice, they will be abandoned with no one to care for them. When I see a friendly elderly person, I can't help but wonder about the ulterior motives behind their "angelic" smiles.

Shortly after we finished the V8 soup, Mother

wrote me a check for fifty dollars that I, with burning shame, gratefully accepted. It is good timing, as I didn't have the funds to pay my electric bill, despite Rainbow's monthly contributions. City living is ruthlessly expensive; it is either pay Angela or have light, and I for one can't spare Angela.

Mercifully, Mother left because it was getting dark and she doesn't like driving at night. After she left, I could smell her familiar Elizabeth Taylor perfume that she's worn for as long as I can remember, and the longing to be a child again—to do it all over—overwhelmed me so much that I crumpled to the floor and cried for what felt like hours. These days I would give anything to feel my father's strong hands around my ankles pulling me from my bed, his face a shade of crimson, his lips mangled up in a sneer of rage. There were so many possibilities back then, so many directions to go, even if at that particular moment, the only direction was straight into town to open his store. It's funny, but with all that Father faced in his life, he never gave up. He never let anything keep him from opening his store and showing his large red face to everyone that walked in. And thanks to him, I had someone to pull me out of bed for so long that I never quite got the hang of doing it by myself.

I checked on Jane after my mother left and

ended up sitting on the floor by her feet watching one of her awful shows while she hummed and patted me on the head. We didn't talk, but despite the Jesus stuff she watches, I think we might have been friends if we had met when she was younger. When I started to cry about Butterscotch, she just kept humming and patting me. I can't explain why, but it was probably the kindest thing that anyone has done for me in a very long time. Rainbow has been a wonderfully uplifting presence, but I think I am not yet healed from the loss of Butterscotch, as all it took was a kind gesture from Jane to bring me to tears. Grief sneaks up like a wave, and most of the time when it catches me, my back is turned.

The new cat comes tomorrow. I am determined not to get too attached.

●●

From: Fawn Birchill
Sent: Sun, Apr 14, 2019 at 12:13 AM
To: Angela Washington
Subject: Volume

Dear Angela,

I was looking over the log from Friday, and I have a question. When you say that three customers came in that day and only one purchased a book, do you count the people that looked in the windows? Perhaps that may count for something. Did this person buy an *expensive* book? Furthermore, there have never been as few as three customers in my store in one day. Are you sure you counted correctly?

Fawn, Owner

From: Fawn Birchill
Sent: Sun, Apr 14, 2019 at 1:12 PM
To: Angela Washington
Subject: Betrayal

Dear Angela,

Yesterday I walked by the Grumpy Mug to see what kind of customer volume they had (surely it would be similar, as we are practically the same store), and not only did I see it packed, but I caught a glimpse of Kyle inside, helping someone find something. Did you know he worked there? Is that why you have been sneaking over? Have you given them your résumé, and should I, in anticipation, just let you go as well? Little did I know this store would not only take my customers but also my employees—I should have had you all sign a noncompete! I should have never let Kyle go over and look for Butterscotch. This, I fear, is how I began to lose him. But go ahead and work for those hippies if that is what you want to do with your life. Just give me enough notice to find your replacement.

Best,
Fawn, Owner

April 14

Dear Rainbow,

Due to Angela's recent dismissal, I am in need of help around the store. You are the first person I thought of, out of all the people I know, who might be perfect for such a role. Please let me know as soon as you can, as I do need to fill the position soon.

Many thanks,

Fawn, Landlord

Advertisement

SEEKING ENERGETIC, ENTHUSIASTIC, AND TALENTED INDIVIDUAL FOR A UNIQUE VOLUNTEER OPPORTUNITY

Looking to better your life in the exciting and romantic world of used bookstores? Look no further! Be part of a growing business with potential for professional advancement and a chance to use your ingenuity on business and marketing projects. Great for anyone from students to young moms and recent retirees. Must have some cashier experience and a love for books. Must be open to cleaning and occasionally working longer hours. Must be available on weekends. Must be willing to *work*. If nothing is below you, there is no telling how far you will rise in this company.

Compensation: Volunteer basis to start, but this could change with a demonstration of excellent skills and dedication!! No benefits at this time. EOE.

Interested and serious applicants, please send résumé and cover letter to email address above. **Must not be allergic to cats**

From: Fawn Birchill
Sent: Tue, Apr 16, 2019 at 1:03 AM
To: Hank Turo
Subject: Wonderful Cat

Hank,

I wanted to write to say thank you for the lovey cat. I have named him and he is doing well in his new suuroundings. It was more than a pleasure meeting you and it was nice meeting your wife.

If you are ever in West Philadelphia, please stop by and visit us! Of course you may bring your wife but it is not necessary, as I daresay I felt less of a connection to her than I did with you. Many women threatened by other women who are strong an business savvy and so I understand where she is coming from if this is the case for her and it seems to be)!

Sincerely,
Fawn

From: Hank Turo
Sent: Tue, Apr 16, 2019 at 9:17 AM
To: Fawn Birchill
Re: Wonderful Cat

Please stop emailing me. Our transaction is over. Also, I don't let anyone insult my wife, mostly for their safety, not for the sake of her feelings. She is a decorated marine veteran, and she doesn't take insults lying down.

Hank

From: Fawn Birchill
Sent: Tue, Apr 16, 2019 at 10:08 AM
To: Hank Turo
Re: Wonderful Cat

Hank,

I apologize; I was inebriated when I wrote that email. You seem to be the newest victim of my late-night drunken correspondences (my mother being the oldest and most seasoned), and for that I greatly apologize. My father did a similar thing when I was growing up. He would nurse a bottle of gin and write letters to his dead relatives whom he hated and then burn them. Clearly he had some issues! I am merely mourning for a lost loved one.

I never meant to insult your wife. I am beyond impressed that she is a veteran. Truly, a strong woman indeed. How wrong I was!

That said, I will respect your wishes and stop emailing you.

Just wanted to say thank you for the new cat.

Sincerely,
Fawn

• •

April 20, 2019

Rainbow has politely declined the offer of being my number two in the store, so I'm currently busy fielding applications. She cited that, though flattered, she does not wish to embark on anything that could get in the way of her passions. In the end, I think it's for the best that I did not hire her for the job. I can't put my finger on why, but there's something about her that doesn't exactly exude responsibility.

So with no replacement at the moment and with Angela gone, the ticking of the clock in this vast, empty space has grown louder and reverberates through my skull. I am going to try hard not to let this happen, but I think I may have to raise the rent on Jane. I hope she won't leave because of it. It seems as if Jane's daughter will pay anything to avoid seeing her. Maybe I'll get lucky and she'll just pay the extra money so I can keep Jane on. Honestly, I don't know what that woman has against her mother or why she's exiled her to a small apartment in Philadelphia. If she was a terrible mother in her younger years, she has certainly calmed down by now. It's funny how people have such trouble letting things go.

Angela was right. Being downstairs in that drafty store for the entire day, I can see how the customer volume has dropped. I get overwhelmed now when there are two customers inside. I am worried they are a team and one is set to distract me while the other makes off with a book—a racket I wouldn't put past the rather resourceful UPenn student body. They are all so smart and appear to be quite innocent—a perfect guise for thievery.

Yesterday I organized the Mark Twain Room and found a dead pigeon under the pile of books. The room didn't even seem to smell funny because of it, which gives me the impression that the whole place has a smell to which I have grown immune. I called Rainbow down to give me her thoughts, but she explained that she only smells auras, so she wasn't much help in that regard. To mitigate the possible odor, I opened the windows and put on the industrial fans. The sound is awful but at least it drowns out the ticking clock. It is so loud lately! As if someone slipped a megaphone behind the mechanism just to drive me insane.

After the store closed today, I cleaned Jane's bathroom because it desperately needed it. It's really my bathroom if you want to get technical, so it wasn't as though I was doing her an enormous favor, but she really seemed to appreciate it. It was a nice change after yesterday when I did practically nothing all day but come across a dead pigeon.

I have given the new cat an atrocious name and have decided that his sole purpose is to eradicate the mice from the building. If he remains utilitarian and practical, then when he eventually passes on I won't be so distraught. That said, my plans to keep an emotional distance from this cat might prove difficult, evidenced by the events of Bert's introduction to Jellybean. Rainbow, rightfully so, was cautious to put them together, but perhaps she saw something in Bert that I failed to notice right away. She released Jellybean onto the floor, and for a moment the little thing froze as if dropped from a helicopter into a lion's den before dinnertime. And then Bert, who is three times the size of Jellybean, took two steps toward her, yawned, and flopped down as if to offer himself for belly pets. Jellybean then sniffed his front paw and hopped away. But I will not get attached to him. I will not.

From: Fawn Birchill
Sent: Sat, Apr 20, 2019 at 11:09 PM
To: Florence Eakins
Subject: A surprise visit

Florence,

Mother stopped by the other day. I could have done without that. I don't know what she told you, but I was on my way out when she surprised me. I had just taken a shower and so was in my bathrobe. I had a date in Old City that I needed to cancel because of her impromptu visit. Have you ever had Cuban food? I know your usual fare is American or Italian, but Cuban is truly something for the worldly. Well, perhaps if you ever visit, I will take you.

Speaking of, once again Mother is imploring that I visit Father. I never had anything to say to him when I was younger, so why would I have anything to say to him now? If I were to visit him, I am sure we would exhaust the niceties and small talk in under a minute and find ourselves in an awkward silence that I simply wouldn't be able to bear. I would choose to leave under such a circumstance.

I had this thought the other day after coming across some words in the newspaper. I thought of Father, and I wonder if you remember how he would allow us to go on mispronouncing words, never correcting us or bothering with one shred of opinion either way about it. I remember believing that the word *fetish* was pronounced "fet*eesh,*" and I repeated it well into my teenage years until I heard someone utter it correctly in class. I grew angry with Father (and with Mother, though she probably didn't know any better either). I wasn't angry because he simply wouldn't correct me. I was angry because he didn't care to take the time to teach me not only how to say it but what the word meant—for a mispronunciation to that extent is enough to make one wonder if I even know what I'm talking about! Why would I spend time with such an undynamic human being who let his daughters run around mispronouncing words? And do you remember that for years the entire family would say "salad" after every sneeze because of my simple misunderstanding when someone said *"salud"*? You, Mother, and Father (who was the worst offender) shouted "Salad!" after every sneeze. And like everything else, I only questioned it when every child in elementary school, as well as the teacher, went into hysterics at my ignorance. He really preferred us to be mindless, didn't he? He must have been quite intimidated when I went to college and actually graduated. I think it's a challenge for a person like him to accept that his offspring has its own original thoughts and beliefs. If he had it his way, I'd be running his general store like a mindless drone to this day, stocking shelves and bending to his every whim as he shouted orders from his hospice bed. No, thank you.

In other news, if there is anything you need to talk to someone about, you know I'm here. Mother didn't tell me anything, so don't blame her. You just tend to never tell me anything but very good news. I shared with you the trouble with my cat, so if you want to use our sisterly relationship for anything, feel free to dump your troubles (if you have any) on me. I'm here.

Fawn

From: Florence Eakins
Sent: Sun, Apr 21, 2019 at 9:17 AM
To: Fawn Birchill
Re: A surprise visit

Hi Fawn,

I didn't know Mom paid you a surprise visit. She hasn't mentioned anything about it to me. And I don't remember Dad letting us run around mispronouncing words. Honestly, it doesn't seem like that terrible of a sin in the big scheme of things.

Mom is only ever looking out for us, as annoying as it can be at times. I think she just needs things to do and worry about. I have enough to do and worry about, so it's kind of nice knowing that someone else is thinking of me. Joseph sure as hell isn't thinking of me.

Speaking of, I'm curious what Mom "didn't tell you" about me, though I'm sure I can guess. She's not the best at keeping secrets. I appreciate you reaching out to help—I really do—but I'm okay.

Flo

From: Mark Nilsen
Sent: Wed, Apr 24, 2019 at 4:11 PM
To: Fawn Birchill
Subject: Magician

Hi Fawn,

I thought you should know that Rainbow came into my store today with her rabbit to do some magic illusions. I had to ask her to either make a purchase or leave. I hate that I had to do this, but she was disrupting business. A little illusion here and there would have been okay, but she started vanishing customers' cappuccinos and coffees. It was impressive until she couldn't figure out how to rematerialize them. Not sure where they went and, by the look on her face, she didn't seem too sure either.

I spoke with her, so I think she gets the message not to do this again. I'm just grateful she didn't try this with one of the cats.

Mark

●●

April 24

Dear Rainbow,

Please refrain from going to Mark's store and performing illusions. Sadly not everyone, it seems, is an enthusiast for the sleight of hand.

Fawn, Landlord

P.S. If you manage to find those coffees, may I try one? I want to know what the big deal is, but I simply can't bring myself to go in there.

●●

May 6, 2019

My world has grown quite small. Besides Jane and Rainbow, I interact with so few people these days, though I'm finding it rather comforting in a strange, melancholy way. If I am to be undone, I blame Mr. Whitney and especially the nefarious Mark Nilsen. If I am to curl up in a hole for the rest of my life, it is thanks to all those who betrayed me, hurt me, and used me. I am not a Greek tragic heroine with hubris; I am a victim of the modern greed-ridden dangers of the world. Whoever thought that such stress could befall a person who just wanted to open an innocent little bookshop?

I read that Mark opened his store because it was his late mother's dream to own a bookshop, but she was never able to get around to it because she had been ill for so long. I question the validity of that only because I know how skilled he is at turning sympathy into business. I suppose I could do the same, but I wouldn't be able to live with myself. To say that Fawn Birchill wanted to open a used bookstore because she found comfort in books growing up with a tyrannical father, an ineffective mother, and a dull sister seems like a cry for pity. I can see the article now: Books allowed her to escape from her meager, militaristic upbringing until college, where she learned a thing or two about business and opened her very own store. There she excelled and watched her family's reaction transition from mild amusement to muted jealousy. And now, twenty years on, she's still sailing along. No, thank you. I'll stick to merit and leave the pity mining to the amateurs.

Part of running a good business is not letting anyone know how bad things have really become. The way I see it, when things are at their worst, that's when you advertise, when you fight. That's when you evolve. Suddenly I find myself worrying that since I've grown quiet, my family and the public have caught on that something is not right. The thing is, I'm fine. Nothing here has changed.

In other news, Bert has caught two mice. The only downside is that he takes forever to kill them. I am left sitting down at my computer busying myself, trying not to focus on the squeaks of terror as he carries the mouse around in his mouth and uses it as his Ping-Pong ball. The last kill took an hour. I should have named him Gestapo.

Yesterday I caught my hand in the bathroom door. I sat down on the toilet seat lid for a long time just focusing on the dull, throbbing pain, and I had the clearest thoughts. Sometimes I think this place is nothing more than a cocoon from which I must emerge. I both love this place and hate it for what it has become—what the poisonous people like Angela, Kyle, Sam, Mark, and Mr. Whitney have allowed it to become. I let them have too much say, too much rein. I should not go back to the way things were before them, but I fear that continuing on this current path might also be detrimental. The bottom line is: I must not allow anyone into a position of decision-making or even give them the impression that their thoughts and ideas could be utilized. What I need are mindless servants who will do what they are told, who are too soft of mind to see that scraping gum from sidewalks is below them, who don't grumble when told to clean the bathroom, who don't get upset when I give my own books away to loyal customers. It is my store! It is my store! And now that the vermin have been rid from the place, it is time to take it back.

●●

Advertisement

SPRING FEVER SALES EVENT

The Curious Cat Book Emporium will hold a once-in-a-lifetime sale through the weekend of May 17 ONLY. Starting Friday at 8 a.m., there will be doorbuster prices on everything from romance novels to travel books. All fiction, all weekend, is 50% off! May 17 through May 19 at 7 p.m.—DON'T MISS IT! Light snacks, coffee, and juice will be free to paying customers.

●●

May 8

Dear Rainbow,

I noticed toward the back of the store that a certain person had made an impressive fort out of some of the books.☺ If it was you, can you please put them back when you are done? I do not wish to get in the way of your creativity, but please be mindful that in my store, my customers do come first.

Many thanks,

Fawn, Landlord

●●

From: Fawn Birchill
Sent: Sat, May 11, 2019 at 10:30 PM
To: Florence Eakins
Subject: Great time

Dear Florence,

I am not sure what to say regarding Little Joe's play and performance this afternoon. It has taken me the train ride to gather my thoughts properly. Let me at least begin by saying that I always knew Little Joe was a talented young man, but I certainly hadn't expected this. He has come a long way from his awkward screeching phase. Either you have found him an excellent teacher or he has come into his own naturally. The show was worth every penny they charged; however, I was pleasantly surprised to find that you had set aside an extra complimentary ticket in my name. I truly felt like the queen of England. What treatment!

I am so grateful for this but also grateful to have shared in a wonderful family moment. Even though I wasn't able to stay long after the show, I am glad I was able to wish Little Joe congratulations. Perhaps he has a future on Broadway? It's hard to get there, but he just might have what it takes!

If interested, I have a book in my inventory called *How to Act & Eat at the Same Time* by Tom Logan. If he'd like it, I can gift it to him. I'm not sure how one can write an entire book on acting while eating, but what do I know about it? Not much! I've oft watched actors such as Robert De Niro and Matt Damon sit down and eat a meal while delivering lines, and I hadn't thought much about it until now. Surely there is an art to it that the layman like me doesn't understand.

Many thanks,
Fawn

From: Florence Eakins
Sent: Sun, May 12, 2019 at 8:07 AM
To: Fawn Birchill
Re: Great time

Hi Fawn,

I'm so glad you enjoyed it! Little Joe was thrilled you were able to make it, even if he was bouncing all over the place after the show. He gets so excited after curtain call.

I asked him if he wanted to read a book on acting and he said he did, so please feel free to send it over or stop by sometime. It's very appreciated! Also, I wonder if the title instead suggests learning to keep yourself fed and bills paid while being a working actor? Either way, great stuff to learn!

Thanks again,
Flo

●●

From: Mark Nilsen
Sent: Sun, May 12, 2019 at 11:21 AM
To: Fawn Birchill
Subject: Regarding Ian McEwan

Hi Fawn,

Did your new employee actually stop by and harass my customer service manager about

Ian McEwan's visit? The price we are paying him is private; we won't share it, so your strange tactics aren't going to work.

Mark

From: Fawn Birchill
Sent: Sun, May 12, 2019 at 2:35 PM
To: Mark Nilsen
Re: Regarding Ian McEwan

Dear Mark,

My new volunteer worker, Jack, was merely asking your employee what they were paying Ian McEwan to come to their store. I'm sure you'll be unhappy to find that Ian and I have been in contact, and he is considering visiting my bookshop as well as yours. This is not harassment but merely a business inquiry from one savvy businesswoman to another (though of course you are a man). I merely don't want to short Ian or perhaps overpay him and embarrass you.

Since I walk by your store on a regular basis, I have in the past glanced in and seen Kyle Krazinsky at the counter or assisting customers; however, the last couple of times I failed to see him. Does he not work on Saturdays, or has he finally been fired? He worked for me for some time in the past and was a fairly competent employee but ended up being a little untrustworthy. I think he was the one who stole thousands of dollars' worth of my books. I always found it a little suspicious that he quit shortly after I asked him to start keeping inventory. He is most likely running a nice racket online. If you haven't fired him yet, keep an eye out.

Best,
Fawn

●●

From: Fawn Birchill
Sent: Mon, May 13, 2019 at 10:09 AM
To: Jack Grisby
Subject: Books in the Basement

Dear Jack,

Please go down to the basement and identify which books do not have mold on them, bring them up, and shelve them in the former Mark Twain Room. It will become the Miscellaneous Room now. I think we have purged enough *Tom Sawyer* books to finally rid ourselves of the "specialist" status.

Fawn, Owner

●●

May 15, 2019

I think the new person I hired is a bit slow. Either that or he doesn't know what to think of me. Sometimes when I speak to him, his eyes become very wide and he just nods as if what I am saying to him is the word of God. As long as he does what he is told, I don't really care what he thinks of me. I am finished trying to be friends with my employees.

I had a most revelatory thought yesterday that Kyle never used me as his reference for the Grumpy Mug. I wonder if he had even put my shop on his résumé to begin with (though he should have, as it would have left a gaping hole in his résumé, and employers hate to see that). I wonder if perhaps he had Angela or Sam give him a reference and if they feigned a managerial position to sound authoritative. I don't understand what frightens Kyle about using me as his reference. I am fair and honest, and I have been in this business for many years. Though, all that said, I would have probably turned down giving him a reference if they had called me, so it's probably for the best that they didn't bother. By law I am not allowed to say terrible things about previous employees; however, I believe my silence would have been more than enough to hammer the nail into the coffin.

I have not heard back from Ian McEwan.

I wonder if my letters go into a dark void in outer space. Or perhaps, because of the Mark Twain incident, all authors have written me off. I wonder if they are all that tight-knit and band together against certain letter-writers and fans. I do hope not.

●●

THE CURIOUS CAT BOOK EMPORIUM

Blog Post #4
Employee Profile: Jack Grisby II

For this blog entry, we are going to do a quick profile on the newest employee, Jack Grisby II.

Jack Grisby II

Hometown: Chestnut Hill

Favorite Book: *The Da Vinci Code*

Favorite Food: Chipotle (the chain)

Favorite Pastime: I can sit for hours and look at my hands and be totally entertained. I also like waiting for toasters to be done.

Favorite Music: Music that's emotional

Role Model: My dad, and Ryan Gosling

Goals and Aspirations: To one day fly in a hot-air balloon, to one day swim faster than my brother

Chuck, to one day be an actor in Hollywood like Ryan Gosling.

Something People Don't Know About Me: I have a hard time memorizing lines so I sometimes write them on the insides of my arms. I hope I never have to do Shakespeare.

Favorite Quote: "Love is like a butterfly. Hold it too tight and you will crush it; hold it too loose and it will fly away." My acting teacher told us this and said you can apply it to acting, but I'm still not sure how they connect. I still like the quote, though. I'd like a girlfriend to try it out on.

●●

Fawn Birchill/*CuriousCatBooks*/4m

Fawn here! What #classic novel do you want to see made into a #movie that hasn't been? #Post your answer!

●●

From: Jack Grisby
Sent: Sun, May 19, 2019 at 7:13 PM
To: Fawn Birchill
Subject: Commercial

Dear Fawn,

I was watching a Big Bang Theory rerun and a commercial for Geico came on and I looked up their annual revinue and they actually do really well as a company so I thought well what if we did something like that? I mean TV commericials, not insurance.

Jack

From: Fawn Birchill
Sent: Sun, May 19, 2019 at 8:17 PM
To: Jack Grisby
Re: Commercial

Jack,

Though that is a terribly smart idea, I do not believe I have the time with all that is going on to write up a script or devise any clever ideas for hooking people. I appreciate that you are thinking of different ways to reach out to a greater audience, however. It is touching to know that someone besides me is strategizing—and on the weekend!

Fawn, Owner

From: Fawn Birchill
Sent: Mon, May 20, 2019 at 8:09 AM
To: Jack Grisby
Subject: The Floor

Jack,

I understand that you were trying to help, and I appreciate your effort, coming in early to “surprise me.” I know very little about wooden floors, but what I do know is that one should never ever take a Brillo pad to original hardwood flooring. I am not sure how to handle this seeing how the entire downstairs floor is now stripped and covered in scrapes. I wonder, Jack, at what point you realized your mistake—or was it only when I pointed it out to you? Clearly, you do not think this is an improvement? I am sorry I am writing this in an email, but I believe a face-to-face talk would result in nothing but a lot of yelling.

Fawn, Owner

From: Jack Grisby
Sent: Mon, May 20, 2019 at 8:15 AM
To: Fawn Birchill
Re: The Floor

Dear Fawn,

I apologize with all my heart for what I have done to your floors I can’t believe I did something so stupid and no I didn’t notice it. Rainbow said maybe it wasn’t the best idea but I didn’t listen to her I should have. I’m in the bathroom very upset. I'm sorry. I will resine immediately.

Jack

From: Fawn Birchill
Sent: Mon, May 20, 2019 at 8:18 AM
To: Jack Grisby
Re: The Floor

Jack,

It will be okay. I'll find a few thrift store rugs for the time being and throw them over the flooring. Please don't resign—you meant well, and I still need your help.

Fawn, Owner

From: Gregory Harris
Sent: Mon, May 20, 2019 at 5:14 PM
To: Fawn Windsor
Subject: Philadelphia

Dear Fawn,

I hope you are well. It just so happens that I am going to be in Philadelphia, about which you've told me so much, in the coming weeks. I have meetings at UPenn, so I will be in the area for about a week. Would you mind sharing your recommendations again on where I should go and what I should see?

How are you, my dear?

Regards,
Gregory

From: Fawn Windsor
Sent: Mon, May 20, 2019 at 9:36 PM
To: Gregory Harris
Re: Philadelphia

Dear Gregory,

Philadelphia!

What a lovely and charming city. It seems that all it ever does is rain, which I find mildly irritating, as it ends up reminding me of England. But the architecture is quite French. If you go to city hall, step inside and look around; you will find yourself in Paris! I do recommend traversing Rittenhouse Square, and if you have time, try the Mütter Museum. It is gruesome but very educational, and I don't believe you will find it all that hard to stomach. Additionally, since you mentioned that you would be in meetings at UPenn, stop by the Curious Cat Book Emporium. I have been to Philadelphia thrice, and each time I have stopped into this little gem of a store.

The owner is lovely, intelligent, and has a cracking good wit. She is also quite pretty, though she is no spring chicken. But, alas, neither are we!

Additionally, if you care for the art of legerdemain, the owner has a magician of great talent staying with her. The last time I was there, the woman—her name is Rainbow—made my Tiffany crystal watch disappear! It reappeared moments later (thankfully!) right before my eyes, but on the other wrist! Truly, you should take a gander. She claims to be from a long line of magicians dating back to the 1700s, when they regularly employed gunpowder in their trickery to thwart the advance of the British army. What they would do is gather in the woods and wait to surprise the redcoats as they advanced across the open fields, and when the time was right, they would burst out of the forest, appearing out of nowhere in a flurry of smoke and fire!

You know, now that I write it out, it sounds more like they were not magicians but regular militiamen. When I revisit the store, I will have to get some clarification on this . . .

Anyway! Here I am going on about Philadelphia when I've said nothing about my life. There is honestly nothing very new. I went up to Scotland last week to look at some horses for sale. I purchased a horse, and he has turned out to be quite dumb. Alas, one doesn't buy horses for their intelligence but for their beauty, swiftness, and/or practicality. This one is quite adorable; however, I often find him with his head pressed against the stable wall, breathing heavily, as if willing the wall to come away. He will also sometimes break out into a sudden gallop only to stop and lie down in the middle of the field, rolling around like a dog. Pierre says it's nothing to worry about and rather silly to assume a horse can't have a personality, even if it's an odd one.

Ah, well, that is really all for now. Do let me know if and when you are planning to go to that bookstore. Incidentally, the owner's name is Fawn as well—just like my name! (Which could be why we got on so famously.) Tell her that her Brit counterpart says hullo!

Regards,
Fawn Windsor

From: Fawn Birchill
Sent: Tue, May 21, 2019 at 8:02 AM
To: Jack Grisby
Subject: Please Clean

Jack,

Bert made another "mistake" in the romance/erotica section. Please clean it up before it starts to smell up the room. Bring it to me when you are done; I have a special place in which I dispose of such messes.

Thank you,
Fawn, Owner

From: Jack Grisby
Sent: Tue, May 21, 2019 at 8:11 AM
To: Fawn Birchill
Re: Please Clean

Hi Fawn,

Do you have rubber gloves and is this safe to do it seems like maybe I could get a infecscious disease.

Jack

From: Fawn Birchill
Sent: Tue, May 21, 2019 at 8:16 AM
To: Jack Grisby
Re: Please Clean

Jack,

There are rubber gloves in the broom closet by the back door, but honestly the cat lives off Friskies and hot dogs, and I assure you that his excrement will not harm you if you simply use a paper towel.

Fawn, Owner

● ●

From: Jack Grisby
Sent: Tue, May 21, 2019 at 6:09 PM
To: Fawn Birchill
Subject: Reconsider TV ad?

Hi Fawn,

I was watching Big Bang Theory reruns again and then Friends and there were so many advertisements during the commercial breaks that I have a feeling that those companies get a lot of customers even though they spent a lot because a lot of there customers like the advertisements. I don't know maybe we should reconsider?

Jack

From: Fawn Birchill
Sent: Tue, May 21, 2019 at 7:18 PM
To: Jack Grisby
Re: Reconsider TV ad?

Dear Jack,

I believe this would be a waste of money.

What we must focus on here are our competitors. What is it that Mark is doing that makes him so successful? I believe the only differences between the two of us are his fancy signage, his bright lighting, and his modern furniture. Oh, and his fancy coffee and beer. And perhaps the open mic readings and book signings.

Honestly, I believe signage is becoming more important these days, for most people are either drawn in by word of mouth or by window-shopping. If you make a place look inviting on the outside, then they will want to come in. So my thought is this: let us buy up some nice potted plants and hanging baskets and set them outside. Also I will ask that you go to the back of the Grumpy Mug and search through their trash to find a couple of posters that we can alter to appear fresh. I believe that if we actually cut the posters into star shapes to remove the Grumpy Mug name, Mark will be none the wiser. He couldn't possibly accuse us of theft if there is never any proof that his name existed on the poster to begin with. Let me know where you get with that. Also, I cannot afford to buy all new lighting for the store, but I will ask that you open the shutters along the side of the building and let some light in. We might have some overdue dusting to do, as the light will no doubt reveal a serious lack of cleanliness toward the back of the store. Luckily, those books are history and foreign language, so we don't get many customers back there at all.

Fawn, Owner

Fawn Birchill/*CuriousCatBooks*/14h
Fawn here! What classic literary character represents you most? Fawn: Daisy Buchanan, Madame Bovary, Caddy Compson all in one!

Fawn Birchill/*CuriousCatBooks*/13h
Fawn here! What classic literary character represents you most? Jack: Bilbo Baggins, Dirk Pitt.

From: Jack Grisby
Sent: Wed, May 22, 2019 at 8:02 PM
To: Fawn Birchill
Subject: Pool party Monday

Hi Fawn,

Can I take Monday off to go to a pool party at my house?

Thankyou
Jack

From: Fawn Birchill
Sent: Wed, May 22, 2019 at 9:23 PM
To: Jack Grisby
Re: Pool party Monday

Jack,

That is completely fine. I didn't know you had a pool—how lavish! Is it aboveground or in-ground? It always makes a world of difference to me. Where in-ground is fashionable and always costs loads of money to install, with aboveground I always feel like a fish in a large, opaque fishbowl, constantly going in circles or small straight shots. The design doesn't wear one out but only gives one the sense of aquatic claustrophobia. Swimming becomes an act of futility, more than anything else. It is my opinion with pools, at least, that one must go big or go home.

Incidentally, growing up it was always my classmates whose parents were lawyers or doctors who had in-ground pools. I envied them greatly—especially since they would never invite me over. Sometimes, in the dead of summer, my sister and I would don bathing suits and leave our dusty yard, biking the five miles with towels draped over our shoulders in the hope that Tiffany (the one with the pool who lived closest to us) would invite us over if she saw us biking in front of her house. One day, Florence and I circled her driveway for so long that her mother came out and told us to "get lost." By that time we were quite hot and thirsty, and the noise of splashing and merriment behind their palatial home was enough to make Florence burst into tears right in front of her. The display did not soften her heart of stone. We went back home after this and resigned ourselves to filling up the bathtub with cold water and taking turns lying there in our bathing suits. Unfortunately, Father was always too cheap to even consider the smallest of abovegrounds. We weren't even the envy of the poorest kids in the trailer down the street, who had one of their own anyway.

Ah, here I am going on! You can see I am sensitive when it comes to talk of pools! Of course you may take Monday off. I will continue on here with no trouble whatsoever, though it is unlikely that anyone will venture in on Memorial Day, so I'm hoping that I may be able to just close. Is this family only or are you also inviting friends? In-ground or above?

Excited for you,
Fawn, Owner

From: Jack Grisby
Sent: Wed, May 22, 2019 at 9:54 PM
To: Fawn Birchill
Re: Pool party Monday

Hi Fawn,

Its inground with a Jacuzzi attached to it and then next to it is a poolhouse and an outdoor wet bar with lots of rum in it.

Jack

From: Fawn Birchill
Sent: Wed, May 22, 2019 at 10:17 PM
To: Jack Grisby
Re: Pool party Monday

Jack,

Ah, *magnifique!* I had no idea your family was so affluent! What do your parents do?

Incidentally, I make a mean cold macaroni salad, so if you are short on them, I can make one for the party and leave it in the fridge for you to take over. I am in no way inviting myself but simply offering to put in some time to make a delicious snack for your guests. Do think on it!

Fawn, Owner

From: Jack Grisby
Sent: Wed, May 22, 2019 at 10:32 PM
To: Fawn Birchill
Re: Pool party Monday

My mom is a prosecuton lawyer and my dad is an heir to an oil fortune and basically now he is a philanthripist and he opens halfway houses in the city.

Oh and I talked to my mom and she said that there is no need for extra food because it will be catered but she says thankyou.

Jack

From: Fawn Birchill
Sent: Wed, May 22, 2019 at 11:14 PM
To: Jack Grisby
Re: Pool party Monday

Jack,

My heavens—I had no idea, Jack! Your parents must be very hard to hate!

Even though you say it will be catered, I recommend you sneak my macaroni salad in among the food. It will be a homemade delight. Who, may I ask, have you hired for the catering? Tell me it is not Fortieth Street Catering.

Fawn, Owner

From: Jack Grisby
Sent: Wed, May 22, 2019 at 11:55 PM
To: Fawn Birchill
Re: Pool party Monday

No we are not using Fortieth Street but someone else I'm not sure.

Jack

From: Fawn Birchill
Sent: Thu, May 23, 2019 at 12:12 AM
To: Jack Grisby
Re: Pool party Monday

Jack,

Phew! You dodged a bullet by not hiring them. Your parents have truly amazing taste for going with someone else. I applaud them.

As you are not catching on to my many hints, I am just going to come out and ask this. Please do not feel obligated to say yes. Even though I am your boss, in no way should you be pressured to think that if you said no, I would consider firing you. Does your pool party have room for one more? Trust me, if you say no, I will definitely not show up on my bike in a bathing suit, circling like a shark until you let me through the gates! Ha ha!

Fawn, Owner

From: Tabitha Birchill
Sent: Thu, May 23, 2019 at 10:05 AM
To: Fawn Birchill
Subject: Memorial Day?

Dear Fawn,

I hope you are well. I wanted to invite you to

a Memorial Day cookout at the hospice center around noon. Can you make it? It will be held in the nursing home section (east wing, next to the koi pond). Food will be provided, and there will be a little fireworks show as well. And, for the main event, someone will sing the national anthem; however, we hear it will be sung by one of the nurses. For some reason they are not having Little Joe sing, even though Florence basically told them it would be in their best interests to do so. This nurse can't carry a tune in a bucket. I don't know what they have against us. Perhaps they are jealous of him? Hope you can make it!

Much love,
Mother

From: Fawn Birchill
Sent: Thu, May 23, 2019 at 10:32 AM
To: Tabitha Birchill
Re: Memorial Day?

Dear Mother,

Thank you for your kind and generous invitation, but I am sadly going to have to decline. I have been invited to an extravagant in-ground pool party in Chestnut Hill, and as I have already accepted, to say no at this point would be more than a little rude. There will be fireworks, a bar featuring rum from all over the tropics, a band, and catered five-star cuisine by Philadelphia's most famous chef. You probably haven't heard of him in your narrow circles, so I won't even bother to tell you who it is, but he is by far the greatest restaurateur Philadelphia has ever seen. And if I tell you that Moritani himself will be there (another *excellent and famous* chef), you wouldn't know what I meant, but just know that this fact alone makes it a big event that I cannot miss. Thank you so much anyway, and have a lovely time with Father!

Fawn

● ●

From: Jack Grisby
Sent: Thu, May 23, 2019 at 10:51 AM
To: Fawn Birchill
Re: Pool party Monday

Hi Fawn,

I asked my mom and she said no its family only so I can't add you to the invite even though I want to. Sorry.

Are the signs I picked from the garbage okay? They stink a littie.

Jack

From: Fawn Birchill
Sent: Thu, May 23, 2019 at 11:13 AM
To: Jack Grisby
Re: Pool party Monday

Jack,

I understand entirely. In fact, my father, who is very ill, has asked that I spend the day sitting with him in hospice. I believe they will have their usual Memorial Day food of burned hockey-puck hamburgers, canned applesauce, and boiled creamed corn. Generally the "events" consist of loading everyone outside onto the lawn (which takes about an hour) and setting off the saddest excuse for fireworks the world has ever known to the tune of a tone-deaf nurse singing "The Star-Spangled Banner" into a microphone. The fireworks last about five minutes. I believe the staff is afraid of setting the building on fire, as they tend to have no idea what they are doing.

I think the signs you rustled up are fine. From the street, no one will see the wet decay on the edges, and by the time they notice it they will be too close to the door to turn back without looking like they're afraid of commitment. And don't worry about the smell. I think if our customers are interested in smelling our signage then they have bigger problems than we do! I am buying the plants today. Please start cutting the old posters into star shapes. Remember, Jack, we need to avoid any evidence that these ever came from the Grumpy Mug.

Fawn, Owner

• •

From: Tabitha Birchill
Sent: Thu, May 23, 2019 at 6:00 PM
To: Fawn Birchill
Re: Memorial Day?

Dear Fawn,

Please reconsider the invite? It would be lovely to see you, and I'm not sure how many more Memorial Days your father has left. Florence will be there with Joseph and her kiddos. Also, I wanted to update you that after much badgering on my part, the nursing home has rescinded and they are allowing Little Joe to sing! Should be a wonderful time.

Love you,
Mother

From: Fawn Birchill
Sent: Thu, May 23, 2019 at 6:50 PM
To: Tabitha Birchill
Re: Memorial Day?

Dear Mother,

Florence's presence on Memrial Day fails to make me feel guilty. In fact, I know for sure that they have very little to do that day as generally Joseph cannot manage a grill on his own without burning himself and their backyard is the size of my bathroom so whats the point in doing anything for Memorial Day but spending it locked up in the ever-exciting halls of the hospice?

And for the the record, I can hear Little Joe sing "The Star Spangled Banner" any time I like. With the way those two constnatly have him performing at the drop of a hat I know there will be no shortage of his rendition of our country's great anthem blasting across the Appalachians. I need only to call them up and request it.

Fawn

From: Fawn Birchill
Sent: Thu, May 23, 2019 at 7:18 PM
To: Tabitha Birchill
Re: Memorial Day?

Dear Mother,

Forgive me. I have been hitting the wine

spritzers and did not mean to send such a scathing email. Please delete and do not tell Florence what I said. I did not mean any of it. It is so unreasonably hot in this city today that I started the chilled wine a little early for a Thursday. (Needless to say, I'm really looking forward to that pool party!!)

Fawn

P.S. Now that we are all adults, I believe you can answer me straight on this one: Why were you and Father always so against getting us an aboveground pool?

From: Mark Nilsen
Sent: Fri, May 24, 2019 at 11:20 PM
To: Fawn Birchill
Subject: Signs

Hi Fawn,

A few things. Those signs in your front window look a lot like ours, only slightly altered. I didn't think too much of it until one of my employees informed me that he saw your employee rooting through our trash bin, pulling out our discarded signage. According to my employee, he appeared as happy and comfortable in there as a flea on a dog. How exactly do you find these people? I'll reiterate that what he is doing is illegal, and I will not hesitate to call the cops if I catch him again.

Also, I like the plants out front. I can't help but notice that you've taken a page from my decorating book. Soon, if we're not careful, no one will be able to tell the difference between our two stores.

Best,
Mark

From: Fawn Birchill
Sent: Fri, May 24, 2019 at 2:36 PM
To: Mark Nilsen
Re: Signs

Mark,

I am too busy to be dealing with these petty matters. I have customers to attend to. However, since I am a good steward of the neighborhood, I will address your blossoming accusations. Are you positive one of your employees saw Jack in the trash? We only took your signage once, and I went through the trash myself. I didn't realize there was anything wrong with doing that at the time until you threatened to call the police, so why would I make the mistake of doing it again?

Do you think I am mad? I will have you know that Jack is from Chestnut Hill and extremely wealthy and would never lower himself to pick through the garbage. Also, anything Jack does in his free time is something that I cannot control. He is a free spirit for sure—a quality that I believe you and I can relate to.

Also, I find it abhorrent that you accuse me of copying you by decorating the front of the store with plants. I didn't realize that the Grumpy Mug patented the act of decorating with plants. Congratulations for this achievement, and I do apologize! I will remove them immediately and also inform Thirtieth Street Station and every restaurant in Philadelphia to bring them inside or face the wrath of Mark Nilsen! It is spring, Mark. Plants grow in the spring. To think that I am emulating your business model is ridiculous, as I was here first and have been putting plants in my storefront from the very first year I opened. It is embarrassing how you have copied my business model from day one, and you further mortify yourself by turning the tables and accusing me of copying you! Thank you; I needed a good laugh today.

Fawn

From: Fawn Birchill
Sent: Fri, May 24, 2019 at 4:56 PM
To: Jack Grisby
Subject: Macaroni Salad

Jack,

I couldn't help myself and decided to make macaroni salad anyway! If you do not want to bring it home tonight since you will be riding your bike and then taking public transportation home, I would be happy to deliver it to the party myself on the way out to my father's drab Memorial Day festivities. I wouldn't stay more than a few minutes!

Fawn, Owner

From: Jack Grisby
Sent: Fri, May 24, 2019 at 5:15 PM
To: Fawn Birchill
Re: Macaroni Salad

Hi Fawn,

Okay I'll take it. Thankyou! I'll put it in my back pack and bring it home after work.

Jack

From: Fawn Birchill
Sent: Fri, May 24, 2019 at 5:35 PM
To: Jack Grisby
Re: Macaroni Salad

Jack,

Do not put the salad in your backpack. As it is in a glass Pyrex bowl with some plastic wrap over it, I believe it would not be a wise move. Within minutes, it will surely spill onto your laptop and books. I sincerely hate Tupperware and all plastic containers in general, and I throw them all out the very first chance I get. I hate them so that I do not even give them the benefit of being recycled! Ha ha! Also, I have lost the rubber lid to the Pyrex bowl, so I must resort to plastic wrap. Please return the bowl after the party.

Many thanks,
Fawn, Owner

May 25

Dear Rainbow,

It's fine that you are learning lock-picking skills, but please refrain from your practice during store hours, as customers need to be able to leave. I noticed that the door was locked from the outside earlier today—a truly problematic pickle we found ourselves in. I was able to guide a customer through the back, and thankfully he seemed to have a good sense of humor about it, but not every customer may see it that way.

Many thanks,

Fawn, Landlord

●●

May 27, 2019

Jack took the macaroni salad and should be enjoying it by his pool right about now. I am thinking about poor Mother surrounded by the family, the stench of the halls, and the smell of burned meat. Though I do not envy her, I can't help but think that it would have been nice to see Florence's little boys, especially the increasingly talented Little Joe. And I'm honestly not sure how much in decline Father is, having only heard it from Mother and Florence, but I would like to see it for myself. Perhaps we could have talked. About what I'm not sure since he was never much of a talker, but I think just sitting there with them and having the freedom to go when I wanted to would have been nice tonight.

I, for one, have snuck onto my roof and am sitting with a bottle of white wine. The sun has begun its descent behind me in the west, and before me I can see the city in its silhouetted grandeur. The Comcast building, the Cira Centre, those hilarious Commerce buildings that look as if they have little horns and . . . all the others that I cannot identify. And somewhere in Chestnut Hill there is a party the likes of which perhaps even Gatsby would envy. For once I would like to be the envy of someone. It troubles me that even someone like Jack could be worthy of envy, simple as he is. But don't we all strive to live happily and simply? Money complicates all things. If Father weren't so strict with money when we were growing up, Florence and I might have had a normal upbringing. Everything we did revolved around frugality. And at times it was downright detrimental. I am reminded of family road trips when my father would refuse to let any of us eat until we arrived at the destination because he thought roadside stops were a total waste of money. Angrily he would hunker over his steering wheel as the three of us complained, knowing that we had hours yet to go in the car. We flew by Roy Rogers after Roy Rogers until I became resentful of Roy, hating the very sight of his establishment. How bitter I was toward all the other families going in and getting themselves pretzels or sandwiches.

During one particular trip I needed to pee terribly, so I told my father. He didn't like stopping for anything, not even bladders, but I began to cry and wail, so I gave him very little choice. He pulled off the highway, and I snuck off into the bushes only to find myself surrounded by blueberries! I picked them, loaded them into my shirt, and took them back to the car. Only after my sister and I had begun gorging ourselves on them did my father ask us what we were doing back there. He promptly lost control of his vehicle after realizing that we were not eating blueberries but enjoying some poisonous pokeberries. As we were on the western border of Pennsylvania, I innocently assumed they were a different variety of blueberry and not another type of berry altogether. Imagine my surprise! My father pulled over and made me knock all the berries onto the ground. By then Florence had begun to cry and ask if she was going to die. By the time we reached the emergency room, we started getting terrible diarrhea. We lost hours on the road, and Father was beside himself for having to pay the astronomical emergency room fees. Mother was furious at our father for not allowing us to eat and then subsequently causing me to take desperate measures. But that is the way I am and always shall be. I am a survivor.

There is some smoke off in the distance, southeast. I hope it isn't a fire. I find that spring tends to make things go a bit sideways in this city.

I can hear Jane moving around in her apartment. Just a walk across the room is a death-defying stunt. I think I'll go check on her since it looks like it might rain anyway. Speaking of stunts, Rainbow is off performing a show at a youth center in South Philly right about now. It is her first official paid gig in a long time, so she was both excited and nervous all day today. Leading up to this event, she had been using me as a mock audience member. To date she has disappeared Bert, some of my books, and my personal laptop. Rest assured that they were returned moments later but in a flourish of cloth and fire. I cautioned her afterward that Bert is quite flammable and that it probably isn't the best trick to do on live animals, but she reiterated her professionalism. Additionally, Jack has been an enormous help to her during his downtime at the store. I often hear the two of them cavorting and can't help but emerge from my quarters and watch. He simply can't get over her tricks and insists she repeat them so he can catch any faults, but alas he cannot catch any. He once spent five minutes examining Rainbow's thumb after she pretended to cut it off. There was no blood or sign of injury, but still he insisted she must go straight to urgent care. Eventually, to assuage his mounting concern, Rainbow agreed to go. Jack kindly footed the bill, but along with that came the inevitable embarrassment. Apparently the doctor, after hearing the story, was not amused and, according to Jack, "yelled at me a little for wasting his time."

Despite my excitement for her, I do wish Rainbow were here, as she, Jane, and I have such fun together. Yes, perhaps I will see how she's doing. Even though we don't have any tapes to watch (because I'm pretty sure I sold every one of them), I'm sure there is something worthwhile on cable.

From: Fawn Birchill
Sent: Tue, May 28, 2019 at 9:09 AM
To: Jack Grisby
Subject: Floorboards

Jack,

Due to the rains last night and the leak in my roof, my floorboards are soaked and warping in the humidity. As I cannot afford a repairman at this time, I am going to hammer the wood back into place and glue it with some wood glue . . . at least until I can afford some help. Please man the register this morning and help anyone who comes in.

Hope you had a lovely pool party, and thank you for bringing the leftovers. It will be nice to have five-star cuisine at lunch today after crawling around on the floor all morning.

Fawn, Owner

From: Fawn Birchill
Sent: Tue, May 28, 2019 at 12:05 PM
To: Jack Grisby
Subject: Macaroni Salad

Jack,

When going into the refrigerator for lunch, I couldn't help but notice how the macaroni salad had made its way back, completely intact save a few small spoonfuls. You do know that when I asked you to return my bowl, I meant sans food? Was there some confusion on your part, or did people dislike my salad?

Fawn, Owner

From: Jack Grisby
Sent: Tue, May 28, 2019 at 12:15 PM
To: Fawn Birchill
Re: Macaroni Salad

Hi Fawn,

The chief Moritani saw the salad I brought and was very upset because it smelled funny to him and also was next to his oysters and sushi platter. He called it peasant food and said to get that disgusting abomanation off his table so I did I put it in the poolhouse. He was upset after that and didn't look at me for the rest of the day and even when he decided to swim he seemed mad I guess swimming couldn't even cheer him up. ☹

Jack

From: Fawn Birchill
Sent: Tue, May 28, 2019 at 1:04 PM
To: Jack Grisby
Re: Macaroni Salad

Jack,

I can't believe Moritani said such things about my salad! And thank you for not sparing any of the gory details. Those are some extremely colorful words that I didn't think he ever employed. Macaroni salad is not peasant food but a delicious, creamy, filling delight. I greatly apologize for causing such a divide at your event.

Fawn, Owner

● ●

From: Fawn Birchill
Sent: Wed, Jun 5, 2019 at 8:59 AM
To: Florence Eakins
Subject: Hooray for sunny days!

Florence,

Ah, what an exciting time! It has been such a rainy spring that I find myself transformed into a whole new woman on sunny days like this. Currently my employee, Jack, is opening the store while I finish my coffee on the roof with my laptop. Mornings like this remind me why I love Philadelphia so much. In late spring, the city glows in the morning heat and the sun beats down on the buildings, sucking up all the dew from the night before. The rivers seem to sigh their vapors up to the sun, blanketing the atmosphere with their questionable contents. Midday a humid smoggy mist falls over everything and walking outside can feel like a sauna, but this is precisely what I love. The heat has always been a welcome sensation for me: like a big hug and not suffocation, as most people see it. Perhaps it is because menopause is hardly affecting me. Who knows? I may never get it and stay young forever! Ha ha!

For sure we will get loads of people in today—perhaps UPenn students that have decided to stay in the city all summer. We have placed a beautiful array of potted plants and flowers out front and have bought all new store signage to grab people as they walk by. My competitor down the street is insanely jealous by the livening up of my store and shows it by accusing me of stealing his posters! As if I would do such a thing.

I am so glad to hear that Memorial Day was enjoyable, and I am so sorry to have missed Little Joe's singing. Please know that you are all welcome here any time. I would love to have you. And tell Little Joe that I won't put him on the spot and make him sing like all his other relatives do each time he visits anyone. I say let the little guy be a kid! For example, Bert is extremely skilled at catching his toys in his mouth. I used to have him do it for customers until one day he realized how degrading it was to be constantly "on" like that, so I believe he purposely "lost" his little toy. Now he just lies around all day and walks off every time a customer approaches him for a pet. This is what happens when we force things. Just a thought!

Fawn

From: Florence Eakins
Sent: Wed, Jun 5, 2019 at 11:12 AM
To: Fawn Birchill
Re: Hooray for sunny days!

Hi Fawn,

Nice to hear from you. I'm really glad you're enjoying the weather. I think I'm going to take a walk during my lunch break—it's been kind of a stressful day here.

Regarding Little Joe, he's the one who insists upon singing all the time. It's not us. It's a little annoying that you think that's something we'd do to him. I'm very protective of my kids and would never be that kind of mom. If you spent more time with us, you'd probably understand that. Sorry if this is harsh. I'm having one of those days.

Flo

From: Fawn Birchill
Sent: Wed, Jun 5, 2019 at 12:34 PM
To: Jack Grisby
Subject: Toilet

Jack,

Please do not use the customer bathroom. I’ve told you, go into my apartment and use my toilet. And do not blame this mishap on the macaroni salad. If your stomach is so sensitive that you can’t handle a little pasta and canned tuna, then you have bigger problems.

Fawn, Owner

From: Fawn Birchill
Sent: Wed, Jun 5, 2019 at 12:56 PM
To: Jack Grisby
Re: Toilet

Jack,

On second thought, I just checked the expiration date for the mayonnaise that I used in the salad, and it looks like it expired last year around this time. I thought it smelled funny a couple of weeks ago but blamed it on being a knockoff mayonnaise brand, not something out of date. I am truly sorry for the inconvenience this has caused on your intestinal system. I suppose it is rather fortuitous that no one at your party ate the salad or you would have all been rushing to the bathroom.

We frugal ones like to keep things a bit longer than we should. Once my father kept a small carton of eggs for months and months until Christmas morning when he decided to surprise us with a scrambled-egg breakfast. Needless to say, we opened our presents between bathroom breaks.

Fawn, Owner

From: Tabitha Birchill
Sent: Fri, Jun 7, 2019 at 5:46 AM
To: Fawn Birchill
Subject: State of mind

Dear Fawn,

Are you doing all right? I tried calling you yesterday, but you didn't pick up. It's been a long time since I've heard your voice. I don't know why you are wondering about the fact that we never bought you a pool when you were a child. It was a long time ago.

If you must know, it was because your father was frugal. I tried to convince him to buy one since you were both such hard workers, but he wouldn't listen. We took you to the Jersey Shore quite often because we thought it was important you experienced swimming and the only cost was fuel and a quick lunch. Cheaper than buying and maintaining a pool, by far.

I heard there was another building collapse in the city. Was it anywhere near you?

In the coming weeks I'm going to be a bit busy with things, but perhaps I can pop in one day after that?

Love you,
Mother

From: Fawn Birchill
Sent: Fri, Jun 7, 2019 at 6:00 AM
To: Tabitha Birchill
Re: State of mind

Mother,

Thank you for your concern, but I'm having a hard time understanding it, as it seems to have come entirely out of the blue. Once again, I must remind you that the one time you came to visit me, you showed up unannounced as if to intentionally catch me in the state in which you found me. I must reiterate that I was on my way to dinner and was having a whirlwind of a busy day. Instead of springing visits on me, perhaps it would be better to plan something. I know you are capable of doing that with Florence almost every weekend.

Thank you for answering my question about the pool. It is funny how finances always got in the way of things growing up when Father ran a mildly successful general store. Yes, I do remember our car trips to the Jersey Shore. It was always the town of Brigantine that we went to, as it was a stone's throw from the Atlantic City casinos where Father could hopefully win back the gas money he spent getting there. He always ended up losing more, however, and wandered back to the car defeated, telling us all rather angrily to "get in, trip's over." And how we cried! And how you remained cold and silent the entire way. Don't you think, in retrospect, that it would have been much easier had Father only bought us an aboveground pool?

Fawn

P.S. Yes, there was another building collapse, but everyone is okay. It happened way over in Northern Liberties, nowhere near my home. I believe the rain has weakened the underground structures of many of the older buildings.

From: Albert Collins
Sent: Fri, June 7, 2019 at 6:10 AM
To: Fawn Birchill
Subject: Regarding A Visit

Good afternoon,

Though we are very pleased to have received an offer to read in your store as well, we are going to politely decline, as Mr. McEwan has quite a full schedule already. I do hope you will stop by, however, and see him at the Grumpy Mug, as you say your store is just down the street.

Cheers,
Albert Collins

From: Fawn Birchill
Sent: Fri, Jun 7, 2019 at 6:40 AM
To: Albert Collins
Re: Regarding A Visit

Mr. Collins,

Thank you so much for responding to my query, though it was less than what I had hoped to garner. It seems silly that you are not willing to allow him another brief appearance at a store that is literally steps away from the one he is officially visiting. How about you ask him directly instead of dictating his every move? Perhaps Mr. McEwan would be interested in doing this, and you are so stuck in your ways that you are unable to see this. And I do understand that if he were to go visit every single bookstore in the vicinity, he would never go home. But please rest assured that we are the only two bookstores in the neighborhood, so it would only be two stops.

Please reconsider?
Fawn

From: Fawn Birchill
Sent: Fri, Jun 7, 2019 at 7:30 AM
To: Jack Grisby
Subject: When you get in

Jack,

Please take the stack of cards I left on the counter by the register and hand them out in front of the Grumpy Mug. They are discount cards for coffee and a book. As I was up on my roof the other night, I realized that people coming from the east are distracted by his store and never make it to mine, so this will be a good way of reminding them of our presence.

I believe Mark can't be upset if you stay on the sidewalk.

Many thanks,
Fawn, Owner

From: Jack Grisby
Sent: Fri, Jun 7, 2019 at 10:00 AM
To: Fawn Birchill
Re: When you get in

Hi Fawn,

Rainbow and I stood outside and handed out the cards and when it wasn't working she did magic tricks and put the cards in there pockets for them to find later. She is so talented omg.

Jack

●●

June 10, 2019

I woke up this morning to discover fresh graffiti on the side of my building. This has never happened before, so I can't help but wonder if it wasn't Mark or one of his jealous employees. I asked Rainbow about it, but she had her door shut all night while working on an "illusion to go down in history," so she was no help whatsoever.

The graffiti itself looks pedestrian and amateur, and it does bear the telltale signs of one who does not do this often. It's really quite a way to wake up on an otherwise beautiful day: get the newspaper, then turn back to your home to see derogatory slang in bold letters sprayed across your siding. To whoever is reading this, please do not judge me. If you have paid any attention to my woes thus far, you would understand that I am at my wit's end here and honestly knew not what else I was to do. Also, I am not a morning person. So I took a can of red paint from the basement and an old brush and walked over to the Grumpy Mug, still in my bathrobe, and wrote "LOWLIFE" in large, bold letters across his building. As I was halfway through, even at that early-morning hour, a tour bus passed and I immediately regretted choosing such a long word. I simply couldn't just leave it at "LOWL" so I hastily finished and ran back inside to the safety of my fort.

I cannot believe that it has come to this. After the vandalizing, I tried to read my newspaper in peace but the graffiti, now on both of our buildings, would not leave my thoughts. It was all I could do not to pace around the room and check the windows.

And then, at about 7:30, Mark rode up on his bike. Through the window, I could see the look on his face change from pleasant to livid bafflement. He immediately turned to my store, and I ducked away from the window so quickly that the act of flitting away was almost as obvious as if I had been standing on the front lawn with a megaphone telling him I did it. That said, he must not have seen me and went inside. He emerged about twenty minutes later with a can of white paint.

Honestly, what is the world coming to that people are so vindictive? Why should I have to deal with this kind of jealous, petty behavior when all I want to do is sell books? And why should I have to suffer the slings and arrows of my customers' judgments on my broken stair, toilet, windows, and floors? Often I feel like John Proctor in The Crucible *or Shylock in* The Merchant of Venice, *desperately trying to make a case for myself before people who have already made up their minds. Selling books used to be such a simple, happy venture for me.*

●●

THE CURIOUS CAT BOOK EMPORIUM

Blog Post #5
Employee of the Year

And the winner is . . . Jack Grisby!

This month we looked back on the year and the many achievements and milestones to determine who among Fawn's employees deserved this illustrious award. It was easy for the committee to decide the winner—not because everyone else is terrible but because Jack is so exemplary, generous, and passionate in his work. He puts everything into the Curious Cat Book Emporium, as if his life depended on it—and we assure you it does not, as Jack is very well-off, with an in-ground pool and an outdoor poolside rum bar, to only name a few of his family's attributes.

So we reward Jack with a certificate, a ten-dollar gift card to the wine store, and a twenty-five-dollar gift card to the Curious Cat Book Emporium. Spend it wisely!

From: Jack Grisby
Sent: Tue, Jun 11, 2019 at 2:12 PM
To: Fawn Birchill
Subject: Rainbow emergecny

Hi Fawn,

Rainbow was doing contorshin stuff on the staircase and now her head is stuck between the banisters and I don't know what to do. I tried olive oil and coco-nut cream but it didn't work. Can you come downstairs to help her.

Jack

From: Jack Grisby
Sent: Tue, Jun 11, 2019 at 2:15 PM
To: Fawn Birchill
Subject: She's okay

Hi Fawn,

Never mind she got her head out. We are going to clean the oil and lotion off the banister now.

Jack

From: Fawn Birchill
Sent: Tue, Jun 11, 2019 at 2:40 PM
To: Jack Grisby
Re: She's okay

Hi Jack,

I'm sorry I missed this, but I'm glad she's okay. Were there any customers in the store when this happened?

Many thanks,
Fawn, Owner

From: Jack Grisby
Sent: Tue, Jun 11, 2019 at 2:48 PM
To: Fawn Birchill
Re: She's okay

Hi Fawn,

Yes, there were four I think and one helped to try to pull her head out and that's when it came unstuck so I thanked him very much and gave him a discount on his book I hope that's okay.

Jack

From: Fawn Birchill
Sent: Tue, Jun 11, 2019 at 3:01 PM
To: Jack Grisby
Re: She's okay

That's fine, Jack. I would have done the same thing myself.

Many thanks,
Fawn, Owner

● ●

June 14, 2019
There is an update on the graffiti. I am embarrassed to write this, but I believe it's important that I acknowledge (even if I don't admit it to Mark) that there has been a slew of vandalism this month in West Philadelphia. Authorities are saying that homes are being targeted and the culprits are most likely kids off school, punchy from the heat and bored with nothing to do.

Apparently the graffiti itself isn't gang related but instead, as I previously opined, amateurish and laced with childish profanities, which points to bored high school kids. Luckily for me, Mark has assumed it was one of the kids.

So yes, I made a bad judgment call by immediately accusing Mark. But with all that he has done, is it really so impossible for me to think that it could have been him? Was that really such a great leap in logic? Still, I really can't believe that I did that.

phillysmallbiz.com
Wed, Jun 19, 2019

Top Review—The Curious Cat Book Emporium
Today when I asked their new employee to help me find *A Moveable Feast*, he took me to the culinary section. I thought maybe he was messing with me, so I was like, "Okay, where is it really?" And he looks at me with this blank expression and goes, "Well, we can order it for you." I would have thought I was being punked, but the kid let me leave without buying anything, so I think his dumbness was for real. Do their employees read at all?

—Brittany G.

phillysmallbiz.com
Wed, Jun 19, 2019

Dear Brittany G.,

I apologize profusely that Jack was not able to show you where we keep *A Moveable Feast*. Please return, and I will be happy to show you. The fact that he took you to the culinary section is perhaps a reflection on the failing education system and not his own lack of interest in literature.

Fawn, Owner, The Curious Cat Book Emporium

phillysmallbiz.com
Wed, Jun 19, 2019

Top Review—The Curious Cat Book Emporium
Um, so their cat scratched me when I tried to remove him from the chair I wanted to sit on. All I did was pick him up by the scruff like a mother cat, and he totally freaked and drew blood! Why are they letting violent animals interact with customers?

—Stefanie C.

phillysmallbiz.com
Wed, Jun 19, 2019

Dear Stefanie C.,

I must ask that you first look to your choice of actions regarding Bert, and do not blame him outright for lashing out at you, as you say. I have known this cat to be nonviolent ever since he came into my life. Sometimes he is found curled up on one of our many chairs, as is his customary habit. If you want to sit in one of those chairs, you have two options: you may either sit in another chair or wait for him to leave the current chair. Pushing him off the chair or grabbing him by the back of the neck and dragging him down are not options. I have never had to ban anyone from my store except the year I opened when an older man came in and regularly slept and urinated on one of the couches (it has since been reupholstered); however, I may need to add another notch to my belt. So that I may sufficiently ensure that you will not come back and harm Bert again, what is your full name, please? Your PSB photo is blurry—perhaps on purpose?

All the best,
Fawn, Owner, The Curious Cat Book Emporium

From: Fawn Birchill
Sent: Wed, Jun 19, 2019 at 7:24 PM
To: Mark Nilsen
Subject: Warning: Cat Bully

Dear Mark,

A phillysmallbiz.com user that goes by the name of Stefanie C. came into my store, threw Bert off his couch, and then complained that he lashed out at her and scratched her. I know Bert to be harmless except to mice, so I take her story rather skeptically. I wanted to warn you about her and to ask that you watch her closely if she comes into your store and interacts with your cats. She might be cruel to them as well and then act surprised when they defend themselves. Looks like this woman might be running a racket where she goes to stores, gets "hurt" by the animals there, and requests reparations. She hasn't yet gone that far with me, but I fear she might so I wanted to give you a fair warning.

Best,
Fawn

From: Mark Nilsen
Sent: Wed, Jun 19, 2019 at 8:09 PM
To: Fawn Birchill
Re: Warning: Cat Bully

Hi Fawn,

Thanks so much for the heads up on this. It's a shame people behave this way.

Best wishes,
Mark

••

From: Fawn Birchill
Sent: Tue, Jul 2, 2019 at 4:09 PM
To: Mark Nilsen
Subject: Apologies

Dear Mark,

Though we spoke briefly, I wanted to also express my apologies in writing. In no way did I ask that Jack go into your store and, when the coast was clear, take down your Ian McEwan sign only to put it up in my store window. This preposterous idea is only something that could have come from the—dare I say—simple mind of this young man. He means well, so I ask that you please forgive him. Because his actions do secondarily represent my store, please forgive me as well.

I hope the sign has been returned in a favorable condition.

Best,
Fawn

July 3, 2019

I worry that Jack winning the employee of the year award has inspired him to take extreme measures in the betterment of this store. It's one thing to go through the garbage to retrieve old unwanted signage, but it's quite another to go to the Grumpy Mug in the middle of the day and take their posters out of the windows. The saddest thing in all this is that, just like the time he ran the Brillo pad over my wood floors, he has no idea what he did wrong. To reprimand him would be like reprimanding a dog for eating his own vomit—it's just in his nature. And it is in Jack's nature to care so greatly about what he is involved in. I believe it is something he inherited from his parents who are nothing but philanthropic.

In a way, Jack did a good thing in that he forced me to face my fears. These many months I have been avoiding that store, refusing to step inside out of fear that I might just love it.

The place simply struck me. I don't know how else to put it. Stepping inside is like stepping into the comfort of your own home. Virtually everyone is friendly. It is well staffed and well organized, and it smells of coffee and paper. Once in a while, interrupting the jazz or classical music, one can hear the espresso machine brewing. I was lucky enough to see all five cats and found them to be absolutely adorable, calm, and friendly. One cat that, according to her collar, goes by the name of Scooch, came up and sat beside me on one of the sofas. She is a longhaired black cat with a white mark on her chest. She simply sat beside me and stared at me, as if peering into my soul. I pet her for some time while leafing through a coffee-table book on Australia. The other cats—Hero, Captain Flint, Lilly, and Shadow—walked by, their tails swishing with purpose. I didn't get a chance to meet them all, but one of the employees was kind enough to tell me their names.

I gave this same employee the stolen sign and asked to speak to Mark, who promptly came down from the second floor to greet me.

He said, "Scooch is never so friendly. She must really like you." It thrilled me to get such a compliment. I immediately apologized for the stolen sign. If he was upset, he didn't show it.

After finishing my business there, I didn't want to leave. And when I walked back up the street to my store and looked at it, trying to see it as a customer and not as a biased owner, something overcame me. It was a sense of desolation—

as if while everyone else went one way, I had taken a wrong turn and found myself abandoned on a middle-of-nowhere road. Rainbow was performing tricks outside at the time and must have sensed my sadness, because she approached me and produced a bouquet of plastic flowers from her mouth. What a kind, thoughtful gesture. She insisted that I keep them, and so they are sitting with me at my kitchen table as I drink a glass of wine.

Sometimes I can't help but see the similarities between Mark and me. Like me, he clearly cares deeply for his business, and so how can I blame him? If the circumstances were different—if we weren't directly down the street from each other, if he didn't make it so difficult—it's possible we'd get along, but I'm afraid I'll never know this for sure. I believe we are kindred spirits, caught on different sides of the battle lines. But alas, battle we must.

THE CURIOUS CAT BOOK EMPORIUM

Blog Post #6

A Tale of Two Kitties!

For our second entry of the month we will compare and contrast the late and beloved Butterscotch and the lively Bert!

	Butterscotch	**Bert**
Hair	Tawny	Gray
Tail	Curly	Fluffy
Meow	High	Low
Friendly?	Yes	Yes
Attack ct. (mice)	5+	3
Attack ct. (customers)	None	1 (questionable validity)
Sleeping place	Books	Chairs, the couch
Food	Everything	Olives, hot dogs
Favorite story	*Madame Bovary*	*Snakes in Suits*
Favorite show	*Murder, She Wrote*	Anything with pandas in it

●●

From: Fawn Birchill
Sent: Thu, Jul 4, 2019 at 3:03 PM
To: Tabitha Birchill
Subject: Father

Dear Mother,

I'm sorry I missed your call, though I wish you hadn't left that message and instead just simply asked that I call you back immediately. And now, after several tries, I cannot seem to get through to you. Can you please tell me when the funeral will be? Will it be Catholic to align with how he was raised, or will it be born-again?

Perhaps we should bury him with his Pendleton blanket? I think he might like that. Call me please.

Fawn

July 4, 2019
My father is dead. My father is dead. My father is dead. My father is dead.

July 4, 2019 (More)
I find it rather humorous and a bit ironic that I am surrounded by books with mostly clean old-fashioned conclusions—where the protagonist struggles against a great burden, is forced against an immovable object, but in the end manages to overcome, to break free and rise above. Or perhaps like in some of my Russian novels (take Nabokov, for example), the protagonist manages to give in to selfishness and childishness and is ultimately crushed under their own hubristic weight. But here, in the real world, we just keep living. Living until we expire. This is the irony: that I live

surrounded by these fantasy-filled, tidy ribbon-and-bow stories where all is either figured out or dashed upon the rocks, and here I must continue to idly muddle through. It's very anticlimactic, being human. Existing not as a grandiose character in a story but as a mere living and breathing animal with veins and gray hair and a bad back.

I sit here in the afternoons, listen to the somber groaning of this building, and eat my ham sandwich lunch to the sobering melody: groan . . . creak . . . groan! Sometimes I put on Mozart. Sometimes a customer falls in through my doors (I call it falling these days because that's the way they now appear to me, as if they've been sucked through a multidimensional wormhole, baffled and horrified to have found themselves here), but mostly it is just the wind I hear, howling through the cavernous empty aisles of my fallen empire. And then, to that terrible groaning, I crawl into bed and hope that I have paid all my bills for the month and that nothing has slipped by. Not exactly the stuff of Nabokov or even Dickens—certainly not Faulkner!!

I have enough left in my savings account to sustain me for three more months.

No one wants to live life ignored. I admit that it is much easier to deal with when it is coworkers or fellow business owners than when it is my own family. But I don't care. I don't care at all. I have learned to accept it and pretend I don't see it and wear it as an invisible cross and lug it around at family functions while everyone fawns over Florence and never me, never me, it's never ever going to be me.

● ●

From: Jack Grisby
Sent: Fri, Jul 5, 2019 at 9:32 AM
To: Fawn Birchill
Subject: Book Shelf Collaps

There was a book shelf collaps this morning. All the books fell. I can't find you what do I do? Also can't find Bert hopefully he's not underneath.

Jack

From: Fawn Birchill
Sent: Fri, Jul 5, 2019 at 9:39 AM
To: Jack Grisby
Re: Book Shelf Collaps

Jack,

For now, please stack the books in a pile until I find a solution. Please take the broken shelf outside for trash. Bert is with me, so nothing fell on him, thankfully. And *collapse* is spelled with an *e*.

Fawn, Owner

THE CURIOUS CAT BOOK EMPORIUM

Blog Post #7
Did you know . . . ?

In this blog entry, we will go through a typical day at the Curious Cat Book Emporium!

At 7:30 I awake, and after a brief beautification session, I have toast, yogurt, and orange juice. I then feed Bert, the cat, and head downstairs to the bookstore. Jack usually arrives at eight, and together we turn on the music (classical) and open the windows if it's a nice day. Jack rolls the discount books onto the sidewalk, and when that's done, he counts inventory. After lunch Jack chooses a section and makes sure it is properly alphabetized while I assist customers. Sometimes I will help Jack with memorizing his lines for a play he is in if we are having a slow moment, though slow moments are quite rare. Toward evening Jack wheels the discount books back in (those that haven't been sold), then we lock up the store and close the windows. Sometimes, when we are feeling extra energetic, Jack and I will do a quick dusting and cleaning, occasionally breaking into raucous dance—twirling through the store, dust flying, Jack careening down the spiral staircase while I pirouette and sashay through the aisles laughing and singing like a child. I doubt many stores have the kind of fun that we do. We may not be rich, but at least we have a blast surviving!

● ●

From: Jack Grisby
Sent: Mon, Jul 8, 2019 at 7:23 AM
To: Fawn Birchill
Subject: Coyotes

Hi Fawn,

Omg did you hear the coyotes last night? They woke me up and then I couldn't sleep so I just watched Big Bang Theory under my blanket because they are so scary omg.

Jack

From: Fawn Birchill
Sent: Mon, Jul 8, 2019 at 8:40 AM
To: Jack Grisby
Re: Coyotes

Jack,

No, I don't think you were hearing coyotes, especially if you live in Center City. Have you ever heard of Occam's razor? Most likely, there were just a few wise guys having fun last night outside your apartment.

It's a nice day, so please wheel out the cart for the sidewalk sale. Include the romance novels. They smell a bit like urine, but it's harder to detect outdoors.

Fawn, Owner

From: Jack Grisby
Sent: Mon, Jul 8, 2019 at 8:45 AM
To: Fawn Birchill
Re: Coyotes

Fawn,

Maybe they were coy dogs or just half wild dogs though I don't know the difference between them and then also wolves do you? I'm still freaking out a little today from it sorry if I seem adgitated.

Jack

From: Fawn Birchill
Sent: Mon, Jul 8, 2019 at 9:01 AM
To: Jack Grisby
Re: Coyotes

Jack,

Coyotes are coyotes, and coydogs are the children of coyotes and domesticated dogs. Don't quote me on that, but I'm fairly certain it's true. I grew up in the suburbs, and we sometimes heard them at night. I promise you: they are neither in Center City nor in Philadelphia at all. Are you this scared of regular dogs as well?

Fawn, Owner

From: Jack Grisby
Sent: Mon, Jul 8, 2019 at 9:05 AM
To: Fawn Birchill
Re: Coyotes

Yes because when I was three a mastiff bit me on the face when my mom said I should say hi to it. That's why I have the scar on my chin which I hate but my dad says it makes me look like Harrison Ford.

Jack

From: Fawn Birchill
Sent: Mon, Jul 8, 2019 at 9:10 AM
To: Jack Grisby
Re: Coyotes

Jack,

The mastiff was probably just as scared of you as you were of it. The only reason it bit your face was because you frightened it. I don't understand why your mother thought it was a good idea to have a three-year-old crawl up to a full-grown mastiff, but that's probably why I am not a parent.

That scar makes you look tough, by the way. I wouldn't be shy about it.

Fawn, Owner

●●

July 8, 2019

Jane's daughter just left. Needless to say, she paid me only a brief visit, announcing that thieves have been robbing her mother of her belongings. Of course, Jane and I acted shocked the entire time. The woman can be quite the actress when she needs to be. I talked her daughter out of calling the police, stating that it's hard to say how long ago the criminals were here. I wanted to tell her that this is what happens when you live thousands of miles away from your helpless mother and never visit, but I decided to keep it civil. Jane is a most excellent liar because the only thing she lamented missing were her aloe plants. I could tell that it was a manipulation to make the whole thing more believable and to distract her daughter from the greater losses, like the furniture. Her daughter became angry with this and rightfully so. I managed to get two hundred for the end table, and she decides to focus on a few crummy plants! I could barely contain my laughter. Clearly she was getting a lot of joy from seeing her daughter like that, so I just stood back and tried not to burst out laughing. Another thing: her daughter, ever the detective, wanted to know what robbers wanted with aloe plants and Richard Simmons tapes. I told her that maybe it was a band of geriatric thieves from the nursing home on Market Street. Perhaps they sneak out at night, don black eye masks, and steal the elderly's pills, VHSs, and whatever else old people like. Her daughter said that I had been watching too many cop dramas. I actually don't own a television. I watch everything on my Dell desktop downstairs, and I've never been interested in cop dramas. Needless to say, the tension wasn't broken by any humor.

One thing I did tell her was that if she was so concerned about her mother, then she should take care of her in Hawaii—an idea I quickly regretted communicating, as her rent is the only thing saving me from bankruptcy and, admittedly, I have grown to like her company very much. Nearly every night when I'm not too exhausted, I'll poke my head in to check on her and sometimes end up sitting with her for a couple of hours, playing games or watching television. We don't talk much, and I think we both prefer that.

I haven't seen Rainbow in a few days. She insists on no interruptions while she perfects her most "shocking and inspiring illusion to date." Still, I knock to see if she is at least alive, which she is always quick to confirm. I don't want to annoy her, but with all the fire tricks, limb removal, and orifice extraction, naturally I worry.

Ian McEwan is officially not interested in coming to my bookstore, but his representative said he might stop by if he has time. I will have to send out an advertisement letting people know just in case he stops by that week. That should lure in a few wallets.

July 8

Dear Fawn,

Enclosed please find the invitation for Dad's funeral, and please RSVP so that we know how much coffee and food to purchase for the wake. I hope you are doing well after the news of his passing. It has been hard for us all here. Charles and Little Joe won't stop crying, and Joseph and I are struggling in general. This only seems to make things worse. I don't know if I told you, but we are seeking the help of a marriage counselor. It's been a lot of work, and when things like Dad's passing happen, it really tests what work we've done.

Anyway, sorry if this is TMI. It's just a tough time right now. Hope you can make it to the funeral and the wake afterward.

Flo

●●

From: Fawn Birchill
Sent: Mon, Jul 8, 2019 at 7:10 PM
To: Florence Eakins
Subject: Funeral

Dear Florence,

Of course I will be at Father's funeral. I didn't know I needed to RSVP, being his eldest daughter.

I am sorry to hear that you and Joseph are having issues, but I'm sure that things will work themselves out. Two people who are as busy as you don't have time to mope about and wait for things to improve. You will just have to make them. You two should go out on a date. When was the last time you did that together?

Did I tell you Butterscotch died? You and

Mother never ask about him, and it isn't like me to bring things up unprompted, so I'm not surprised if I haven't yet mentioned it. I briefly considered bringing his ashes and doing a combined funeral, but I don't think Mother would allow it. It's a shame how animals, which are sometimes closer to us than any humans, rarely get the same amount of pomp and circumstance upon their deaths.

Regardless, I will be there. See you Sunday.

Best,
Fawn

P.S. I don't have to go up and say anything, do I?

●●

July 8, 2019
Jane has passed.

They say death happens in threes, so I hope that is all I have to endure this year. She did not deserve to be so alone. But then again, I suppose she wasn't, not at the very end. I had gone in as I usually do in the evenings with a bottle of wine and two glasses (her glassware is never cleaned very well), looking forward to a game of gin. I found her in her chair, eyes closed, while a televangelist screamed on the television. I touched her shoulder to wake her, but she didn't wake up. So I put my hand on hers, and it was cold to the touch. I stood there in disbelief for some time, the televangelist shouting in the background about how when you are in heaven you are never alone. Your loved ones surround you, and you will never know sadness. That didn't sound very comforting to me, for what's the point of existing, even in heaven, if you don't feel anything aside from bliss? And without the compass of sadness, how do you even know what real happiness feels like? I shut off the television and just watched her for a little while, profoundly shaken. I poured myself some wine and called the ambulance as well as her daughter, who will be flying in from Hawaii first thing tomorrow. I didn't cry because I thought she didn't want to die, but instead I cried for all the time she sat here alone. Being alone isn't bad unless you don't want to be alone, and I don't. I don't think she did either. And that is why I sat there and wept.

It's funny how, when people die, you think about all the things you didn't get to talk about. Not necessarily what you never said—that's something entirely different—but rather what conversations you never had. For instance, my father and I never discussed penguins or architecture or the Berlin Wall. Not once. If we had, I wonder how different things might have been between us. We never discussed astronomy or politics or literature. Never paintings, never opera. I must admit that he was so wrapped up in getting through every terrible moment, or cherishing the time he could close his eyes and shut us all out, that I have a difficult time mourning him. However, in a funny way, it makes me miss him more. One could argue that it's hard to miss what was never there, but I disagree.

I wish I had gotten to know Jane sooner so I had the opportunity to know her longer. I miss her so much.

●●

From: Florence Eakins
Sent: Tue, Jul 9, 2019 at 7:30 PM
To: Fawn Birchill
Subject: A few words

Hi Fawn,

It would be great if you could say a few words at our father's funeral. After all, you are his eldest daughter.

Flo

From: Fawn Birchill
Sent: Tue, Jul 9, 2019 at 9:08 PM
To: Florence Eakins
Re: A few words

Florence,

As far as many funerals go, they tend to be on the verbose side. Most people want to get in and out as soon as humanly possible, as they are simply too difficult to withstand—especially if you liked the deceased. So I'm smart to the idea of someone asking me to say "a few words," as you well know you'd rather have me give a speech. Yes, I am quite eloquent, being surrounded by literature each day; however, I wish not to participate in the morose proceedings. Not only do I bristle at the idea of public speaking, but also I quite honestly have nothing to say about Father. I can say literally a few words (as you requested), and they would go something like this: "As fathers go, he was an interesting one." And I would leave it at that. Surely you do not want me to speak, for, given our childhood history (something you've managed to squash down into the recesses of your brain), there is little good that I can talk about.

I could mention that after Aunt Tilly took us shopping at the King of Prussia mall and bought us high-end clothing that fit us, Father made her return all of it so we would "stop walking around like little prima donnas." Or the time you had a friend over for dinner and Father wouldn't let her leave the table until she had finished all her peas. Do you remember how she cried afterward? I believe you consoled her by taking Father's toothbrush and rubbing it around inside the toilet bowl. Or all the times he prayed in the checkout line at the grocery store "just to kill time" instead of talking to his daughters like a normal person would. Or the time our cousin from Wilkes-Barre (the smelly one) took me to prom, and when he tried to kiss me and I called Father to pick me up, he didn't believe me and instead left me there with him. Or that time the young marine kept coming around to take you out and Father chased him off with a shotgun. He was actually a decent-looking man. Or, perhaps worst of all, how he made you sit in the back room of the store for years doing the books instead of letting you do your homework while he forced me to clean, run the register, and take deliveries. It's a shame how you forget these things, Florence, and act as if none of it ever happened.

All that said, clearly I have come up with a litany of phrases for his funeral, so if you are in dire need of a speech, I suppose I am your huckleberry.

Fawn

From: Florence Eakins
Sent: Tue, Jul 9, 2019 at 9:41 PM
To: Fawn Birchill
Re: A few words

That's fine, Fawn. You don't have to say anything.

Flo

● ●

July 11, 2019

I have an update on Rainbow. This morning I awoke to find her door ajar. Careful not to disturb her, as I know her work is very sensitive, I snuck over and gently knocked with only the tip of my finger. When she didn't answer, I called to her, but still there came no response. I waited a few breaths and informed her in a kind tone that I was coming in. I only wanted to see if she was all right, as she has had this door securely shut for days and has only emerged to use the bathroom, find food, and dispose of Jellybean's poo.

Ever so carefully I eased the door open, and what I saw nearly knocked me over. I stood at the threshold of her small bedroom to find it completely emptied of her belongings. There was no trace of her and Jellybean; it was as if she was never there to begin with. My heart sank. At first, of course, I thought that she had left in the night, upset with me over something, but she was never the kind of person to take offense to anything at all—a quality about her that I found both rare and refreshing.

So, feeling rather dejected and still reeling over the loss of Jane, I steadied myself on the doorjamb and took some deep, cleansing breaths. I couldn't understand how I managed to lose her, this ray of sunlight in my life. I should have told her sooner how much she meant to me; perhaps then she wouldn't have left. Immediately I thought of Jack and how he wouldn't take her sudden disappearance very well. I walked into her room and stood with my back to the window, trying hard to find a clue—anything that would tell me what the hell had happened—when I noticed an envelope taped to the wall beside the outlet.

Hungrily I opened it to find a letter and one hundred dollars cash enclosed. I would have included the letter verbatim in my journal, but soon you will understand why this was not possible. Unfortunately, I am forced to re-create what I read within. Here is the best my memory can do:

Fawn,

It was such a pleasure staying with you in your lovely home. I enjoyed the time we spent together, as well as meeting and getting to know the late and fabulous Jane. But it is with a heavy heart that I must perform my last great vanishing act and leave this fine place behind. Please know, Fawn, that though we have reached the end of our time together, though the rainbow must eventually fade, there is always another to be admired elsewhere. This rainbow is thrilled to announce that she is currently headed to Atlantic City to perform in her very first casino show. Because of your support and willingness to take me in for not much money at all, I was able to perfect my craft in a way that fits AC's standards. I am closer than ever to reaching my Vegas dream and will forever count you as a dear friend who played an important role in that. I hope my last two months of rent will help as you find another occupant.

All the love and a pot of gold,
Rainbow and Jellybean

If I do say so myself, I think I did pretty well capturing what she wrote before the disappearing ink she used rendered all her words extinct. (Thankfully, the cash did not go the way of the ink.)

I will now tell Jack the news. I know he won't take it well, for I think he might have had a little crush on her.

From: Mark Nilsen
Sent: Fri, Jul 12, 2019 at 8:32 AM
To: Fawn Birchill
Subject: Coffees

Hi Fawn,

I'm a little baffled this morning. I walked in to find two freshly made cappuccinos and two black coffees (the exact drinks that were vanished by your magician friend) steaming on the coffee counter. I was the only person here this morning to open, and after checking last night's footage, I have no explanation for how they suddenly appeared on the counter.

This is kind of freaking me out. I am not accusing you or her of doing anything because the footage definitely proves no one was here. On top of that, the alarm never went off. What do you think?

Mark

From: Fawn Birchill
Sent: Fri, Jul 12, 2019 at 10:16 AM
To: Mark Nilsen
Re: Coffees
Hi Mark,

Rainbow has gone off to AC to perform magic tricks in one of the casinos, so I'm not sure how this is possible. Perhaps she was paying her debts, though I, too, remain entirely perplexed as to how this could have happened, unless you are spinning me quite the yarn. That said, I'm not sure why you'd lie about this.

Equally baffled,
Fawn

PSB Classifieds

1br—800-sq-ft Gorgeous Victorian-Era Apartment—West Philadelphia—$1,200/mo (Utilities Included)

Laundry in the unit. Small balcony off bedroom overlooking a tennis court (not ours, someone else's). No AC, but stays cool in summer. Hardwood flooring throughout. Reliable appliances. No bugs, no bats, and very few mice. Some closet space. No basement access. Great for college student or single person, or perhaps a couple that likes cozy quarters. Lots of sunlight. Kitties allowed!

<LOCATED IN WEST PHILADELPHIA>

Fawn Birchill/*CuriousCatBooks*/1m
Fawn here! The #CCBE: chock-full of personality—literally by the thousands! Come meet them all at the #CCBE!!

●●

To: Jack Grisby >
12:20 PM

Funeral started. How is everything going?

To: Fawn Birchill >
12:25 PM

OMG A sink hole took store

To: Jack Grisby >
12:30 PM

What? What do you mean?

To: Jack Grisby >
12:35 PM

Is it gone? Get Bert!

To: Fawn Birchill >
12:36 PM

Why?

To: Jack Grisby >
12:37 PM

WHY?? Don't ask why, just get him! I am leaving.

To: Jack Grisby >
12:38 PM

Are u okay? Sry I didn't ask!

To: Jack Grisby >
12:38 PM

Jack???

● ●

From: Mark Nilsen
Sent: Mon, Jul 15, 2019 at 7:16 AM
To: Fawn Birchill
Subject: Thank you

Hi Fawn,

Writing from home today—if I was in the area I would stop by, but it's hard to come up there right now. I just want to say again, thank you from the bottom of my heart for saving my cats. I honestly don't know what I'd do if I had lost all of them too. I don't know how to repay you or what to really say here. Just know that I'm thinking of you and hoping all the bruises and scrapes that you and Jack have endured heal quickly. You're a really good person. Don't let anyone, especially me, ever tell you otherwise.

See you soon,
Mark

From: Fawn Birchill
Sent: Mon, Jul 15, 2019 at 9:09 AM
To: Mark Nilsen
Re: Thank you

Mark,

You need not thank me, but instead thank Jack. If he hadn't texted me and made me think my own store had fallen into a hole, I probably wouldn't have run from my father's funeral to try to rescue the store. Imagine my fright!

Anyway, the cats' agility and Jack's quick timing really had everything to do with it. And then, climbing over fallen shelves that had poured onto the street, retrieving the animals, grabbing them by the scruff of their necks and pulling—I have never felt more useful in my life. It is a nice feeling, rescuing cats. I should do it more often! Next time, however, I'll try not to get scratched so much.

Yes, I walked away with a few scrapes, and the firefighter who grabbed me off that one shelf certainly gave me quite a bruise, but it was all worth it! My bad back didn't even cry out in protest. Even when the fireman yelled at me and said that what Jack and I were doing was extremely idiotic and dangerous, I didn't regret a moment of it. I am so happy that we were able to save all five cats, even though most of your books were lost. Still, just think if you were open on Sundays. You might have lost not only books but all your loyal customers to the hellmouth. What a thought!

It is oft believed that firemen are the ones who save cats from precarious circumstances, but alas, I believe yesterday proved that it is only a fable, for those firemen didn't seem interested in pulling any cats out of the store. I think they were hoping there would be people inside to rescue, so they became bored when they arrived to find there were only cats to save. Either that or all of them are dog people.

I can't imagine the amount of duress you must be under right now. But! You are now in the safety of your home, where you can lick your wounds and hold your cats a little tighter tonight. Tomorrow will be a new day. An obvious notion, but inspiring all the same.

Also, you are young. You will simply take it on the chin and fight another day. Perhaps at another location?

Sincerely,
Fawn

From: Florence Eakins
Sent: Mon, Jul 15, 2019 at 9:40 AM
To: Fawn Birchill
Subject: ANSWER YOUR PHONE!!

From: Fawn Birchill
Sent: Mon, Jul 15, 2019 at 10:03 AM
To: Florence Eakins
Re: ANSWER YOUR PHONE!!

Dear Florence,

After listening to your scathing voice mail, I wish not to subject myself to one of your ranting phone calls. No doubt you made sure that people were around to hear you—another reason I am abstaining from feeding your "heroic," self-righteous displays in front of the family.

I feel as if I am in a position to defend myself for my "troubling behavior," as you put it, at Father's funeral. I wasn't merely "texting," as you say, as if I were an insolent teenager sending love notes. And the fact that you describe my physicality as "fidgety" is insulting at the very least.

I will have you know that halfway through the dreadfully morose proceedings, I received a text from my employee informing me that the store had fallen into a sinkhole. Now Jack, in his haste, failed to give proper context, and I was left to assume that my store had been destroyed when really it was my competitor's store down the street. Still, I didn't know this, so I ran out to save my business, my livelihood, and of course Bert. And you tell me that I was needlessly texting? You tell me that I was rude? I am only sorry that I didn't explain it to you at the time. I wish I had known how important your opinion is, especially since (as you admit) you made sure the entire family knew just how I behaved at “my own father’s funeral.” Feel free to clear my name with the rest of the family. No doubt you will to save face. I’m sure you wouldn’t want me to go around putting out your fire.

Best,
Fawn

••

From: Jack Grisby
Sent: Mon, Jul 15, 2019 at 10:12 AM
To: Fawn Birchill
Subject: Day off

Hi Fawn,

Is it okay if I don’t go to work today and get a tetnis shot? Mom says I need one. How was the funeral? Do you like that I’m using more punctuation?

Jack.

From: Fawn Birchill
Sent: Mon, Jul 15, 2019 at 10:30 AM
To: Jack Grisby
Re: Day off

Jack,

Yes, of course you can. I am sorry you have to go and get a tetanus shot. Let me know how everything goes.

The funeral was fine, thank you. Mother was a wreck and foolishly flung herself over his casket in the middle of church. Who does she think she is, Meryl Streep? The nicest thing my father ever did for her was tell her when she had food in her teeth. I am grateful to have been pulled out of there.

Fawn, Owner

P.S. You are doing a great job on the punctuation. Your emails no longer make me feel as if I'm on a roller coaster operated by Jake Barnes on a bender.

PSB Classifieds

1br—800-sq-ft GORGEOUS, STUNNING Victorian-Era Apartment—on Clark Park —$1,200/mo UTILITIES INCLUDED!!!!

Laundry in the unit! Small balcony off bedroom overlooking a tennis court! Stays cool in summer! Hardwood flooring throughout. Reliable appliances. No bugs, no bats, and rarely mice! Closet space! No basement access. Great for college student or single person, or perhaps a couple that likes cozy quarters! Lots of sunlight! Kitties allowed!

<LOCATED IN WEST PHILADELPHIA>

From: Gregory Harris
Sent: Tue, Jul 16, 2019 at 8:00 AM
To: Fawn Windsor
Subject: Update

Dear Fawn,

That's it; I've done it! I have purchased myself a ticket to Philly, and you better believe a visit to the emporium is on the books. I am very excited to see it and your American counterpart. How are you doing, my dear?

Regards,
Gregory

From: Fawn Windsor
Sent: Tue, Jul 16, 2019 at 11:13 AM
To: Gregory Harris
Re: Update

Gregory,

I am ever so excited that you will be in Philadelphia in August! Not that I will be there to greet you, but that you have solidified your plans. One mustn't go through life never experiencing this city. And contrary to what I told you, Fawn's store is doing so much better because, you see, a sinkhole has taken her nemesis's store. It wasn't a terrible sinkhole where everything was just gone—but it was almost that bad. The back of the store fell in first, causing the front of the store to topple back and out. Fawn and her first mate (as she likes to call him), Jack, ran in and rescued all the cats with expert speed—or so I've been told. The owner truly owes her a great debt of gratitude. And you should have seen him! The day after she rescued his cats, he paid a visit to her store, bringing with him a large bouquet of wildflowers. It was just about the kindest thing that has ever happened to her.

And since then, due to his store's vanishing act, customer volume has gone up! It's funny, when it comes right down to it, how tenuous loyalty can be.

In my news, life is dull. The mornings are hot and foggy, and most days it has rained. I may take a trip to the south of Spain just to get away from this dreadful British weather.

Much love,
Fawn Windsor

●●

Advertisement

BRING YOUR PET TO THE BOOKSTORE DAY!

Stop by the Curious Cat Book Emporium this Saturday, July 20, for our first annual Bring Your Pet to the Bookstore Day! Just because the Grumpy Mug Bookstop is no longer with us does not mean we can't sit around some precious tomes and cuddle with our beloved pets! Every participant gets a free cup of coffee. Free dog treats will also be available.

Animals must be leashed or restrained at all times. They MUST be housebroken. The following animals will not be allowed in the store: snakes, rats, mice, squawking birds, monkeys, hamsters, horses (oversize animals of any kind), and ferrets.

●●

From: Jack Grisby
Sent: Sat, Jul 20, 2019 at 6:45 AM
To: Fawn Birchill
Subject: Animals

Hi Fawn,

I am really worried about today. Will the dogs be leashed? Will they be with their owners all the time? I am really worried about this. Can I stay in the basement.

Jack

From: Fawn Birchill
Sent: Sat, Jul 20, 2019 at 7:46 AM
To: Jack Grisby
Re: Animals

Jack,

There is nothing to worry about. If they "go" in the store, please be ready to clean it. I will, of course, then ask the guilty party to leave.

Fawn, Owner

From: Fawn Birchill
Sent: Sat, Jul 20, 2019 at 7:18 PM
To: Jack Grisby
Re: Animals

Jack,

Thank you for your help and your bravery today. I know being around that little poodle was hard for you. Even though we only had that one participant plus Mark who brought Scooch, it was still well worth it.

Fawn, Owner

●●

From: Tabitha Birchill
Sent: Sun, Jul 21, 2019 at 11:01 AM
To: Fawn Birchill
Subject: Will

Dear Fawn,

I hope you plan to attend the reading of your father's will on the twenty-fourth. If you need it, Florence and I would be happy to pick you up at the train station before and drop you off there after.

Life has been so strange without him. Often when I lie in bed at night, I can still feel the weight of his body beside me, and I can still smell his Preferred Stock cologne. I know he wasn't in bed with me the last few months, but he was at least alive. In my heart I think

I hoped he would come home. But now it is clear he will not, so that missing weight beside me is all the more difficult. I hope that you are faring all right through this. Know that you can always talk to me. I know you had a complicated relationship with him, but he loved you very much—even though he showed it in funny ways.

Love you,
Mother

From: Fawn Birchill
Sent: Sun, Jul 21, 2019 at 2:12 PM
To: Tabitha Birchill
Re: Will

Mother,

Of course I'll be there, although I can't imagine there is much to be gained for any of us. As Father promised, he wanted to give his money to the church, and he keeps his promises. This is the same church that has a brand-new playground, gorgeous facilities, and state-of-the-art sound system for their concerts. The pastor of this same church drives around in a Benz, I believe—or so he did the last time I saw him a few years ago. Is he invited to hear the will as well? He might as well be, since I'm sure he will be reaping the benefits of my late father more than you, Florence, or I will.

Fawn

●●

July 21, 2019

It would be refreshing to hear that Father has given his inheritance to Florence and me, but that would be far too perfect. So it will never happen. With a little money, I could repair the store: fix the rotting foundation, buy a new heating system, eradicate the mold problem, hire a maid, fix the wooden floors, repair the sagging steps on the stairs, repair the shutters, fix the few smashed-in windows, landscape the small lawn outside, buy a nice new sign, purchase some new books to sell. I could turn a corner. I could rise like a phoenix from the ashes of my father's death and be whole again, and Mark Nilsen would be nothing but a blip in the distant dark past. And with all of that, I wouldn't be ashamed to invite Florence and her family over. I wouldn't be ashamed to bring a romantic interest around.

But how could I be ashamed of my little empire? Though it isn't perfect, it is not worthy of shame. It is perhaps a reflection of who I am and what I have worked so hard for, and maybe my great expectations have imploded in my face. But isn't that reality? Do we ever live up to what we thought we would be? And so here I am, but am I ashamed? Was Father ever ashamed? His store was a disaster even in its heyday. And then, those last hard years when he started to cognitively decline and I had to do everything to keep the store running so my parents could pay their bills. And Florence, who did nothing to help but instead found excuse after excuse, hiding behind a voice lesson for Little Joe or a work event at the office. And even in those hard days, my father was not ashamed. He ran his ship into the rocks with more pride than was good for him. And when I didn't want his failing store, it hurt him more than I would ever know. That was to be my inheritance, so the reading of his will is going to be pointless for me because the one thing he ever wanted to give me was that store, and I didn't take it. Instead, I forged my own path, and I know it broke his heart to see that. And a part of me is sorry that I made him feel that way.

●●

From: Jack Grisby
Sent: Mon, Jul 22, 2019 at 8:09 AM
To: Fawn Birchill
Subject: The Sale Cart

Hi Fawn,

The sale cart lost it's wheel. I can't attach it again so I don't know what to do.

Jack

From: Fawn Birchill
Sent: Mon, Jul 22, 2019 at 8:55 AM
To: Jack Grisby
Re: The Sale Cart

Jack,

Simply drag it outside and prop it upright with a book. I'll be down in a moment.

Fawn, Owner

From: Jack Grisby
Sent: Mon, Jul 22, 2019 at 9:07 AM
To: Fawn Birchill
Re: The Sale Cart

But what if someone wanted to buy that book? That is a lost sale. Or if they see it they will pull it out and look at it and then the book shelf will topple maybe. Can I put a not for sale sign on it?

Jack

From: Fawn Birchill
Sent: Mon, Jul 22, 2019 at 9:23 AM
To: Jack Grisby
Re: The Sale Cart

Jack,

I doubt anyone will notice the book and want to buy it if it's shoved under a mobile bookshelf, but if it would make you feel better to put a **NOT FOR SALE** sign on it, then by all means do so.

Fawn, Owner

From: Fawn Birchill
Sent: Mon, Jul 22, 2019 at 11:40 AM
To: Jack Grisby
Re: The Sale Cart

Jack,

Please don't put the sign on the cart itself, as the books within it are most certainly for sale. I have moved the sign and placed it only on the book. Was it like that this whole time?

Fawn, Owner

Fawn Birchill/*CuriousCatBooks*/6m
Outdoor sale today on romance books! Come peruse the Love Cart! Always 20% off!

PSB Classifieds

1br—800-sq-ft GORGEOUS, ELEGANT, SUNNY Apartment—on Clark Park—$1,050/mo UTILITIES INCLUDED!!!!

Laundry in the unit! Small balcony off bedroom overlooking a *tennis court!!!* Can fit a grill!! Stays cool in summer! Antique hardwood flooring throughout! Beautiful appliances! Closet space! Great for college student or single person, or perhaps a couple that likes cozy quarters! Lots of sunlight! Dogs and cats allowed!

<LOCATED IN WEST PHILADELPHIA>

From: Fawn Birchill
Sent: Tue, Jul 23, 2019 at 7:00 AM
To: O'Hare Repair
Subject: Basement Flood

Dear Cahill,

Hello! Remember me? It has been too long—which is a good thing, I daresay, as I haven't needed your services until now! How are the boys? I am requesting a quote for a basement flood. Do you handle those? The rain last night did a number on the basement and ended up saturating nearly every old book that I have stored down there. My employee, Jack, has been wading through five inches of water all day pulling the books out and dragging them up to the empty apartment adjacent to mine for the time being. The water smells terrible, so I wonder if all of it isn't rainwater and perhaps Jack has been wading in some questionable fluids. Can you let me know what you would charge to suck up the water and reinforce the basement so that this does not happen again?

Many thanks!

Fawn, Owner, The Curious Cat Book
Emporium

P.S. You must be making a lot of money this year! Philadelphia has been falling apart at the seams. Did you hear about my neighbor who lost his business in a sinkhole? Tragic!

From: O'Hare Repair
Sent: Tue, Jul 23, 2019 at 8:19 AM
To: Fawn Birchill
Re: Basement Flood

Hi Fawn,

Sorry to hear about your basement issues. I've attached a quote here, but it would probably be best to stop by and give you a quote in person. This estimate is probably on the low end of what it would be. I'd have a better idea if I took a look at it myself. Let me know if you'd like to schedule a time for me to stop by.

Cahill

From: Fawn Birchill
Sent: Tue, Jul 23, 2019 at 10:04 AM
To: O'Hare Repair
Re: Basement Flood

Dear Cahill,

That is simply out of my price range. Is there something else we can work out? Perhaps I can make you a delicious home-cooked meal? Do your boys like reading yet? I have many great books that they can just have for free. Please consider. I have very little to give, but this must be resolved. I believe every day that the water is sitting there, it is ruining the already questionable foundation.

Many thanks,
Fawn

From: Fawn Birchill
Sent: Tue, Jul 23, 2019 at 9:18 PM
To: Jack Grisby
Subject: Shop-Vac

Jack,

Thank you for offering to bring in your Shop-Vac from home. I fear it will be a lot of work, as the basement is enormous. If you are up to it, I would appreciate your effort, but please understand that I cannot pay you.

Fawn, Owner

July 24, 2019
I have left Jack to the mess downstairs, but I fear he will not be able to take care of it all. The books in the now-empty apartment have such a horrible, rotten smell to them. I am tempted to throw them out. It's a minor blessing that no one has responded to my PSB ads for the apartment, since upon entering they would most likely turn

around and leave due to the offensive smell. It is evident, even from the first floor.

I am back from the lawyer's office. Where do I begin? I wasn't surprised to find the pastor sitting there with us, and he was among the appointed beneficiaries along with Florence, my mother, and me. Surprise, surprise, he made out with the jackpot: $14,000 to go toward that pristine church. The pastor, a very nice man who just happens to be wealthy, was humbled and grateful for my father's generosity. I looked at him, hungrily, hoping that he would give the money to the family—the rightful owners, the ones who suffered through knowing Father for fifty-plus years—but alas, it was not in the cards. He just sat back and listened as Florence was bestowed Father's gun rack, worth about $5,000, and I was left with his gold watch and high school ring, worth only about $300. Mother, of course, got the house and apparently a small but helpful IRA that none of us knew about.

I said my goodbyes to everyone and headed for the train station alone, trying not to burst into tears right there on the street. The watch was heavy in my shorts pocket, and his ring barely fit my slender thumb. None of us wanted these things. We didn't want a gun rack or watches or even money. We just wanted a dad.

I'm not sure how I almost missed his store. I suppose I was thinking about too many things, so

I didn't notice that there before me stood the gray, decrepit, boarded-up old building—a building that I had walked to most of the years of my young life but hadn't revisited in over a decade.

His sign had been left up, weathered over the years: **BIRCHILL'S GENERAL STORE**. *The gray-blue paint that my sister and I slapped onto the building during the span of a few weeks over the summer when we were in middle school had nearly chipped completely off. Underneath was the rugged brown skin of bare wood. It almost looked as if it was leaning into the building beside it (a Domino's Pizza), as if it were too weary to hold itself up anymore. And then, it hit me all at once like a stack of falling hardcovers: I wasn't looking at a store. I was looking up at my father.*

I touched the building, and the paint flaked off in my hand. I held my father, small and fragile. That flake of paint, this moldy building that had long belonged to the bank, this thing that no one wanted, was more an embodiment of him than his own skin, or perhaps now, his ashes. I went up to the front door and breathed in the stale air through the tiny cracks. My old life came flooding back to me: boots on the dirty front steps, the creak of the freezer unit door, the cold smell of the stone basement, the ding of the cash register, the distinct staccato laugh of the postman. I sat on the front stoop for a moment, the odor of decades past whirling around in my brain. Images of my father sweeping became so real I could almost see it. The early-morning odor of his cheap coffee wafting through the aisles and out the front door, hanging in my mouth, clinging to my hair. The slam of a new stack of newspapers each morning brought in by Smoking Joe, the delivery guy.

As I sat there, I realized that it wasn't for lack of money that he became the way he did. It was simply the fact that we Birchills don't know when enough is enough. We are too caught up in our memories of what was rather than our dreams of what could be. I certainly don't want to end up with this as my legacy: this husk of a dream that once was, this monstrosity of peeling walls and warped floorboards, of broken windows and a waiting bed in hospice. All my life I've been proving to my father that I'm nothing like him and that I'm better in every conceivable way, but where has it gotten me? My god, I've spent my whole life in a pissing contest with my family. My whole entire life.

And the last thing I want is Florence's little boys to grow up and come across my old building and say, "That Aunt Fawn, she had a nice idea, but can you believe she ended up going mad over it?" No, I don't want to become Miss Havisham—clinging to the hope of a doomed dream.

And in the same way I have clung to this idea, I

have also carried with me the heaviest burden of all: the inability to let the past stay in the past. If I'd had a car, I would have driven to Florence's and then to my mother's and asked if we could all start over again. Here I am, clinging to a bad childhood, letting it sully everything new. Right now, with all my bitterness, I am no better than Jane's awful daughter.

When I returned, Jack had managed to break his mother's Shop-Vac. Surely I'll be paying for that. He thinks it's simply clogged, but the burning smell gives me the impression that he has ruined the motor. I asked him if he was aware that he should be using a filter, and he just gave me that blank look again like he had forgotten something very important.

●●

From: Florence Eakins
Sent: Sat, Jul 27, 2019 at 11:26 PM
To: Fawn Birchill
Subject: Will reading

Fawn,

It has taken me since the will reading to find the words to tell you that I think your behavior was awful. That pastor and his church have been a beacon of light and happiness for our dad for many years, and if he wanted to give him his money then let him.

I don't understand why you never liked Dad. He was a good dad to us. I loved working back there, balancing the books, doing my homework (which I was allowed to do), talking with friends on the phone, and just being a kid. I'm sorry you found the work to be so awful, but you always took things too seriously. Maybe if you had relaxed a little more, you would have seen that he was only showing us important life skills? I know it was probably harder being in the front and dealing with all those customers. I'm not going to pretend that I didn't have it easier, and I know he could be tough on you at times, but he meant well, Fawn.

He did the best he could. I'm sorry that was never good enough for you.

Flo

From: Fawn Birchill
Sent: Sun, Jul 28, 2019 at 10:30 AM
To: Florence Eakins
Re: Will reading

Dear Florence,

I'm sorry I didn't accept the invite to go to lunch with you, Mother, and the pastor, but I just couldn't be around that man for another minute. Mostly my anger was and is directed toward him and not you and Mother, innocent pawns in the game of exuberant and unnecessary monetary gift giving.

I'm a little surprised Father let you talk on the phone with friends and goof around, but I suppose I should have known better. He was always infinitely harder on me for some reason. And yes, I'm sure his intentions were noble—and maybe you were mostly spared the brunt of this—but overall he was about as warm to me as a block of ice. Hardly the definition of a good dad.
Fawn

●●

July 28, 2019

I just ended a phone call with my mother that concluded, oddly, with her apologizing to me. It's a new feeling, being apologized to. It's not something that normally happens for me.

Florence and I both struggled in school due to our respective lack of sleep, but she always struggled more than I did. It was known in our immediate family that I was smarter and worked harder, but I never thought Father paid much attention to this fact. To him, I believed his daughters were faceless, soulless workhorses put on the planet to better him. Little did I know. Florence remained in the back goofing off because Father knew that she'd actually study if put in a boring office with books all around her. And to an extent, it seemed to help. She was rewarded with comic books, candy, and games, while there were no rewards for me. According to Mother, Father believed that I was the one who would make something of myself, and so I was the one who learned how to count inventory, run the cash register, handle the orders, and work with people both face-to-face and over the phone. According to my mother, I was his favorite. I was his pride.

And it hurt him immensely that I never visited as an adult—that I saw those years in that store as pure torture and not a necessary foundation to building work ethic and business acumen. Mother told me not to blame myself because it was his fault he never told me "how special you are" and "how much he loved both of you girls." Though he might have loved me, it would have taken nothing for him to tell me this. I wonder how different things would be now if he had only said the words. If he had embraced me and said he was proud.

I sit here too emotionally drained to bring a glass of wine to my lips. And so instead I'm lying in bed, angry with my father but sad for him too—sad for the man that, because he couldn't open up a smidge, lost his eldest daughter and caused her to lose a father before he was even gone from this world.

• •

From: Fawn Birchill
Sent: Mon, Jul 29, 2019 at 9:29 PM
To: Mark Nilsen
Subject: Idea

Dear Mark,

I'll begin by admitting that I have probably started this email about ten different ways before resorting to this confession, because I truly have no idea how to put any of this into words. And here I am, usually well armed with an arsenal of adjectives and hyperbole! What I can say is that my decision yesterday has made me a bit speechless. Yes, speechless over my own decisions. I find it comforting that even at fiftysomething, I can still surprise myself.

Here goes! Mark, I would like to sell you my store for indefinite use. No doubt you have insurance money for such a venture elsewhere; however, I believe the reason you haven't bounced back so quickly is that it isn't a buyer's market right now. I can imagine that you have been scouting for vacant businesses all over Philadelphia to move into so as not to lose further revenue. I understand how hard it is to go a day without making money, and even though we started out on rather unsavory terms, I can empathize. I will give you my store at an excellent price. I won't lie to you: it needs work. We recently had a basement flood, our heating unit is broken and needs to be replaced, the customer bathroom is a nightmare, and the foundation is questionable. And I admit that there is in fact a rodent problem, but I believe with five cats you can easily take care of it. Bert was helpful in that regard, but he is only one cat and a rather lazy one at that. I'm sure you know of the cosmetic problems with the building: the ruined hardwood flooring, the broken windows, and the chipped paint. You certainly wouldn't be buying perfection. But if you are interested, are you free to meet over coffee, perhaps tomorrow, to work out the logistics?

For decades I fought a cold war with my father, trying to show him that I could excel in business far better than he, but I realize now that if one goes into business out of spite, insecurity, or a selfish drive to be admired, then it will end up in heartache, as it did for me. I had something to prove, Mark. And for many years I felt that I succeeded in that—

that is, until you came along and showed me what it looks like to open a business out of love.

I must apologize for the way I behaved toward you this past year. I don't understand why we, who have such similar appreciations, must be enemies. We should not be pointing cannons at each other across seascapes but in fact should be a fleet, sallying forth into the uncertain waters of the business world. So please, consider my offer. I feel fortunate that I can finally see the good your store has done for this community.

As a side note, I know you couldn't have caused a sinkhole to take your store on purpose, but I must admit that in the darkest of times I have fantasized about setting my building on fire for insurance money. I imagine you get a nice chunk of change and that it is worth it if you don't get caught!

Sincerely,
Fawn

●●

From: Fawn Birchill
Sent: Sat, Aug 3, 2019 at 3:14 PM
To: Albert Collins
Subject: Mr. McEwan's visit

Dear Mr. Collins,

I understand that the reading had to be postponed due to tragic events at the Grumpy Mug; however, I would like you to know that Mark Nilsen has agreed to buy my establishment and will move into my store very soon—in a matter of weeks, I believe. So I am writing to request that you please add the Grumpy Mug back onto Ian McEwan's schedule. Mark does not know that I am writing this to you, for I believe he has given up hope that he could convince such a busy writer to change his schedule under such short notice, but I had to try.

To turn down this opportunity now would almost be adding insult to injury after Mark lost his store to the terrible sinkhole. I know that removing the Grumpy Mug from the tour list would not be an intentionally malicious move; however, I wouldn't be able to see it any other way. Can we all agree that the poor man has lost enough as it is?

Please reconsider,
Fawn Birchill, Owner, The Curious Cat Book Emporium

From: Mark Nilsen
Sent: Mon, Aug 5, 2019 at 8:37 AM
To: Fawn Birchill
Subject: You and Jack

Hi Fawn,

I am officially offering you the job of store manager, if you want it, when you return from your trip. We can work out the details if you are interested, when you get back. For now, don't answer but think about it. There is no rush on the decision. We'd all be really happy to have you. We are also looking forward to fostering Bert while you're away. He will be a sweet addition.

How would you feel about us hiring Jack as well? Would you recommend him? We'll interview him, of course, but I want to get your thoughts on how he is as a worker and as a person.

Thanks so much,
Mark

From: Fawn Birchill
Sent: Mon, Aug 5, 2019 at 2:12 PM
To: Mark Nilsen
Re: You and Jack

Mark,

Thank you very much for the offer. I'm not sure exactly how to respond, be it yes or no, so for now I will simply say thank you. If I return to this fine city, we can take it from there. Also, thanks ever so much for watching Bert while I am away. No doubt he will get along famously with the other five cats, as he is not territorial at all. In fact, he moves so little that sometimes customers confuse him for a throw pillow.

In answer to your second request, yes, it would mean a great deal if you would hire Jack. I am not sure what he will do once I close for good and hand the building over to you. There is a dedication and kindness to him that I cannot explain. It is as if he has no concept of how filthy rich he is, an excellent quality in an employee and in a person. He is very willing to do almost anything to help. He even went through the garbage for me once without hesitation—mind you, it was not to retrieve your posters!

Many thanks,
Fawn

From: Fawn Birchill
Sent: Mon, Aug 5, 2019 at 8:00 PM
To: Gregory Harris
Subject: This is I

Dear Gregory,

I grew up in Pennsylvania, just outside Philadelphia, with a younger sister, an undynamic mother, and an overbearing father. We saw very little of the money my father made from his general store in Norristown and so led very simple, threadbare lives. Put to work constantly, we were forced to wake each morning before dawn and assist him before going to school. There, I would struggle to keep my eyes open throughout the day. Sleep became my favorite thing to do aside from pretending I was someone else, anywhere else. So I must confess that I am not who you think I am. All these years, since our very first exchange through letters, I have been untrue to you.

I have never left the country. I have never really been in love. I have never really been happy. There. Now you know me better than most anyone in the world. I have been ashamed that my business could not live up to the expectations I had put on it, so denial became an easy coping mechanism, as did lying to you about my life. I must admit that I had so much fun writing to you, creating all these wonderful scenarios that I wanted to be true. And I thought that perhaps someday it all would come true. Denial is the gateway to perpetual fantasy, and when you get deep enough into the fantasy, extricating yourself becomes an act of herculean proportions. It took many things to free me from this—things not even worth getting into. However, if you are still planning on coming to Philadelphia to visit the old Curious Cat Book Emporium, I would be truly humbled to have you meet Fawn Birchill. Perhaps then we can get into the nitty-gritty.

Gregory, you are a true friend, but a friend that still barely understands who I am. And that is my disservice to you. Please, consider meeting me. It would be an honor. I am sorry if I've made you angry, and I understand if you have no interest in continuing our correspondence.

Sincerely,
Fawn Birchill

Advertisement

SPECIAL ANNOUNCEMENT

The Curious Cat Book Emporium announces its Going Out of Business Sale this Monday, August 12, through Saturday, August 17. Every paperback 75% off. Every hardcover 60% off. Sales on already reduced prices!! Don't miss out!!

THE CURIOUS CAT BOOK EMPORIUM

Blog Post #8

The Last Entry

Dear beloved customers (especially Sybil C.), fellow local business owners, and friends:

It has been a wonderful run, but with a heavy heart I must say my goodbyes. My life has been so full and rich, but I have found no happiness greater than the satisfaction of opening my store each day. How lucky and privileged I have been to serve each one of you. With my newfound freedom and a little extra cash from the building sale, I may just travel the world, searching out the geographical influences of writers such as Dickens, Conrad, Shelley, and Chekhov, to name only a few. Perhaps I will even write a book on it!

Please do not hesitate to come in and say your farewells as we wrap things up. Feel free to peruse one last time—we will be having some unforgettable sales.

I must stress that this is not a declaration of failure but a new opportunity. As many of you know, the Grumpy Mug Bookstop will be moving into this location and continuing its business as usual after the tragic events earlier this summer forced it to close. So like a phoenix rising from the ashes, we are not ending but evolving. I gave up the silliness of being Wiccan years ago, but I still hold on to the idea that all things are cyclical, ever changing, and therefore never truly ending.

I bid you all adieu and thank you for your years of patronage.

Sincerely,
Fawn Birchill

From: Florence Eakins
Sent: Fri, Aug 9, 2019 at 5:43 PM
To: Fawn Birchill
Subject: The bookstore

Hi Fawn,

Are the rumors true? Mom tells me that you are selling your store and traveling the world or something. Are you sure this is the right decision? I tried calling, but you didn't pick up as usual. What is going on? Is everything okay? Can we talk?

Flo

From: Fawn Birchill
Sent: Fri, Aug 9, 2019 at 6:55 PM
To: Florence Eakins
Re: The bookstore

Florence,

Yes, the rumors are true. I do not have an exorbitant amount with which to travel, but I believe it will be enough to have fun and live a slightly bohemian lifestyle throughout. It would be lovely to live as Hemingway did in *A Moveable Feast*. The last time I read that book, I was filled with jealousy, for all that his protagonist did was drink and talk about literature all day! Clearly, he lived a highly evolved life. Sorry, you are not much of a reader and probably don't know what I am talking about. Moving right along!

It was wonderful seeing you and Mother yesterday, and thank you for the impromptu and delicious barbecue on your patio. I don't think I've ever seen Mother so happy. I'm not sure if it's a direct correlation to our father's passing or just the fact that we were all together with everything finally out in the open. Regardless of the reasons, it was wonderful to see. And it was so nice, as always, to see your boys and husband. It seems that every time I see Little Joe, his voice improves tenfold. He will look back one day and appreciate all that you sacrificed for him so he could reach his goals. Let's just cross our fingers and hope it's not all in vain and that he doesn't become an accountant or something horribly dull like that!

I plan to see many countries and eventually settle somewhere—possibly England. While I'm traveling you are all, as always, more than welcome to visit me. And you're absolutely right. I won't really know if giving up my store is the right decision, nor do I know if it will make me a happier person, but I won't know any of this unless I try.

One day I will return for another visit, but for now I will send you postcards!

Farewell for now, and much love to you and the family,

Fawn

●●

From: Gregory Harris
Sent: Sat, Aug 10, 2019 at 7:18 PM
To: Fawn Birchill
Re: This is I

Hi Fawn,

I'm shocked, but not as shocked as I thought I'd be, as I've suspected something was up through the years. Thank you for sharing this with me. I know it wasn't easy. I know Fawn Windsor's life was glamorous and lackadaisical; however, your life doesn't sound so bad either. I think you are too hard on yourself. And, since we're being honest . . .

It's only fair that I tell you that I am not in real estate. I am a waiter in Old City at this place called Bloo. It's a new joint that serves cocktails that glow in the dark. It's terribly gaudy, and I have to wear iridescent rings around my neck and wrists like a prisoner in some cheap sci-fi movie, but it pays the bills. I always wanted to get into real estate, but it was always too scary a leap to take. Like you, I've never been outside the country except for one bad excursion to Mexico that I should tell you about sometime. I had a crazy boyfriend in my twenties, ha ha. What else? I'm not married, I'm not dating anyone at the moment, and I live in a small apartment in South Philly over a bubble tea joint.

It sure was fun to pretend, wasn't it? I'd still love to meet you. To think we were only a couple of miles from each other this whole time.

Much love,
Gregory

From: Fawn Birchill
Sent: Sat, Aug 10, 2019 at 7:32 PM
To: Gregory Harris
Re: This is I

Dear Gregory,

I don't know what to say. I'm shocked to learn that we've both been playing each other like Stradivarii. I daresay that we've gained much joy from these letters, and now that I know the truth about you, I feel slightly guilty for ending this fantasy. I suppose this means that you never went to Harvard and you don't have an apartment in Paris and a house on the Caspian Sea? For years I have secretly hoped that one day you would take me there, but I suppose it is not in the cards.

Honestly, it does make me feel better that you were always a little suspicious of what I was writing about my life. I admit that it all was a little too rosy. I tried to muck it up with my constant boredom and my family never getting along (true, by the way), but I suppose it wasn't enough.

I am so glad you still want to meet me. Would you like to see my bookstore? It is soon to change hands, but you will be able to catch it in its last days. I am thinking of traveling the world with the money I have made on the building. I won't be able to buy an estate in England with it, but it's better than nothing. Do you know that I've never even been to Canada? Perhaps I will start there as, due to our proximity, there is simply no excuse to skip it.

Fawn

August 13, 2019

I am not sure where I'll go or what I'll do outside of traveling. Just the thought of waking up somewhere else is a bit daunting. No longer seeing the seasons change outside those old drafty windows, nor hearing that familiar creaking in the middle of the night, nor smelling the scent of the lilac bush outside the first-floor kitchen window makes it difficult, and sometimes I just want to break down in tears. But I'm keeping busy in these last days—too busy to think too much about it.

Father would be disappointed. He would see this as admitting defeat, but unlike him I know when to walk away. I don't want his legacy. I don't want to look back on my life and realize that I could have saved myself but didn't out of stubborn pride. It's not always admirable to go down with the ship, contrary to what my father believed, and there was never any question that this ship was going anywhere but down. And though I have no fear of being alone or dying alone among my aloe plants and Kleenex boxes, I will choose not to do it here, in this romantic but drafty place that holds the kind of memories that can stifle a person to death. I have spoken so much of seeing England, but the Dalmatian Coast sounds far too ridiculous to pass up, so I think that will be my second experience after Canada. Much like myself, the most exotic place my father ever traversed was Philadelphia's Chinatown, and that's only because he made a wrong turn. I don't think he even got out of his car. As much as I detested him all my life, I need to do this for him almost as much as I must do it for myself.

Mark Twain is supposed to have said: "Go to

Heaven for the climate, Hell for the company." I have had enough good company, I think. It's time for some fair weather.

From: Fawn Birchill
Sent: Fri, Aug 30, 2019 at 2:08 PM
To: Jack Grisby
Subject: Gold watch

Dear Jack,

Tomorrow I am leaving on a flight to Montreal where I will be sitting at an outdoor café sipping wine and eating delightful cakes. With me I will have a last-minute addition: my childhood friend, Gregory, who has also never been outside the country (except a stint in Mexico that I can't wait to hear about). We are not lovers, as he prefers the male gender for romantic companionship. And to think, all this time through my letters, I have been subtly wooing him! I digress.

In a matter of days, you will find a gold watch in the mail that once belonged to my father. He won it during a poker game at an Atlantic City casino when I was very young. A lawyer had put his gold watch in the mix and my father, on one of his rare moments of fortune, happened to win! With the watch he also won $1,000—money that was swiftly lost moments later at the blackjack table.

In the twenty years I've been in business, I haven't had an employee quite like you. No one has ever been so loyal—almost to a fault—so I simply couldn't think of a better person to receive this. If the watch doesn't fit, you can bring it to a watch repairman who will take out the extra links. My father had wrists like a bull.

I hope you enjoy working for Mark. I know it will not be the same, but stiff upper lip! I will send postcards of my travels, so keep an eye out.

Sincerely,
Fawn

● ●

From: Fawn Birchill
Sent: Sat, Aug 31, 2019 at 10:15 AM
To: Mark Nilsen
Subject: Reading

Mark,

Thank you for the voice mail, and sorry I missed your call. I am at the airport and only have about thirty minutes before I have to catch my plane, so I will be quick! I am glad

Mr. Collins reached out to you and changed his mind about the visit. I am sad to be missing the great author, but I believe he will be back as long as he feels welcomed and it is a successful, well-attended evening—however, I can't imagine it wouldn't be.

I do not know when I will be back. Gregory mentioned staying and getting a work visa in Ireland, and I may join him; however, I've always wanted to live in England so we might end up parting at some point. I hope getting those visas is easy. I know nothing about the process at all. Once I get a more permanent address, I will send it to you (and also send for Bert). Please text me photos of the store and keep me updated on all your adventures. Oh, and please don't forget to feed the alley cats while I'm away.

I wish you much happiness. It is all that matters.

Fawn

●●

From: Sybil Crawley
Sent: Sat, Aug 31, 2019 at 10:30 AM
To: Mark Nilsen
Subject: Be True

Mark,

As a longtime customer of the Curious Cat Book Emporium, naturally this is a difficult transition for me. And as my beloved bookstore owner sets sail for new waters—as she gazes off into the sunset, the golden rays reflecting off her sunglasses, her eyes squinting toward an unfamiliar but exciting future—I cannot help but be extremely happy for her. All that said, I am saddened by change, but I also welcome it. Fawn has sold her building and her store to someone who, I think, is a man worthy of receiving it.

I obviously can't see inside her soul, but I have the feeling that Fawn knows as well as I do that life is short and that sometimes the best way to live is to learn to let things go—like pets, money, seriousness, lovers, and sometimes one's business. In the time I've spent in that place as a loyal customer, I can say with honesty and with a heavy heart that you very well may have purchased the most wonderful bookstore there ever was. And perhaps the saddest thing of all is that there will be no great sending off, no dramatic conclusion, no orchestral denouement. Just a quiet cessation, as there is in real life: the folding of the hands upon the chest, the closing eyes, the wintry end—a new silence in an unruly world.

But then, it isn't all ending, is it? You have pulled the curtain aside to reveal a new life hidden between those dusty walls. I am eager to patronize your store just as I did the Curious Cat Book Emporium, but remember that you have been given an opportunity to rise again, so you must be careful. Take her out slowly, sail with the wind at your back, keep your shipmates close and happy, and always, always be fair and true.

Your future customer,
Sybil C.

From: Mark Nilsen
Sent: Sat, Aug 31, 2019 at 10:45 AM
To: Fawn Birchill
Fwd: Be True

Hi Fawn,

I know you wrote this email. All the same, thanks for the well wishes and your signature hyperbole. I'll miss receiving it on a regular basis.

Take care,
Mark

From: Fawn Birchill
Sent: Sat, Aug 31, 2019 at 11:13 AM
To: Mark Nilsen
Re: Fwd: Be True

Mark,

No, I most certainly didn't write this. Do you really think I'm so sneaky that I would think to open two email accounts just for the purpose of emailing you as someone else? This is why we had trouble in the beginning. You must think me completely mad.

Unfortunately I don't have time to settle this, as my flight is boarding and Gregory is standing over by the windows chewing his fingers and gesturing like a mime for me to get going. He is actually quite entertaining. I'm surprised people aren't throwing coins at him.

We will settle this later. Besides, I don't see why you care either way since Sybil was nice this time.

Much love,
Fawn

Acknowledgments

First I would like to thank my incredible agent, Elizabeth Copps, who believed in this project way back in 2013 when Fawn's story was in its infancy. Thank you for sticking by me, for fighting for me, and for never giving up hope. I am fortunate to have you as my agent, my champion, and my friend. And to Maria and the entire team at the Maria Carvainis Agency—thank you a thousand times for your support.

To my wonderful, insightful editor, Alicia Clancy, thank you for your vision, talent, and sense of humor. And to the entire team at Lake Union—thank you for your creativity and hard work throughout this process.

Thank you, Cindy Johnston, my mother-in-law, who was one of the very first beta readers for this book. You have become my friend and also one of my greatest champions. Your constant support means the world to me.

Andrea Lynn Green, my talented and beautiful sister, thank you. You've been creating with me since we were old enough to scribble sketch comedy out on scrap paper and insist that everyone watch. Laughter got us through a lot and allowed me to see the importance of it in art, life, and relationships. Without you there infusing your unique sense of humor into all things, I'm not sure I would have made such a realization. You are a huge anchor in my life and one of my best friends.

Mom, thank you for encouraging my creativity, allowing me to try anything I wanted to try, and always accepting me for who I am. You have always been there for me, sacrificing and cheering me on, and I will be eternally grateful.

Dad and Linda, you have shown me encouragement through the years and have pushed me to keep going, to not lose heart, and to remember what is important. Thanks, Dad, for passing down that Green fighting spirit. It keeps me in the ring.

Huge thanks to the rest of my family, particularly Grandma Connie, who continues with her vivaciousness and love to be a source of inspiration and support.

And for my late Grandma Betty and late Pop-up, who showed enormous love to my sister and me and also let us get away with (almost) anything. Words can't express how much I miss you.

Thank you to the extremely talented and driven Brian Morgan and Sarah Longhi, and your writers' retreats. Brian, my chosen brother, you have been one of my greatest champions through the years, and you are a huge reason why any of this has been possible, why I kept going, and why, because of an encouraging word from you, I started in the first place.

A thousand thanks to my early readers for this project and others: Beth Gorman, Brittany Gaines, Liz Ursell, and David Pham. Beth and Brittany, you have been there, without judgment, for all my ups and downs. I don't know where I'd be without you both.

To Alex Sando and Andrew Feierabend, I love you guys. You have been with me from the beginning as constant friends whom I could always count on and who always encouraged me to keep going. Enormous thanks as well to Katie Simpson, Sebastian Göres, CJ Brooks, and the rest of my hilarious, wonderful, beautiful Philly family. Doobies forever, though Matt would never.

Thank you to the incredibly talented and driven Lisa Conn, Andres Cruciani, Lee Bacon, and Rachel Morgan—may we always cheer each other on.

Also, immense gratitude to my work friends and colleagues who have been incredibly supportive through the years.

Thank you to the University of the Arts for the teachers who enriched my life and pushed me to be a better artist. Endless love and gratitude always to Ernie Losso for being a friend and fostering my writing early on and to the late Jared Martin for his support and encouragement. To Elise Juska and Aimee LaBrie for their wisdom and excellent teaching. Thank you to Emmanuelle Delpech for teaching me to play and create without barriers.

A huge thanks to the New York Pitch Conference and Writer's Workshop and all the amazing writers and mentors I met there. Our group was a little family by the time it was done and, though we are scattered across the world now, I think of you often and am grateful for your support and feedback.

To my entire aikido family, you have been vital in keeping me going, especially during the harder times. Even a small word of encouragement to a writer is huge, and you all delivered and then some. I can't express enough how much it means to me.

Ed Shockley, who walks in both the aikido and writer world, thank you for everything.

Last but not least, Matt Johnston, more than anyone you know the journey I've taken with this book. You have been there with me fighting for years, celebrating my accomplishments, and sticking with me through the darkest of times. You always believed in me, even when I didn't believe in myself. Thank you for your tough love, for our long conversations about writing, and for being someone I could turn to when I needed a critical eye. May we always be there for each other. As Tim Canterbury wrote to Dawn Tinsley: "Never give up."

About the Author

Elizabeth Green graduated from the University of the Arts with a BFA in theater arts. They have contributed to McSweeney's Internet Tendency, Hobart, Wigleaf, Necessary Fiction, fwriction : review, and others. Their hobbies include native gardening and aikido. Hailing from Upstate New York—Greenwich, to be specific—Elizabeth now lives outside Philadelphia with their husband and two cats.

Center Point Large Print
600 Brooks Road / PO Box 1
Thorndike, ME 04986-0001 USA

(207) 568-3717

US & Canada:
1 800 929-9108
www.centerpointlargeprint.com